# DARK OF NIGHT

# SUZANNE BROCKMANN

# DARK OF NIGHT

A NOVEL

BALLANTINE BOOKS • NEW YORK

Copyright © 2009 by Suzanne Brockmann

Published in the United States by Ballantine Books, an imprint of The Random House Publishing Group, a division of Random House, Inc., New York.

BALLANTINE and colophon are registered trademarks of Random House, Inc.

Library of Congress Cataloging-in-Publication Data

Brockmann, Suzanne.
Dark of night : a novel / Suzanne Brockmann.
p. cm.
ISBN 978-0-345-50155-4 (alk. paper)
1. Government investigators—Fiction.   I. Title.

PS3552.R61455D37 2009
813'.54—dc22          2008045393

Printed in the United States of America on acid-free paper

www.ballantinebooks.com

9 8 7 6 5 4 3 2 1

FIRST EDITION

To my hero, Paul Newman

When I was in my early teens, I went to a matinee of *Butch Cassidy and the Sundance Kid*—a movie that remains, to this day, my all-time favorite. I've since seen it more times than I can count, but I'll always remember my very first viewing. Because I went into that theater a little girl—a rough-and-tumble tomboy—but when I walked out, I was a woman.

Even though, at that time, Robert Redford was being touted as the hot new star, it was Paul who caught my young but discerning eye on that momentous day.

And, as if the sky had opened and a thousand-voice choir of angels had broken into a resounding and fiery chorus of Barry White's "You're the First, the Last, My Everything," I sat in that dark theater, transfixed by all that was Paul. And I suddenly and absolutely got it. I understood—*completely*—why boys existed, and what they were good for.

I was thirteen, he was forty-something, but this was not a schoolgirl crush. It was true, abiding, long-lasting love. (The salad dressing, popcorn, and lemonade, with all proceeds going to charity, only cemented my adoration.)

Thank you, Paul, for being wonderful, talented, generous, smart, funny, and wickedly gorgeous. You made the world an immensely more beautiful and better place, and you will be missed.

# ACKNOWLEDGMENTS

A special thank-you to the enormously supportive team at Ballantine Books, especially Jennifer Hershey for suggesting that Dana Isaacson fill in for her as editor while she was busy adding to her family! And thank *you*, Dana, for being so wicked awesome. Thanks also to Courtney Moran, Crystal Velasquez, Kim Hovey, Kate Blum, and Libby McGuire.

Snaps to Steve Axelrod, the world's best agent.

Thanks to the home team: Ed and Jason Gaffney, Eric Ruben, Apolonia Davalos, Fred and Lee Brockmann, Kathy Lague, the fabulous Kuhlmans, and the world's most awesome schnauzer puppies, CK Dexter-Haven and Lil' Joe.

Thanks to my first-draft readers: Ed Gaffney, Lee Brockmann, Deede Bergeron, Patricia McMahon, and Scott Lutz.

Thanks also to the members of my political "debate club"—Bill, Jodie and Joan Kuhlman, Randy Divinski, Deede Bergeron, Patricia McMahon and, of course, Ed. You guys helped make campaign season bearable.

A big shout out to my steadfast gang of readers/volunteers—Elizabeth and Lee Benjamin, Suzie Bernhardt, Stephanie Hyacinth, Jim and Beki Keene, Laura Luke, Jeanne Mangano, Heather McHugh, Peggy Mitchell, Dorbert Ogle, Gail Reddin, Erika Schutte, and Sue Smallwood.

As always, any mistakes I've made or liberties I've taken are completely my own.

# DARK OF NIGHT

# PROLOGUE

Sophia kissed him.

Dave Malkoff sat there, on a standard-issue stool in a generic travelers' bar off the lobby of an equally unremarkable Sacramento hotel, as Sophia. Kissed. Him.

It wasn't an accident. She hadn't lost her balance and bumped into his lips with hers. No, no, that *was* her tongue lazily but quite intentionally exploring the inside of his mouth, her fingers in the hair at the nape of his neck, her lovely, lithe body pressing against him until she hit the barrier of the wooden seat between his open legs and could get no closer.

She tasted both sweet and salty, like the wine she'd been drinking mere moments ago, like the tears he knew she'd shed when the news had come down that James Nash was dead.

Dave's stomach twisted and his heart clenched, and he almost— almost—pulled away to ask Sophia if this—this kiss, this embrace—was some kind of knee-jerk reaction to her grief over the loss of their friend and co-worker.

Co-worker.

The word made it sound as if he and Sophia and Nash had adjoining cubicles in some fluorescent-lit office somewhere. Instead, their *co-worker* had been gunned down as a result of their Troubleshooters Incorporated team—with Dave as reluctant leader—having taken on a no-pay assignment that went bad.

And yes, thanks in part to Nash's sacrifice, the rest of the team was finally safe—including all of the hostages that had been taken.

Hostages that included Sophia Ghaffari.

Who was now kissing him.

*Him.* As in David Malkoff.

She was kissing him as a direct result of his having, earlier that day, blurted out the fact that he was in love with her, making this entire situation even that much more bizarre.

It was only in his wildest dreams that he'd ever imagined confessing his feelings. He and Sophia were friends, buddies, pals. For years, he'd been terrified of ruining their comfortable relationship by revealing the pathetic truth. For years, he'd convinced himself that he was content to love this incredible woman from afar—to keep his feelings for her hidden, unrequited and pure.

And in those wildest dreams, if he did fantasize summoning the courage to speak his heart, he'd never imagined her reacting with anything other than kindness. She'd wince at the thought of hurting him, then gently pat his hand while telling him how much she valued his loyalty and friendship.

The idea that she might actually consider his announcement something of value, and then try to touch his tonsils with her tongue, had never, *ever* crossed his boggled mind.

And yet, this was the reality in which he now lived.

A reality in which her breasts were soft against his chest. A reality in which she angled her head and opened her mouth wider so that he could lick his way into her mouth. And dear God, the sensation of Sophia's tongue against his own flooded him with a wave of heat and need so intense his knees went weak—thank God he was sitting down.

And still she kissed him, right there in that extremely public bar, in the very hotel where a large number of their other co-workers from Troubleshooters Incorporated were also staying. Anyone could walk in and see them. Their boss, Tom Paoletti. Tom's second-in-command, Alyssa Locke. Their mutual friend and James Nash's former partner, Lawrence Decker.

And okay, thinking about Decker instead of focusing his full attention on the fact that he was kissing Sophia was probably not the smartest thing Dave had ever done.

Sure enough, as if she'd read his mind, Sophia finally ended the kiss.

She pulled back, the tip of her tongue a pink flash against her lips, as if she were savoring the taste of him—though she was more likely cleaning up any excess saliva he'd left behind because, face it, when it came to kissing, he was sorely out of practice. But then there they were, his heart damn near pounding out of his chest, that soft lower lip he'd just thoroughly and intimately enjoyed now caught between Sophia's teeth as she gazed searchingly at him, a question—or maybe it was just blanket uncertainty—in her crystal blue eyes.

Dave had to laugh, because the idea that she could kiss him like that and remain at all doubtful as to his enthusiastically positive response was ridiculous.

His arms were still around her. She was still standing between his legs, her fingers still playing with his hair, which felt about four million times better than he'd ever imagined. She smiled then, too, laughter lines crinkling the corners of eyes that both glistened with sadness and sparkled with life. She was so beautiful—and even more gorgeous inside, in her generous soul—that he couldn't speak.

So he kissed her again.

As he lowered his mouth to hers, before he closed his eyes, he caught a glimpse of Sam Starrett—a co-worker from the San Diego office and husband to company XO Alyssa Locke—in the mirror behind the bar.

"Whoa," he was pretty sure he heard Sam say as the kiss Dave had intended to be as sweet and tender as the one Sophia had just given him turned into something else. Something molten and powerful and scary as hell—or it would have been had this woman not turned to fire in his arms. She was kissing him back with the same amount of need, molding herself to him even as he damn near crushed her in his arms.

And when he pulled back—because, God!—she was breathing as hard as he was. Again, she just stood there, this time her forehead pressed against his as she labored to catch her breath.

"We should probably . . . um . . ." Dave couldn't do more than whisper, couldn't really figure out *what* they should do, other than get out of there, because, yes, that was Alyssa in the lobby right outside the bar door, talking on her cell phone.

"Go." Sophia finished his sentence for him, pulling back to nod her agreement.

Somehow Dave let go of her, and she gathered up her jacket—a huge

Windbreaker that one of the paramedics had given her some hours ago, to ward off the chill of the evening in the mountains. She also took her wineglass and his mug of beer, both of which had magically been refilled, no doubt by the attentive barkeep, and headed briskly for the door.

Dave couldn't walk out of there without adjusting his pants, so he tried to do it surreptitiously—and failed. It was a stare-into-space, grab-and-pull kind of move, only he managed to meet Sam Starrett's eyes in the bar mirror. Dave quickly looked away, but it was too late. He saw speculation in the former SEAL's eyes. Surprise was there, too—a heavy dollop of *Sophia's with Malkoff? No way*... But it was the speculation—where were they going and what were they going to do when they got there?— that bothered Dave and made him stop at Starrett's bar stool instead of following Sophia out the door.

"It's been a long day," Dave told his immediate superior's husband. "I'm just going to see Sophia up to her room."

Almost as handsome as James Nash had been, Starrett was Texas-born and -raised, with a cowboy drawl and good ol' boy attitude, both of which came and went at whim. He'd draped his long, rangy frame on one of the stools, his booted foot claiming possession of another for his wife—no doubt his version of "save, save, super-save." His Texas-sky eyes were guarded as he met Dave's gaze, as he tactfully didn't call Dave's obvious bullshit. "I'm sorry for your loss, Malkoff. I didn't know Nash all that well, but he was . . ." Sam cleared his throat. "He'll be missed." He looked at Sophia, who'd come back into the bar to see what had slowed Dave down. "I'm glad you're safe, though. You must be feeling, uh . . ." Another throat clearage. "You know, relief can be a pretty consuming emotion, so—"

"Which is why I'm seeing Sophia to her room," Dave cut him off. "Good night."

As he turned and headed for the door, his hand against Sophia's back, he could feel Starrett's gaze following them.

She was silent as they went toward the elevator, as they joined two elderly women, one with a walker, who were waiting for the lift to arrive.

Dave took his mug and had a healthy slug of his beer. The door opened with a ding, and after the little old lady faction had boarded, he let Sophia go first. He didn't need to ask what floor she was on. They'd checked in at the same time—he knew they were both on four.

The door closed and as the elevator groaned its way upward Dave felt Sophia reach out and touch him, her fingers hooking on his belt at the back of his pants. He didn't dare look at her, didn't dare touch her, didn't dare say a word. He just kept his eyes on the numbers appearing above the door. Two. Come on. Three. God, this thing was slow.

Four. Finally. The number lit but the elevator seemed to hover in limbo for eons before a bell rang and the doors opened.

And then they were alone in the hall, and the elevator door was closing, and Sophia finally spoke. "What you told Sam," she said, leading him down the corridor as she fished in her pocket for her key card. "You weren't . . . Were you . . ." She laughed and started again as she took the card from its paper folder and slid it into the lock. "He's right, you know. About relief being . . ." The green light flashed and the lock clicked, and Sophia grabbed the handle and opened the door, holding it there as she turned to look up at him, her pretty face somber. "That's not what this is."

Dave nodded as he looked, hard, into her eyes. "I know," he whispered. He also knew what—precisely—this *was*. The first runner-up could still get the prize if the real winner bowed out.

*If* had become *when* over the past few weeks as Troubleshooters team leader Lawrence Decker had made it profoundly clear that he had no room in his life for Sophia, who'd fancied herself in love with him for years. No doubt about it—the man was a moron to have pushed her away.

But he had. And now Sophia claimed that she'd come to terms with the fact that sitting around and waiting for Decker to get a moron-ectomy wasn't going to get her the things she wanted. A home with a man who loved her. A family.

"You coming in?" she asked, holding the door open and turning back to look at him as he leaned there against the wall.

With her shimmering blond hair, delicately featured face, gracefully shaped mouth, perfect nose, huge blue eyes, that fairy-princess point to her chin, Dave found her to be so beautiful, his throat ached. Or maybe it was aching because he knew—as her best friend and confidant for so many years—just how damaged she truly was. He knew how hard she'd worked to regain the semblance of a normal life, to overcome the violence and tragedy of her past.

He also knew that she hadn't had sex in years.

Neither had he. Which she, of course as *his* best friend, also knew.

This was going to be . . . Dave searched for the correct adjective. *Terrifying* was up there with *amazing* and *miraculous*. Was there a word that included all three? *Thrilling* wasn't quite right and . . .

"You don't have to if you don't want to," she said, and he realized that his delay in response had retriggered her uncertainty.

"I'm an idiot," he said, coming inside and closing the door behind him, leaning on it so that it latched, throwing the bolt and the night lock, too. "I was just relishing the moment and—"

"Are you scared?" she interrupted.

He blinked at her directness. "Yes, but not for the reasons you think." She smiled at that.

Dave had to smile, too, as he looked around the room for a place to put down his beer mug. "We don't exactly have a lot of secrets, do we?"

"I still have a few," she admitted as she put her jacket over the desk chair and kicked off her shoes. "And I'm betting you do, too."

The room was standard as far as hotels went. Nice enough in size, with a neutral décor that neither pleased nor offended, and a king-sized bed that he forced himself not to look at. There was a cluster of furniture—a small table and several chairs—over by the windows, and he headed toward its relative neutrality.

"I'm not scared," she told him as she set her wineglass down on the bedside table. "At least I wasn't while you were kissing me. Which is something I desperately want you to do again. Which is going to be difficult with you over there and me over here."

"I'm trying to give you space," Dave told her through a heart that was securely lodged in his throat. She *desperately* wanted him to kiss her again.

"No, thank you," she said.

"Because, see, we should probably talk and I'm not sure I can do that with your tongue in my mouth. Which is not to say I didn't *completely* enjoy—"

"We can talk more later. If we need to. I mean, we've talked for years." She held out her hand to him and his feet moved toward her of their own volition.

So he spoke quickly. "It's occurred to me that it's been a while since either of us have taken a shower."

Sophia went still. It wasn't so much that her expression changed, because it didn't. She didn't move, she didn't say anything, but Dave stopped short, knowing that he'd somehow said the exact wrong thing.

And in a flash he remembered her telling him—haltingly—about her captivity, about how the other women would bathe her. They'd put perfume in her hair and on her body, dress her completely in white—the better for the blood to show, should a man prefer that sort of thing.

"I meant me," he added hastily. "I'm pretty sure I reek—"

"I love the way you smell," Sophia told him, tears in her eyes because she knew he knew. And likewise he knew *she* knew he was now—absolutely—terrified of making another insensitive blunder. "I've always loved the way you smell."

"Really?" Dork that he was, his voice actually cracked, but she didn't seem to notice or care as she nodded. He took her hands. "Soph . . ." *Tell me what to do, what you need. . . .*

She answered his unspoken question. "Just kiss me the way you kissed me downstairs."

He pulled her close, and she went up on her toes to meet him halfway as he covered her mouth with his own. He didn't try for tender, didn't go for sweet—not that it would have made a difference if he had, because trying to wrangle the heat that sprang up instantly between them would have been as futile as trying to put out a five-alarm fire with a baby blanket.

He wasn't sitting down this time—there was no bar stool to keep her from pressing herself fully against him, so she did and it was all he could do to keep standing. He was still aroused from those first kisses, a fact that he was no longer able to hide from her. Not that she seemed to mind.

In fact, on the contrary, she looped one leg around him, as if she wanted him closer, and God, now his hands were on her perfect rear end, pulling her more tightly against him as he kissed her and kissed her.

He could feel her pull his T-shirt free from his jeans, feel the coolness of her hands against his back as she pushed the shirt up in an obvious attempt to get it off.

It made sense that she would want to undress him—she was in control, this was her choice. And he had just decided that he'd stand there, doing the one thing he was certain she liked—kissing her—when she pulled her mouth free to whisper, "Help me."

So he did, yanking his shirt up and over his head, while she rid herself of her own shirt, then kissed him again, as if she couldn't bear to spend too many seconds without his mouth on hers.

He was living his most cherished fantasy. He'd been granted his heart's one desire. No doubt about it, at some point during this past total suckfest of a day, he'd done something really right to be here now. His mind raced as he ran his hands across the softness of her back, her shoulders, her arms, aware as hell—despite the fact that his eyes were closed—that Sophia was pressed against him, nearly skin to skin, in her bra. Which, for the record, was white and sweetly lacy with a tiny pink flower sewn between her perfect breasts.

He could feel her hands at the waist of his jeans. She opened his belt buckle like a pro—okay, don't think that—unfastened the button, found the zipper pull and. . .

Famine, disease, drought. Dave fought to focus, but it wasn't until he conjured up a picture of James Nash, with a white sheet being pulled over his head, that he knew for sure that he wasn't going to embarrass himself by coming in Sophia's ridiculously soft hands.

Of course, now he had to fight not to cry, and he was certain, without a doubt, that bursting into tears would be far more embarrassing than ejaculating within three seconds of Sophia's touch. Although both were to be avoided, if possible.

So he gently moved her hands to a less sensitive spot, as he lifted his head and admitted, "It's been a while, and I'm . . . afraid that . . ."

She stepped back, stepped out of her pants while he did the same. She hesitated, though—even if only briefly. Anyone who didn't know her as well as he did might've missed it. But she *did* hesitate, glancing over her shoulder at the mirror behind her before unfastening her bra and slipping her panties down her smooth, perfect legs.

The mirror behind her. . .

The light was dim enough that he could barely see the scars from her captivity—the largest one being on the small of her back. But he knew—as she did—that they were there.

And Dave also knew, with a seemingly brilliant stroke of insight, what to do, what to say to this gorgeous, naked woman standing there, so vulnerably, before him. "In truth," he said, his voice raspy, hoarse to his own ears, as he pulled her close and touched her, skimming his hands across all that gorgeous, gleaming skin, across her breasts, her stomach, her back, and yes, even her fading scars, "it has nothing to do with how long it's been and everything to do with you. I've always found you completely irresistible. Always."

She lifted her head to smile up at him, but her trepidation was still there, in her eyes.

So he kissed her—kissed her and tugged her back with him, so that they fell, together, onto that bed. Deep in the recesses of his brain, he knew he should be careful not to be on top of her. He should loosen his grip so that she never felt restricted or overpowered. He should let her remain in control.

But she clung to him, opening her legs to pull him closer, wrapping her arms and legs around him, her hand on his butt, pushing him even more tightly against her, her breath hot against his ear as she reached between them with her other hand. "Dave. I want . . ."

Her fingers closed around him, leaving no doubt in his mind exactly what she wanted and when she wanted it—him, and right now. She shifted her hips and he felt her yield to him. She was soft and slick and tight around him, and as he slid into paradise he knew there was something he had yet to do or say, but when he opened his mouth, "God, I love you," came blurting out.

They were the exact same words that had gotten him here, and once again, it was the right thing to say. Sophia laughed, but there was a catch in her voice, and he lifted his head to look into her eyes as she held him there, tightly inside of her, as intimately joined as two people could possibly be.

"Thank you," she whispered. "For saying that."

"It's true."

Her eyes filled with tears, and she reached for him, pulling his head down and kissing him, moving against him, beneath him, as best she could with his weight on top of her.

But the sight of those tears haunted him and he had to ask. "Are you sure you're—"

"I'm good," she said. "I'm great. I'm unbelievably . . . Oh, Dave, I need . . . More . . . Of you. . . . Please . . ."

More of him. Okay.

He moved with her then, carefully, slowly, and she seemed to like that—"Oh, yeah . . ."—so he didn't speed up. The friction was incredible, the sensation sheer bliss—as if he were being stroked by the softest of hands, except not really, because it was even better than that.

Kathy/Anise had liked sex hard and fast, and she'd always, *always* been running the show, even when she'd been beneath him. It had been 180 degrees different than these long, slow withdrawals, and equally endless deep, *deep* thrusts that made Sophia moan—dear God, much more of this and he was going to lose it—except what the hell was he doing thinking about Kathy now when he was making love to Sophia—Jesus, he was making *love* to *Sophia*. Dave wondered inanely if she were thinking of Decker or maybe her dead husband, Dimitri, or even some distant, long-ago lover that she'd let slip away, and there was no way he could compete against any of them, except now he was *way* too much inside of his head so he tried to clear his thoughts of everything but this intense, mind-blowing pleasure he was feeling—that she was feeling, too.

"So good . . . ," she breathed. "So good."

Good didn't begin to cover it, but good was better than bad, it was better than get me out of here, don't touch me, get your fucking hands offa me. . .

Good couldn't kill you, except Dave *was* dying, he was choking, he was *drowning*, and he didn't want to die, but Jesus, he didn't want to go back to that basement with the bright light and the questions and the pain.

They'd taken all of his fingernails off his right hand and had made it clear they were ready to start on his left because they hadn't caught on that he was stronger than anything they could throw at him. The waterboarding, the electric shocks, the blows to his face and body. . .

He just ran to Sophia in his mind, losing himself in his vivid memories of the too-short time they'd shared. Seven weeks. It had been slightly more than seven weeks since that first night.

His favorite escape was to go back to that night, to that very first time they'd made love. While it wasn't the best sex they'd had—because God, they'd had a lot of sex in seven weeks, even with both of them out of town for part of that time—it was, for him at least, among the sweetest.

Although this time the monsters had gone too far but then pulled him back before he'd had the chance—in his mind—to reach his very favorite part. To make Sophia come. Which pissed the shit out of him.

They yanked the rag from his throat, hauled him up, and bent him over so the water they'd forced into him left his stomach and lungs as he coughed and choked and vomited his way back to reality—which sucked ass.

He fucking hated it here, yet his body gasped for air, tears streaming down his face as he puked even more, as he spit out a tooth that he must've broken as he'd savagely bit at that rag they'd stuffed in his mouth.

Here in the land of light and pain, those beautiful weeks that he'd spent with Sophia seemed distant and blurred, like a rapidly fading dream—only he knew it had happened. He knew that, in her own way, Sophia loved him, that she'd been ready and willing—and yes, even eager—to spend the rest of her life with him.

Dave clung to that truth, like a distant echo of the most beautiful, pure music cutting through the cacophony of angry demands and the shrill buzz of pain.

It was his love for Sophia, his memories of their time together, that was keeping him sane, keeping him alive, although it wouldn't help him for much longer—he knew that, too. He could feel his already damaged body weakening—the infection from his knife wound getting more severe with each passing hour. And each time it was harder to come back.

But back he was, and he waited, still gasping and coughing, for the questions that would come. And for the blows that would follow when, once again, he failed to give his captors the information they wanted.

His world had shrunk to four absolute truths.

He loved Sophia—heart, body, and soul.

He would die before betraying his teammates, his friends.

He *was* going to die. He knew that when these monsters who were torturing him finally realized that they could not break him, they would, unflinchingly, put a bullet in his head or slash a knife across his throat.

And the fourth truth?

Dave knew that Sophia was—at that very moment—in the company of Lawrence Decker. Deck—who loved her almost as much as Dave did.

And the jealousy and resentment he'd always felt, the green monster that, for years, Dave had never quite been able to tame, had changed. Over the past nightmarish blur of hours it had been twisted and crushed and turned into something hard and gleaming and clean. A gem of emotion—pure and brilliant.

It shone through his pain, brighter even than any of his other truths.

Because Dave knew with faith as solid as stone that Decker would keep Sophia safe from harm.

And for that, Dave would be eternally grateful, even after his last breath had left his lungs.

# CHAPTER ONE

I f Dave had known, before he'd picked up the phone, how much trouble this one call would cause, he would've let it go directly to voice mail.

But it was Sunday morning, and he was enjoying—very much—the experience of surfing the cable TV news channels from the comfort of Sophia's bed.

He loved hanging out in the bedroom of her little apartment, and not just because most of the time he was in here of late, he was in the process of taking off Sophia's clothes.

Though she'd lived in this tiny second-floor walk-up for far fewer years than he'd inhabited his spacious and still-spartan condo, she'd turned this place into a real home. Her furnishings were unique—quirky, mismatched pieces she'd picked up in flea markets and painted in the vibrant colors of the Mediterranean. Rich blues in a variety of shades mingled with bright yellows, warm reds, and a green that brought to mind the newness of spring. Artwork—some of it her own, and quite good—hung on the walls. The open windows were covered by full, gauzy curtains that shimmered and breathed with the breeze. A ceiling fan was kept always running, moving at its lowest, laziest speed.

Last week Sophia had moved the TV into the room for him—an admitted news junkie—and as the phone rang again, he pushed the remote control's mute button as he shouted to her, in the bathroom, "You want me to get that?"

Sophia had just turned on the water, and as he heard the shower door clunk shut, she called back, "You don't have to."

Dave should've ignored it and turned off the TV and gone into the bathroom to help Sophia wash herself in those hard-to-reach places, but he was an idiot. He was still on a high from last night, when his plane had landed and he'd turned on his phone to find that she'd called him while he was in the air. Five times.

She'd gotten home several days early from her own business trip to Denver and—of course, because he had purposely neglected to tell her of his own international trek—was wondering where he was. She was cooking dinner, although, honestly? After four days apart? They were going to be eating late.

Dave had called her immediately, headed straight to her place, where she'd jumped him the moment he'd walked in the door—as if she'd been as starved for his touch as he'd been for hers.

Incredibly, it wasn't the fabulous sex they'd had right there in her living room that had made his day, week, year—no, *life*. It was later, after dinner, with Sophia drowsy, her head on his shoulder, as they were about to fall asleep, telling him that she'd missed him, and that she slept much better—as in, she didn't have her usual nightmares—when she spent the night in his arms.

It seemed the perfect segue for him to ask her about those nightmares—a topic they'd both shied away from, for years. And this time, he was ready for it. This time, he knew the questions to ask.

But then she'd added that, in the morning if he wanted her to, she'd clear out a drawer for him, maybe make him some space in her closet . . . ?

If he *wanted* her to?

Dave had answered by kissing her, and she'd kissed him back, and they'd made love again—slowly this time. Sweetly. She'd breathed his name on a sigh and she'd fallen asleep almost immediately after, leaving him holding her in his arms, with his heart so full his chest actually hurt.

But now, in the light of morning, the TV, the empty drawer, and the closet space weren't enough for Dave. Nuh-uh. No, sir. He had to further stake his claim here in Sophia's life by answering the telephone on her bedside table at 10:37 on a sunny Sunday morning, with a voice still rusty and deep from a satisfying night made up only partially of sleep.

"Hello?"

There was a hesitation—an indrawn breath—as if the person on the other end were surprised to hear someone male pick up the phone. That's right. Uh-huh. He was so the man. He was the dude with the cojones grande who was going to get his very own drawer here in Sophia's pretty bedroom.

"May I speak to Sophia?" The voice, when it finally came, was female, older, with a hint of Great Britain in its precise enunciation.

"I'm afraid she's indisposed," Dave said. "May I take a message?"

"Please. Will you ask her to call her Aunt Maureen?" She pronounced it *ahhnt*, rather than like the insect. "Maureen Miles. I'm her father's sister . . . ?"

Oh, no.

"Yes," Dave said. "Of course. Hi. Sophia's, um, told me about you. From Boston, right? I'm Dave. Her . . ." What? Boyfriend? Lover? Bedroom-drawer guy? They'd talked about a lot of things over the past weeks, but they'd never precisely defined what their relationship now was.

Maureen Miles didn't seem to care. There was more to her message. "Will you let her know that her father's back in the hospital?"

Shit. "I'm sorry to hear that," Dave said. "Mass General again?"

Another brief pause. "Yes. The doctors have given him only a few days this time, and he would like, very much, to see his daughter. I should think she owes him at least that much—"

"I'm sorry," Dave cut her off. "With all due respect, ma'am, do we live in the same universe? Because in the reality-based one where I reside, Sophia owes him *nothing*."

"He's her father," the woman said.

"He may have contributed his sperm to the creative process," Dave said tartly, "but in my opinion he lost the right to call himself *Daddy* a few decades ago."

She was silent again for a moment, but she was just regrouping. She hadn't given up. "Please tell her that he's being moved into hospice in a few days."

"I'll give her the message," Dave said, a *but* heavy in his tone, and the woman hung up without a thank-you.

He dropped the handset into the phone's cradle and flopped back onto Sophia's pillows, staring up at the spinning ceiling fan.

From the bathroom, he heard the sound of the water shutting off, the shower door opening. Sophia's melodic voice. "We need to get moving if we're going to make it to Encinitas by noon."

What? Dave lifted his head and aimed his voice toward the bathroom door. "Noon? Wait a minute, why?"

She appeared in the doorway, gloriously naked, drying herself with a towel, her wet hair slicked back from her face. She was one of those women who were even more beautiful when not wearing makeup.

Or clothes.

It was hard to think or listen when Sophia was naked, and he'd obviously not heard her response to his question, because she gave him her *I'm repeating myself because you're staring at me blankly* smile and said, again, "The main parking lot'll fill up by noon."

"Seriously?" Dave sat up, struggling to make sense of her words. "Are we talking about the same thing? The parking lot'll *fill up*? For a *flea* market?"

"Antique show," she corrected him, heading out of sight, back to the sink, where she kept a collection of bottles and jars of lotion, each one of them smelling sweeter than the last. If he hurried, he could watch her smooth some onto her arms and legs, her stomach and breasts.

As he skidded to a stop in the bathroom, she met his eyes in the mirror. "You know, we don't have to go."

"I want to." He opened the shower door and turned on the water. "The thrill of the hunt, the excitement of finding a treasure hidden in with the trash, the hours tromping through the brain-meltingly hot sun with the four million other people who helped us fill up the main parking lot before noon, who are hoping to find the exact same perfect cabinet for the kitchen before we do, so maybe we'll have to win a duel or probably a spelling bee in order to gain ownership . . . I'm totally there, T-H-E-R-E."

Sophia had turned around to look at him, her gaze traveling below his waist, her lower lip caught between her teeth as she tried not to smile — and failed. "You either *really* love antiques, or you're lying through your teeth." She reached out and wrapped her fingers around him as she gave up and laughed. "I'm going to go with lying through your teeth."

Dave laughed, too, as she stroked him, as she smiled up into his eyes. "Obviously I'd anticipated a different morning agenda," he told her. "But I'm a grown-up. I can multi-task. I can both be your antique-hunting partner *and* spend the day imagining all the ways I'm going to make you come after we get home."

"Hmm," she said, swaying closer, the tips of her breasts brushing his chest as she pressed his erection against the softness of her stomach. "Or we can say the heck with the main parking area, and take the PITA shuttle from the south lot."

"South lot," he repeated, unable to keep himself from touching her, his fingers sliding across her silky, clean, lotion-sweet skin. "There's a south lot?"

Sophia nodded, then jumped up, wrapping her arms around his neck, her legs around his waist, like a piggyback ride in reverse.

"I love the south lot," Dave told her as he grabbed her to keep her from slipping off him, her perfect derriere filling his hands. And God, this was unlike any other piggyback ride he'd ever given anyone, because she shifted and pushed him hard and deep inside of her. "Holy *shit*."

She pulled back to look at him, laughter lighting her face and making her eyes sparkle and dance. "New one, huh?" she asked as she began to move against him.

He nodded. "Oh, yeah." His experience with sex, pre-Sophia, was ridiculously limited, and she knew it because, well, he'd told her the truth.

They'd talked about a lot of things in those first few days A.S.—after Sacramento—and while he hadn't been ready to go into full, gory detail about his farce of a relationship with Kathy-slash-Anise, he *had* confessed to Sophia that his full sexual oeuvre was limited to five interactions with one woman who didn't particularly like him, even though she'd pretended otherwise.

Sophia hadn't fainted at that news, no doubt because her own baggage was also quite cumbersome when it came to sex.

That first morning they'd woken up in each other's arms, they'd made a promise to be honest in regard to their intimacy—since it was a potential minefield for both of them.

So, yes. Having sex standing up in the middle of the bathroom *was* a new one for him. Although there really wasn't much he could do but stand there holding her, the muscles in his arms and shoulders getting quite the workout.

Which maybe meant he was a wimp, because she was petite and didn't weigh more than a hundred pounds. But Dave was discovering that holding on to a hundred-pound woman was a very different experience than holding on to a hundred-pound woman while having sex with her. "Ah, God," he said. "Soph . . ."

"Thumbs up or down?"

"Oh, up," he told her. "Big up."

"Me too," she gasped, her breath warm against his ear. "But feel free to, you know, set me on the counter, by the sink, if you need to—"

"Not a chance." Dave loved where his hands were, loved the sensation of her legs and buttocks straining to push him more fully inside of her, but when he shifted slightly to get a better grip, he discovered—eureka!— there *was* something he could do besides simply stand there and not drop her. He shifted again to hold most of her weight with his left arm, freeing up his right hand to touch her again, with slightly better aim.

She sighed his name, and that, combined with the increased speed of her rocking motion, was enough to bring him teetering to the edge of his release, so he touched her harder, deeper, and she came with a moan and a shudder that he loved as much as he loved his new drawer and closet space. And in that fraction of a heartbeat, in the brief instant of time between his knowing that he, too, was going to orgasm—*now*—and the deep rush of mind-blowing pleasure that was already starting to surge through his body, he remembered the phone call.

He'd yet to tell Sophia that her father was in the hospital.

Dave came with a crash, with a shout—"God, I love you!"—pulling her warm, pliant body more tightly against his, as she kept coming around him, urging him, as always, to give her more, *more.*

It should have diminished his pleasure—his remembering the unhappy message he'd promised to deliver. It should have made him ashamed for forgetting something so important in the first place.

It should have, but it didn't.

Sophia's father was a rat-bastard and few besides his sister Maureen would miss him when he was gone.

"*Sweet* Jesus," Dave said when he got his vocal cords working again.

Sophia just laughed, still clinging to him, nuzzling his neck, ankles locked just beneath his butt.

Arms shaking, knees wobbly, he carried her out of the bathroom and dumped her onto the bed, collapsing beside her. "That was a solid thirty on the fun scale."

She laughed again. "When is it ever *not* a thirty?"

In an effort to lighten things up—mostly for his own sake, since the simple fact that he was in a relationship with the woman of his dreams was often enough to get him choked up—Dave had suggested a rating system, one to ten, for each new-to-him sexual position, of which there were many. And yes, in all honesty, it was a way, too, for him to acknowledge his lack of experience—by addressing it straight on, with humor.

"Sweetheart"—he opened his eyes to do his best Bogart—"for me, just being in a room with you is a twenty."

She had her head propped up on one elbow so that she could look down at him, her eyes wide and serious as her smile slowly faded.

"You know that I love you, too, right?" she finally murmured.

He gazed back at her for several long moments before he responded. He waited until he knew for sure that his voice wouldn't vibrate with emotion. "You don't have to say that."

"It's true," Sophia insisted. "These past few months have been . . ." She shook her head. "Sad, because of Nash dying, but . . . Also . . . I don't know if I've . . ." She looked down toward the jumble of bright blue sheets beneath them and started again. "I can't remember ever being this . . ." She searched for the right word as Dave waited, his heart in his throat. She met his gaze again, her eyes guileless and nearly as blue as the sheets. "Content."

Not *quite* the word he was hoping for. Still, he smiled because he was okay with it. Fact was, he'd be okay with a wide variety of *less than* words. Such as satisfied. Comfortable. At ease.

At peace.

Dave knew he was Sophia's second choice. He'd accepted that weeks ago, the very first night they'd made love. It *would* be enough. It *was* enough.

"I'm glad," he told her now, reaching up to push her hair back behind her ear, and it wasn't a lie. He let her look long and hard into his eyes so she would know that he meant it, that he accepted her words for what they were—something good, if not fairy-tale perfect.

Her mouth quirked up into a smile. "You have no idea how hot you are, do you?"

"What?" Dave laughed as he realized what she'd said, and then rolled his eyes. "Yeah, actually," he said, "I'm pretty sure I do. I fall somewhere between pickled and poached. Maybe, right after I get a haircut, for about two minutes, I can pass for steamed and . . . As fascinating as this discussion is, can we save it for tonight? Because—and I should have told you this before, but you stupefied me with your nakedness. . . ."

"I'm still naked," she pointed out, that lip again between her teeth as she played with the hair on his chest, and dear God, Dave could see a whole lot of *as long as we're going to park in the south lot dot dot dot* in her eyes.

"Right," he said, as his body stirred at the thought of staying in bed with this woman—his woman—for the rest of the morning, "so I better talk fast. That was your Aunt Maureen on the phone, Soph. Your father's back in the hospital."


Jimmy Nash had been dead now for nearly two months, and he could confirm, absolutely, that being dead sucked.

And, yeah, it was true that *not* being dead had its occasional negative moments, too. For example, getting out of bed for the first time, after the surgeon removed a small but deadly chunk of lead from his chest. That had been unpleasant.

And watching his memorial service via webcam—that hadn't been as much fun as he'd imagined it might be. In fact, he'd been stunned—and deeply moved—by the sheer number of operators from the SpecWar community who'd shown up to pay their last respects. It was SRO inside that church. On top of *that* shock, it had bothered him immensely to see friends like Dave and Sophia mourning his passing when he was sitting right here, alive if not quite well, in a hospital bed.

But most of his not being dead was positive. Waking to find Tess Bailey curled up in the chair beside his bed. Waking to find Tess reading in the chair beside his bed. Waking to find Tess running her fingers through his hair or holding his hand as she sat in the chair beside his bed. . . .

All by itself, waking was pretty positive, particularly when Jimmy thought about how close he'd come to never waking again. But with her freckles and her sunshine-filled smile, with that palpable love for him in her eyes, Tess made his waking miraculous.

Deck made it pretty damn good, too. Yeah, Lawrence Decker spent a shitload of time on watch in another chair on the far side of that hospital room. And he always knew exactly what to say, each time Jimmy had surfaced from his narcotics-induced haze.

"Tess is safe. You're safe. We're all safe."

It didn't matter how many times Jimmy came up out of the fog. Decker would reassure him, over and over again, that they were safe. Until Jimmy finally believed him.

An FBI agent named Jules Cassidy had helped Deck fake Jimmy's death—a con that had been brilliantly realized. Of course, circumstances had provided the perfect setup. Jimmy had been critically injured in a firefight with some very bad men—although not, ironically enough, the same bad men who now wanted him dead. He was rushed to a hospital in Fresno via medevac chopper and had, in fact, flat-lined on the flight. This gave additional teeth to the idea that he might not survive his surgery and, in fact, that was the very story Decker and Cassidy had used.

James Nash, aka Diego Nash, was pronounced dead on the operating table at Cedar Vista Hospital in Fresno, California at 6:14 P.M., Wednesday, 30 July 2008.

Only a handful of people knew otherwise—and Jimmy trusted them all, completely. There wasn't even a surgeon floating around out there as a potential liability because Cassidy had worked some kind of voodoo at the hospital. Jimmy suspected it involved hacking into and changing medical records, which was probably some kind of a felony, since the agent was acting on his own accord. But Cassidy was purposely keeping his FBI superiors and the entire Bureau out of the loop when it came to the fact that Jimmy was still alive.

In fact, Jimmy's new identity—one Lloyd Howard—had been fabricated without the help of any kind of government protection program. Decker and Cassidy agreed that it was important to hide the fact that Jimmy was alive from any and all government agencies.

Because at this point? They were pretty sure that the very nasty men who wanted Jimmy dead had access to government records—even those labeled top secret.

They were pretty sure that the bad men they had to take down—in order for Jimmy to very literally get his life back—worked for the mysterious and clandestine no-name Agency's black ops sector.

They were pretty sure about that because, at one time, Jimmy Nash had worked for the Agency's black ops sector, too.

"Good morning."

Tess smiled as she looked up from her book. "Hey," she greeted

Decker, who came to the end of the bed and actually reached out and held on to Jimmy's left foot.

"You ready to blow this popsicle stand?" he asked Jimmy.

Who laughed and then winced at the surge of pain. "Yeah. I wish." He held up his arm, IV tubes still attached. "I'm still attached to the mother ship."

Before the words were out of his mouth, Deck turned to the door, where one of the nurses—Paula, buxom and jolly, a proud new grand-mother—came bustling in. She shut off the drip, and almost before Jimmy could blink, she'd extracted the needle from the back of his hand.

"This goes back in, Mr. Howard," she warned Jimmy sternly, which was countered by the permanent twinkle in her lively brown eyes, "at the least little sign of dehydration. You want to go home? You'll push fluids. Do it right, we'll release you tomorrow."

"Tomorrow?" Tess spoke for him, disbelief in her voice.

Decker was grinning. "Blood test came back clear."

"But . . ." Tess was still concerned.

"It'll be easier for him to rehab off-site," Deck told her, not saying more than that, since Paula was still in the room. It wouldn't just be easier, it'd be safer. For all of them.

Truth of the matter was, as safe as he'd been made by the news of his "death," Jimmy still worried every time Decker or Tess left his room. He knew he was safe, and they were, too—when they were with him. But the only way he'd ever be fully convinced that the threat was completely gone, would be for him to identify and track down the men who'd threatened and then tried to kill him.

Right now he knew barely nothing. Several vague clues. An e-mail ad-dress that he'd already tried to track, that had gotten him nowhere. A shirt that he'd worn on one of the days they'd tried to eliminate him—stained not only with his own blood, but with the blood of the man who'd tried to take him out. The vaguest of descriptions of that man, who'd attacked him in the darkness of a moonless night.

Jimmy hadn't gotten a visual, just a sense of the man's size: average height and weight, medium build.

Which narrowed his search down to, oh, about a quarter of the world's population.

A DNA test on the shirt could provide far more specific answers, but it would also tip his enemy off as to his current still-alive status. Decker and Cassidy had agreed about that. Their plan was to wait to do that test until Jimmy and Tess were out of this hospital and ensconced in an even safer place. Which was looking to be tomorrow. Saints be praised.

"Don't worry," Deck was reassuring Tess. "We'll get him back up to speed in no time."

"He'll be getting into trouble before you know it," the nurse reassured Tess, then turned to give Jimmy a mock evil eye, "if he pushes fluids."

"Yeah, yeah," Jimmy said as she left the room, as Decker made certain that the door was tightly shut behind her.

"Are you *sure* . . . ," Tess started.

"The infection's gone," Decker told her. "He's healing nicely. It's time." He turned to Jimmy. "Cassidy wants to bring in additional security for the move to the safe house. He's going to give me a list of names. I want you both to go through it. If anyone on his list makes you at all uneasy—"

"I don't care who's on the list," Jimmy interrupted, "as long as it includes Dave Malkoff."

But Decker was already shaking his head.

"Why?" Jimmy asked. "Deck, I have two friends on this entire planet. You and Dave. And Dave thinks I'm dead. He also happens to be one of the smartest operatives we know."

Decker's smile was gone—he was back to his usual grim.

Tess leaned forward to take Jimmy's hand, but it wasn't just to calm him down. She had something to tell him, and he could tell from her face that it wasn't going to be good news.

"Oh, shit," Jimmy said, looking from Tess to Deck and back again. "What happened to Dave?"

"No, no," Tess quickly reassured him. "He's fine. He's just . . ."

"Sophia happened to Dave," Decker told him, and the words didn't make sense.

"Dave and Sophia hooked up," Tess translated, and Jimmy realized that the concern he'd seen on her face had been for Decker, who'd had some kind of twisted thing for Sophia for years now. Fool that he was, he'd never acted on it. And now, apparently, Dave had intervened. Jimmy's disappointment for Deck was curiously mixed with a sense of "you go, boy" for old Dave. Dave and Sophia. Holy Mother of God.

"It happened the night that, you know . . . ," Tess continued, but he didn't know until she added, "The hostage rescue outside of Sacramento . . . ?"

"Are you kidding me?" Jimmy asked.

She shook her head. Not kidding. "They've been hot and heavy ever since."

"Wait a minute." He needed her to clarify. "Are you telling me that the night that I *died*, Dave and Sophia decide to skip the grieving and fuck like bunnies?"

Tess winced at his verb choice, glancing quickly at Decker, who was shaking his head.

"Sorry." Jimmy realized what he'd just said. "I just thought that, you know, Dave would be a *little* upset. Sophia, too. Christ."

"People deal with grief in all kinds of ways," Tess reminded him. "And I'm also sure that Sophia knew . . ."

She didn't finish her sentence. She didn't have to.

What Sophia had known was that her last hope of starting something with Decker had died with Jimmy Nash. Sophia had believed—as had the rest of their friends and co-workers—that with Nash out of the picture, Deck would insert himself into Tess's life, dick first.

And everyone also believed that, without Nash and all of his bullshit around to distract her, Tess would instantly recognize how terrific Decker was, and how perfectly suited they were for each other.

And Jimmy's fiancée and his best friend would get married and live happily ever after, leaving Sophia out in the cold. Jimmy, too—but his cold would be the six-feet-under kind.

"Look, I'm . . . happy for her," Decker said now, about Sophia—proving what a Boy Scout he was. Because he meant what he'd said. "I'm happy for Dave, too. He's wanted this for a long time." He cleared his throat, obviously uncomfortable with this entire discussion, because at the bottom of it lay a truth they all studiously worked overtime to avoid mentioning: that Decker had, once upon a time, had feelings for Tess.

"Seeing them together is . . . This whole thing is . . ." Deck shook his head and started again. "It's harder than I thought."

Jimmy knew his friend wasn't talking merely about seeing Sophia with Dave. Decker was talking about being seen in public with Tess, pretending that he and his dead best friend's fiancée had turned to one another for comfort. *That* was what was harder to do than Deck had thought.

No shit, Sherlock.

And Jimmy would've wagered the entire contents of his bank account that Sophia's watching Decker pretending—yeah, right—to want to be romantically involved with Tess was at least partially responsible for her propulsion into Dave Malkoff's waiting arms.

But wait. The festival of jealousy didn't stop there.

Jimmy was guilty of having a carnival-load of it himself—watching the footage of Deck putting his arm around Tess's shoulders at the memorial service, holding her hand as she leaned toward him for comfort. He'd gotten pissed off, imagining Decker kissing Tess good-night so that those fuckers who'd tried, numerous times, to kill Jimmy would believe he truly was dead.

It sucked the biggest dick ever.

*Oh, what a tangled web we weave. . . .*

"I'm sorry," Jimmy said again, because he was the spider who'd started this multi-level charade spinning in the first place.

"I just think we all need a little space," Decker told him quietly, pouring a cup of water from the pitcher on Jimmy's tray.

"Fair enough." Jimmy nodded. "We don't tell Dave. And sorry if I brought an unwanted picture to mind."

Decker handed him the water. "Drink," he ordered as he headed back out of the room. "Lots. I want to get the hell out of here."

Jimmy drank.


The place really was perfect.

Eight bedrooms, ten baths, indoor and outdoor swimming pools, outfitted gym with a climbing wall, home theater, chef's kitchen, fully furnished and equipped—all sitting like a castle atop the summit of a mountain.

And FBI agent Jules Cassidy had the key to the front door in his pocket.

And, okay, this probably wasn't a mountain for most people, but Jules had grown up in the Northeast where the mountains were ancient and tree-covered and worn. Here in California—home of that nifty geological phenomenon known as the Sierra Nevadas—this thing jutting up between two desert valleys really was just a very steep, ragged little hill.

But for Jules's intents and purposes—which were many and varied—a hill of this magnitude was mountain enough.

"Two million dollars," Sam Starrett mused as he stood at the wall of sliders that opened onto a deck overlooking the scenic desert valley to the south. "He's working for a month, and they're paying him two *million* dollars. That's . . . what? Over sixty-five thousand dollars a day. A *day*."

"Yeah, but you see," Jules pointed out, "after his agent takes his cut, and after taxes and expenses? It works out to be only about half that much, so, you know, it's not that big a deal."

Sam turned and looked at him, eyebrows up.

"Kidding," Jules said, laughing at his friend. "It's a huge deal. It amazing."

Jules's husband, Robin, had come ridiculously far in the years since he'd publicly acknowledged that he was gay, and had gone into rehab for his alcoholism. His had been a coming-out of epic proportions, since he was on the verge of becoming one of Hollywood's leading action-adventure stars.

And while Robin's two-million-dollar paycheck for his role in this film was impressive, there had been a time, right before he first came out of the closet, that he could have demanded five times that amount. But Robin hadn't cared. He'd chosen sunlight and honesty over guaranteed fortune and fame. He'd chosen Jules, and had worked his ass off to stay sober. It was never going to be easy, but he now had over two alcohol- and drug-free years under his belt.

The naysayers had assumed his career was over.

The naysayers were not only freaking nincompoops, they were, as it turned out, seriously *wrong* freaking nincompoops. Proof was in the Emmy that sat on the mantel of the home Jules and Robin shared in Boston.

Robin was psyched to be doing this movie—a science fiction action-adventure—during his hit TV show's summer hiatus. He was pleased to be making that much money, but he was *most* excited about using this opportunity to help out Jules with what they'd been referring to lately as "his little extracurricular project."

The film was shooting nearby in the desert as well as six hours away in San Diego. Robin wouldn't be staying at this fabulous fortress of a house every night, but he'd be here as often as he could. And he'd be footing the bill—a fact that he generously shrugged off as "no big deal."

"Do you think we should form a search party and go after Alyssa and Ash?" Jules asked Sam now.

"I was checking out the security room." Alyssa's voice carried up the stairs before she appeared, little Ashton—nearly six months old—on her hip. With his baby-smooth mocha brown skin—as beautiful as his mother's—and his father's blue eyes, he was a remarkably cute baby, with a gleeful smile that was all his own. "May I state for the record that this place has a *security* room? There are forty-two video cameras and God knows how many motion sensors, not just out by the fence, but around the house as well." She exhaled a laugh and added some attitude. "*If* you can call this castle a *house*."

Sam took Ashton from his wife and sat on the leather sofa with the baby on his lap, putting his cowboy-booted feet up on the heavy wood coffee table. *Clunk, clunk.* "I myself couldn't help but notice the industrial-strength backup generator," he drawled, heavy on the Texas—*he'p* instead of *help*—as he made a face at his son, who chortled with laughter.

"And by the way, that fence? Electric," Alyssa informed Sam as she sat down next to him, fishing in her bag for Ash's binky. "The gate's the kind the government uses at embassies in countries that tend to end in *-stan*. You will *not* be getting visitors dropping by unexpectedly."

"You can see for miles from that deck." Sam turned to Alyssa. "What do you figure? About fifty clicks on a clear day?"

"At least. Anyone who wants to get through that gate without permission"—Alyssa wasn't done talking about the fence—" is going to have to use a substantial amount of C-4. And once they do, they've got, what? Two miles of completely exposed driveway up to the house?"

"One and eight tenths," Jules corrected her.

Both of them turned to look at him with nearly identical concern as he made himself comfortable in the easy chair across from them.

Alyssa put voice to their question. "Is Robin having trouble with another stalker?"

Jules shook his head. "No. I mean, yeah, there're always the fans who go too far, so we've learned to be careful, but this is—"

"A freaking fortress," Sam finished for him.

"Yes, it is," Jules agreed.

"What's going on?" Alyssa asked.

Jules cleared his throat. Crossed his legs. "Before I tell you this," he said, "I want to state that it's both an advantage and a disadvantage that you guys are my best friends."

Sam looked at Alyssa and covered Ash's little ears. "Why can't he ever ask us for a favor without having to make a fucking speech?" Despite the covered ears, he only mouthed the F-bomb.

"I have no idea." Alyssa settled back on the couch, getting comfortable. "But part of being a good friend is letting your friends talk, so . . ."

Sam turned to Jules, clearly not willing to climb aboard Alyssa's train of serene acceptance. "Yes," he said. "Whatever you're gonna ask us to do? We'll do it."

"But see, that's my point," Jules said. "I don't want any of us to feel as if I'm taking advantage of our friendship—"

"Help me out here, Ash," Sam told his son as he turned the baby to face Jules. "Tell your Uncle Squidward that we're happy to assist." He spoke in a squeaky baby-voice that was just too funny. "We're happy to assist."

Laughing, Jules shook his head as he looked at his friends. Alyssa had been an officer in the Navy before she joined the FBI. She'd worked for the Bureau for years—as Jules's partner. She'd left at about the same time she'd married Sam, who'd served as an officer in legendary U.S. Navy SEAL Team Sixteen. Sam had managed to get himself into some trouble, and rather than take a desk job, he'd retired from the military. At which point the pair of them went to work for former SEAL Tom Paoletti's civilian personal security firm, Troubleshooters Incorporated.

Alyssa was Tom's XO, or second-in-command, which made her Sam's boss, go figure.

Jules persisted. "When I say *any of us?* I'm including me. And I kind of feel as if I'm—"

"If you're asking us to camp out here to help keep the crazies away from Robin," Sam interrupted, "it's not exactly going to be a hardship."

"I already picked out our suite," Alyssa added.

Sam looked at her. "The one with the blue drapes?"

She nodded. "With the extra room that could be the nursery. You see that bathroom? I think it's bigger than our kitchen."

"Nice shower." He nodded. "*Very* nice shower. Although the suite on the third floor—"

"That one's ours. And this isn't about Robin," Jules said again, interrupting them. "He's renting this house, yes. And he'll be staying here, with me, part of this month, and possibly even longer, if the situation doesn't rectify itself and will you please let me tell you what this is about before you say *yes?*"

"I'm pretty sure that ship has sailed," Sam pointed out.

"What situation?" Alyssa asked, silencing her husband with an amusedly pointed look.

"I'm just saying," Sam said with a shrug.

And with that, alleluia, they were now sitting there quietly, waiting for Jules to explain, finally giving him a chance to talk.

"I've got an operative in hiding, who needs a safe house to rehab and regroup." He chose his words carefully, because until they signed on he couldn't tell them too much. "He worked in the black ops sector of a government agency and believes that he's been marked for what he calls *deletion*—which is exactly what it sounds like. I've kept him separate from any of the official protection programs, because we haven't identified the person or persons who've tried to kill him. But we do believe that whoever they are, they have access to top secret, high-clearance-level information."

"Shit," Sam covered Ash's ears to say. He glanced at Alyssa before asking Jules, "You're absolutely certain that your operative isn't, um, how do I put this? The problem?"

"He's not, and I am," Jules said. "Certain."

"Black ops create . . . certain pressures for operatives," Sam pointed out. "Some agents go rogue."

"Oh, he's rogue, all right," Jules said. "But not the way you mean. I trust this man. Completely."

"Enough to risk your career," Alyssa said. It wasn't quite a question, but it wasn't quite not, either.

So Jules answered as if it were. "Yes."

"What career?" Sam scoffed.

"Hey," Jules told him. "S-squared, SpongeBob. I happen to love Boston."

"I can't help but notice, Toto," Sam said, "that we're not in Boston anymore."

Jules sighed, exasperated. "I'm on vacation. May I please continue?"

"There's more?"

"Yeah," Jules said a tad sharply. "The important part. The part where—"

"We might find ourselves investigating corruption deep inside a government agency?" Alyssa interrupted this time. "That's basic math, Jules. I think we've already figured that out. At least I have." She looked at her husband.

"Durrr," he said.

"This could be extremely dangerous," Jules had to tell them.

"Eek," Sam deadpanned.

"You said *rehab*," Alyssa asked. "Your man's been injured?"

He nodded. "Gunshot wound to the chest. He's gonna need a month of hard work to get back to speed. Maybe a little less because he's . . . who he is."

Alyssa glanced at Sam before asking Jules, "I assume you're going to take the utmost precautions when you move him in here."

"That's one of the things I was hoping you could help me with," he told them. "My plan was to bring him in when Robin arrives tomorrow."

"We do this right," Sam said, with a glance at Alyssa, "and no one will know your man is here. It'll look to the world like we're taking a high-end vacation with our fruity and very rich friends."

"Without Ashton?" she asked.

"I say we bring him," Sam said. "The alternative is to see if Mary Lou can take him, but . . . After seeing this place, I'm convinced he'd be safer here with us." He looked at Jules. "You okay with that?"

"Of course."

Alyssa asked, "How actively is your operative being hunted?"

"We're pretty sure they think he's dead," Jules told them. "Whoever *they* are."

"Define *pretty sure*," Sam said.

"His own friends think he's dead," Jules said. "I can count the number of people who know that he's not, on the fingers of one hand."

"So the goal," Alyssa clarified, "is both to keep your man alive and to find out who wanted to 'delete' him."

Sam laughed. "You know, some people actually go to Disneyland when they take a vacation?"

"Are you in?" Jules asked.

"Absolutely," they said in unison, then looked at each other and added, "Owe me a . . . Coke," also at the same time, down to the pause before *Coke* and the smile that followed it.

Euphemism, anyone?

"One condition," Sam said, reluctantly pulling his attention away from his wife's loaded smile. "If we meet him and don't get the same warm fuzzies you obviously feel for him, we walk away and keep our mouths shut."

"Deal," Jules said.

"Who is he?" Alyssa asked. "Do we know him? Oh, my God, Jules—"

"Gunshot wound to the chest?" Sam spoke over her, putting it together at the same moment. "Son of a bitch! Is it . . . ?"

"James Nash," Jules told them. It no longer surprised him that out of the two of them, it was Sam whose eyes instantly filled with tears.

"Ah, Jesus," he said. "Does Tess know?" He answered his own question. "Of course she knows. And Decker. . . . Holy. . . ." He held Ash out for Jules. "Will you . . . Please . . . I gotta . . ."

Jules took the baby and carried him down the stairs. "Come on, Ashton, let's find the playroom, see what kind of toys come with this joint," he said, drowning out Sam's voice as he embraced Jules's good news with a resounding "Holy, *holy* fuck!"

"I don't think you should go. Not for him," Dave told Sophia, as calmly and evenly as he always sounded. "I think you should go for you."

Her Aunt Maureen had tracked Sophia down a few years ago. She hadn't even realized she *had* an aunt before that startling call—and she wasn't at all sure she wanted one at this late date. But the brusque, stern-voiced woman now phoned every few months, trying to guilt, shame, or bully Sophia into visiting her dying father.

Of course, Paul Miles had been dying for quite a few years now.

"You honestly think I'll find *closure*?" Sophia asked Dave as she stepped into her panties and put on her bra, her movements jerky with her frustration and anger.

"No," he said, reaching for her, catching her arm and tugging her back to the bed, where he was still stretched out, still naked and extremely male, and yet still solidly Dave. Her champion, her hero, her lover—and her best friend. "I doubt you'll ever find closure. I just think—"

"I have nothing to say to him," she interrupted. It was what she always said to Maureen—and to Dave, too—whenever her aunt called.

It was funny—the turmoil caused by Maureen's phone calls had always made Sophia run straight to Dave. They'd talked about her father frequently over the past few years, and about whether or not Sophia should go to Boston to see him before he died.

But never while Dave was naked and sprawled on her bed.

"Maybe you don't have anything to say," he told her now. "Or maybe you just think that you don't. Maybe going to Boston to see him will—"

"I was eleven years old," Sophia said flatly.

He blinked, then blanched. "What?"

"Eleven years, one month," she said. "It was four weeks to the day after my birthday."

"You told me you were a teenager. I thought—"

"I lied," Sophia informed him, but then had to turn away from the maelstrom of emotion in Dave's usually bemused hazel eyes. "Because I didn't want you to look at me the way you're looking at me right now."

"Let's go to Boston," he said quietly. "So I can kill him."

Sophia shook her head. "That's not funny."

"I'm not kidding." Now his eyes were hard, almost flat. She'd spent most of her life around dangerous men, and she'd seen that look before, but rarely-to-never in Dave's eyes.

"Don't," she said. "If I'd wanted a caveman, I never would've given up on Decker." And okay, she'd not only spoken too sharply, she'd spoken too thoughtlessly. She immediately apologized. "Sorry. *Sorry.*"

Too late.

But her harsh words had done the trick. Dave was back. Kind, warm, smart and funny, slightly goofy Dave. Who, as usual, pushed his own hurt feelings aside in order to focus on her. In order to take care of her. To make sure she knew that she mattered to him—more than anything else in the world. To make sure she knew she was safe and loved.

"Your parents never came back?" he asked. "Not even to . . . to . . . pick up their things?" She shook her head, but he still couldn't believe it, saying, "So from the time that you were *eleven* . . . ?"

"I was on my own," Sophia verified for him. "Yes."

Maureen had insisted that her darling brother had left his only child in Katmandu, believing her to be in her mother's care, and that Sophia's crazy mother, Cleopatra Farrell—she'd legally changed her name from

Cynthia—had left, believing Sophia to be safe with Paul. It was a simple mistake. An unfortunate accident.

But a month after her eleventh birthday, Sophia had woken up to find herself alone in an unfamiliar country, with no money, no passport, and only enough food to last a scant few days.

She was too young to know that she could go to the embassy. It never occurred to her that the consulate might be able to help. There was only their angry landlord shouting about the money her parents owed, and pushing her out into the street when she couldn't pay him. She'd cried—*What will I do?*—and he'd slapped her and told her to be a man, to do what other boys her age were doing: get a job, become an apprentice to a craftsman.

She could tell that Dave was imagining a nightmare of a different kind for a little blond girl alone on the streets, so she quickly reassured him. "I dressed like a boy. All my clothes were hand-me-downs, and . . . About two months earlier, I had a bad case of lice, and my mother . . ." She tried to make it a joke. "Thanks to her work ethic, which was *if you don't have to, don't,* she didn't try to, you know. Comb out the nits. She just shaved my head. My hair was still short so . . ."

Left to fend for herself, even at eleven, she'd instinctively known she'd be better off not advertising the fact that she was a girl.

"Everyone thought I was a boy, so I played along," she told him.

"Miles Farrell," Dave said. It was the name by which he'd first known her, back in her previous life—back when her husband, Dimitri, was still alive. "Your father's and mother's last names."

Sophia nodded. She knew from his eyes that *he* knew she'd called herself that because part of her had naively hoped one or the other of her parents would come back. She'd hoped that they would search for her and find her.

"I'm so sorry," Dave said, his hand as warm and gentle as his eyes as he smoothed back her hair.

"I survived," she reminded him.

But he shook his head. "Eleven-year-olds shouldn't have to survive something like that."

"I like to think I'm lucky," Sophia told him, leaning against him, grateful for his solid presence as he continued to stroke her hair. "My mother didn't move to the hard-core drugs until *after* I was born."

Dave laughed. "Whoo-hoo. I wonder if Hallmark makes *that* card. *Happy Mother's Day. Thanks for not mainlining heroin until I was nine.*" His hand paused. "And *there's* a question I'd like to ask your father. What the hell was he thinking to leave you with a woman who could well have sold you to a local warlord to get her next fix?"

"Maureen said he didn't know. Which is . . ."

"Bullshit." He finished for her.

They sat for a moment in silence, Dave lost in his own thoughts as Sophia tried to think of a single item for the Go-See-Her-Father "pro" column, and came up only with *if she went, Maureen would stop calling her.*

No, she had to change that *would* to a *might.* There was no guarantee the phone calls would stop. They might even increase. Maureen might start asking for money. Or her father might make a "miraculous recovery"—assuming he truly was sick in the first place. He could well follow her back to San Diego and . . . the thought made her sick to her stomach.

"I don't want to go," Sophia blurted out. "To Boston."

"Then we don't go," Dave said without hesitation, as if it were an absolute. His use of the plural got to her, too. *We* don't go, as it if were a given that he'd go with her.

She tipped her head back to look up at him. "I'm sorry that I said what I said about—"

"Shh." He briefly pressed his lips to hers before she could say *Decker.* "It's done. Forgotten."

But she couldn't let it go. "You deserve better."

"What I deserve," Dave told her quietly, "is honesty. You never need to soften the truth for me, Soph. Never."

"Sometimes," she admitted, just as quietly, "I soften the truth"—it was a good description of what she regularly did—"for me."

He was silent then, the tension in his body the only sign that her words had impacted him.

"Well, whenever you're ready to talk about . . . anything," he said, unable to keep his voice completely steady, "I'm here and I'm ready to listen. I know you've . . . been through a lot and . . . Just because you survived it doesn't mean it doesn't haunt you." He cleared his throat. "You know, we haven't talked about Dimitri once since Sacramento."

Sophia closed her eyes.

"That wasn't meant to be a reprimand," Dave continued. "I'm just pointing it out. I'm sure it's subconscious on your part. I mean, we make love pretty frequently. Which isn't a complaint," he added quickly. "Believe me. But chances are strong that *I'm* not going to say *Let's talk about your husband's death* when you're on the verge of talking off my clothes. Which I'm happy to have you do anytime."

"Please," Sophia said. "Let's not talk about Dimitri now."

"I wasn't suggesting that we do," Dave responded. "Just pointing out that . . . Okay, I just wanted to mention it and I did, so . . . Enough said." He paused. "About *that*, anyway. But at the risk of pissing you off, I do have something else I want to say to you. About your father."

Sophia opened her eyes. "Dave . . ."

"Just listen," he urged her. "I'm not saying you should change your mind. In fact, I'm virtually certain you're going to be sorely dissatisfied with his answers to any of your questions, but I do know—absolutely—that once he's gone? He'll be *gone*, Soph. And your chance to talk to him, to tell him whatever you might want to tell him? That'll be gone, too. Dead is forever. And you're going to be on this planet for years after he's passed. As crazy as the idea might seem right now, you might reach a point, later in your life, where you'll be able to forgive him. I don't want you to regret letting this last chance to see him slip away."

She managed a laugh. "Yeah, that wasn't you trying to change my mind."

"It wasn't," he argued. "I'm just saying *be certain*. And if you're not, well heck, let's go to Boston. I'll be with you the whole time, I promise you. If we get there, and you look at him through the doorway to his room, and you decide you want to turn around without letting him know you're there . . . ? I'll lead the way home.

"And if you *are* certain, and you want me to call Maureen back," Dave continued, "and say that your father's already dead to you so stop calling, be-yotch? I'll do that. I'll help you change your phone number, if you want. I'll help you move. And if you want to say the hell with everything and just get in the car and go to that flea market, find that perfect cabinet? Give me two minutes to shower."

All the complicated emotions Sophia was feeling—her frustration with Maureen, decades of hurt and anger toward her father, and the complicated mix of everything she felt for Dave—swelled in her chest and rose up, filling her throat. She had to work hard to speak. She had to squeeze her words out, so she said as few of them as possible, hoping that Dave would understand.

"Kiss me."

And he smiled at her as only Dave could smile, with a mix of amusement, chagrin, and what could only be called pure adoration. It lit him up, made his eyes even warmer, and took about ten years off a face that most people wouldn't call handsome.

But most people had never seen that smile.

"Or we could go with Plan D," he said, and obeyed her command.

# CHAPTER TWO

Whenever Tracy Shapiro lugged her groceries home, she found herself wondering *what* she'd been thinking to get a two-year lease on an apartment that was a "mere" four blocks from a grocery store.

The idea had seemed wonderful. Red-dot savings and smart shopper specials, just a short walk away.

And four blocks *was* nothing when she was dressed in workout gear and her running shoes.

But in a skirt and heels, coming straight from work, her laptop bag over her shoulder, four blocks was torture.

Of course, it was her choice, so to speak, to take the bus to and from the Troubleshooters Incorporated office, where she worked as the company's trusty receptionist. Assuming that choosing *not* to take the bus and instead spending her entire paycheck on gas, having nothing left with which to buy food, and starving to death was a viable option.

And it was her fault entirely that she'd been unable to pass up this week's smart shopper special on a particularly healthy brand of soup, in microwavable containers that she could take with her to work. The walk would've been a pleasant one if she'd stuck to her plan of picking up only a bag of salad and some halibut to grill on George.

Foreman, that is. Not her other George—a thought that made her smile grimly.

If she'd had a hand free, she would've fished her cell out of her handbag and called her friend Lindsey, to leave a message on *her* cell about how she'd just realized her two favorite appliances were both named George.

She'd leave a message, because Lindsey was probably having dinner with her husband, Mark—while basking in his love and adoration.

Or maybe Lindsey would actually pick up the phone, starved for female conversation because *her* very best friend, Sophia, had slipped into dark-side-of-the-moon mode—that zone of zero communication that often happened in the first lustful, free-fall weeks of a new romantic relationship.

Sophia was too busy to talk to anyone because she was getting busy with Dave Malkoff.

Tracy hadn't seen *that* coming. Not from Sophia's end, anyway. From Dave's, absolutely. But Tracy had always believed that Dave had a better chance of being struck by a random falling anvil or getting bitten by a radioactive spider than of ever winning the pleasure of beautiful Sophia Ghaffari's company.

Dave had a relatively high nerd factor, sure, but he was a very nice person, and he wasn't unpleasant to spend time with. Tracy had cut his hair for him a time or ten. She'd taken him clothes shopping, too. And yes, they'd had a post-tailor-visit dinner—and several glasses of wine—at the Cheesecake Factory, and Tracy had let him know that if he'd made the suggestion, she would've gone home with him.

But he hadn't, so she didn't, and the moment had passed.

Which was just as good, because she didn't seriously like him, not that way. She was just looking for a distraction, which, yeah, sounded sluttier than it really was.

In her defense, at the time she'd been on the rebound from That-Creep-Michael, who'd gone from *I love you, I love you* to *Later, babe, I'm moving to Maine*, practically overnight.

And *that* fiasco was after the world's most embarrassing one-night stand ever, with Navy SEAL Irving Zanella, who'd immediately left for six months of punishment duty because he'd gone UA—the Navy's version of AWOL—to save Tracy from a psycho-killer who'd wanted to use her corpse for an art project.

Which was something she absolutely could *not* think about while walking alone down a dimly lit city street.

Tracy picked up her pace, her shoulders screaming, the handles of the plastic bags cutting into her hands as she hurried the last few blocks. And then she was turning the corner onto her street, in sight of her building where—oh, good!—Tess and Jimmy were home, light streaming from their open living room window. They would surely hear her if she screamed loudly, and if there was one thing she was good at, it was being loud and. . .

Shoot.

She slowed her pace, looking up at that brightly lit window, at the ceiling fan she could see spinning, at Tess's once jungle-worthy collection of house plants, now brown from neglect.

Tess and Jimmy weren't home.

Tess and Jimmy would never be home again, because Jimmy Nash was dead.

Really.

For weeks, Tracy had held her breath, waiting for someone in the office—Jimmy's good friend Lawrence Decker, or maybe even the boss, Tom Paoletti—to give her a wink and a nod, letting her in on The Big Secret. Which was, of course, that Jimmy was only pretending to be dead.

For a while, she'd found clues and hints in nearly everything.

The coffee mug in the office, for example.

For as long as Tracy had worked at Troubleshooters Incorporated, Jimmy and Deck had had an ongoing competition for the coffee mug with the smiley face. It had nothing to do with the silly artwork, and everything to do with its super size. It held more coffee—ergo, they would steal it from each other's desks.

It had been sitting on Jimmy's desk, half full with cold coffee, the morning Tracy had come in to the office after word had gone out that he'd died.

The sight of it had made her cry, but she'd washed it out and carefully set it back on his desk. It seemed somehow wrong to put it in the cabinet with the other mugs. And there it had sat, in an office that no one used, that everyone walked a little bit faster to get past, because Jimmy was gone.

But on Decker's first day back, some weeks after the memorial service, he'd headed for the coffee station, which was out in the waiting area near Tracy's reception desk. And as he poured himself a cup, she'd realized that he'd swiped that smiley face mug off Jimmy's old desk.

It seemed weird that he would have done that—as if seeing that mug sitting there should have made him cry, too. Inwardly, of course, because he *was* an alpha male.

But he hadn't even looked upset—he hadn't look *any*thing—and Tracy had found herself holding her breath again, waiting for Decker to glance at her, toast her with that mug, and give her a *we both know Nash isn't really dead* nod.

But he hadn't.

And okay, it wasn't just stupid things like coffee mug usage that fed Tracy's fantasy.

She'd asked both Lindsey and Troubleshooters XO Alyssa Locke if didn't they think it was strange that Decker had delivered Tim Ebersole, leader of the neo-Nazi group called the Freedom Network, to the authorities in close to one healthy piece?

Neither of the two women had understood her question, so she'd clarified. Decker could just as easily have delivered Ebersole's lifeless body to the FBI. He absolutely could have killed the murderous SOB—claiming self-defense and ridding the world of Ebersole's evil—and no one would have questioned him.

Tim Ebersole was directly, *absolutely* responsible for Jimmy Nash's death. No one doubted that.

And yet Decker had let the man live.

Lindsey had agreed that it was a little weird, but Alyssa had told Tracy, "That's what makes Decker Decker," which made a certain amount of sense.

Lawrence Decker *was* one of a kind.

He was also an enigma. Just when Tracy thought she'd figured him out, identifying him as a man of certainty and consistency, always ordering the exact same type of pizza or coffee, he'd go and do something completely unexpected.

She, however, *was* as predictable as a stone.

Even when the cold hard truth was staring her in the face, she "what if-ed" her way into believing improbable and ridiculous possibilities.

What if Jimmy were just *pretending* to be dead . . . ?

And yes, it was probably the fact that, before Decker had caught him and brought him to justice, creepy and evil Tim Ebersole had faked *his* death, that had made Tracy come up with that ridiculous idea.

It created a far nicer scenario than the one in which Jimmy was forever gone.

But the truth was, as much as she wished otherwise, that this was real
life, not some Hollywood thriller where Jimmy would emerge from hiding
when the time was right.

No, Jimmy Nash was dead—his ashes contained in a pathetic little
urn that now sat on the mantel of the gas fireplace in the apartment he'd
once shared with Tess.

Tracy knew, because she'd found it there. She'd recognized it—it had
sat on the altar of the church during his funeral.

*The memorial service was lovely.*

Why were some people so unbelievably stupid?

Someone—a client—had said that, just today, to Decker, in the lobby,
right in front of Tracy's desk.

The memorial service *wasn't* lovely. A good friend had *died.* Violently.
And Tracy was sorry, but there were no comforting words or musical selec-
tions that could make anything even remotely connected to that tragedy
into something that could ever be described as *lovely.*

She sighed as she humped her groceries up the stairs past Jimmy and
Tess's, to her own apartment, remarkably fatigued after what had been an
unusually quiet day at Troubleshooters Incorporated.

She hadn't created an incident, although she'd been tempted to. Instead, she'd sat at her desk and bit back the words she wanted to say—
*Personally? I thought the memorial service sucked*—as she'd forced a smile
at the imbecile who'd uttered that crap.

Decker had shown the king of the buttholes to the door and headed to
his office, hand on the back of his neck as if he'd had a killer of a
headache.

"Can I get you some coffee?" Tracy had asked him, and he'd actually
looked surprised. Or maybe that had been fear she'd seen in his usually
steady eyes, so she added, "Tom just made a fresh pot." Subtext: Someone
else me made it—not me.

She'd long since learned how to make a proper pot of coffee, but those
first few months she'd worked as Troubleshooter's receptionist, she'd gotten it really wrong, too many times.

And the myth that her coffee was unpalatable lived on.

"No thanks," he'd said. "I'm all set."

"I'm sorry about . . ." She'd pointed to the door. "*Lovely*. God."

Deck had smiled ruefully, and disappeared back into his office, leaving her to the scheduling, which was becoming quite the challenge.

Sam and Alyssa had just gotten the boss's permission for a solid month of lost time—what was he thinking? And Dave was going to Boston with Sophia, whose father was in the hospital. Their return date was unknown. Tess was still on medical leave, and Decker, too, was only working part-time and if anyone else called in with some excuse not to show up, they might as well shut the office down for the entire rest of September.

And maybe they should. They could all use a break.

Tracy set her grocery bags down in the hall as she unlocked her apartment door. She went inside, kicking it shut behind her as she hustled the groceries into the kitchen, where she put the salad and the fish in the fridge, because dinner could wait. She hurried into her bedroom, dumping her laptop on her bed so she could change into a T-shirt and jeans.

It had to be Lawrence Decker down there in Tess and Jimmy's apartment. He was probably—finally—helping Tess by clearing Jimmy's clothing out of the place.

His doing so would put the final nail in the coffin—*bad* analogy, wow—of Tracy's fading hope that Jimmy was still alive. For a moment, before she zipped up her jeans, she paused, and considered pretending that she hadn't seen the light, so that she wouldn't have to help, wouldn't have to know.

But throwing out Jimmy's clothes was not going to be an easy task for Deck, who'd been friends with the dead man for more than ten years.

The very least Tracy could do was help get the job done, twice as quickly.

Slipping her sneakers onto her bare feet, she grabbed the laundry basket that was in the corner of her bedroom, and went to do just that.


Jimmy was having a nightmare.

It was a frequent occurrence—and had been, even before he'd been shot and nearly died.

Tess had learned through the years they'd been together that it wasn't always necessary to wake him. Sometimes it was enough just to put her arms around him and hold him tight.

But here, a half-day's drive from San Diego, in this remote desert safe house that Jules and Decker had set up, she was still sleeping on a cot that she'd placed in the corner so as not to disturb him.

He awoke with a shout. "No! *No!*"

Tess scrambled to his side. "Jimmy. Jim, it's all right. We're safe."

"Oh, Christ," he gasped as he clung to her. "Oh, Tess . . ."

"I'm here," she said.

"Where?" he asked. "What . . . ?"

"The safe house," she told him. "Remember?" She fumbled for the unfamiliar lamp on the unfamiliar bedside table, finally found the switch and clicked it on.

"Shit!" Jimmy turned away, closing his eyes against the light. "Don't!"

She switched it back off, but not before she saw that his face was wet with tears—as if she would somehow think him less of a man because he'd wept in his sleep? Still, over the past long weeks of his recovery, he'd been more vulnerable than he'd ever been before—at least in his adult life. Confined to a bed, hooked up to monitors and an IV, unable to move, forced to accept help for his most basic needs . . .

The ride from the hospital had not been an easy one, and he'd been sleeping pretty much continuously since arriving here early Monday.

His wounds, both from being shot and from the surgery that had saved his life, were still painful. And the infection that had riddled him for weeks had not only made him weak, but had prevented him from moving around, which Tess knew made his back and legs ache all the time.

Not that he'd complained.

Not in the hospital, and not in the cargo van in which he'd ridden here, on a stretcher. FBI agent Jules Cassidy himself had been driving, with Alyssa riding shotgun and Tess in the back.

They'd pulled right into the spacious five-bay garage at the base of this amazing hilltop castle, and closed the door tightly behind them.

Sam Starrett was already there, waiting for them, playing the tough-guy former SEAL even though everyone at Troubleshooters knew that he was an emotional pushover, and that the idea of bunnies falling in love in the spring made him choke up. He'd hugged Tess a little too tightly in greeting before clearing his throat about fourteen times and telling Jimmy that he looked like shit warmed over, which, for a guy who'd been dead for a few months, was pretty damn good.

They'd wheeled Jimmy into an elevator—this place had an elevator!—and gone to a gorgeous two-room suite with floor-to-ceiling windows looking out onto the harshly beautiful desolation of the desert. The windows were one-way—no one on the outside could see in—but Tess had noticed Jimmy's trepidation as he looked at them, so she'd shut the drapes. With the push of a button on the wall by the bed, they'd closed with the softest motorized purr, and Jimmy soon relaxed into sleep.

Over the past day and a half, he'd roused only for meals.

But now he was awake and struggling to control his still-uneven breathing as Tess carefully stretched out beside him. She rested her arm across his stomach as she took his hand and interlaced their fingers, her leg across his thighs.

The full body contact seemed to soothe him, and it wasn't long before he moved—to wipe his eyes with the heel of his other hand.

"Shit," he said again, but softer this time. "It's the same fucking nightmare, every fucking night."

That was more information than he'd ever given her, but of course they hadn't been able to talk freely in the hospital, with the nurses constantly coming in and out. Here, however. . .

Heart pounding, Tess quietly asked him, "Can you tell me . . . ?"

Jimmy was silent for a long time—which was not a surprise. Talking about himself—his feelings and fears—was not one of his stronger skills, and she'd all but given up on his ever answering when suddenly he spoke.

"Did we get the DNA results back from that shirt?"

Tess sighed at his change of subject. "Not yet. Maybe in the morning."

"But we sent it out to the lab?" he asked.

The shirt in question was the one he'd been wearing when some unknown person had tried to kill him. It was, apparently, only one in a number of recent incidents in which Jimmy had nearly ended up dead—and Tess couldn't think about that too much or her head would explode.

But the shirt didn't just have only Jimmy's blood on it—it also had the blood of his attacker.

That shirt was—and Jimmy hadn't told her this, but she'd figured it out by doing the calendar math—one of the reasons their apartment had been searched and trashed last July. His attacker had wanted his DNA sample back.

"We sent it on Monday morning," she told him, her frustration leaking out in the terseness of her reply. "Early yesterday."

"It's Tuesday?" He was surprised and disgusted with himself. "What the hell have I been doing?"

"Sleeping," she informed him. "It's what bodies do when they need to heal."

"We need to back down on my pain meds," he told her, "because those dreams . . ." He shook his head—a rustle against the pillow in the darkness.

"The dreams are all yours. Last meds you took were . . ." She had to think about it. "Before we got into the van."

He sighed heavily. "Great."

"I wish," Tess said so softly she was almost inaudible, "you could tell me. . . ."

He was silent again, and she closed her eyes, knowing that if he weren't still so weak, this was where he'd kiss her. Make love to her. Try to tell her, through touch and eye contact, all the things he couldn't bring himself say.

"It's okay," she said, "if you don't—"

But Jimmy spoke, cutting her off. "I'm on assignment," he said, his voice barely more than a whisper in the dark. "Another black op covert from the motherfuckers at the Agency."

She was surprised—and a little confused. "In your dream," she clarified, the words falling out of her mouth even as she realized she should just zip it and let him talk.

But he seemed okay with her question. "Yeah. But the assignment in the dream has the same MO as the others. The real ones. A phone call to tell me where and when. Background information in a file in a bus station locker. Whoever it is on the other end of the phone, he knows my travel plans, my schedule at Troubleshooters—sometimes before I do."

Tess hardly dared to breathe, praying that he'd keep talking.

He did. "This time I'm in New Mexico—some little town called Kettleston—and I can't believe I've gotten a call, but it's not a deletion, thank God." His voice shook. "God, Tess."

"I'm here," she said, through a throat that was tight from the sudden tears that sprang up—tears she didn't dare let escape. "It's all right."

"No," he said, "it's not."

"It's over," she reminded him.

"Sometimes I think it'll never be over." His voice was rough with emotion.

"But it is," she insisted.

"After all this, you still have faith we're going to live happily ever after," he said, with a sound that was half laughter, half despair. "I don't know why."

"You're in Kettleston," she prompted him, tempted to shake him because she was sick and tired of his *lack* of faith — in her, in them. "What do they want you to do?"

Jimmy sighed. "Almost nothing. A simple B&E for a hard-drive download from a computer that isn't connected to the Internet."

Hence the hard access via breaking and entering. Even a secure wireless setup could be hacked by someone with fairly rudimentary skills, but if a computer didn't have an Internet connection. . .

"The target's not in Kettleston," Jimmy continued, "it's in Albuquerque — a three-hour trip. I've got a rental car, so I make the drive."

Troubleshooters Incorporated had a client based out of Kettleston, New Mexico. Harrison & Sons. It was one of their many paranoia accounts — businesses run by CEOs who feared terrorist attacks despite being HQ'd in the land of cattle or corn.

Sometime over the past year — Tess couldn't remember exactly when — Harrison & Sons had hired Troubleshooters to redesign their security system, and Jimmy had been in charge of the project. It was an easy job at a high rate of pay — the drawback being the travel and the days spent away from home, housed in a crappy hotel.

"The intel in the file I've been given," Jimmy continued quietly, recounting his "dream," if that's what it really was, "is limited. Brief. I'm entering the home of Ronald Fenster. He's a bank manager, thirty-nine years old, divorced, no kids, heavily in debt, suspected drug use, currently in Phoenix, Arizona, at a real estate investment workshop."

"In other words, he's not home," Tess said, and felt Jimmy nod.

"No one's home," he confirmed. "It's a simple job in an empty house. A cakewalk. I'll be in and out inside of thirty minutes, depending on how long it takes to copy his files to my flashdrive. According to the intel, the computer I'm targeting is in the southeast bedroom on the second floor.

"The McMansion is dark," he continued. "I drive the neighborhood, but it's after midnight and the whole development is rolled up tight. So I leave the car about a mile away and walk in. Disable the security system and enter through the back door.

"I'm halfway up the stairs when I know something's wrong. Really wrong. I don't know how I know—maybe I smell blood, maybe I hear something. I draw my weapon as I keep going—if I stop they'll know that I know they're there. So instead of going into the southeast bedroom, I head for the master, where I goddamn nearly trip over Ronald Fenster, who's tied to a chair. He's been . . ."

Jimmy stopped, and Tess just waited, holding her breath, praying that he'd do it—that he'd trust her enough to tell her.

"He's been beaten," Jimmy whispered. "Tortured. The ends of his fingers are . . . Christ, he's a mess. His throat's been cut and I slip in the blood, which slows me down. I can hear them now, they're coming for me, and I discharge my weapon at the bedroom door, and I think maybe I hit one of them as as I kick out the window screen. I jump and by some miracle I don't break my ankles, and I'm running as they shoot at me. And I'm hit, but the bullet's spent, and I know I'm not badly hurt. I can get away as long as I don't leave a trail of blood. Except then the dream shifts, and I'm back in the bedroom, only this time it's not Fenster in the chair."

He took a deep breath, and it sounded raspy and loud in the darkness, but then he whispered, "This time, it's you."

Oh, God. "I'm here," Tess said again, unable to keep her voice from shaking. "I'm right here." She *didn't* tell him that maybe—just maybe— her showing up dead in his dreams was his subconscious fear that his deceit could still kill their relationship. After all, he'd lied to her for *years.*

It seemed he might be out of the woods in terms of his physical injury—which meant it was getting close to the time to tell him that the emotional damage she'd sustained from his dishonesty *had* nearly been fatal.

"I know what you're thinking," he said, and she waited to see if he really did know. "How much of the dream is a dream and . . . Obviously the last part, with you, is just . . . But the rest of it is . . . It's kind of a conglomerate of . . . What I'm trying to say is that it happened, but not that way. The assignment in Albuquerque *was* just a computer download. But the intel in the file they gave me was faulty. Fenster was home. He was very much alive. He heard me break in, and he had a gun, and when I went out the window, he shot at me. He didn't hit me, though. The getting shot that I dreamed about was from another black op, in Kansas, about a month later—but I was out of range and the bullet was spent, so . . ."

A spent bullet was one that had run out of force and energy. It didn't do as much damage. But it still could do plenty of harm.

"Kansas?" Tess asked, working hard to keep her upset out of her voice. He'd been *shot* last year—not in a dream, in *reality*—while in Kansas. "Smallwood?"

She felt him nod in the darkness. "Yeah."

Jimmy had been part of a "red cell" team at another client's corporate headquarters in Smallwood, Kansas, last winter. He'd come home from that assignment and immediately gone out on another. And then another. And another.

It hadn't made sense because he hated spending so much time on the road, but now Tess realized he'd been waiting for his *gunshot wound* to heal before sharing a bed with her.

She had to grit her teeth in order to hold her tongue. Chastising Jimmy—or slapping him—would only shut him up, fast. And this was not the right time to roll out her list of demands. Mostly because she still hadn't recovered enough from nearly losing him to be reasonable. She recognized that *promise you'll never go anywhere without me again* wasn't going to fly. Although *from now on, you* must *tell me when you've been shot* was a definite add to her list.

"At least that's what I thought at the time—that the intel was bad," Jimmy added, and it took her a second to make sense of his words. Unlike Tess, he'd already dismissed his injury. "I suspected I'd been set up, but it wasn't until later—until Smallwood—that I knew for sure. I was supposed to die that night in Albuquerque. Fenster was supposed to shoot me as an intruder. *That's* what the dream's about. It's my subconscious telling me that I should have known back then that it wasn't a mistake, that they weren't just getting sloppy. That they wanted me dead."

"Who did?" Tess asked. "Who's *they*?"

He laughed—a burst of frustration that made him wince and curse. "Tess, believe me, if I knew who they were, they'd no longer be a threat to anyone. With luck, when the DNA report from the shirt comes back . . ."

He was quiet again for a while, just breathing.

But then he said, "After Smallwood, I went back to the Agency. I walked into Dougie Brendon's office and I made him take me in to the head of the black ops division, where I told them both that I was done. They denied sending me out on missions, at least not in the past two years, but they would've denied it, you know? Considering some of the shit they made me do."

Tess did know. She'd worked for the Agency's support unit for several years herself. Black ops were called *black* ops for a reason. The assignments were never acknowledged, and tended to be well outside of the limits of the law. There was never a paper trail, never a record, never a prayer—only instant distance and disassociation from the Agency—for the black op agent who was unlucky enough to be apprehended by the "enemy."

"Same night I went to see Brendon," Jimmy continued quietly, "I got a phone call. The son of a bitch who called told me that it's too late. That I can't back out now, that if I go in to the Agency again, if I talk to *anyone* . . . I'll end up back in prison.

"I tell him to go fuck himself, and I hang up the phone. And then I went back to Albuquerque. See, I knew that, whoever they were, they were monitoring my travel. Anything the government knew about me, they somehow knew it, too. So I figured I'd send them a little message."

Tess nodded. She knew exactly where his story was going. Straight back to Ronald Fenster.

"They called me the next day," Jimmy told her, "and I bluffed. I said that I'd gotten one of their compatriots to talk to me and that I was well on my way to tracking them down so I could rip out their throats and end this bullshit. And then I waited for them to show up at our old friend Ronald Fenster's house.

"Only somehow, they got to him first," he whispered. "Somehow, they knew. I sat there for three days, Tess, and nothing moved outside or inside of that house. Finally someone shows up, but it's a realtor, putting a FOR SALE sign out front. She leaves, and as soon as it's dark, I go inside. And the house is empty. No furniture, new carpeting, fresh paint.

"And I finally go back to my hotel room—I'm already freaked out—and there's a DO NOT DISTURB sign on my door. So I'm careful when I enter the room and. . . ."

"Fenster?" Tess asked quietly, bracing herself.

"Yeah," Jimmy told her. "They put him in the bathtub. He was tied to a chair, and . . ." He had to clear his throat. "Tortured. To make it look like they'd tried to find out what he'd told me—which was nothing, because I hadn't even talked to the man. They *knew* I hadn't talked to him—they'd probably contained him the day after he failed to kill me. They knew I'd figure it out and come back for him. And they wanted to send me a message. So they cut his throat, probably ten minutes before I got back to the hotel. His body was still warm, Tess. For all I know, I fucking walked past them in the lobby."

Oh, God. "He was in the *bathtub*," Tess repeated, clinging to the facts. She didn't want to think about how close the killers had come to Jimmy.

"Thoughtful of them," Jimmy said. "I only had to get rid of a body. I didn't have to tear out the carpeting and repaint the walls."

Tess sat up. Something here didn't make sense. She could understand why Jimmy's mystery men wouldn't have tried to kill him as he'd waited outside of Fenster's house. Jimmy had surely been on high alert at the time, and they no doubt knew him as an operator well enough to recognize that going after him then would be a deadly mistake. But . . .

"If they wanted you dead," she asked, trying not to let her voice shake, "why not just wait for you at the hotel and kill you there? They were *in* your room."

"Or why not take me down with a sniper rifle, in the CVS parking lot? Or at the gas station, or outside our apartment or . . ." He shook his head. "I don't know. Best I can figure is they didn't want me dead by assassin. At least at that time. Later, I think they just wanted me dead, but back then, they seemed to want me dead at the scene of a crime—"

"And Ronald Fenster, with his throat slit in the bathtub?" Tess couldn't help it—her voice was getting louder. How could he *not* have told her about this when it had happened? She wasn't just angry at the men who wanted him dead—she was angry at Jimmy, too. "Didn't *he* make your hotel room the scene of a crime?"

"Well, yeah." Jimmy gave her that. "But they would've had to wait for me in the room, and someone might've heard the gunshots."

Oh, God.

"Why didn't you say something?" Tess couldn't keep the question inside any longer. "Why didn't you tell me—"

"Because they pinned a note to Fenster's shirt that said: *Don't go to the authorities, don't talk to anyone. Go home and wait for instructions, or . . .*" He choked the words out. "*Tess is next.*"

"So . . . what? You decide to come home and . . . and . . . break up with me?" Suddenly Jimmy's erratic behavior over the past year made sense—in a backwards, twisted, utterly imbecilic way.

"I didn't know what else to do. I thought you'd be safe if I—"

"You should have come to me, or, God, at least told Decker!"

"I thought—"

"That I'd just let you go?" Tess asked him. "*Oh, well? Thought he was the love of my life, but I guess it didn't work out?*"

He was silent again, for such a long stretch of time that she stood up, putting some distance between them, afraid that if she didn't, she'd smack him.

But he didn't answer her and he didn't answer and she got tired of waiting. "Don't you shut down on me now," she said, all of her anger and fear and frustration coming to a boil. Her voice got even louder—she couldn't help it. "Don't you dare!"

"I was scared," he shouted back at her. "All right? I was fucking terrified. I've never gone up against anyone like these motherfuckers. I have never searched so hard and so long and come up so empty. That doesn't happen to me, Tess. I can do this job with my eyes closed. I'm better than everyone—except for these guys. They want me dead, and they'll go through you to do it!"

There was a knock on the door. A voice from the other side. "Everything okay in there?"

Great. It was Jules Cassidy, come to see what all the shouting was about.

The fastest way to get rid of him would be to give him a visual, so Tess quickly crossed to the door. Opened it. The light was on in the hall, and she squinted in the brightness.

The FBI agent was actually wearing Mighty Mouse boxer shorts, a Juicy Fruit T-shirt, and a rueful smile, his hair charmingly rumpled and his feet bare, as if he'd rolled out of bed.

Stopping on his way to get his sidearm, which he held loosely but with total authority.

"Jimmy's feeling better, but I don't think he's quite ready yet to be shot for being a jerk," she told Jules. "But thank you. I'll stick to yelling at him for now."

He laughed his surprise, even as he looked past her to do a quick visual sweep of the room. Tess, too, glanced back to where Jimmy was in bed, his arm up, covering his eyes, his nose tucked into the crook of his elbow, his misery apparent.

"We're clear," Jules said, and Tess realized that he was wearing his miniaturized headset—an earpiece that was about the size of a large hearing aid, with a microphone that was aimed vaguely toward his mouth.

She and Jimmy had been given similar headsets, so they would always be in the communications loop.

"I'm sorry we woke everyone," she apologized.

"Nah," Jules said, good-natured as always. "It's barely nine o'clock. I turned in early because I'm still on eastern time. I figured it'd be better for me to stay on that schedule. That way I can take the morning watch and not have it, you know, kill me."

"Still," Tess said.

"The timing was good," Jules reassured her. "We'd scheduled a drill for nine thirty, so . . . We're going to be running worst-case scenarios pretty much constantly over the next few days. Tomorrow, if Jimmy's up for it, we'll do several where we get the two of you, plus Robin and Ash, into the security room. See how long it takes us."

The security room doubled as a panic room. Once its door was locked, it would take a tank to blast through the reinforced walls.

"Late morning's probably best for that," Tess said. "Let Jimmy sleep in as long as he can."

Jules nodded, his smile kind. "We'll figure it out tomorrow. Hey, as long as he's awake, take his blood pressure and temp, okay?"

"I will."

"Tell him I'm glad he's feeling better enough to get the verbal asskicking he deserves. And be sure to throw in a *you're a freaking idiot* or two for me, while you're at it." He nodded at the door. "Don't forget to lock it."


Sophia was going to be sick.

The man in the hospital bed was a stranger—a frail, desiccated old man who looked as if he'd lived far longer than the slightly-less-than-sixty years she knew her father to be.

Of course, considering his years of drug abuse, plus nearly two decades of hard time in a foreign prison, it was amazing he was still breathing.

It was only if she squinted and tilted her head that she could see a shimmering ghost of the vibrant, laughing man with the long, sun-bleached, dirty-blond hair that she'd known all those years ago.

The rush of memories was dizzying—playing Frisbee with him in what looked like a park but was, in fact, royal gardens, her father turning the potential trauma of getting chased away by soldiers on horseback into just another game. It was he who insisted she dress in boys' clothes, giving her precious freedom as they traveled through countries where women and girls were treated as second-class citizens.

She remembered him reading to her, always reading, his voice slow and lazy, but still melodic even when he was stoned. She remembered him singing to her, too—Lord, he'd loved his guitar.

She'd carried it with her for months after he'd vanished. She'd nearly died fighting to keep it from being stolen, and, badly beaten, she'd wept—not over her scrapes and bruises, but over the guitar's loss, over having failed him.

And over her realization that he was never coming back.

"Hey," Dave said, his voice in her ear, in tune with her as always. "Okay, it's okay, I've got you. Hold on to me and just breathe, all right, Soph?"

She nodded, closing her eyes against the nausea that swirled around her, as he pulled her down the hall, all but carrying her, his arm strong and warm around her waist.

He was speaking to someone in his team-leader voice—commanding, authoritative—and within seconds, he'd found her some blessed privacy in a bathroom, and had closed and locked the door behind them both.

Sophia went right to the sink and ran cool water on her hands and wrists, splashing it up onto her face, her makeup be damned. Dave hovered, pulling paper towels from the rack on the wall and holding them out for her.

"How can I help you?" he asked as she dried her face, his voice as filled with his concern for her as his eyes. "Tell me what you need."

Sophia had to laugh—it was either that or cry. "You mean, besides a trip to Hawaii and a new car? A Prius, I think. Or maybe one of those cute little Smart Cars."

Dave smiled, but it wasn't enough to hide his worry as he pushed a stray lock of her sodden hair behind her ear, his fingers gentle against her cheek. "Seriously, Soph. Just say the word and we're out of here. Seeing your father shouldn't make you physically ill."

"I'm okay," she said. "It was just . . . weird. I'd hated him for so long that . . . I'd forgotten how much I loved him."

Her eyes filled with tears, and he didn't hesitate. He pulled her close and tucked her in against him, enveloping her in his arms, his chin against the top of her head. "I'm so sorry," he murmured, his voice a rumble in his chest. "I can only imagine how hard this must be. It's completely okay if we just go to the hotel—"

"No." She shook her head. It had taken her a day to decide to come to Boston, another day of travel—heading east, they'd lost three hours of daylight. She was jet-lagged and nauseated and needed a shower, a hot meal, and some seriously tender lovemaking, followed by a full night of sleep. But only after she did this. "I want to see him. *Talk* to him." She pulled back to look up at Dave, wiping her eyes with the crumpled paper towel in her hand. He didn't look convinced, so she said it again. "I *want* to."

"He'll still be here tomorrow," he pointed out.

But she shook her head. "No. We're here now. And I don't want to tempt fate. Will you do me a favor and—"

"Absolutely," he cut her off. "Whatever you need."

She had to smile at that. "One of these days, you're going to say that, and you'll find yourself repaving my driveway."

"With a smile on my face, and a song in my heart," Dave told her. He was dead serious, too. "What do you need me to do right now?" He figured it out before she could answer. "Distract Maureen."

Sophia nodded. "I don't want to do this in front of her," she said. "I'm sure I'm going to do it wrong; I mean, I haven't read Miss Manners recently, so I don't know the correct etiquette for a reunion with a long-lost father."

Dave smiled as she'd hoped he would. "Consider it done," he promised.

And then, because he was so solidly Dave, she dared to ask for more. "Do you think you can keep her out of the room and still . . . come in with me?"

"You want me in there?" he asked, as if he didn't quite believe her.

"Very much," she whispered.

He nodded, holding her gaze. "Then I'm there," he said, as if it were a given, written in stone.

"She's extremely . . ." Sophia searched for the right word.

"Domineering?" Dave volunteered. "Pushy? Bossy . . . ?"

"I was going to say *bitchy*," she told him. "Entitled and a little mean."

"Frightened," Dave countered, "because her little brother, whom she loves, really is dying this time."

He was right. The nurse had told Sophia that her father was going to be moved into their facility for hospice care in the morning. "That, too," she admitted.

He kissed her—a sweet brush of his lips against hers. "Nurses, bless their souls, have expert level ratings when it comes to the world's Aunt Maureens. Give me about twenty seconds to delegate, and I've got your back."

"Thank you," Sophia told him, and he kissed her again.

"Anytime."

He released her, and she turned to check her hair in the mirror over the sink. Her eyes were red and swollen and most of her makeup had been washed away.

"You look beautiful," Dave told her—another absolute. "Let's do this."

"I'm ready," she said, although she wasn't quite sure she meant it.

But when Dave held out his hand, and she took it?

She was.


Someone had definitely been in Tess and Nash's apartment.

Decker went through the place carefully, but found no sign of robbery, no sign even that the place had been searched. Which didn't mean it hadn't been. It just meant that whoever had done the job had chosen a covert method—as opposed to a toss-and-run.

He probably should have used his secure satellite phone to call for backup, except there wasn't anyone to call. Jules, Sam, and Alyssa were all precisely where he wanted them to be—guarding the safe house, where they'd moved Nash and Tess yesterday morning. The last thing Decker needed was for any of them to leave their posts.

Besides, what would he say? *Nothing's been moved. Nothing big, that is. But I'm pretty sure I sense a molecular disturbance. Someone—besides me—has been in this apartment, sometime in the last week, moving the air around.*

Back in the hospital, Decker had spoken to Nash only briefly about the men who'd tried to blackmail and then murder him. The conversation had been short not only because Nash was easily exhausted, but because he honestly didn't know much about them. He believed they were somehow connected to the Agency, an organization for which Deck, too, had once worked. But Nash didn't know that for sure. Whoever they might be, they were, he'd stressed to Decker, the most formidable of opponents.

So after Deck had walked through the apartment twice, he'd gone out to his truck to get the bug sweeper that he kept behind the front seat. It wasn't until he went over the place thoroughly—and found no electronic surveillance devices—that he got the duffel bag down from the shelf in the master bedroom closet. It was exactly where Tess had told him it would be, above a tidy row of her clothing—mostly dresses and feminine versions of business suits.

He refused to let himself get too distracted, although there was one dress—formal, floor-length and slinky—that made him stop and look. It was gold and it glittered, with a set of string-like straps that he couldn't quite figure out, but that he guessed, when positioned properly, would leave most of Tess's back exposed. Most of her front, too—the neckline of the dress was cut almost down to the waist.

And yeah, perv that he was, he couldn't not touch it, and the soft fabric slipped seductively through his hands before he left the closet and set to work opening the drawers in the big dresser beneath the front window, doing what he'd come here to do—pack up a few things for his friend.

Not a lot, and nothing that would lead anyone who came in to search the place to believe that Nash was still alive. A stack of his favorite, comfortably faded T-shirts in rich colors, and an old sweatshirt—things that Tess might've wanted to wear to bed.

Deck then went through his friend's underwear drawer, searching for the Holy Grail of boxer briefs—a pair that was red-and-blue-striped.

Several weeks ago, Decker had gone to Target and bought Nash new socks and underwear. No way was he going to come here and remove clothing that Tess herself would never wear—not after taking such great pains to make sure their enemy believed Nash to be dead. But the substitute briefs Deck had purchased were apparently "ball-crushingly uncomfortable" and "like wearing sandpaper."

Despite his delicate hindquarters, Nash couldn't remember the brand or style of briefs that were his favorites—only their red and blue color. Hence Decker's current scavenger hunt.

And there they were, red and blue, in the middle of an impressively huge stack of underwear. As Deck pulled them out, he had to admit that they *were* exceedingly soft to the touch. And yet they were cotton—truly a miracle of modern science. He made a note of the brand and the size, re-folded them, and put them back on top of the pile.

He'd head for the mall in the morning, on his way out to the safe house. Nash was also going to need workout gear. Shorts. Sweatpants. Jeans.

The irony there was that Nash had more pairs of jeans on the shelf in the closet than a man would need in an entire lifetime. And Deck was going to be buying him yet another pair.

And they probably wouldn't be soft enough, either.

Next item on his list was . . . He found the pile of novels right where Tess had said they were—on the table next to her side of the bed—and put them into the duffel. She'd also wanted her bathing suit—he'd have to re-member to pick up a new one for Nash, too. Her favorite slippers, her run-ning shoes.

He'd found everything and was zipping the bag when he heard it.

A sound from the living room that signaled more than a mere disrup-tion of air molecules.

Deck grabbed his sidearm from his shoulder holster as he both dove for cover and spun, weapon raised, to face his attacker.

Who screamed, dropped the laundry basket she'd been carrying, and fell backward onto the tile floor, her hands in the air. "Don't shoot, it's me, don't shoot!"

Jesus, it was Tracy Shapiro, the Troubleshooters receptionist.

Decker immediately stood down. Figuratively. In reality, he slipped the safety back onto his weapon and flopped back on the plush carpeting, closing his eyes as he waited for the buzz-rush from the adrenaline at least to stop surging. With the jolt he'd gotten, it wasn't going to start to fade for a good long time.

"What," he managed to ask, "the hell . . . ?"

"I'm sorry," Tracy gasped. "I rang the buzzer, but I guess you didn't hear me."

He turned his head to look at her. There was no way he'd missed hearing a buzzer. Was there? Damnit, if he had . . . He rolled up into a sitting position as he holstered his weapon beneath his short-sleeved overshirt.

"Maybe it's broken," she continued to prattle. "I mean, I pushed the button, and I assumed it buzzed but that I just couldn't hear it from out in the hallway so—"

Decker cut her off. "How did you get in?"

She fished in the front pocket of a pair of jeans that were right out of 1972. They fit her like a second skin, cut low on her hips but flaring out at the bottoms. "I have a key," she announced, pulling one free and holding it up as Exhibit A. "Tess gave it to me when they—when she—moved in."

As she re-pocketed it, her T-shirt rode up, exposing a smooth expanse of tanned, toned skin and, yes, a belly-button ring in a bright shade of blue. It figured Tracy would have one of them. As if those jeans weren't enough to turn the hetero male portion of the population into one giant hard-on.

Back when Decker was ten, he'd had a babysitter named Mary Kate Sullivan who wore hip-huggers nearly identical to these. Over three decades later, and he still hadn't recovered.

"I live upstairs . . . ?" Tracy now reminded him.

"I know." Deck nodded as he pushed himself to his feet. She'd helped Tess and Nash find this apartment. Tracy and Tess had been friendly. Not good friends, not particularly close, but certainly neighborly.

"Are you here to get Jimmy's things?" she asked.

He felt himself go still. Why would she think he was here for *Nash's* things?

"Because I can help," she continued, gathering up the clothes that had fallen out of the laundry basket when she'd dropped it, quickly refolding some of the T-shirts. "There's a Goodwill box at the grocery store down the street, although you might want to take his shoes to a consignment store. There's one that specializes in designer brands. Shoot, I forget the address, but it's over near the zoo."

And Decker realized that when Tracy had said *get Jimmy's things*, she'd meant *get* as in pack them up and move them out of the apartment—which is what people did when someone died.

"No," Deck told her. "Thanks, but I'm just here to pick up some stuff for Tess."

Tracy believed him, her eyes somber. "How is she?"

"Hanging in," he lied as he held out his hand.

Again, she bought it as she let him pull her up. "How are *you?*"

Most people didn't dare to ask him that. But the concern in her eyes was genuine.

And warm.

And for several long seconds, Decker found himself thinking about a phone conversation he and Tracy had had nearly two months ago. She'd told him she was available, if he ever needed anything, and being male, he'd thought she'd implied something else entirely. Something that included the exchange of bodily fluids. And while he'd stayed silent, figuring out what to say in response, she'd realized that her words could have been taken as a sexual invitation, and she'd furiously backpedaled, letting him know that that *wasn't* what she'd meant at all, that she'd meant she was here if he should ever need to *talk.*

He'd told her not to worry, that he hadn't gone there and thought that, but they both knew he was lying.

On the other hand, he'd believed her. She honestly hadn't meant her words as a disguised *come hither and I'll do you.*

Not consciously. Subconsciously, though, was an entirely different story. Decker was fully aware that Tracy Shapiro noticed him on a purely animal, biological, female-to-alpha-male level.

And animal attraction being what it was, they'd both been careful, from the start, to keep their distance.

Which was why Tracy now pulled her hand free—damn, was he still holding it?—and took a step back at the exact same moment that Decker did.

And wasn't that awkward?

He forced a smile that no doubt came out more like a grimace, and answered the question she'd asked. "I'm hanging in, too."

"Well, I'm happy to help however I can. With the packing," she quickly clarified. Which only served to let him know that the thought of a different kind of help—one that put her atop him and naked—had flashed through her mind as well.

He pushed the thought away, slamming the lid on a box that he'd kept carefully shut for so many years that he'd lost count.

Tracy picked up the laundry basket and carried it into the bedroom, setting it on Tess and Nash's bed. "Just say the word," she added.

Decker leaned in the doorway, watching her put the clean clothes into the dresser drawers, careful to keep his gaze off her exquisitely shaped ass. "I don't want to move any of Nash's things out before Tess is ready," he lied easily.

"Of course." Tracy seemed to know where everything went, which wasn't that big of a surprise. She had something of a reputation for being inquisitive.

He couldn't resist saying, "I had no idea you did laundry on the side."

She shot him a humorous *oh no you dih-n't* look, and in that moment, before she answered, Decker realized that *that* was what was different. Tracy, who had a key, had been in this apartment since his last visit. And she'd taken the dirty laundry that had been overflowing from the hamper in the corner of the bedroom. She'd washed and folded it and was now putting it back.

"Tess and I have a deal," she told Decker. "It's supposed to be a mutual thing, only I almost never travel, so . . . Anyway, if we find that we're unexpectedly out of town, which happens—happened—to her and Jimmy pretty often, the other one of us goes into the fridge and takes the perishables. We also make sure the garbage isn't turning into toxic waste in the kitchen. I realized, about a week ago, that I hadn't done that, so I came in, you know, wearing my hazmat suit? Not that I'd needed it."

"I took care of the garbage," Deck told her.

"I figured," Tracy said. "But then I saw the hamper and I thought that's gonna suck, you know, if Tess comes home to find a pile of Jimmy's dirty clothes and, um . . ."

She'd opened one of the drawers and was standing there, staring into it, distracted.

"That was thoughtful of you," Decker told her. "Thank you."

"I also checked the washer and dryer," she said as she turned to look at him. "There was a load of socks and underwear in the dryer. I folded that and put it away."

Tracy was extremely easy to look at, with long auburn hair and a classically beautiful face with perfect, even features and big blue eyes. Decker had seen her personnel file when Tom had first hired her, and even though she dressed younger, he knew her to be in her early thirties.

She was slightly shorter than he'd thought, with yes-there-is-a-God curves to a body that she kept trim but not overly so.

It was easy to forget, when looking at her, that there was a highly functioning brain in that pretty head. There was a question now on her face. She was trying to keep it hidden from him, but he could see it.

"Is, uh, Tess staying with you?" she asked.

"No," Decker said. It was nice to not have to lie while she was looking at him like that. "She's just taking some time to . . . You know."

"Oh," Tracy said, as if what he'd just said made sense, "because I'd love to see her. I thought you were, um, together. Not that that's any of my business. But you know how rumors fly. Dave's pretty much moved in with Sophia—although that's not a rumor—and you and Tess are . . . whatever you are."

Decker forced himself to not react. What exactly was she digging for? And she was definitely digging. Had they come full circle back to the sexual attraction thing? He made himself shrug. "It's . . . complicated."

She nodded, and the sudden compassion in her eyes was not feigned. "I bet."

It was definitely time to go. Deck picked up the duffel and headed for the door. "I want to check that door buzzer. Make sure it's working."

Tracy followed, carrying her now-empty laundry basket. "How's this weekend?"

"I'm sorry?"

"I'd like to visit Tess and I thought—"

Jesus, that would never work—a visit from Tracy? "I'll let her know," Decker said, "but she's probably not . . ." He shook his head as he opened the door to the corridor and used words that made his *no* more definite: "She's still not up for visitors."

"Then maybe you shouldn't tell her. Don't give her a choice," Tracy said. "If I just dropped by . . . It might be good for her."

As Decker kept the door propped open with his boot, he pressed the button for the buzzer. Nothing. Which was a relief, because it meant he hadn't been distracted beyond imagining, nor was he losing his mind. He tried to look apologetic as he turned back to Tracy, who was still inside the apartment. "I don't think that's a good idea. She's still pretty fragile."

"All right," she said, "then I'll send her a card. What's the address?"

"Just give it to me," Decker said. "I'll pass it along." He motioned for her to exit through the open door.

But she didn't budge. "Funny how I knew you were going to say that."

He'd used both body language and word cues to end their conversation, but it hadn't worked, so he finally went point blank. "I've got to go. Will you lock up? Get the lights and the fan?"

"Sure, but . . ." Tracy turned back into the living room, raising her voice so he could still hear her. "Don't forget your . . . whatever this is." She came back to the door holding the bug sweeper that he'd left—damn—on the table next to the sofa.

"Thanks. Yeah. Right. I, uh, got a spark from one of the outlets in the kitchen last time I was here." He was lying his balls off, but she was nodding.

"Oh, my God. That must've been scary."

"Yeah," he said as he opened the duffel's zipper just enough to slip the device inside. "I broke a glass and used the vacuum to clean it up, and . . . I wanted to check the grounding on the outlet and . . . Turns out it's fine. It must be the vacuum, so be careful if you borrow it."

"I will," she said, still planted solidly in the apartment.

"Take care."

"You too." But before he could leave, she stepped forward and caught his arm with one well-manicured hand. "Ooh, Deck, wait. Since you're going to see Tess, is it all right if I write a note for her right now?"

He made an apologetic face as he gently extracted himself from her grip. "I really need to get moving."

"It'll only take a second. Just let me grab a paper and pen." She was already heading back into the kitchen.

"I'll be back in the office on Thursday," he called after her. Damnit. "Tracy, I've really got to go. You can send Tess an e-mail. Her e-mail's still the same."

"But a note makes it so much more personal," she said, coming back with a pad that Tess had kept near the phone. "Didn't your mother ever tell you that?"

Decker sighed as she tore the note she'd written off the pad and held it out to him. "I'm sure Tess will appreciate . . ." He read the words that she'd written in her round, girlish handwriting.

*Did you use that thing out in the hall, too?*

He looked up at her in surprise, and she looked up from writing another note to shake her head at him, in obvious disgust and disappointment. She finished and tore that second sheet off the pad.

*Last month Tom put me in charge of cataloging and keeping track of field equipment. I know exactly what a bug sweeper is, thank you very much.*

She reached out and used her pen to tap the first note, because he hadn't answered her question.

He shook his head, *no*. He hadn't swept the hallway.

"Are you sure you have everything?" she asked. "Oh, wait. Don't leave yet. Didn't Tess want that DVD . . . What was it, again?"

Decker just kept shaking his head. She obviously wanted him to come back into the apartment, no doubt to ask him why he'd swept the place for bugs. But that was a discussion he absolutely did not want to have. Not now, not ever. "I'll check with her and get it next time."

"*The Philadelphia Story*," Tracy said, quickly scribbling a third note on that pad. "It's her favorite movie. Well, that and *Casablanca*. Oh, and *Moulin Rouge*, of course, although it's probably best if she stays away from movies where one of the lovers dies. At least for a little while longer."

She tore that third sheet from her pad and thrust it at him.

*Who is Tess hiding from???* she'd written. *And why are you bringing her some of Jimmy's T-shirts and underwear?*

Decker looked up at her, and he saw hope mixed with the disbelief on her pretty face.

"I'm not," he said, answering her second question half-honestly. But he knew, try as he might to hide it, that she could see the truth in his eyes—that she was right, and that Nash was still alive.

"Oh, my God," she whispered as her eyes filled with tears. "Oh, my God . . ."

Ah, hell. Really?

Out of an entire team of highly skilled, super-elite operatives, it was Tracy, their allegedly ditzy receptionist, who'd figured it out?

As Decker watched, she tamped down her emotional response, blinked back her tears, and pushed the door open even wider. "Come inside," she said, in a voice that didn't so much as waver. It was a command, not an invitation. "And help me look for that DVD."

Decker folded all three notes and, hefting the duffel bag and shaking his head, went back into Tess and Nash's apartment, where Tracy closed the door, tightly, behind them both.

# CHAPTER THREE

S omeone was following him.

Years of working for the CIA had definitely made Dave paranoid, but there was no doubt about it.

Someone *was* following him.

At this late hour of the night, the top floor of the vast hospital parking
garage was deserted—except for Dave and the person who was following
him—and he was glad he'd suggested Sophia wait in the lobby. Seeing her
father again had been hard enough—no need to add to the misery by having to schlep to the car through the relentlessly chilly New England rain.

Still, the father-daughter reunion had gone well. Sophia had been gra-
cious in her acceptance of the old man's tearful apologies. She'd even
gone so far as to grant him forgiveness, of sorts. And her father had actually
started breathing more easily. Sophia had seemed to feel some relief, too
and—

Dave heard the footsteps again and glanced over his shoulder, half
hoping it was Sophia's Aunt Maureen, but knowing, just from the sound of
the footfalls, that it was someone much bigger than she was.

And it was, indeed, someone much bigger—than Dave even.

Male, Caucasian, mid-thirties, 250 pounds, about six-six. Gang tatts—
teardrops on his face, but faded—as well as inked letters on both of his
hands, between his knuckles and the first joints of his fingers. Dave wasn't
close enough to read what they spelled out.

He kept moving—his rental car was just ahead in the far corner of the lot, alone save for a dark blue pickup truck right next to it. He reached into his pocket for his cell phone as he glanced back at the big man again.

Shaved head, pale eyes—it was hard to tell their color in the low-wattage fluorescent streetlights—pierced eyebrow and nose, mangina beneath his lower lip.

Leather jacket slick with rain, jeans, biker boots.

He hadn't increased his pace at Dave's double-take, but he also hadn't angled off toward the only other cluster of cars. He just kept moving, parallel to Dave now—closer to the two vehicles. It was entirely possible that the blue truck was his, and that coincidence had brought them into the parking garage at this exact same moment in time.

Judging a man from his appearance was neither nice nor PC, but before Dave could comment on the weather—*hell of a night for a trip to the hospital*, at which point the big man would proudly announce that his wife had just had a baby girl, their first child—he heard the unmistakable metal swish of a switchblade knife being unsheathed.

He looked again, and sure enough, the dim light glinted off a nasty-looking blade held with a distinctly non-amateurish grip in the behemoth's extra-large hand.

Running for his car was not an option—knife-guy was planted neatly between it and Dave.

So Dave stopped, too. He stood there, in the rain, and said, "Are you sure you want to do this?" as he took out his cell phone and dialed 9-1-1. "Because I've already had a difficult day—after a bitch of a week—and this is not going to make it any better."

The big man smiled, exposing a gold tooth, like he was some kind of villain from a James Bond movie.

"Seriously," Dave said, "I know I don't look like much, but I'm former CIA. Plus, I just called for help and . . . Yes," he said into the phone to the emergency operator. "David Malkoff, formerly with the CIA? I'm on the top floor of the Fruit Street garage at Mass General, with a thug with a knife. Police backup would be nice—ASAP." He closed and pocketed his phone, then directly addressed the man. "If you start running now, I won't come after you."

The man's response was to feint forward, then swipe from the left, which sent Dave dancing back, untouched, landing in a defensive crouch as he put it into plain language even an ogre such as this one could understand. "Don't fuck with me."

Another swipe, and Dave timed it, turning and throwing his entire body into a roundhouse kick that knocked the knife from the fellow's colossal hand. It clattered and skittered across the tarmac as Dave scrambled—not very gracefully but so what, there were no judges here giving them points—to put himself between the giant man and the blade.

And yet the goliath was still between Davy and his rental car, which sucked since he'd left his slingshot back in San Diego. And then it sucked even more, when the last little bit of him that wasn't yet wet got soaked as the skies opened up and the rain came down even harder.

*Cssshhhht.* The sound was almost hidden by the rush of the falling rain.

"Oh, come *on*," Dave said, as he saw that, yes, his attacker *had* opened another switchblade. "This is where you run away."

The man finally spoke. "Not yet."

"It should be obvious that I'm not giving up my wallet," Dave pointed out.

"I don't want you to," the man said, his voice a lilting Irish brogue, a surprisingly musical tenor for such a monster. "Come, man, defend yourself." He smiled, revealing another flash of that tooth. "Or not."

He rushed Dave then, and it was like facing down a freight train that was barreling down a mountain. There was no point in trying to pick up that other knife—Irish's arms were much longer.

But a charge of this sort had no finesse, so Dave stood his ground until the last split second, waiting to see, from the way Irish tensed his wide shoulders, which way that knife was going to go. And again, Dave kicked into it, and *again* it went sailing, but then Irish crashed into him, which wasn't as painful as it would have been had the knife been in the man's hand, but was still quite the body slam.

They hit the ground with Dave already bringing his elbow up, hard, into Irish's ugly-ass face. He heard the crunch of a broken nose even as the bigger man wrapped one huge arm around him, pinning him, too, with a leg like a tree trunk, keeping him from rolling and scrambling away.

It was then, even as Dave scraped and ground the heel of his shoe down the front of Irish's leg, even as he went for the bastard's eyes, that he felt the piercing cold in his side. Cold and hot at the same time, and he froze for a split second, knowing his mistake had been in letting the big man get too close.

"A man who carries two probably carries three," Irish breathed in Dave's ear, then drew his third blade out. "Give my best to Santucci."

Santucci? Who the fuck was that?

But Jesus, now it hurt.

It wasn't cold, it wasn't hot, it was just brain-explodingly painful, and Dave knew he had to move or he was going to get sliced to shreds, so he hammered back again with his elbow as he grabbed for the monster's balls, but the man rolled, pulling his lower body away, which freed up Dave's legs, so he kicked and he scrambled and he bit and he flailed, and he turned his head and saw the crazy glint of light reflecting off that first switchblade knife that he'd knocked out of Irish's hand.

Dave reached for it, rolled toward it, his fingers closing around the handle even as he pushed himself to his hands and knees.

It was only then, gasping for air, wet hair in his face, blood pouring from his side onto the rain-soaked tarmac, that Dave realized Irish was gone.

He heard the sound of approaching police sirens—no doubt it was they that had saved his life—as he grabbed again for his cell phone and dialed Sophia's number.

He dragged himself toward the rental car—ready to lock himself in, in case Irish decided to come back—as Sophia picked up.

"Hey," she said. She sounded fine—thank you, Almighty Father. "What's taking so long?"

"Are you all right?" he gasped.

Her voice changed, turning crisp, efficient. "Yes. What's going—"

"Stay where you are," he ordered her. "In the lobby. Is there a security guard?"

"By the door to the ER," Sophia reported. "Yes. Dave, what's—"

"Stay with the guard," Dave told her. "I'm okay, but I was attacked in the parking lot—"

"Oh, my God, Dave!"

"I'm all right," he said again. "Stay with the guard—I'm going to come to you. The police are on the scene." He had to shout over the sirens. "They're going to bring me into the ER. Meet me there."

He shut his phone, hanging up before she could argue.

And then, thank God, the police *were* there, a woman in uniform drawing her sidearm as she scrambled out of the cruiser that had squealed to a stop closest to him. "Hands where I can see 'em! Drop the weapon!"

Dave pushed himself back onto his knees, leaving the knife on the ground as he held out his empty left hand.

"Both hands!"

He pulled his right hand from his side—it was covered with a ridiculous amount of his blood, like some kind of horror-movie special effect.

"Jesus!"

"My name is Dave Malkoff," he told her. "I made the 9-1-1 call. I'm former CIA. I was attacked by a man with a knife—that's his knife. I've been wounded." Obvious, but sometimes in duress, people needed help getting past their initial shock. "I could use an ambulance."

"I need an ambulance!" the female cop shouted.

"We need one over here, too," someone shouted back, and Dave turned to see another uniform—had to be a rookie; the kid was maybe twenty—on the other side of his rental car. "Oh, fuck," the rookie said, then scrambled away.

Dave could hear the unmistakable sound of vomiting, as the female cop said again, even more horror in her voice, *"Jesus!"*

He held his side as he pulled himself forward, so he could see around the car and . . .

Dear God.

The female cop shouted something that seemed to be directed at him, her words a dissonant blur.

Dave didn't answer. He couldn't answer. He had no idea what the answer was. He was suddenly dizzy—maybe from the spinning blue lights atop the police cars or the loss of blood—and try as he might to stanch the flow, he couldn't keep it from slipping out between his fingers.

The female cop's weapon was up again, almost in his face, waving in his peripheral vision as she shouted at him, "Is this the man who attacked you?"

The question finally penetrated, and Dave looked up from the grisly sight of a man with his throat slit, lying in a puddle of blood, half underneath his rental car.

It wasn't the big Irish man, but what the hell . . . ?

"No," Dave tried to tell the cop. "No . . ."

The dead man was Barney Delarow, a fellow CIA agent, a real sonuvabitch who'd led the murder investigation against Dave, all those years ago, back when Kathy-slash-Anise's body had been pulled out of the Seine, just outside of Paris.

"Dave! *Dave!*"

He turned to see Sophia, running toward him across the parking lot, another woman beside her, and he tried to stand up, to show her he was okay, that he could walk into the ER for the stitches he was going to need, but somehow the driveway smacked him in the face, and he realized he'd fallen.

She was beside him then, on her knees in the rain and the blood. "Help me!" she was shouting. "He needs to get over to the hospital *now!*"

And then he was being lifted, but he had to tell her, he had to make sure she knew. "I didn't kill him, Soph. That's not the man—"

"Hang on," she told him, tears or maybe it was just rain running down her face. "Dave, damnit, don't you leave me!"

Oh, shit, did she really think . . . ?

"Never," he tried to tell her, reaching for her through the darkness that was trying to swallow him, and connecting with her hand. Somehow he couldn't quite squeeze it. "Never . . ."

"You have to put his underwear back," Tracy told Decker as he set his bag down on Tess and Jimmy's living room floor, as she forced herself not to burst into tears. Jimmy Nash was *alive*. He had to be alive, otherwise Deck wouldn't have come back in here.

She had a million questions—what was going on, was someone after Nash and if they were, were they after Tess, too?—but she focused on the problem at hand. "If *I* noticed that you took some of his things," she told Decker, "someone else could, too."

"I didn't take any of his underwear," he countered quietly. "I just moved it a little. And the T-shirts . . . Tess could wear them. You know, to bed?"

What, was he crazy?

"You've been trying to make people believe there's something going on between the two of you," she pointed out. "And yes, it's bound to be incredibly complicated—your guilt, her guilt. But do you really think that she's going to ask her new lover to bring her some of her old lover's—her dead lover's—T-shirts so she can wear them? To bed, no less, where she could presumably occasionally bump into you?"

He shook his head, but it wasn't in response to her question. It was more of a rejection of this entire conversation.

So Tracy pushed on. "You know I'm right. Buy him new ones," she told Deck. "Buy him new *everything*. And we really do need to box up all of his stuff and get it out of here. Because if I were one of the people you wanted to convince that he's dead . . . ? I'd be wondering why you haven't done that yet. But I'd stop wondering if you delivered those boxes to Goodwill. Give his clothes away—don't put 'em in storage, okay? If his life is in danger—and it must be if you've gone to all this trouble—just give it all away."

Decker swore under his breath.

"I know it's a big expense," Tracy started, but he stopped her.

"No," he said, "that's not . . . You *are* one of the people we wanted to convince that he's dead. And if *you* figured it out . . ."

She had to turn away, because his words stung. She took the opportunity to pick up the bag and carry it back into the bedroom. Some of the operatives at Troubleshooters believed her to be less-than in the brain department—she was well aware of that—but she hadn't thought that Decker was among them. He'd never talked down to her, or treated her with anything other than respect.

"I figured it out because I live upstairs," she reminded him as he followed her, as he watched her set the bag on the bed. She unzipped it and took out the T-shirts that he'd put in there. There were a half dozen of them, and she made sure she got them all. "Because I guessed. Because I *hoped*. And because I'm *not* an idiot."

"I didn't say you were," Decker countered, as she put the entire pile neatly back into the drawer.

"Didn't you?" she asked, glancing up at him.

He was standing there, still watching her, arms crossed, feet about shoulder-width apart. He wasn't a big man, but he was extremely solid—a fact he usually tried to hide by wearing clothes that were not only drab and dull but just a smidgen too large. Today he was dressed in faded blue jeans, with an olive-drab T-shirt that was more form-fitting than usual, since it was hidden beneath a white, brown, and green plaid summer button-down shirt that looked like something Ben Affleck might've worn back when he was making *Good Will Hunting*—before he'd won an Oscar and had money to spend on clothing.

It was kind of funny. There were quite a few very handsome men working at TS Inc., and anyone who didn't know Lawrence Decker probably wouldn't have included him in that subset. But they'd have been wrong.

The fact of the matter was that the man worked it—hard—to be nondescript. He tried to blend in with his nothing-special brown hair and his seemingly average light brown eyes that were, in truth, a fascinating mix of green, blue, and brown. Tracy even suspected that he refrained from smiling too often, because his smile was a killer and took him instantly over into the hottie pile.

"You're an extremely intelligent receptionist," he told her now in his accentless, average-guy voice. "The key word there being *receptionist*." He swore again as he looked at his wristwatch. "Damn it."

"If you have somewhere to be," Tracy told him, "we can talk more about this tomorrow. I'll help you with the shopping. And I'll get this stuff packed up. Lindsey can help—"

"No," Deck cut her off. "Lindsey can't know."

Which meant Lindsey Jenkins, one of Troubleshooters' best kick-ass operatives and a former detective with the LAPD, didn't *already* know. Which made Tracy feel a little better. Less odd woman out.

She nodded as she went through the rest of the items in the bag. The only other troubling piece of clothing was a sweatshirt that had to be Jimmy's. She removed it. "Understood. I won't tell her."

Deck was still shaking his head as she rezipped the bag. "I'm sorry," he said. "This is too important."

"Okay then," she said, finding the right shelf in the closet for the sweatshirt. She raised her voice so he could hear her. "I'll do the packing by myself. Tomorrow, after work." But as she came back out of the closet, she saw that Decker's head-shaking hadn't stopped.

He just stood there as he looked at her with a full boatload of chagrin in his eyes. "Honey, I'm really sorry, but you're not going in to work tomorrow."

"*Excuse* me?" Tracy stared at him.

Decker didn't repeat himself. He was obviously aware that she both had heard him and knew precisely what he'd meant. "It's best if you call Tom from your home phone or your cell—don't use this line."

"And my excuse is *what*?" Tracy couldn't believe this. "I'm suddenly sick? Like, *Hello, Tom, even though I was perfectly fine when I left work this evening, I seem to have come down with . . . with . . . West Nile Virus*?"

Decker shook his head yet again. It was getting old. "More like you're taking a vacation with a new boyfriend."

"With no notice?" She was horrified, and made an *are you insane, Napoleon Dynamite*-worthy sound. "I would never do that. Not even for . . . Johnny Depp."

"Most of the staff is on vacation or taking lost time," Decker pointed out. "There's not going to be much to do over the next few weeks. It's last-minute, yeah, but it's good timing. Tom'll agree."

"And if he doesn't?"

Decker sighed. "Then you apologize and tender your resignation."

"*What*?"

"I know, and I'm sorry—"

"Sorry?" she said. "You're *sorry* that because you don't *trust* me to keep my mouth shut, I'm going to lose my job?"

"It's not that simple," Decker told her. "Think about it. If you were me, would you let you walk around, knowing what you now know?"

"Absolutely not," she said, heavy on the sarcasm. "Because you know me. I can't keep a secret to save my life. Plus, I'm none too bright. You never know, it might just come flying out of my mouth at any given moment."

"That's not what I think," he told her quietly.

"Isn't it?" she asked. "And what exactly does it mean—you're not going to *let* me *walk around*? Am I under arrest? Are you going to, like, lock me up? Word of warning: I don't do well locked in basements. Or closets. Although I've never actually *been* locked in a closet, so on that one, I'm just guessing."

Decker was shaking his head again, his eyes dark with understanding. "We've got a safe house," he said. "You'll stay there for the duration. It's comfortable—"

"Stay," she said. "Involuntarily, though, right? Like, if I want to, say, go to the mall—"

"Pack a bathing suit—there's both an indoor and outdoor pool."

"With a half-naked cabana boy named Rico?" Tracy shot back at him. "Serving drinks with little umbrellas? With enough daiquiris and exotic . . . *dancing* from Rico, ditzy, shallow Tracy won't remember that not only is she in jail, but she's *lost* her *job. . . .*"

He was trying not to smile, which was infuriating. "If you lose your job, I'll make sure you get it back when this is over and done."

"And when, exactly, is that going to be?" Tracy asked, arms crossed. He'd mentioned *the duration.*

"I don't know," Deck admitted with that same point-blank honesty that she'd always admired. It wasn't quite so charming tonight.

"Will you also pay my rent and utilities until that as-yet-undetermined time?"

"Yes," he replied without a hint of hesitation.

She blinked, because okay, that surprised her. "Seriously?"

"Honey, you have my word."

And there they stood, just gazing at one another.

Tracy had Decker's *word.* It was stupid, but his saying that impressed her. Bottom line, she liked this man. She admired him, very much—even when he'd hurt her feelings and pissed her off.

And then he went and did a double-Decker by voluntarily bringing up the volatile topic she'd tossed out a few moments ago with her locked-in-the-basement comment. "I understand that the idea of having your freedom restricted is a frightening one for you, because you've been locked up against your will," he told her quietly. "But the safe house is huge—you'll have your own private suite of rooms. There's a chef's kitchen, a home theater with an extensive collection of DVDs—"

"I'm a reader," she informed him. "A voracious one."

"We'll make sure you have all the books you want," he promised. "You can relax by the pool and read. And if it gets too restrictive for you, we'll figure something out. I'll get you to the mall. I won't be able to do it often, but . . . No one's locking you in the basement, okay? Never again. Not as long as I'm alive."

And okay, when he said things like *that*? As if they were absolute? *Not as long as I'm alive.* It was hard not to get a little gooey inside.

"Let's go to your place and make that phone call," Deck said, grabbing the duffel bag by the handles, "and pack your bag."

Wait a minute. Tracy trailed after him, into the living room. "Why not just tell Tom the truth—that I know about Jimmy and I'm going with you to . . . wherever this safe house is."

"He doesn't know," Decker told her, the fact of which floored her.

She had to repeat it, because it seemed so unlikely. "*Tom Paoletti* doesn't know."

"Nope," Decker said. "Sam and Alyssa do—but only because they're part of the security team guarding . . . you know."

Tracy did know. Guarding Jimmy Nash. Whatever was going on, Deck was spooked enough to not want to say his name aloud, even in a surveillance-free zone.

"Tess knows, obviously," he continued. "Jules Cassidy, from the FBI. And his, um, husband Robin? But only because he's providing the cover for the house. Me, and now you. That's pretty much it."

Tracy stared at him. Even more astonishing than the fact that she was going to be sharing a safe house with movie star Robin Chadwick Cassidy was the fact that so few people knew that Jimmy was alive. And she hadn't missed the fact that Dave and Sophia weren't on that list. Sophia—whom Tracy had been certain was just going to show up at work, one of these days, married to Decker. Like, they were going to leave the office—separately—some Friday night, and return happy and together on Monday, after a weekend spent risking their lives and thwarting some dangerous terrorist.

But Tracy had stopped being so certain of that when Jimmy had died.

Everything had changed after it became obvious that Decker was applying for Jimmy's old position in Tess's life. Except *that* was just another brick in the wall of his attempt to convince the world that Jimmy was dead.

And like most of the world, Sophia had believed Decker. And she was now playing house with Dave Malkoff.

Which really had to stink for Deck—despite his joy over Jimmy's not being dead.

"For the record," Deck told her now, "you're the only person who figured out what was really going on, so . . . I'm pretty sure that makes you the opposite of an idiot."

"I have no idea what's really going on," Tracy admitted. "Just that Jimmy is—"

"Don't say it," Deck stopped her. "When we get to the house, we'll fill you in on the details of the situation. You can help with support. In between the books-by-the-pool thing. If you want."

Tracy shut her mouth, which had dropped open when he said the word *support*. "I want."

"Good," he said. "And please don't take this personally, but until we get to the safe house? I'm going to be glued to your side."


Dave was in some kind of serious trouble.

He was still under from the anesthesia he'd been given while the doctors cleaned out and stitched up the knife wound in his side, but when he awoke, there were going to be a slew of questions.

Dear God, the sight of all that blood. . .

It had sent Sophia hurtling back, to Dimitri's death, to the violence that had violated their lives and left her a widow.

There'd been so much blood that day, too. It had caked beneath her fingernails and stained her clothes, and she'd sat, numb and shaking, then as now.

Back then, she'd been powerless, helpless—much as the men in the dark suits were trying to make her feel tonight.

But she wasn't helpless—not anymore—and she stood up, digging in her purse for her cell phone. A big sign was posted on the wall of the hospital waiting area, saying NO CELL PHONES ALLOWED, but to hell with that.

She needed to make this call.

Because just as she was no longer helpless, Dave hadn't suffered Dimitri's fate. His injury had been messy, but far from fatal. Fortunately, there had been no internal damage done by that knife, and his condition, post-stitches, had quickly gone from stable to solidly good.

They were keeping him in the hospital overnight, but really only because his stitches were being called "surgery," and the facility had rules about what constituted an inpatient or an outpatient procedure. The nurse had told her they'd want to keep him in, too, for observation because of the loss of blood. It didn't warrant a transfusion, but they were giving him fluids—and painkillers—intravenously.

Dave was, the nurses had all told her, an incredibly lucky man. A fraction of an inch in any direction . . .

But he was going to be fine. Which was unbelievably good news.

On the other hand, the guards at Dave's hospital room door, the crowd of dark suits waiting to question him further about the dead man in the parking lot, and the seemingly fact-conflicting answers he'd given to their questions when he'd briefly roused in the ER . . .

That wasn't so good.

Sophia sought control over her hands, forcing them to stop shaking so that she could dial her phone. She had the private cell number of Jules Cassidy, who worked—high level—at the FBI's Boston office. He wasn't so much *her* friend as a friend of many of the other operators at Troubleshooters.

It rang and rang, but he finally answered, thank God. "Cassidy." His voice was thick from sleep.

"This is Sophia Ghaffari, from Troubleshooters? I'm so sorry to wake you, sir," she said. "But it's rather urgent."

"I'm sorry," he said. "*Who* is this . . . ?"

"Sophia—" she started.

He finished with her. "Ghaffari, right. Sorry. Of course. I'm having one of these nights where the phone rings every twenty minutes, and each time I wake up with fewer brain cells firing. It's okay, sweetie, go back to sleep," he soothed someone in the room with him, no doubt his husband, Robin. "Just let me . . ." It was clear he was moving, closing a door behind him. "What's going on?"

"I'm sorry to bother you, but I'm over at Mass General," she told him. "Here in Boston. With Dave Malkoff. He was attacked in the parking lot by a man with a knife." Her voice shook. "He was stabbed."

"Is he all right?" Jules asked, the warmth of his concern palpable, even through the somewhat shaky cell phone connection.

"He lost a lot of blood, but he's . . . Yes," Sophia told him. "He's going to be fine."

"Has he ID'd the perp?" Jules asked. "And, wait a minute. Did you say he was stabbed in the *hospital* parking lot?"

"We were visiting my father," Sophia said. "He's dying and . . ."

"I'm so sorry," Jules said. "And . . . This isn't meant to be funny, even though it's going to come out sounding like a sick joke, but . . . Your father's not some Tony Soprano type, is he?"

"No," Sophia said, laughing despite her worry, despite the tears that kept forming in her eyes. "Not a chance."

"FYI, muggings outside of hospitals aren't uncommon," Jules pointed out. "There've been cases of addicts trolling emergency room parking lots, hoping to score an OxyContin prescription off some poor schlub who broke his ankle."

"That's not what this was," Sophia said.

"Are you worried for Dave's safety?" Jules asked. "Because I can call and have a guard put on him—"

"He's got plenty of guards," Sophia said. "But they're the other kind. The kind who are there to make sure he doesn't go anywhere. And to keep me out. They won't let me sit with him. I'm in the waiting room."

"Okay," Jules said. "I'm just going to shut up now and let you tell me what's going on."

She took a deep breath, exhaled hard. "Dave says he was attacked by a big man—a skinhead—who ran away when the police arrived. But there was another man at the scene, and I don't know for sure, but it's possible he was a CIA operative. A very dead CIA operative. His throat was cut."

"Oh, crap," Jules said.

"Yeah. Whoever the dead man is, I'm pretty sure Dave knew him, but he swears he didn't know he was there until the police found the body. Regardless of that? The dead man was neither big nor bald. I'm also pretty sure there were two knives found—but Dave said his attacker had three. One of the knives was in Dave's hand when the police arrived, the other was on the pavement by the dead man. They're testing them for prints and blood—you know, DNA."

Jules was silent for a moment, then said, "This incident. It's out of the blue? I mean, from your point of view? Dave hadn't mentioned an old friend or, I don't know, an old . . . enemy?"

"No," Sophia told him.

"Any secretive phone calls?"

"Not that I noticed," she said. "No."

"Mysterious trips?"

"We both travel for work," she answered, although a small warning bell chimed in the back of her mind. She still didn't know where Dave had gone just a few days ago, while she was in Denver. She'd assumed it was work-related, but he'd said something about taking several additional days off to come here, to Boston. It hadn't struck her as odd—*additional* days— until now.

"What?" Jules asked, perceptive as always.

"No," she said. "Nothing. We just . . . In our business, we don't talk about our assignments. Not outside the security of the office." But they did talk about it *in* the office. Dave had known she was going to Denver to close a deal with a new client. But he hadn't told her about any impending trip. Which, of course, didn't mean something hadn't come up while she was away.

Still, with a dead CIA agent in the hospital parking lot, Sophia had to wonder.

She put conviction into her voice. "This *is* completely out of the blue. I mean, come on. This is *Dave* we're talking about."

To her own ears, she didn't sound completely convinced, but Jules chuckled.

"I hear you. And okay. I'm going to look into this, see what I can find out."

"He's not supposed to regain consciousness until morning, but . . ."

"This is Dave we're talking about," Jules finished for her. "Check."

"Can you . . ." Sophia hated to ask, but she wanted in, to Dave's room. "Please, will you come down here, to the hospital, and throw your weight around?"

"Sweetie, I would if I could, but I'm in California. Robin's doing a movie out here and . . . Even if I could break away from my current . . . situation, it would be tomorrow night—at best—before I could get to you."

Sophia couldn't help it. She started to cry, pulling the phone away from her mouth so that Jules wouldn't hear her.

Somehow he knew anyway. "Here's what I'm going to do," he told her. "I'm going to call Yashi. Joe Hirabayashi, okay? He's one of my best agents—a really great guy. He'll make sure that, whatever happens, Dave isn't shipped off to Guantánamo, all right?"

Dear God, she hadn't even thought of *that*.

"That was a joke," Jules said.

"Was it?"

"Yeah, okay, not really," he admitted. "Let me go and call Yashi. He'll participate in any further questioning, make sure it's all kosher."

"Thank you."

A nurse came hurrying down the hall, glancing into the waiting area where Sophia was pacing. "Are you Sophia Ghaffari?" she called.

"Excuse me," Sophia told Jules as she called back to the nurse, "I am."

"Mr. Malkoff's awake," the nurse reported, "and he's asking for you. He's extremely agitated—we're afraid he's going to hurt himself."

Sophia was already running. "Please, hurry," she told Jules as she hung up her phone.


The world was a blur of pain and color and sound, and through the confusion and chaos, Dave was certain of only one thing.

Sophia wasn't there.

And the only conceivable reason he could come up with for why she wasn't sitting at his bedside, was that something terrible had happened to her while he was getting stitched up. That whoever was giving orders to the giant Irish skinhead had attacked again, this time going for her.

So Dave ignored the team of suits, most of whom drew their sidearms and shouted at him not to move as he pulled the IV needle out of his arm and swung himself over the metal rail on the side of the hospital bed.

The time for talking was over. He'd tried that, tried shouting, too, but it hadn't given him what he'd wanted—the reassurance, with his own bleary eyes, that Sophia was alive and in one piece.

He could feel a breeze in a place where breezes didn't often blow—no doubt because he was wearing one of those ridiculous hospital gowns and his ass was hanging out.

"Ask me if I give a shit," he said to a nurse, who was backing away from him, her hands out and down, as if she were trying to calm a wild animal.

"Dave! Dear God!"

It was Sophia, thank the Lord. She pushed her way into the room, past the suits and the guns, glaring at them in outrage and disbelief.

"What are you, going to shoot a wounded man? Get those weapons out of here!" She turned toward Dave and added, just as disapprovingly, "Are you out of your mind?"

"I thought . . ." With his anger and fear dissipated, with their numbing properties drastically diminished, his world had turned into a rather large ball of pain. "Maybe you . . . needed me."

"Help me get him back into bed," she commanded someone—the nurse—who appeared and took his right arm as Sophia took his left.

She was there, she was real, she was warm, she was solid.

And that was *his* blood staining her shirt and pants.

A second nurse lowered the railing—it was much easier getting in and out that way—and Dave settled back into the hospital bed, where it didn't hurt quite so much. "I'm so sorry," he told Sophia.

"Shhh," she said, her eyes filled with tears. She held tightly to his hand and brushed his hair back, out of his face, as the nurse checked his wound, rehooked him to his IV bag, and added a second bag to the cocktail. "*I'm* sorry that I let them kick me out."

"What happened?" Dave asked. "Was that really Barney Delarow—"

"Excuse me, Ms. Ghaffari," one of the suits stepped forward to say, "I'm going to have to insist that you leave. Until you've given your statement to the authorities . . ."

His voice trailed off, because Sophia had turned to look up at him, giving him her full attention—which often resulted in grown men being struck dumb. Even with blood on her clothes, hair bedraggled from the rain, she was angelic. "And you are . . . ?" she asked.

He cleared his throat—not once, not twice, but three times. "Special Agent Bill Connell. I'm in charge of this investigation."

Dave focused his eyes, and . . . yup, it was Connell, with his florid complexion and hard-drinker's vein-riddled nose. Bill was nearly as big of an asshole as Barney Delarow had been. Wasn't this just swell?

"Good," Sophia said, "then I'll give my statement to you, right here and now. It's pretty simple. Dave and I flew to Boston to see my father, who's in this hospital, in the cancer ward. We came in late, and likewise, it was late when we were finally ready to leave the hospital to go to our hotel. It was also raining, so Dave went to get the car. I waited in the lobby, which is where I was when he called me on my cell phone. He made certain I was okay, and then told me he'd been attacked in the parking garage."

Whatever was in that new IV bag was making him even more woozy, so Dave used his right hand—the one that Sophia wasn't tightly holding—and pulled the little tube under the hospital blanket. He folded it in half, effectively stopping the drip, even as he forced himself to focus.

"He told me to stay with the security guard," Sophia continued, turning to look at Dave, "which I did, since she went into the garage herself, to assist the police as they arrived on the scene. Dave was trying to get to his feet when I got there, but his injury was severe and he fell. He seemed to recognize the dead man, whose throat had been slit, and who was lying partly under our car." Her voice didn't shake or wobble but her words became slightly more precise, and Dave cursed himself for putting her through this. "Dave insisted—quite emphatically—that this was not the man who'd attacked him. He said that his attacker had been large, with a shaved head. Dave also insisted that he was unaware of the dead man's presence until the police brought it to his attention.

"Because Dave was bleeding heavily," she continued, "I was, at this point, focusing on getting him onto a stretcher and over to the ER. You now know everything I know, Special Agent Connell. Although surely there's footage from a security camera."

"Conveniently, there's not," Connell said. "Camera went out of order a few hours earlier. That's something you know how to do, isn't it, Malkoff?"

"As does nearly everyone in this room," Sophia countered.

"Except we weren't on the premises earlier," he pointed out, looking from Sophia to Dave, looking at their hands, which were tightly clasped together. "You work with Malkoff at Troubleshooters Incorporated?"

"That's correct," Sophia told him. "But he's also my fiancé."

What? Dave looked at her, but she squeezed his hand and shot him her *don't argue* look, disguised behind a sweet smile.

"Really," Connell said on a laugh that was a mix of amusement and disbelief. "Malkoff, you old dog, you. What is it with you and obscenely beautiful women? You must be hung like a horse." He turned to Sophia. "He tell you he has a habit of killing his fiancées?"

Color had already been rising in Sophia's cheeks over that *horse* comment, but now her demeanor turned positively icy. "If you're referring to Anise Turiano, yes, he's told me about her. About how she found out he worked for the CIA and tried to sell him to the highest bidder. About how he nearly died, thanks to her betrayal."

"He tell you that her body was pulled out of a river, wrapped in plastic?" Connell asked. "Which was nice, since it preserved some of the forensic evidence. His DNA was all over her, inside and out—"

"I was cleared of those charges," Dave interrupted. "Sophia knows that, yes."

"She know that Turiano's throat was slit?" Connell asked him. "Much as Barney Delarow's was tonight? Or how about the fact that your semen was found in Turiano's body, with forensic evidence indicating ejaculation occurred *after* she was dead?"

Oh, shit.

"Yeah," Dave said, giving Sophia an apologetic smile, although it probably came out more like a wince. She was moving her thumb across the back of his hand—just the slightest of caresses. It was both soothing and reassuring. "That didn't come up, because, you know—and you *do* know, Bill—that it was verified, through extensive testing, that the *minute* amounts of my . . . DNA found inside the body contained chemicals— spermicides and traces of latex—indicating that sperm had been taken from a used condom and—"

"That's right," Connell said. "I forgot. According to your statement, you and your first fiancée *always* used condoms. Mr. Careful."

Sophia's thumb stilled, and as Dave met her eyes he knew instantly what she was thinking.

One of the few things that he *had* told Sophia about his brief but tumultuous love affair with Kathy-slash-Anise was that the woman had given him an STD. Which implied that there had been at least *some* unprotected sexual contact.

Connell just kept on flapping his mouth. "Your story was that you *didn't* murder Anise Turiano and then fuck her dead body in a homicidal rage, but rather that you were framed. Right."

Dave shook his head as he looked at Sophia in silent apology.

But the CIA agent wasn't done. "Dave passed a lie detector test," Connell continued, speaking to Sophia now, "and since no one's *ever* bullshitted their way past one of *those* before . . . Case closed."

"It *was* closed," Dave said quietly, just wanting the asshole to leave the room, so he could talk to Sophia. Try to explain. "So if you're done—"

"Interestingly," Connell said, "Barney Delarow kept the Turiano file active on his computer. He accessed it just this morning."

Okay, so *that* wasn't good news.

"You know anything about that?" Connell probed.

Wearily, Dave shook his head. "I haven't seen Barney in years."

"Phone contact?" Connell asked. "E-mail?"

"None," Dave said.

"That's easy enough to verify," Connell pointed out.

"Yes," Dave said. "I'm very aware of that and I'll say it again: I've had zero contact with Barney Delarow since I left the CIA. And I'm sorry, but shouldn't you take advantage of the fact that I'm relatively alert by getting my description of the man who knifed me—and probably killed Delarow, too? Maybe bring in a police sketch artist, get a picture for a BOLO?"

But Connell had turned to Sophia. "Whose idea was it to come to Boston yesterday?"

"My Aunt Maureen's," she told him flatly. "My father took a turn for the worse, we got a call Sunday morning, so we came. I came. Dave came with me."

"I'll bet he did," Connell said with a smirk. "I bet he *comes* with you a lot."

And that was it. Dave was done. He sat up, ripping pain in his side be damned. "Get out of my room," he spat. "Your superior will be hearing from me about your disrespectful—"

"Relax," Connell said. "It was a joke. She doesn't mind—"

"She minds," Sophia said curtly, even as she tried to push Dave back. "Nurse!"

One of the nurses came bustling back in, frowning at the IV bags, which, of course, weren't dripping as they were supposed to. Dave let go of the tube just before she pulled back the blanket to check both it and his stitches. But she wasn't fooled. "You're going to be one of *those* patients, aren't you, Mr. Malkoff?"

"Soph, you got a pen and paper?" Dave asked, and she released his hand to search through her purse.

"Go," she said a moment later, clicking her pen open.

"White, male, six-six, two-fifty, gold tooth, Irish accent, although that could've been faked," he told her even as he felt the sedative or painkiller or whatever they'd given him slipping through his veins. "He mentioned a name. Santucci. *Give my best to Santucci.* I don't know a Santucci, do you?"

She shook her head, and he went on to describe the man completely as she wrote it all down, even as he felt his eyes start to roll back in his head.

He could hear her then, speaking to someone—no doubt Connell. "FBI agent Joe Hirabayashi from the Boston office will be here at any moment. I'll give this information to him, since it's clear you're not really interested in a true investigation."

Connell: "It doesn't alarm you, even a little bit, that Anise Turiano's killer was never found?"

"No, it doesn't. She apparently had dealings with a number of dangerous people—"

"Including David Malkoff."

"I'll thank you to get out of this room. Dave's asleep and can't answer your accusations—"

"And you don't worry—"

"If you have any additional questions for me"—Sophia's voice was sharp—"you can ask them *after* Mr. Hirabayashi has arrived."

"Ma'am, I'm not the bad guy here."

"Yeah?" Sophia laughed her disdain. "Coulda fooled me."

Another voice then, the nurse, insistent: "The patient needs his rest."

There was the sound of a door closing, and then Sophia was back, her hand gentle on Dave's forehead, her fingers interlacing with his. She leaned over him and kissed him, and he breathed in the sweetness of her perfume.

He wasn't asleep, not yet—there was a reason he'd fought to stay awake. There was something he still had to tell her. But it took such effort to move his mouth and he couldn't squeeze her hand no matter how hard he tried.

"Soph," he breathed, and forced his eyes open.

Her face was right there, above him—beautiful and surprised.

"Oral," he said. "Sex."

He could see her confusion, and he knew she didn't understand.

"Didn't . . . kill her. Wanted to."

"Shhh," she said. "It's okay. Go to sleep. I'll be right here."

"Would have," he told her. "Didn't."

"It's okay," she said again, and Dave surrendered to the darkness, hoping that she was right, but knowing that they were in for a very bumpy ride.

# CHAPTER FOUR

D ecker hadn't showered or even changed his clothes, and he was hyper-aware of his high scruff factor as he held open the door to the Starbucks so Tracy could go in first.

Then again, he almost always felt scruffy and vaguely underdressed when he encountered the Troubleshooters receptionist.

This morning, she both looked and smelled dangerously good— which, again, was nothing new. Her long auburn hair shone as it bounced around her shoulders like a living shampoo commercial.

She was wearing a sleeveless top, a pair of those ridiculous pants that ended mid-calf, and sandals. It was meant to be casual-wear, but on her it seemed elegant. Classy. The pants were khaki and had pockets everywhere, none of which looked as if they could hold anything useful, since they, like the pants, hugged her curves. They weren't too tight, but they were very nicely fitting. Very.

Ditto for the shirt, which was a shimmering shade of blue. Probably silk—although he hadn't let himself touch her. Despite that, he knew it certainly wasn't cotton like the one he was wearing beneath his overshirt.

And her sandals? Heels, of course. With the exception of last night, when she'd been in white and pink sneakers, Decker couldn't remember ever seeing Tracy in anything but heels. High ones, that brought her closer to his not-particularly-impressive height.

Not that he was exceedingly short.

But he'd made note last night—and this morning, as she'd emerged from her bathroom, wrapped in a towel and barefoot—that without the heels, Tracy was. Or at least she was significantly shorter than he'd thought.

Which was probably why she nearly always wore heels.

And yeah, he'd absolutely been thinking only about her diminutive height as she'd come out of the bathroom wearing a towel. Kind of like the way he'd only been thinking about the best mall to hit on their way to the safe house this morning, as he'd sat outside her bathroom, listening to her take a shower.

Right.

She'd accepted the fact that she was going to have to be contained at the safe house, and had made the call to Tom from her cell phone, negotiating a week of paid vacation, with two more at lost time. Lost time was exactly that—lost. Which meant she wouldn't be paid for those weeks, so Decker would absolutely be paying her rent next month.

That was going to suck, but then again, there were worse ways for him to spend his money. Like buying funeral wreaths to lay on a good friend's grave.

Last night, Tracy hadn't blinked when Deck had told her they'd leave for the safe house in the morning, and that until then they'd stay in her apartment, with him sleeping on her couch. But his rule about her leaving the bathroom door slightly open whenever she used the facilities had gotten him a disbelieving stare.

"What exactly do you think I'm going to do while I'm in there?" she'd asked.

"I'm sorry," he'd said, which was the refrain of the day, "but—"

"Just . . . whatever," she'd cut him off. "You're worried about Jimmy, you don't trust anybody, including me. I get it."

She'd been uncharacteristically silent out in the hall and on the stairs, unlocking the door to her apartment and gesturing him inside.

And still she didn't speak, having correctly deduced that he'd need to sweep the place for surveillance devices. She was right—he'd unzipped the duffel and gotten to work.

Her place was smaller than Tess and Nash's, but had the same light, airy feeling, with big windows overlooking the street.

It was messier than he'd imagined, with books overflowing the one enormous bookshelf in her living room, stacked in towering piles nearby, and scattered across her coffee table. Catalogs were everywhere, too. Unlike him, she apparently didn't immediately throw them away when they came with the mail. She actually looked through hers—some were open, with pages marked by bent corners and Post-it notes.

Her bathroom was cluttered, too—the sink counter filled with bottles and jars. The room itself was thick with recently hang-dried nylons and lingerie in a rainbow of colors and styles, which, as far as décor went, absolutely worked for him.

But Tracy brushed past him and quickly gathered it all up as he went over the area thoroughly with the bug sweeper. A bathroom—particularly that of a beautiful woman—was a favorite place to hide a mini-cam.

"Please don't tell me if you find anything in here," she said as he pushed back the shower curtain and encountered the equivalent of a drugstore's inventory of shampoos and conditioners—and, whoops—a neon green dildo balanced artfully on the handle atop the in-the-wall soap dish. It had an on-off switch at its base, which, probably, technically made it a vibrator.

It was a disconcerting discovery, but only because it was so absolutely in the shape of an enormous penis, as if someone had taken a knife to the Jolly Green Giant. For Deck, as for most men, *knife* and *penis* didn't work well together in a single sentence. On the other hand, the thought of Tracy in the shower, using that thing, was a gleaming, golden, five-star, confetti- and balloon-falling winner.

"Oh, shoot," she winced, her arms full of silk and lace panties and bras. It was clear that, were he not standing between it and her, she would have grabbed the thing and run. Instead she just laughed her dismay. "I'm going to pretend you don't see that, okay?"

"See what?"

It wasn't the first time Decker had seen her green . . . friend. It had once fallen out of one of her bags, back when the entire office had gone on a winter training exercise in New Hampshire. He'd ignored it then, too.

But he couldn't hide his smile as he moved on down the hall to her bedroom, where he stopped short in the doorway. "Whoa." Clothing was everywhere—on the floor and covering the unmade bed. It looked as if the room had been tossed—possibly by the extremely un-jolly giant, searching for his missing dick.

Tracy, however, didn't indicate that anything was out of the ordinary.

She kicked aside several pairs of jeans and a random shoe or two as she brought her underwear to a dresser and dumped it into the top drawer. "Sometimes I have a problem deciding what to wear."

No kidding. Decker dodged the larger piles and began to sweep the room, as she folded and put away her clothes with the speed and skill of a lifetime Gap employee. She quickly threw the bed together, too, moving her laptop case onto the floor in order to pull a colorful quilt up over an array of comfortable-looking pillows.

Her bedside tables contained more books, along with candles of all shapes and sizes, their wicks black from use. And yes, Tracy in candlelight would be something to behold, and that was a fact, not any kind of wishful thinking.

More nylon stockings hung from a ceiling fan, and as she stood on her toes and reached to pull them down, her T-shirt separated from those low-riding jeans. And Decker had to be honest because okay, yes, maybe there *was* a little wishful thinking going on right then, inside of his head.

"I've really got to get one of those drying racks," she told him, as if he gave a flying shit where she hung her underwear.

"This is your place," he pointed out. "You're allowed to live your life the way you want."

"As long as I leave the bathroom door open at all times," she reminded him.

"That's just for tonight. When we get . . . where we're going," he said, being vague because he hadn't swept the entire place yet, "you'll have your privacy back."

Her privacy, but not her freedom. She was silent as she led the way into the eat-in kitchen, as he tried to convince himself that he had to look at her—she was in front of him—but that that didn't mean he was watching her ass. But Jesus, the attitude in the way she walked was outrageously attractive, and the fact was, he liked the woman. He had right from the start.

Tracy had grown into her job as Troubleshooters receptionist, although truth be told, she was really functioning now as office manager. She was also the face of the company. She was the first person clients saw when they walked into their San Diego office—similar to the way Sophia Ghaffari was the face of the company with clients out in the field.

In the United States, that is.

The international "field" was another story—one that required a completely different kind of face. Something a little less lipsticked and a little more cammie-painted, equipped with the latest weaponry and technology—and the skill to use it. For years, that had been what Decker—and Nash—had provided.

Decker, for one, itched to get back out there. And the sooner Nash rehabbed and was on his feet again, the sooner they would find the men who wanted him dead—which would get them back to work, hunting down terrorist leaders and making dangerous places a little bit safer for the diplomats and the humanitarians, who were essential participants in the Western World's ongoing war against terror.

And okay, there. He'd made it all the way into the kitchen without thinking solely about sex or Tracy or sex *with* Tracy.

Except, great—she'd just asked him something, and was waiting for him to respond.

"Sorry," he said, "what?"

"I have some fish I was going to grill for dinner. Have you eaten?" she asked. "Would you like some?"

Dinner. Jesus. The reminder made his stomach rumble, and she smiled. "I'll take that as a yes."

He forced a smile, too. "Thanks. That would be great."

Her kitchen was cluttered, too—the counters crowded with more books and unopened junk mail and a couple of bags of groceries that she hadn't yet put away—but it was squeaky clean, the sink shiny and white, no dishes piled up.

Like the rest of the place, it was also free of surveillance devices. But Deck reset the bug sweeper and went through the apartment again, as Tracy cooked the meal.

"Can we talk freely now?" she asked as he came back into the kitchen, as she set two salads topped with grilled fish on the table, as they both sat to eat.

It was delicious—Alaskan halibut over locally grown greens—but seriously lacking in heft. Decker resigned himself to going hungry—it wouldn't be the first time and it sure as hell wouldn't be the last.

"Let's not," he answered her as he tried not to wolf down the food. "I know you have a lot of questions, but there are such things as long-range listening devices. And yeah, I seriously doubt anyone's tuning in, but I'd still rather wait until we get to the safe house."

She nodded as she ate slowly, delicately wiping her mouth with her napkin. "We could duct-tape George to the window pane and turn him on." She laughed at his confusion. "George. Green. Large? In the bathroom?"

He was surprised—and not just because she named her dildo *George*, but because taping a vibrator to the window absolutely disrupted that kind of surveillance. "How do you know to do that?"

"I don't watch much TV these days," she told him, which seemed a complete non sequitur until she added, "but I do TiVo this one really good show about this really hot former spy who practices something he calls *grunge tradecraft*. He did the personal-massager-taped-to-the-window trick in one of the episodes."

*Personal massager.* Was that really what she called it? When she wasn't calling it *George* . . . ?

A picture of Tracy in her shower sprang to mind and he knocked it aside, but not quickly enough.

Because as she leaned forward, curiosity lighting her face, to ask, "Does it really work?" he had to take a moment to remember that she was talking about duct-taping George to the window. As opposed to its more traditional function.

Decker nodded as he used his tongue to fish a piece of lettuce from between his teeth. "Yes, it does."

"Good to know," she said with a nod. "I'll make sure I pack it. You know, just in case."

She was trying not to smile, but one slipped out, making her eyes sparkle, and he laughed. "I thought we were pretending I didn't see . . ."

"We both know exactly what you saw," she countered, pointing at him with her fork. "And it was the elephant in the room. Or one of them, anyway. I think there might be a full, bright green herd in here with us."

Deck laughed again, even as he agreed. "There *have* been a lot of secrets these past few months."

"Like the whole budding romance thing with you and Tess," she said. "How's Jimmy feeling about that?"

He shook his head again. "Don't use his name."

"Sorry." His reprimand shut Tracy up for about ten seconds, but then she spoke again. "It must have been weird," she noted. "But you did it really right. I honestly believed you were . . . You know. Conflicted. It felt vaguely like shoplifting because it was so soon, and yet . . . It was very well done."

Shoplifting. Damn. Decker wondered what Tom, his boss, thought of him, seemingly going after Tess mere days after Nash's death, but then pushed that far away. It didn't matter what Tom or the rest of the world thought. The only thing that mattered was Nash—alive in that safe house, in Tess's arms, healing and getting stronger every hour, every day.

"And yet you had doubts," Decker pointed out. He still couldn't quite believe that, out of everyone, *Tracy* had figured it out.

"Hope," she corrected him. "I had hope and—"

He stopped her. "I definitely want to talk about this more—tomorrow."

Tracy nodded. And ate in silence for another ten-second stretch. Which apparently was as long as she could go without talking.

"Since you don't want to talk about . . . the thing you don't want to talk about," she said, "then maybe we should discuss George."

He laughed his surprise, because, Jesus. "Is there really anything left to say?"

"Aren't you surprised?" she asked. "Or even just curious? About why my longest-term relationship is with a sex toy named after George Clooney?"

She completely cracked him up. "Clooney, huh?"

Tracy nodded. She was trying her best to treat this seriously, but another smile slipped free. Goddamn, she was a beautiful woman.

"Well," he said, slowly, choosing his words carefully, because he suspected that this sex-toy talk was her testing the water, so to speak.

They'd start with a discussion of her dildo and then move on to cock rings and genital piercings, and then over to hard-core bondage. And he'd end up spread-eagle and tied with scarves to her bed, a hood over his face as she first whipped him and then rode him hard, and yeah, as appealing as that was, thinking about it was not a particularly good idea. At least not right now, while trying to eat dinner without spilling it down his shirt.

"It's been my experience that romantic relationships," Decker continued, "especially sexual ones, are complicated. Too much so. And as far as sex for the sake of sex goes? The guilt can be a bitch, because even if she says she's on the same page, she's either lying to herself, or *you* are. Lying to yourself, I mean. So . . . There's just too much room for misunderstanding."

She was nodding, in complete agreement.

"I think you're smart," he told her, "for sticking with George. For right now, anyway. Until you meet someone who's . . . a good fit, for more than . . . generating heat." He forced another smile. "Me too, you know? I have my own . . . handy solution."

She smiled her understanding of his wordplay but then looked away, maybe because she was embarrassed for him. Or maybe she was disappointed because she'd understood his subtext: *Honey, despite the weird spark between us, we are absolutely not going to spend tonight or any other night having screaming-hot, bag-over-the-head, tied-to-the-bed sex-for-the-sake-of-sex.*

Although—and this didn't happen often, because he had better control than that—he'd once again given himself the solid beginnings of a hard-on, just by thinking about it, about her. He shut himself down, willed it away. He'd lived without sex for a long time. There was no reason on earth his physical needs should interfere now.

Except shutting it down wasn't working for him tonight.

Tracy was sitting there, across the table from him, quietly finishing her salad, taking a sip of water. She met his eyes as she set her glass down. "I'm sorry about Sophia."

Jesus Christ, this woman had no fear. Either that, or no idea of personal boundaries. "I don't know what to say to that," he admitted.

"You can say whatever you want," she told him evenly. "And it won't leave this room. You can pretend otherwise, but I know that you cared about her. And I'm pretty sure that she's with Dave because of . . . your pretending you're with Tess."

Decker stood up. Took his plate to the sink. "Now, see, you're oversimplifying what is—was—a complicated . . . thing."

Thing? It was never a *thing*, not in the way most people would use the word, but it wasn't a relationship, either. It had been a non-relationship. A relationship version of a demilitarized zone.

"I'm sure there's a lot I don't know," Tracy agreed, clearing her dishes, too. "But I think you should consider bringing both Sophia and Dave into the loop, before this thing between them goes too far."

Before? "Word is, he's moved in with her."

"That's just sex," Tracy scoffed. "He hasn't *moved* in moved in. He's just getting his happy on every chance he can get, and— Look at you.

Don't get all uncomfortable, like you're living in some G-rated world where all they're doing is holding hands and chastely kissing good night. That could've been you, twirling her around her bedroom every night—and you know it. She gave you the green light for *years*."

"You better go pack," he said, because this conversation had gotten completely out of hand. Plus, he was still slightly aroused, which was freaking him out, because in the past all it took was the *thought* of Sophia and the horror that she'd been through—the murder of her husband, her captivity in Kazabek, her abuse at Decker's own ignorant hand—to exorcise any errant, inappropriate sexual cravings.

Tracy didn't leave the kitchen. Instead she walked over to the wall phone, heavy on the attitude, which, again, really worked with those jeans. She picked it up, and when he moved to stop her, she shot him a *get real* look. "I'm just ordering you a pizza," she told him, "so you don't fade away from lack of carbs." She squinted her eyes at him, as if trying to read his mind. Or to remember the type of pizza he always asked for whenever the crew at TS Inc. put in a late night. "What are you, pepperoni, with black olives and . . . ?"

"Mushrooms." Decker nodded. "Thank you."

She placed the order, hung up the phone. "It'll be here in ten minutes. They always say twenty, but they're right up the street."

She vanished down the hall to the bathroom, but was back in a flash, waving giant green George at him, which was an image he really didn't want lingering in his brain, thanks—a dick of any kind or color in those smooth, well-manicured hands.

"Don't want to forget my boyfriend," she announced, and went into her room to pack.

As he'd eaten that pizza, she'd filled two very large suitcases. But Decker had bitten his tongue rather than chastise her or even mock her, because really? Traveling light wasn't a priority here. They would be driving the six hours to the safe house. Let her take as much as she wanted.

She'd left her door ajar as she went to bed, as he'd stared at the ceiling from his vantage point on the couch. He'd slept only lightly, with one eye open, listening for any sound or movement from Tracy. The fact of the matter was that he *did* trust her. If he didn't, he wouldn't have slept at all.

What he didn't trust was that she wouldn't make a mistake and inadvertently blow Nash's cover.

So this morning, he'd lugged her luggage out to the back of his truck, locked the cargo cover down, and—without any additional talk of green dildos, thank you, Jesus—they were finally on their way.

They'd stopped, briefly, at his apartment, to pick up his bag—one and small—because his intention was to spend a few days at the safe house, goading Nash into starting his physical therapy.

Decker and Tracy were just a few blocks from his place, heading for the 5, when she spotted the Starbucks.

"Ooh. Ooh, ooh," she'd said. "Last chance at civilization."

"We're not going to the moon." But he'd pulled into the lot, because why the hell not. Because the truth here was that she *was* going to jail. And yes, the safe house was luxurious and spacious with its swimming pool and gorgeous views. But once there, Tracy *wouldn't* be able to leave.

It wasn't going to be as bad as getting locked in a basement by a psychopath, which was something that had happened to Tracy a few years back, right after she'd started working for TS Inc. Decker knew that after that experience, the idea of being locked anywhere had to be difficult. And yet, here she was.

Trusting him completely.

He followed her now to the counter, where she ordered for both of them. Which made sense, just like with last night's pizza. As Troubleshooters receptionist, Tracy had been called on often to pick up a Starbucks order, on those days when regular coffee just wouldn't cut it. Still, she must've noticed his surprise, because she glanced at him. And then smiled.

"You have no clue that you order the exact same thing every time, do you?" she said.

What? "No, I don't."

"Yes, you do. And it's pretty boring, too. Medium roast, grande, black."

"Sometimes," Decker said, a tad defensively, "I have a scone."

Tracy laughed as she held up a little bag that the barista had handed her. "*Honey*," she said, using the not-very-PC nickname that slipped out of him from time to time when he spoke to women, especially those whom he found appealing, "you *always* have a scone."

Jesus, she was nicely put together, and as Decker laughed his acknowledgment of his own mundane-ness, their gazes held and sparked, and there it was again, that fricking heat that, for years, he'd worked overtime to ignore. Not just with Tracy, but with everyone. He'd met quite a few attractive women since Khobar, since his fiancée Emily had become his ex-fiancée. But after learning his lesson the hard way, he'd always backed away.

Maybe he was tired from that night of little-to-no sleep, tossing on her freaking uncomfortable sofa, worried about the way that, despite his best efforts, the number of people who knew about Nash was growing. And he knew it was a mistake, but this time, here in the safety of Starbucks, when that connection sparked between them, he didn't immediately look away.

Instead, he let himself take the briefest of moments—three short seconds of fantasy—to pretend that he actually had a real life, and that those suitcases in the back of his truck were there for a different reason. Such as he and this gorgeous young woman were going to spend a few days at a rustic B&B, where they wouldn't get out of bed until it was time to come back home.

Which was pretty much the way his relationship with Em had started. With nonstop sex. Next thing he knew, they were visiting an animal shelter and adopting a dog.

And then she was moving out, taking Ranger with her.

Here and now, Tracy looked away first, flustered, and Decker knew with a flash of insight that he was playing with fire. She *was* his for the taking, which, okay, was an extremely egotistical thought, but that didn't make it any less true.

Like him, she was starved for contact with someone—anyone. Old George just wasn't getting the job done. But if Decker thought his breakup with Emily had been messy, anything he started here and now would surely end in a bloodbath.

So he looked away, shifted his position, and shut down any body-language *Yes, ma'am, I would absolutely love to fuck you's* he might've been sending her.

But Tracy apparently didn't get that memo. "One of these days," she told him, glancing at him from beneath her eyelashes, "you're going to have to take a chance and try one of their blueberry muffins."

And yeah, he wasn't just playing with fire here, he was playing with a live nuke.

When they got back into his truck, he was going to have to go point-blank. *I have to be honest here, honey, because I find you incredibly attrac-*

*tive, and every now and then I slip and it leaks out, but you need to know that I will never, ever act upon it. Even if I didn't have a multitude of other women on my mind—for a variety of reasons—I would never fraternize. I would never have a relationship with someone I work with, let alone someone like you, who might be perceived to be a subordinate.* "It's not my thing," he told her now.

"And a scone is?" she countered. "You know, I tried one once? And it was kind of like eating a spoonful of flour. Except maybe not as flavorful."

The barista interrupted them by handing them their coffees, and Decker dug into his pocket for his wallet.

Tracy stopped him, a cool hand on his arm. A hand she let linger there, sweet Jesus save him. "I paid when I ordered."

How the hell had he missed that? He stepped back, which shook her hand free, and took his wallet out anyway. "Let me pay you back."

"Not necessary," Tracy said. "You are, after all, paying my rent."

"Lawrence Decker, what a surprise."

Deck recognized the voice and turned, and sure enough—holy fuck—it was Jo Heissman standing there. And the world went into high definition as he slammed to full alert, Defcon Two—launch codes out and ready.

Dr. Josephine Heissman. Shrinker of heads. A specialist in PTSD, she'd worked with counterterrorism operatives throughout her extensive career—a career that included an extended stint working for the Agency.

The very same Agency which may or may not have been behind the attempts to erase Jim Nash from the face of this planet.

The doctor was looking from him to Tracy, speculation on her far-too-intelligent face. "And . . . Tracy Shapiro, right?" She held out her hand for Tracy to shake.

Tracy did just that, a smile of real pleasure lighting her face. "How are you, Dr. Heissman?"

"I'm fine, thank you," the older woman said. "I have an appointment down the street, and . . ." She gestured to the room around them. "Gotta have that morning java jolt."

This *was not* a coincidence.

It couldn't be.

It wasn't.

Jo Heissman had worked as psychological support at Troubleshooters

Incorporated for a very brief time, right before Nash had "died." Upon news of his death, she'd immediately resigned.

Decker had been nearly certain that the doctor had maintained her Agency ties. He'd suspected, but had never proven, that she'd taken the job with TS Inc. in order to spy on Nash for her real bosses—the Agency masters to whom Deck was sure she was still a minion.

When he'd confronted her, *she'd* claimed she'd taken the TS Inc. position, with its significantly lower salary, because she was doing a study and writing some paper dealing with the mental health of counterterrorism operatives.

But the bottom line was this: Nash had "died," and she'd left.

Decker didn't think *that* was a coincidence, either.

His mind raced as he played back his conversation with Tracy. What had the doctor overheard? What had she seen?

As a psychologist—and not just any psychologist, but *his* psychologist, who'd crawled around inside of his remarkably fucked-up and noisy head for a number of intense sessions—she could surely read his body language. And for a few seconds there, he'd put his attraction to Tracy on a platter for the entire world to see.

But he was both human and male. It could be argued that any hetero man—even those in committed relationships with their dead best friends' fiancées—would have to be both blind and three years without a pulse not to find Tracy steaming hot.

It was the words the receptionist had said that were going to be the problem. *You are, after all, paying my rent.*

Deck had to assume Dr. Heissman had heard that. And he also had to assume that the doctor had followed them here—from his apartment.

She'd no doubt been waiting there, staking the place out.

What he didn't know was *why*.

Not why she would follow him—he was pretty certain it was to see if she could find out any information that would convince her masters that Nash truly was dead.

He couldn't figure out, though, why she would follow him only to reveal that she was doing so, here in this Starbucks.

"Things have been really slow at the office," Tracy told Jo, in that easy way some women had of instantly reviving lapsed friendships, as if it had been days rather than months since she'd last seen the older woman. "It's been quiet and . . . well, ever since Jimmy passed, it's . . ." She made a face as if shaking off her maudlin emotions. "Everyone's taking vacations and even lost time, to, you know, deal with the loss."

"It's natural to want to step back a bit," Dr. Heissman agreed, glancing at Decker. She was wearing her hair down around her shoulders—hippie hair, Dave Malkoff had called it. It was long and thick and obviously its natural color, with streaks of unhidden gray among the rich darkness. She dressed to match it, in loose, colorful, flowing clothes. A gauzy tunic with dark, wide-legged pants, flat sandals on her feet, a small leather backpack over her shoulder in place of a handbag.

She looked a little pale, a little gaunt, and she glanced over her shoulder when the door to the coffee shop opened, which was a classic signal that she was afraid someone had followed her. Which didn't make sense.

Of course, the fact that she herself had followed *Decker* here didn't make any sense, either. She was truly skilled as a head-shrinker, but as a covert operative sent to tail a professional . . . ? She was seriously lacking.

Not that he'd spotted her car following his truck before he'd pulled into the Starbucks lot. But he would have, given enough time. Certainly before he'd gotten onto the 5. Thirty seconds of mildly evasive driving, and he would've been able to shake her, no question.

"I hope you're doing the same," the doc was saying to him. "Taking some time . . . ?"

But he didn't have to answer, because Tracy was there, ready to intercept the conversational ball. "Everyone's bringing it down a notch," she told the doctor. "I'm taking a full month, myself. I have a friend who just had a baby—her second—and she could really use help with Mikey; he's barely two. So I'm going to her place—to celebrate new life, you know? It seems, like, perfect. I mean, considering."

The doctor nodded, but Tracy didn't let her speak.

"Chica, my friend, well, that's her nickname from high school—*her* high school; I didn't meet her until college—she's got limited parking at her townhouse, so Deck's giving me a ride over there. He's also helping me out by subletting my apartment." She turned to look at him, with such an expression of concerned appreciation that he nearly smiled. She lowered her voice slightly as she turned back to Dr. Heissman, as if conveying a secret. "He's going to clear all of Jimmy's clothes and things out of their place—we were neighbors, you know, same apartment building—and then Tess is going to move back in. On her own timetable, of course. We just thought"—she looked at Decker again, including him in that *we*—"it would be easier for her, if Decker were living upstairs, in my place. He didn't want to just, you know, move in *with* her. Too many ghosts. Plus, it's too soon—at least some people think so. And you know the way everyone talks. Tess doesn't need that. Neither of them do."

She was brilliant. She'd explained the words Dr. Heissman had overheard, and she'd given the two of them a reason to be here, in this Starbucks together.

"How *is* Tess?" the doc asked, addressing Decker.

He gave her his stock answer. "She's hanging in."

Again Tracy took the ball and hit a perfect, clean serve. "So what are *you* up to these days, Jo?"

What was she up to, indeed?

Decker got another glance from behind the doctor's trendy, rectangular-shaped glasses before she turned her attention back to Tracy.

"I've been establishing a solo practice," she answered. "And doing a lot of volunteer work at the VA downtown. I'll be over there for most of the day. I probably won't get to my own office until, oh, three thirty or four."

And wasn't she the angel of all that was good?

"I have a patient who was recently released, whose parents live a few blocks from here," she continued, apparently determined to tell them her entire schedule for the day. "I'll be working with him for a couple of hours this morning, before I hit the hospital."

"A house call," Decker commented. "That seems . . . unusual."

She smiled, albeit sadly. "Unusual measures for unusual times. This patient is a triple amputee. Iraq War vet. PTSD." She looked at Decker, her gaze almost palpable. "A high suicide risk."

"I once told Dr. H. that I was thinking about killing myself," Decker told Tracy. "In case you were wondering about that loaded look she just shot me."

He'd rendered them both speechless, which was quite the trick considering they were both conversational black belts.

"Why are you here, Doctor?" he asked her quietly, taking care not to draw attention with either his voice or his body language. He kept his shoulders loose, his arms held non-threateningly, a pleasant smile pasted on his face. His words, however, were anything but. "What the fuck do you want?"

He'd caught her off-guard, the muscles in her throat working as she nervously swallowed, as she took several steps back from him. Although it was entirely possible that all of it—including her peaked look and the way she'd glanced over her shoulder at the door—was just one big act.

"Nothing," she said, quickly regaining her composure, but he could tell she was lying. "I just saw you come in as I was driving by and . . . I thought I'd stop and say hello."

"Well, you said it," Decker said. He looked at Tracy, who was clinging, wide-eyed, to her Venti Latte as if it were a life preserver. Enough of this bullshit. "We don't want to keep Chica, Mikey, and the new baby waiting."

Tracy didn't move, so he reached to push her slightly, to steer her toward the door, and yeah, both her skin and her shirt were decadently soft to the touch.

They'd barely even turned when Dr. Heissman stopped him with a hand on his arm. "I'm sorry if I upset you," she told him. "That wasn't my intention."

"We really have to go." He looked pointedly down at her hand and she quickly pulled it back.

But apparently she still had more to say. "Wait, I want to give you one of my new business cards." She pulled one out of thin air—she must've had it in her pocket—and held it out to him. "In case you ever need to, you know, reach me?"

There was no way he was taking that. There was not and would never be a single reason he would need to "reach" her.

But before he could tell her to go fuck herself, Tracy played intermediary. She snatched the card from the doctor, and cheerily called, "Nice seeing you, Jo," as she grabbed Decker by the elbow and all but pulled him out the door.

She was silent as she climbed back into his truck, focusing on settling in for the long ride. She put her coffee into the cup-holder, tossed the doctor's card into the well between the two seats, and fastened the belt across her chest, as Decker jammed the transmission into reverse and got them the hell out of there.

They rode in silence for several miles, his fingers tight on the steering wheel, before Deck even allowed himself to glance at her.

Tracy took it, of course, as an invitation to speak. "So, have you, like, slept with every woman that you've ever met?"

Decker laughed aloud at the irony of that.

But she wasn't kidding.

"Believe me, I didn't sleep with Jo Heissman," he told her.

"Then why is she stalking you?" She took a sip of her coffee. "That was both pathetic *and* creepy. I mean, yeah, beneath your bad haircut, you're smokin', but someone needs to tell her *Learn to accept no, batch, and move it along.*"

"That wasn't . . . ," he started. "It's not . . ." Tracy thought he was smokin'. Again, he couldn't keep his laughter from escaping. Thank God they were going straight to the safe house. If they weren't, he would be so fucked.

"I'm pretty sure she works for the people who tried to kill Nash," he told Tracy.

She sat forward at that, turning fully to face him, reaching down to pick up the business card she'd taken from the doctor. "Are you serious?"

Decker nodded. "Yeah."

"Oh, my God," she said. "Oh, my *God*. Decker, stop, *stop*—you've got to stop and look at this."

She was holding out the business card, but waving it so he couldn't possibly read it while he was driving.

So he pulled into a gas station, squealing to a stop as he took the card from Tracy's elegant fingers.

The thing was pretty standard-looking—one of those self-printed jobs with a blue and green design. The doctor's name was in a clear, black font, followed by a variety of letters—her degrees—and then her office address, her e-mail address, and her phone number.

But Jo Heissman had also handwritten a message for him, in her neatly perfect cursive.

*Please help me.*

# CHAPTER
# FIVE

Jules knocked on the half-open door to the suite, peeking in to see Nash sitting up in bed, finishing breakfast and watching cable news. "Mind if I come in?"

"Of course not." Nash picked up the remote and muted the TV.

Tess was sitting curled up in a chair across the room, doing Sudoku, and she smiled—tightly—at Jules. "Checking in to make sure I didn't kill him last night?"

"I was pretty confident you'd draw the line at something relatively benign, like leaving the bedpan out of his reach," Jules countered, "so, no. I wish that was why I'm here."

"Uh-oh," Nash said, glancing at Tess, who uncurled herself and stood up. "I don't like the sound of that."

Dressed as he was in red plaid pajamas, with his dark hair still rumpled from sleep and in need of a shave, Jimmy Nash looked charmingly vulnerable and not at all like the government-owned-and-operated hitman that Jules knew him to be. He pushed back a bowl of oatmeal as he visibly braced himself, no doubt waiting for the next shoe to drop, right on his handsome head.

"Dave Malkoff is going to be all right," Jules told him, and Tess, too, "but he spent last night in the hospital. In Boston. After being attacked—stabbed—by a man with a knife, in a parking garage at Mass General."

"Oh, crap," Tess breathed.

"What the hell was Dave doing in Boston?" Nash asked.

"He was with Sophia," Jules answered, "visiting her father, who's dying of cancer."

"And you think this is somehow related to me," Nash correctly deduced. His eyes narrowed. "That it's some kind of backlash because we tested the DNA from the shirt . . . ?"

"I'm pretty sure that it is," Jules told him. "Yes." He closed the door.

"Did we get results back from that yet?" Nash asked.

"Yep. We found out that the man who tried to kill you last winter has been dead since 1988," Jules said. "The name Kenneth Labinsk ring any bells?"

"Yes and no," Nash said. "Not the name itself, but the strategy."

"It's a standard Agency MO," Tess chimed in. She'd worked in the Agency's support division for years.

"You're in the field, you get into a scuffle, you maybe get a ding," Nash told Jules.

"A *ding* being Jimmy's expression for anything from a hangnail to being gutshot," Tess interrupted.

"Getting gutshot's not a ding," he countered. "Even I know that."

"I'm glad to hear it," she said.

Jules cleared his throat.

"The point being," Nash brought them back, "if you're on an op, and you unexpectedly leave behind some DNA, support steps in and alters some records. Your DNA comes up as belonging to some long-dead civilian."

"The procedure started in the black ops division," Tess said. "It was how the black op agents got the name 'ghosts.' Can we please rewind for a sec, back to Dave?"

"He's going to be fine," Jules told them. "Well, at least in terms of his injury. I've been monitoring the situation all night, because it's kind of crazy, and . . . DNA backlash or not, I'm pretty certain this is your blackmailers reaching out and sending us a message."

Tess pulled a second chair over to Nash's bedside, so they could both sit. "Well, we're listening," she said. "What's going on?"

Jules sat down. "How well do you know Dave?"

"Not very," Tess said, even as Nash contradicted her with, "Well enough to trust him with both mine and Tess's lives."

She turned to look at her longtime fiancé. "Really?"

"Without hesitation." Nash was absolute.

Tess didn't seem as convinced.

"Are you familiar with the reason Dave left the CIA?" Jules asked, and again they looked at each other.

Clearly both of them were hesitant to speak, but finally Tess cleared her throat. "Well, the nonofficial reason is that he was burned out on the bureaucracy," she said. "But I'm, uh, pretty certain that his private file says otherwise."

Nash was genuinely startled. "You hacked into Dave's CIA file?"

She glanced pointedly at Jules—the FBI agent in the room—and answered evasively. "That's illegal. And close to impossible to do."

But everyone here knew that Tess was a computer specialist of legendary ability—able to break into the most intricately guarded files, without leaving even the tiniest cyber-footprint behind.

"We're working together," Jules pointed out. "I'm aware of what you're capable of doing, so let's not play games."

He knew, even as the words left his mouth, that that was the dead-wrong thing to say to this woman who'd been lied to, repeatedly, by the man she loved. If anything, she was the playee, not the player.

"Wow, I'm sorry," Jules apologized immediately, as Tess's mouth got even tighter and her fair skin began to flush beneath her girl-next-door freckles. "That was thoughtless and completely uncalled for. My excuse is fatigue—I spent most of the night on my phone and at my computer and . . . You're one of the most up-front, honest people I've ever met, Tess, and you have every right to be cautious, but let me say this again: We're working together—against a formidable enemy that may well turn out to be a sanctioned part of the Agency's black ops division. We all need to be completely honest with each other. Starting right now."

She nodded. And answered Nash's question. "Yes, I hacked into Dave's file several months ago."

Nash was perturbed. "Why?"

"You were behaving oddly. Something was really wrong, and yeah, okay, I suspected someone was pressuring you. So I checked out everyone you had contact with. *Everyone*." She looked at Jules. "Congratulations on winning second chair clarinet in All-State, back in high school."

Jules had to laugh. Was that really in his file? "Thank you."

Nash, meanwhile, was still securely focused on Dave. "I've heard rumblings that Dave left the CIA after he was looked at—hard—for murder and treason. It was pretty sordid, but these things usually get warped— exaggerated way beyond truth."

"According to Dave's statement," Jules told Nash, because clearly Tess was familiar with the minute details, "which *I* read for the first time last night, he met an American woman named Kathy Grogan while he was in Paris, on assignment for the CIA. It was love at first sight—for both of them. At least that's what she led him to believe. Anyway, it turned out that Grogan was neither American nor named Grogan. She was Anise Turiano, an Eastern European con artist, who targeted men, preferably Americans, got into their good graces—usually via their beds—and ended up robbing them blind.

"In Dave's case," he continued, "she discovered—somehow—that he was with the CIA, and because of that she thought she'd hit the mother lode. They were engaged within a week, but that ended when she tried to auction off his identity and turned up dead—nearly killing Dave in the process."

"Christ," Nash murmured.

"And you're right—it was sordid," Jules told Nash. "There were semen samples and DNA tests and . . . allegations of, um, necrophilia."

Nash was nodding. "That's what I heard, too."

"Dave said he didn't kill her," Tess chimed in. "But it's hard to believe he didn't."

"So what if he did," Nash countered. "She outed him—and blowing his cover could've been a death sentence. It's the equivalent of attempted murder." He turned to Jules. "So how is this connected to his getting knifed last night?"

"The CIA operative in charge of the investigation into Turiano's death was a cheerful fellow by the name of Barney Delarow," Jules explained. "He was convinced Dave had been Turiano's willing cohort, and that Dave had killed her to keep her from becoming a witness against him, for those pesky charges of treason. Even after the case was officially closed, Delarow kept the file active on his computer.

"Dave claims that last night he was stalked and jumped in one of the Mass General parking garages by a skinhead gangbanger-type with an Irish accent. He says the man pulled a knife, which he knocked away. Dude pulls a second knife which, again, Dave dispatches. But now they're down on the tarmac, fighting hand-to-hand, at which point, the perp pulls a third knife and sticks Dave, saying, *Give my best to Santucci*."

"Oh, my God," Tess whispered as Nash closed his eyes and shook his head.

"I take it you know someone named Santucci," Jules said.

"You're looking at him," Nash admitted. "Is Dave really all right?"

"Yeah," Jules said. "Are you saying that *your* name is—"

"Was," Nash corrected him.

"The Agency often assigned new names and identities to operatives with questionable pasts," Tess explained. "Before his name was changed to Nash—and it *was* legally changed—Jimmy was James Santucci and . . . Can I just say that that's information that's considered highly classified? In order to protect their operatives, the Agency wouldn't share that information, not even with the FBI."

Which was why this all was news to Jules.

"Whoever we're up against," Tess continued, "their access to Agency files goes deep." She glanced at Nash. "And I think it's safe to say that Dave's mugging wasn't random."

"But how does it connect to Anise Turiano?" Nash asked.

"You're going to hate this," Jules said. "But after Dave gets stabbed, he fights off the skinhead with, shall we say, renewed vigor, and—remember that first knife the guy pulled? The one Dave kicked away? Well, Dave now rolls over to it and picks it up—which of course puts his prints all over it."

"Oh, fuck," Nash breathed—he obviously saw where this was going.

"In the brouhaha, Dave manages to call 9-1-1," Jules continued, "and the skinhead runs when he hears the approaching sirens. He's gone by the time the black-and-whites show up. There's just Dave, with that knife in his hand, bleeding. But then one of the cops discovers another body—this one's dead, his throat slit. And oh yeah, it's good old Barney Delarow."

Nash didn't say a word, but Tess reached over and took his hand.

"Next to the body is a knife which, natch, bears both Delarow's prints and Dave's blood. As for Dave's knife? It's mostly clean, but there are trace amounts of Delarow's blood and, uh, well, trust me on this—it's clearly the murder weapon."

"Someone's trying to frame Dave," Nash deduced.

"Or Dave's lying and there never was a skinhead," Jules felt compelled to point out.

"Why would Dave lie?" Nash asked.

"You tell me."

"He wouldn't." Nash was certain. "For one thing, he doesn't know my name was Santucci."

"You're sure of that?" Jules asked.

"Yes."

"If Dave slit Delarow's throat," Tess argued, "wouldn't he have been covered with his blood?"

"Not necessarily," Nash answered her. "There are ways that . . . You don't want to know."

"Yeah," Tess said snappishly, releasing Nash's hand, "actually, Jimmy, I *do* want to—" She cut herself off, shaking her head in disgust.

And Jules found himself wishing he had access to the Bureau's vast array of departments. Particularly counseling and mental health services. If he had, he would have recommended some hard-core couples counseling. He knew—firsthand—what it was like to love someone who kept secrets and told lies. Before he'd met and married Robin, he'd spent too many years trying to maintain a relationship with a man who hadn't included honesty among his top values. That had sucked, but even so, it had taken Jules years to recognize that he deserved better.

It was entirely possible that Tess was nearing that breaking point. Which meant that unless Nash wised up and found some serious religion, so to speak, their relationship was circling the drain. Which was a freaking shame, because it was beyond obvious that they loved each other more than life itself.

Jules didn't know Nash well enough to provide the necessary asskicking. Of course, when it came to kicking . . . He made a mental note to ask Sam to pop in and talk to Jimmy, privately. For someone who wore cowboy boots and meant it, Sam was remarkably sensitive and almost freakishly astute.

"Is this something the people who were after you might do?" Jules asked Nash now. "Try to shake you out of the tree by going after your friends?"

Nash nodded. "Yeah. This sounds like them. Someone needs to call Decker and give him a warning. If they went after Dave . . . Deck could be next."

"I tried calling Decker's sat phone," Jules told them. "But got bumped to voice mail. I didn't want to leave a message, even on a secure line—"

"Message," Tess said. "Let's back up a second and really think about the message they were sending—I mean, if this really is the Agency's black ops department trying to shake you loose." She turned from Nash to address Jules. "We did that DNA test, so we've got to assume they know we're looking for them. But now they're also trying to figure out if it's possible that Jimmy's still alive. Because really? What if he *had* died, and someone went through his things and found that bloodstained shirt? What if they found other evidence—records or, I don't know, a list of names of people he'd . . . contacted or . . . You know . . ."

"Deleted," Nash interjected. "Just say what you mean."

Tess laughed at the irony of that, but didn't let it slow her down. Jules knew what she was heading for, and it was a freaking great idea.

"You could set up an FBI investigation," she told Jules.

"Of me?" Nash asked. "If I'm already dead, there's no—"

"Of me," Tess interrupted. "And Decker, too. The FBI could investigate to see if we were somehow involved in whatever crimes Jimmy committed."

Because without the Agency's authority, the jobs Nash had done *would* have been crimes.

"The subtext of *that* message," Jules said, "being *yes, Nash really is dead.* It gives us an additional opportunity—to see if I get a call from Max, my boss, saying *he* got a call from someone at the Agency, asking him to let the entire case drop."

Tess, the smarty-pants, was nodding. But she wasn't done. "Before we get ahead of ourselves, we also have to think about the message we send with our reaction to Dave's attack. Do we hunker down, and bring everyone into the safe house—Decker and Dave and Sophia and, God, Tom and Lindsey and everyone we've ever called *friend*? Because if we do that, if everyone we know suddenly vanishes, and *I'm* the scumbag who hired that skinhead to attack Dave? I'm thinking, *There we go. James Nash is definitely alive.* But if Jimmy really *were* dead? And Dave got attacked like this? Decker would be first in line to assist. And you know, *I'd* even come out of mourning to go to Boston, to help him."

"Over my dead body," Nash said.

"Yes, Jimmy," Tess told him tartly. "Exactly. That's the point. And it's the message we want to give them. That you really are dead."

Nash wasn't happy about that.

"There's another possibility here," Jules pointed out before the man could argue with Tess. "And yes, it's likely that our adversaries are going to be watching closely to see what we do next. But it's also possible that they think Dave's in the loop—that he knows for sure if you're dead or alive. And if he did know you were alive, wouldn't it make sense for him to contact you? I think it's likely they're going to be watching Dave closely, too—to see what *he's* going to do next."

Dave knew that his next move had to be to find the Irish man who'd stabbed him.

Providing that he *had* a next move. It was entirely likely that his discharge papers from the hospital—which according to the nurse, he'd have in hand in about thirty minutes—would allow Bill Connell to swoop down, arrest him, and take him into custody. And in a jail cell, Dave wouldn't be able to move very far at all.

Sophia was still sleeping in a horribly uncomfortable-looking chair across the room when another nurse came in to free him from his final IV bag. Dave sat up after the young man left the room, cautiously getting out of bed to test his still-wobbly legs and, yes, to use the privacy of the bathroom instead of that hideous urine jug.

He relieved himself without waking Sophia—or falling down and peeing on the wall—and on the way out of the bathroom, he poked his head into the hallway, to test the reaction of the guards. Much could be learned from their response to him—which could be anything from them drawing their weapons and shouting for him to back the hell up, to a nod and a polite request to stay in the room with a *please* and a *sir*.

But Dave didn't anticipate the total non-reaction he received—on account of the guards being gone.

The guards were *gone*.

He moved quickly, back into the room, on legs that weren't quite ready for moving faster than a slow shuffle. "Sophia, help me," he said, and she snapped awake, leaping from the chair.

"What are you doing out of bed?"

She headed for the nurses' call button, but he stopped her.

"We're getting out of here," he told her. "Now. Where are my clothes?" The words weren't even halfway out of his mouth when he opened a cabinet and saw them, folded neatly atop his shoes. They weren't the shirt and pants he'd been wearing last night—those had been ruined—but rather a pair of jeans and one of his polo shirts with a collar, a clean pair of briefs, and socks. Someone, probably Sophia, had gotten this out of the suitcase that was no doubt still in the trunk of their rental car—on account of their never making it to their hotel last night. He scooped the clothing into his arms. "Get your things. Let's go. *Now.*"

He didn't know whose snafu this was. But whether it was Bill Connell's, the local police chief's, or the individual uniformed officers who'd apparently left their post unattended, it didn't matter.

What mattered was that, for this brief, shining moment in time, Dave could walk out of this hospital, completely unchallenged.

He opened the door and, glory alleluia, the hall was still empty. The nurses' station seemed to be off to the right. To the left was a long corridor—and a door marked AUTHORIZED ACCESS ONLY.

"This way." Sophia brushed past him, taking his arm and leading him left, but she didn't take the mystery door. Instead she went down the hall and took another left and then another. She led him through a set of double doors and around another corner, this time to the right, finally ending at a bank of elevators. She pushed the down button as he juggled his shoes, trying to shake free his briefs, because the last thing he needed was to get picked up for indecent exposure.

There was a sign for stairs on a door across from the elevators, and Sophia pulled him toward it, not missing a beat as she scooped up the shoe he dropped.

And then, thank God, they were in the quiet isolation of the stairwell and she was helping him get dressed, efficiently but gently, careful not to bump his bandaged wound.

It was the first time since the attack that they'd had any kind of real privacy. In fact, it felt like the equivalent of a planetary alignment or the sighting of a comet—exceedingly rare and not likely to happen again in his lifetime. Especially since he fully expected the missing guards to come bursting into the stairwell at any moment.

So Dave grabbed hold of the opportunity with both hands, jumping into the deep end of what should have been a delicately approached, one-toe-into-the-water-at-a-time topic.

"I caught the gonorrhea from oral sex," he announced as she helped him on with his jeans. "It was the only time we didn't use a condom. Kathy—Anise. And me."

Sophia's response as she pushed him to sit on the stairs so she could put on his socks and guide his feet into his shoes?

She laughed.

And immediately apologized. "I'm sorry. It's just that . . . you said that last night—*oral sex*—and I had no idea what you meant. I was pretty sure it wasn't a request, because you were extremely upset—not to mention nearly unconscious—so . . ."

He caught her hand, forcing her to look into his eyes. "I didn't kill Anise Turiano, Soph. And I didn't—"

"Shhh." She gently broke his hold on her to pull down his shirt and straighten his collar, as he fastened his belt. "We can talk about this later. Are you good for the stairs, or should we take the elevator?"

"I'm good," he lied, starting down, leaning heavily on the banister. "I just wanted you to know—"

"Stop talking and move."

Back when he and Sophia were in their "just friends" mode, he'd told her about the week he'd spent with Kathy-slash-Anise. He'd confessed that it had been his first-ever sexual experience—about time for a man already in his thirties—which had been hard enough to admit. The fact that he'd ended up catching an STD was icing on the embarrassment cake—and proof that life could be a real bitch.

But of course, life had then turned around and caught him completely off-guard by giving him Sophia, so, truly, how could he complain?

"I lied to the investigators," he couldn't not tell her. "It's true. But mostly by omission—"

"It doesn't matter," she told him, helping move past a door that was labeled 3RD FLOOR.

"Yes it does," he insisted.

"No," she said, emphatically, "it doesn't."

"It would've complicated things," he told her as she continued to support him. They headed down to the second floor, and then the first. "I was treated anonymously, at a clinic, so there were no medical records. And it was a week between the time I thought she'd left me and her body was found, so . . . Her autopsy revealed that she had the disease, but by that time I was clean. And I know they tested me for it—I was in the hospital with a punctured lung, courtesy of the same ex-KGB thugs who snuffed her. Although there was no hard proof of *that*, so . . ."

Dave's insistence that he'd never had unprotected sex with Anise Turiano, either before or, God, after her death was confirmed by his clean bill of health. He'd been dropped as the prime suspect—due to insubstantial evidence—although the agents in charge of the investigation remained convinced of his guilt and wrongdoing.

Sophia didn't say anything so Dave kept going. "And as far as Barney Delarow—"

She cut him off. "There's a taxi stand near the main entrance," she said, "but they could be watching for us there. My gut is to get to the street and just keep moving, try to pick up a cab down toward . . . what is it? Cambridge Street?"

"No, Charles. Soph, please, if you have any questions at all, about anything—about Anise Turiano—I'll make sure you get the case file so you can—"

She stopped outside the door to the first floor and got right in his face. "David. We'll talk about this later. Can we walk through the lobby, please, without you shouting about all the murders you didn't commit? Let's keep this low-profile, all right?"

Dave gazed into the crystal blue of her eyes, searching for . . . something he didn't find. He honestly couldn't tell what she was thinking, and that made him feel sick. "What are you doing?" he whispered. "Helping me break out of here, when you don't even believe me?"

She turned away.

What he'd wanted—no, *needed*—for her to do was look him in the eye and say, *I believe you, Dave. I believe everything you say*, but instead she'd turned away.

"Yeah," she said, and he realized that her cell phone had vibrated, and she was taking a phone call.

Great. It was probably Bill Connell himself, telling them that the stairwell was surrounded, and to come out with their hands up.

But then Sophia exhaled hard and said, "Oh, thank heaven," and then, "Uh-huh. Yes, wait, hang on, let me write down the address." She pulled her notebook and pen from her handbag. "Albany Street," she said. "Got it. No, the rental car has a GPS, so . . . We'll be there—probably in . . ." She glanced at her watch. "I want to say an hour, but it'll probably be before then." She laughed at something said by whoever was on the other end of the call. "See you then and . . . Thank you so, *so* much." Snapping her phone shut, she put both it and her notebook back in her bag.

And turned to Dave. "That was Joe Hirabayashi, from the FBI. He wants us to come to the morgue, so you can identify the man who stabbed you last night."

"The morgue," Dave repeated, shifting to sit on the flight of stairs they'd just come down. People generally didn't go to the morgue to appear in a police lineup.

Sophia nodded. "The man from last night? Bald, tattoos, leather jacket, biker boots, gold tooth? He was found a few hours ago, in some park—someplace called the Fenway—with a bullet in his head. Blood splatters on his clothing are a match both for you and Barney Delarow. Your story pans out—you're no longer a suspect."

And that was why the guards had vanished from his door. That bastard Bill Connell had pulled them and left—without having the decency to inform Dave that he was in the clear.

Sophia sat down next to him on the stairs, and she looked so exhausted, he swallowed the words he was about to say: *So . . . About that Anise Turiano thing. Do you believe me now?*

"How about we take the elevator back upstairs," she said, "so you can sign all the papers you need to sign to be officially released. I'll go get the car, pick you up out front, and we can go to the morgue and do . . . whatever needs to be done."

Dave nodded. "Identifying the skinhead would be a nice step toward finding out who tried to frame me."

Sophia nodded, too, but then asked, "Why would someone want to frame you?"

"That's definitely the question of the hour. If we find out *who*, *why* might come for free, like a two-fer."

She laughed, but it was weary. "You said he mentioned a name—Santucci."

"*Give my best to Santucci*," Dave repeated.

"How can you give your best to someone you don't know?"

"I don't know." But whoever Santucci was, Dave was going to find him. Or her. He sighed. "Come on," he said, tugging at her hand. "You slept in a chair—after talking to your father for the first time in decades. Let's ID the perp, then go someplace where you can get some rest."

"I just want to go home." But she didn't move. In fact, she leaned her head against Dave's shoulder and sighed. "Seeing my father again was nothing," she told him quietly. "Not compared to seeing you in that parking lot, and thinking . . ." She drew in a deep breath, and when he turned to look at her, she had tears in her eyes. "When I saw all that blood . . ."

"Hey," he said, pulling her chin up so he could kiss her. Her lips were so sweet, so soft. "Come on. You should know better. I'm harder to kill than that."

She nodded, forcing a smile. "I sometimes forget that you are," she admitted. "It's just that you're Dave. You're . . . Dave."

"Yes, I am," he said. "I'm not sure what you mean by that but . . . I gotta agree. Although these days I'm calling myself Lucky Dave."

Her smile became more real as she held his gaze, but then it faded. She touched him, her fingers almost cold against his face. "I didn't *not* believe you, you know."

Which wasn't the same thing as her believing him.

"We're both tired," Dave said. "Let's just get going. Maybe Yashi'll have more information when we get to the morgue."


The trip to the safe house was going to have to wait.

Tracy knew that wasn't the only reason Decker was antsy as they sat in his truck, in the quiet parking lot of the medical complex that housed Dr. Heissman's new office, waiting for her to show up.

Which wasn't going to be too much longer. In Starbucks, the woman had given them her entire day's schedule—for this very purpose, no doubt.

The parking lot at the VA was too busy, too crowded, too vast—not a good place to connect with the doctor. So here they sat, waiting for her to arrive, as the hands of Tracy's watch moved from 3:45 to 3:46.

But Deck had even more things on his mind besides finding out the details behind that *help me* message.

His secure satellite phone had stopped working, which made it difficult to communicate with any of his fellow operatives.

They'd stopped over at the Troubleshooters office, and the place was empty and locked up tight, which had felt strange. Much to Decker's disgust, there were no replacement sat phones available. Tracy tracked one down—Lindsey Jenkins had it—but she was in a meeting and wouldn't be able to drop it off until later in the day.

It was while they were there, using the secure landline to get in touch with FBI agent Jules Cassidy, that Decker had really had his cage rattled. He'd called Jules to report the weird new Jo Heissman problem, and in the midst of that conversation, he'd found out that last night, while he and Tracy had been having the world's most unsatisfying sleepover, trouble had come to call on the East Coast.

Apparently, Dave Malkoff had gotten into a knife fight outside of the Boston hospital where he and Sophia had gone to visit her ailing father.

And yes, the idea of Dave—uncoronated king of the nerds—in a knife fight was enough to send anyone's incredulometer rocketing sky high. But it was the fact that Sophia had actually met with her horror-show of a father that had made Tracy pause.

Decker, too.

Of course, that wasn't entirely unexpected, since every breath he took was all about Sophia. Every heartbeat murmured her name to him. Every nose whistle, every belch, every fart, and okay, now Tracy was just being mean. But she had to admit to feeling envy for the blonde. Although envy plus mean thoughts equaled jealousy, which was unattractive in a woman of a certain age. As in anyone over eighteen—*months.*

And, realistically? While it was fun to flirt and to daydream and to play a muted version of *That Dawg Would So Totally Cut Off His Left Nut to Do Me* with many of the men at Troubleshooters—including Lawrence Decker—the man had been ragingly right last night. Having a fling with someone she worked with would be crazy complicated.

And also, Tracy knew darn well that she didn't fling. She relationshipped. Upon full penetration, she bypassed logic and reason and went directly to I-Love-You Land. Which was massively stupid—she knew that, too.

These days, though, Tracy was a realist. Or at least she'd started trying harder to be a realist in the wake of her bewildering breakup with Michael-the-Creep, who'd ripped out her heart after she'd just barely gotten it sewn back into her chest. She'd still been vulnerable and emotionally raw following the fiasco with her cheating ex-fiancé Lyle and then that bastard with his Navy SEAL muscles, Irving Zanella. His nickname was

Izzy, but it helped, in getting over him—which had taken far too long, considering it had been only one night—to think of him as *Irving*.

So yes, she'd been neither realistic nor smart when she'd gotten involved with all three of those losers. And she definitely hadn't been realistic or smart last night at dinner with Decker, when she'd gone on a fishing expedition, using George as bait.

*Hello, extremely attractive, slightly older, and hopefully more mature man sitting at my kitchen table. I've always found you hot. I also haven't had sex in a very, very long time, and well . . . here we both are. I know from my mirror that many men think that I'm both beautiful and sexy. So if you put in just a small amount of effort, I will let you talk your way into my bed tonight.*

But Decker apparently was *too* mature—to the point of recognizing what an awful mistake *that* would have been. Or maybe he was simply too in love with Sophia ever to dally, even briefly, with any other woman.

Either that or he was totally gay.

And yes, all right, *that* was Tracy's inner jealous crybaby bubbling forth.

She had plenty of gay friends, and although observation and gaydar could never provide a completely accurate verdict—not like asking "Are you gay?" and getting back an answer, "Yes"—she was virtually certain Decker's orientation was strictly hetero.

Although picturing him naked with, say, Izzy Zanella? It worked for her in a rather odd way.

"You're awfully quiet," Decker said, interrupting her wayward thoughts.

She laughed as she glanced at him. With his sunglasses on, he was harder than ever to read. Still, she was pretty certain that telling him she was imagining being in the middle of a Zanella-Decker sandwich wouldn't go over well. So instead she switched on the signal jammer and said, "You really need to tell Sophia the truth."

Of course, he started shaking his head the moment Sophia's name crossed her lips.

They'd picked up the jammer when they'd stopped in at the TS office. If anyone was trying to listen in with long-distance microphones, it would screw with the signal, but make it appear to the listener as if the problem was radio interference from passing trucks or taxis.

It wasn't as creative or colorful—both figuratively and actually—as taping George to the window and flipping on his shower-safe switch. But on the other hand, it wasn't likely to get them arrested, either. And it did allow them to talk freely without fear of being overheard. And over the past few hours, Decker had filled her in, completely, on the situation with Jimmy Nash.

Well, probably not *completely*.

But Tracy knew there was a plan afoot to make the bad guys who tried to kill Jimmy—whoever they were—believe that the FBI had opened an investigation to see if Decker and/or Tess weren't somehow connected to potentially criminal activities that Nash had engaged in. It had something to do with a bloodstained shirt and a list of people whom Jimmy had apparently deleted while he'd worked black ops for the Agency.

Tracy hadn't asked exactly what that meant—to *delete*—but really, she hadn't had to.

She chose now to talk of less violent but no less volatile things. Such as Sophia.

"You need to tell her," she persisted. "You bring this with you"—she pointed to the jammer—"when you pick them up at the airport tonight. You get them into the truck and . . . You tell them both the truth." That Jimmy was alive.

Decker just shook his head.

"Okay," Tracy said, shifting so that she was turned more toward him. "Yes. Dave's going to get hurt. It's unavoidable, but—"

"It's not about that," he said.

"Sure, you can believe, if you want, that—"

"Look, I know you'd rather think that this is about personal feelings, rather than decisions based on strategy and logic—"

"Oh, please," she scoffed. "Now you're pretending it's *logical*, not to—"

"Honey, why do *you* think Liam Smith was found dead, in a deserted part of a Boston city park?" Decker asked, adding, as if she might not remember who Smith was from their earlier conversation, "The man who attacked Dave last night?"

Tracy paused, thinking about it, while Deck just waited, watching her. "Because he was . . . an unsavory person," she guessed. "Who went unsavory places, where he got himself killed in an unsavory way." Assuming there were savory ways to get oneself killed.

"On the very same night he knifes Dave." Decker's voice was loaded with skepticism. "Come on, Tracy, use that big brain I *know* you've got. What do we know—from the fact that Smith was shot, point-blank, in the face? The man had a powder burn on his chin."

"I didn't know that," she said.

"Well then, I'm telling you now," he countered. "What does it tell us?"

She wished she could see his eyes, but they were securely covered by those dark glasses. He thought she had a big brain, which was refreshing. Most men combined the word *big* with *boobs* when they referred to her. "That . . . whoever shot him was standing very close to him." She realized as she spoke the words what *that* meant—and Decker was right. This wasn't that hard to deduce. "That he probably knew whoever shot him— well enough for the shooter to get that close."

"Good girl," he said, and she felt an absurd rush of pleasure. It was particularly absurd considering his word choice.

"I'm not a girl," she felt compelled to point out. "I'm a woman. And it still *could* be a coincidence."

"Liam Smith was found with his clothing stained with both Dave and Barney Delarow's blood," Decker told her, a muscle jumping in the side of his jaw, as he no doubt thought about what that had meant to Sophia. If Smith had had Dave's blood on him, Dave must've been bleeding badly. Which couldn't have been a happy sight for Sophia. "He was lying there like the perfect little get-out-of-jail-free card for the police and other investigators to find."

Tracy struggled to understand. "So you think whoever killed Smith wanted Dave *not* to be charged with Delarow's murder. But . . . why? After going to all that trouble to frame him?"

He didn't answer. He just waited for her to reach her own conclusion.

She knew Decker thought that the Agency was behind the previous attempts on Jimmy's life. And if the Agency *was* the all-seeing, all-knowing organization they were reputed to be, then they surely knew that Dave had been friends with Decker and Nash. So . . .

"You think the *Agency* thinks that *Dave knows* whether or not Jimmy's alive." Tracy kept going, because Decker was nodding. "They hope Dave's . . . going to . . . lead them to him?"

He smiled at her. "Correct for two points."

"Only two?" she said.

"That one wasn't as mind-stretching as figuring out Nash was, you know," he told her. And she did know—Nash was *still alive*. And Deck was still unable to say it aloud, despite their cone of silence.

"For which I won an all-expenses-paid vacation," she reminded him. "To the world's most upscale jail. Provided I ever get there." She returned to where this conversation had started. "So you're using the fact that the Agency is probably watching Dave's every move as an excuse to not tell him and Sophia the truth."

Decker laughed his exasperation. "Will you please just let that drop?"

"What if the Agency goes after Dave again?" Tracy asked. "Or what if they go after Sophia this time?"

That got her a flash of his eyes over the top of his glasses.

"Frankly? I think you don't want to tell them because you prefer wallowing in misery," she said.

"You're out of line," Decker said quietly, which meant she was finally pissing him off. She'd noticed that about him through the years. He rarely raised his voice. In fact, she'd only seen him get crazy-loud once, when he and Nash got into a physical fight in the Troubleshooters parking lot—shortly before Nash had "died." She'd stood there, with her mouth literally hanging open, astonished at the sight of Decker beating the crap out of Nash.

"I think you wouldn't recognize happiness if it came up and bit you on the butt," she countered now. "Or maybe you would, but you wouldn't know what to do with it."

"I do know what to do with it," he said. "I know exactly what to do. I leave it the hell alone."

"You think Sophia's happy with Dave," she realized.

He sighed—an exaggerated expulsion of exasperation, meant to shame her into letting it drop.

She didn't. "You do," she accused him. "You actually believe—"

"Look, she *is* happy," he told her. "I know it. All right? He's good for her. I've seen them together and she's—" Deck swore pungently, as if at himself.

And using her big brain, Tracy realized exactly what he'd just said. He'd *seen them together.* "You spied on them?" She couldn't keep her delight from showing in her voice, on her face.

"No," he said tersely.

She just looked at him, eyebrows raised, and he added, "I wasn't spy-ing. I was just . . ."

"Spying. You're a spy," she pointed out. "You spied. It's okay. You couldn't help yourself, it's what you do, but . . ." She paused, a little icked out. "Not, like, through Sophia's bedroom window, right?"

"No! Jesus." He took off his sunglasses and rubbed his eyes. "I wanted to make sure she was okay. And she *was*. She was, yeah, happy. Okay? I heard her laughing and it was real laughter. And I would never do *any*-thing to take that away from her."

"And you don't think she'd be even happier," Tracy felt compelled to point out, "with you? I mean, considering she's in *love* with you?"

He was back to shaking his head, after, once again, hiding his eyes be-hind his shades.

"So that's it," Tracy said. "You're just going to quit?"

That got her another flash of his eyes. "Believe me, I quit this game a long time ago."

That didn't just surprise her—it annoyed her. "So . . . what then? You're just never going to have sex again?"

He laughed, but then stopped abruptly. "That's *really* none of your business."

He'd told her that he hadn't had sex with Dr. Help Me, and he sure as heck hadn't had it with Tracy, last night. She knew something had hap-pened between him and Sophia, but was now starting to believe it had oc-curred over the course of a single, accidental night.

Tracy had always known that Decker held himself apart from everyone else at Troubleshooters Incorporated, but she was starting to realize that she'd never imagined just how wide that self-imposed gap was. "Did you honestly tell Dr. Heissman that you were thinking about killing yourself?"

He smiled at that—a flash of straight white teeth in his tanned face. "Only you would dare to ask about that. Tracy, honey, you are absolutely a piece of work."

"Is that a compliment or a disparaging comment?" she mused, forcing herself to pretend that his *honey* didn't make her heart beat harder. "I've never quite figured that out."

Decker just laughed—and she couldn't quite tell if it was in despair or amusement.

"You didn't answer my question," she said, calling him on it. "I think

you *did* tell Dr. Heissman that. But I also think you were totally BS-ing her."
On account of the doctor having worked for the Agency. Decker had filled
Tracy in on his suspicions that Dr. H. had *still* worked for the evil overlord
of the Agency as recently as a few months ago, even while she was em-
ployed as the one and only member of the psych department at Troubleshooters Incorporated.

It was creepy to imagine, but Deck seemed to think Dr. H. had taken
the job at TS Inc. to keep an eye on Jimmy Nash. And apparently the
woman now needed help, so maybe his paranoia was accurate. But did she
really need help, or was she digging for information? That was, hopefully,
what they were going to find out—if and when she ever appeared, here at
her office.

Tracy glanced at her watch: 3:52.

"What if I told you I wasn't?" Decker asked, but again Tracy couldn't
see his eyes through his sunglasses. "Bullshitting her."

"Well," she said slowly, aware that this enigmatic man was holding
open the door to some extremely personal territory. "I'd make sure you
knew that, from my perspective? The world's a better and much safer place
with you in it. I'd make sure you knew that you were loved, and that you'd
be missed. Badly."

He didn't respond. They both just sat there for many, many long seconds as she gazed at her own reflection in his sunglasses. But then he
turned to look away from her, staring out the front windshield at the deserted parking lot. He shook his head again. And finally spoke.

"I don't get you," he said. "I just don't. Is it because . . . I'm here? I'm
human? I'm male? I have both a pulse and a dick?" He turned to look back
at her, taking off his sunglasses so that she could finally see his eyes. Just
like that fraction of a second that she'd thought she'd imagined back in the
Starbucks, he let his attraction for her show. Only this time he didn't hold
back. "What the hell would a girl like you want with me? You into danger,
Tracy? Is that what it is? Because you are playing with fire."

"First of all?" Tracy had to push to speak past her heart, which had securely lodged in her throat. "I'll say it again: I'm a woman, not a girl. Let's
get *that* straight."

"To me," he shot back, "you're just a curious little girl, looking for a di-
version. For a fancier toy to play with. Honey, do yourself a favor, and stick
with the one you've already got."

She exhaled her outrage. "I'm sorry. Did you miss something here? Like the part of this conversation where I've been trying to talk you into telling *Sophia* that you *love* her? Get *over* yourself." She forced a laugh. "Wow, that's part of the problem. You're so completely my type. A pulse and a dick, yes, but a giant stone in place of your heart. If I'm sending mixed signals, it's because I *am* drawn to you, like a moth to a flame. But I'm smarter than that, and I am *not* doing this."

"That's right," he said, putting his sunglasses back on and turning back to the deserted parking lot, "but only because *I'm* not 'doing this.' "

"Oh, my God," Tracy said, "could you *be* any more arrogant? Better stop that, *honey*, because I'm a headcase and it *totally* makes me want to fuck you."

He sharply turned and looked at her again, and this time, despite the sunglasses, his smolder came through. She was afraid, for several long heartbeats, that he was going to yank her to him, and kiss her. Hard.

But then the fear was suddenly diminished by a clean, clear *ping* of shining hope—that this man would, in fact, do exactly that.

Instead he jumped—and Tracy did, too—as Jo Heissman knocked on the passenger-side window.

Decker swore, starting the truck with a roar—and flipping off the signal jammer; wasn't that interesting?—as Tracy unlocked and pushed open the heavy door.

"Are you crazy?" the doctor said, clearly frightened. "This lot has a security camera—"

"I disabled it," Decker told her. "You want help? Get in, and get down. On the floor."

Tracy slid over on the bench seat to make room for the older woman, who hesitated only briefly before she climbed in. Decker, meanwhile, put the truck in gear and pulled out onto the street—almost before Jo had pulled the door shut.

"If you're going to sit that close," he told Tracy, his voice tight as he looked into the rearview mirror, no doubt to see if anyone was following them, "at least try to look like you mean it."

# CHAPTER
# SIX

The alarm signifying a security breach went off, two hours after Tess and Jules had left the safe house, making Jimmy's pulse kick into overdrive and his vision damn near start to tunnel.

They'd been running drills all morning—working on getting down to the panic room as quickly as possible—and his first thought was that this couldn't possibly be another exercise.

No, this was it. Jules had sent Jimmy's shirt to the lab for that DNA test, and the death squad from the Agency believed that he wasn't dead. The attack on Dave had been the warning shot across his bow, and now they were coming for him.

In a fortress like this, Jimmy's response should have been a resounding *Oh, yeah? Suck my balls*, only he currently had no clue where Tess was—or Decker—and that scared the living shit out of him. It sent him, spiraling, back toward the place where he'd spent the past year—alone in an emotional darkness, as he'd tried to convince himself that the only way he could keep his fiancée and friends alive was to keep both the truth and himself far away from them.

It was a bad place to be. He knew it—even as he felt himself slipping, as he found himself thinking the same damning thoughts. *This wouldn't be happening if I just disappeared. . . .*

Tess had once laughed as she'd told him how hard it was for her to visit her mother—whom she loved very much—without having at least a tiny part of her turn back into a belligerent thirteen-year-old. It happened, she'd said, upon stepping through the door to her mother's San Francisco art gallery—which was the only way to get into the apartment upstairs. *Why can't you be like the other moms back in Iowa? Why did you leave Daddy to live like this? A fifty-eight-year-old woman really* should *stop painting for the forty-five seconds needed to run a comb through her hair, and—oh yeah—maybe put on a bra every now and then . . . ?*

It happened, Tess had told Jimmy, regardless of how much she prepared herself in advance of each visit. It happened regardless, too, of how appreciative she now was, as an adult, of the fact that her mother had followed her heart and had insisted upon living a life that was true to herself.

Those old feelings were just ghosts, Tess had said to Jimmy, quite a few months ago. Her voice had been soft and warm in the darkness of their bedroom as they lay together, their bodies still connected after making love. Jimmy was pretty sure she'd been trying to get him to open up and talk about his own mother, which he'd done only superficially. It helped, Tess had gone on to say, to identify those ghost feelings for what they were, and gently push them back into the past. Because they didn't belong here in the present.

That was definitely what Jimmy was feeling right now. Ghosts from the past, made stronger by this crazy fear that Tess was going to die because of his mistakes. And while he recognized both the fact that he was having these ghost feelings *and* the fact that the situation had changed, dramatically, between those days of darkness and now, he couldn't stop himself from running old patterns.

If the Agency was coming for him, then screw it. He was going to give them what they wanted—his undeniable silence through death—and end this bullshit here and now.

But then Sam Starrett rapped on his door. The former SEAL must've correctly interpreted the look on Jimmy's face, because he quickly said, "Just another drill. Once more with feeling, you know?"

The relief made Jimmy light-headed—a fact that Starrett obviously realized, because he came all the way into the room and looped Jimmy's arm around his shoulders. He had Ash in some kind of front-pack sling thing, and the baby gave Jimmy a happy, if soggy, grin.

"Y'okay?" Sam asked.

And Jimmy nodded through the haze. "I can make it to the chair."

"Not this time," the taller man announced, and sure enough, there was no wheelchair waiting for them in the hall. "We're running the no-available-chair scenario."

Didn't it figure? All morning long, Jimmy'd bitched and moaned about having to sit in a wheelchair and be pushed to the panic room. Tess and Sam had actually carried him from his bed to the chair. They'd transferred him into another chair that was designed to carry handicapped people down flights of stairs in emergency situations, took him down those stairs, and then transferred him again to a second regular wheelchair to make the final run along the basement hall. They'd quickly learned how to move efficiently together, as a team.

*They* were the team, that is. Jimmy was the burden. And a true pain in the balls, because he'd insisted—all morning—that he could make it under his own steam. Even though he damn well knew he could never move as fast as those wheels.

But now Sam was giving him a chance to do the run without the chair, and the prospect seemed daunting. It didn't help that Tess wasn't there—if she were, he'd be bluffing his ass off, pretending that this didn't hurt.

"Ow—Christ!"

If Tess were there, he'd at least try to fool her into believing he wasn't a complete candy-ass crybaby.

"Think of this as a drill combined with physical therapy," Sam said, annoyingly cheerful as he all but carried both his son and Jimmy down the hall. "Plus a little distraction to keep your mind offa Tess being gone."

"Yeah," Jimmy said through gritted teeth. "Nothing like a good torture session to while away the time. Thanks *so* much."

Sam laughed, but thankfully didn't make any other idiotic comments as they attacked the stairs.

If Ash hadn't been with them, Jimmy would've said a heartfelt *fuck me* on each bone-jarring step down.

It was obvious that Sam knew this because he was chuckling—typical Navy SEAL asshole sense of humor—as he dragged Jimmy the last few feet into the panic room and kicked the door shut behind them.

"We're secure," he announced into his headpiece microphone as he helped Jimmy onto a soft leather sofa and sprang Ashton from his parachute-like halter—plopping the kid onto Jimmy's lap.

"What? No, don't—"

But Sam had already let go, leaving Jimmy no other option besides holding on to the baby. He was surprisingly heavy, and yet still kind of squishy and soft as he solemnly blinked at Jimmy with eyes that were startlingly blue.

During this morning's drills, Jules's husband Robin had had possession of the little boy, keeping Sam's hands free. But Robin had gone to San Diego with Jules and Tess.

Despite their fear that the Agency was trying to shake Jimmy loose by going after his friends, the movie star was keeping to his schedule. He was going to start filming tomorrow, in the city. One of the many things Jules was doing today was upping Robin's security on the movie set.

Jimmy knew that the FBI agent wasn't happy about that. Kind of the way Jimmy hadn't been happy about Tess leaving the safe house without him. But like she'd said, if Jimmy really were dead, she'd come out of her self-exile to help Dave. Which was why she and Decker were planning to meet Dave and Sophia at the airport.

Crossing the room, Sam went to the array of monitors that displayed clear pictures of every room in the house—huh, there was the bed Jimmy was eager to start sharing again with Tess. Note to self: Block that camera before getting her naked.

As Jimmy watched, Sam used one of his currently baby-free hands to push an intercom button so that they could hear his conversation with Alyssa, who was still upstairs, over the main speakers.

"How'd we do?" Sam asked in his good ol' boy Texas drawl.

"One minute, thirty-four seconds." Alyssa came through clear as a bell. Ash burbled, clearly pleased to hear his mother's voice.

"Not bad for the first time." Sam was the eternal optimist as he grinned, delighted with his son. "That's right, Big Guy, that's your mama."

Alyssa stayed on topic by laughing her derision. "We've got to do *significantly* better if we want to—"

"We can definitely shave it down," Sam interrupted the woman who was both his wife, his boss, and the mother of his child. How the hell did he handle that? "And we will."

Even harder for Jimmy to imagine dealing with was the fact that they'd just locked Alyssa on the wrong side of that panic room door. And Sam had done it without blinking. Of course, this *was* just a drill. . . .

"Maybe I should sleep down here until Tess gets back," Jimmy suggested, raising his voice to be picked up by Sam's microphone, so Alyssa could hear him, too.

This may have been a panic room, but it was decked out with comfortable furnishings, a flat-screen TV, and a virtual storeroom of supplies. There was enough food and water in here to survive the end of the world.

Although why anyone would want to do that was beyond him.

Ash was starting to wiggle and, again, it was astonishing how strong the kid was, so Jimmy turned him around so they were both more comfortable, with that sturdy little back warm against his chest. He kept one hand on the kid's belly, and Ash took hold of one of his fingers with a warrior's grip.

"I don't think that's necessary," Alyssa said. "Gentlemen, you're cleared to release the door. Sam, it's your turn tonight in the kitchen, I have some paperwork to do." She paused, and when she spoke again, amusement was in her voice. "Unless you'd rather trade?"

"Nope, I'm good with what I've got," Sam answered. "But thanks for asking, ma'am. Over and out." He switched off both the speaker and his headset, then opened the door with a hydraulic-sounding swoosh. "She always knows *exactly* what to say so I don't complain. At least not in her earshot. I'd rather spend an hour in the pool than cook, but I'd rather hit my thumb with a hammer over and over for a full day than do paperwork, so . . . Don't look so scared, Nash—I'm not half-bad in the kitchen. I learned from a master—my Uncle Walt, who spent a few years in Italy during World War Two."

As he spoke, he went out into the hall, pulled a wheelchair back inside with him, set the brake on it, then deftly lifted Ash from Jimmy's lap. "Need a hand?" he continued in that same neighborly tone.

"No thanks." But Jimmy was worn out from the scramble down the stairs, and he *did* need Sam's help—one strong hand catching him under his elbow, keeping him from falling back into the chair.

As it was, he landed a little too hard, ringing his pain bell.

He would never say it aloud, not in front of Ashton, but the words *fucking wheelchair* were probably written all over his face. He hated sitting here, but right now he was glad for it.

And he hated it twice as much because of that.

"You'll be outta this thing in no time," Sam reassured him, plopping the baby back in Jimmy's lap.

He hadn't fully recovered from that brain-jarring peal of pain, but he knew enough to cling to Ash as Sam swiftly wheeled them both out into the hall.

"Barbecue or lasagna?"

It took Jimmy a moment to realize Sam was asking about dinner. "I don't care."

"Then it's grill time tonight. That way I can cook *and* swim."

The elevator was open and waiting for them, and Sam backed the chair inside. He pushed the button for the first floor.

"I'm on two," Jimmy reminded him.

"I know," Sam said. "But with Jules and Tess gone, we're shorthanded. I could use a baby wrangler while I'm making the sauce, so it looks like you got yourself a job. This is real Texas barbecue, by the way—I don't just open a jar."

"I'm kind of tired."

But the elevator door opened off the spacious living room, and Sam pushed him out, wheeling him over to the couch that was closest to the open kitchen area. "It *has* been quite a day and . . ." He stopped talking, cleared his throat, and started over. "What say we cut the bullcrap and I just tell you up-front that Jules asked me to talk to you. And frankly? I'd far rather let you go back to your room to mope and drive yourself into a panic over Tess. But I promised Jules, so . . ." He took Ash off Jimmy's lap and put the baby on his back, on the couch, penning him in with a pillow. "You don't have to say a word in response—I didn't promise I'd force you to talk, too, so if you want, you can just sit here and keep Ashton company while I both cook and talk at you. Deal?"

"Do I have a choice?" Jimmy said, as the SEAL all but lifted him out of the wheelchair.

"Nope." Starrett helped him onto the sofa, next to Ashton, who was starting to whimper. "He likes to be picked up, so he can see what's going on. He also likes it when you make faces."

Faces. Ash was starting to demonstrate his Navy SEAL–worthy lung capacity, so Jimmy reached over and carefully picked up the kid, his hands under both of the baby's now-flailing arms. The T-shirt thing he was wearing—it fastened with snaps between his pudgy legs—felt . . . damp?

"Or he could need a change." Starrett raised his voice to be heard over his son as he plopped a bright blue-and-yellow-striped bag on the couch next to Jimmy. "Go wild."

Jimmy held the baby up and out. "I'm not changing his diaper."

"What, you'd rather just sit there like a giant load, while we do all the work?" Sam said cheerfully as he went behind the huge granite-covered island that separated the bulk of the kitchen from the living room. He began getting out a collection of cutting boards, saucepans, and knives. "If it's anything more toxic than plain old wet, I'll take over. Otherwise, I'll talk you through it. There's a waterproof pad in the side pocket of that bag. Put that down on the couch first. No need to provide Lys with a reason to give us her *renting this place doesn't give us the right to pee on the couch* speech. It's a good one, but I've already heard it twice. Even though, considering the rent Robin's paying, I remain unconvinced that she's right. You owe the Boy Wonder a huge *thank-you*, by the way."

Jimmy didn't move and Ash's wailing became halfhearted as he looked over at his father with interest, as Sam serenely got a pile of tomatoes and peppers from the refrigerator and began washing them in the island's little sink.

"One of the reasons you're sitting down here instead of up in your bed, like a little whining girl," he told Jimmy, "is because we got clearance from your doctor to start some strenuous PT. Jules's been sending your vitals back to the doc, and you finally got his green light." He pushed the faucet's handle down and off with his elbow and carried the clean and dripping vegetables to the cutting boards.

"Which means, in case you haven't figured it out yourself," he added as he began cutting up the tomatoes, glancing up at Jimmy with a flash of a grin, "that you're also cleared for other strenuous, non-PT-type activities."

The man was talking about sex.

Of course, Tess was not only not here, but she was very not happy with him. Just because the doctor gave his green light didn't mean she was going to do the same.

"I know exactly what you're thinking," Sam continued, and he actually did. "It's not an automatic when you piss off your woman the way you've done of late. But picture this: She comes back, tonight or tomorrow—and it will be soon. I know you're worried about that, but she's gonna be just fine, and she'll be here before you know it. So she walks in, and you're not only up and sitting on the sofa, but you're hanging with Ash. You go, *Hey, I think the baby needs a change*, I'm like, *Thanks, man*, and I stand up, but you're all, *No, I'm right here, Starrett, I got it—let me*. And I toss you the diaper bag, and Tess, with her chin on the floor, watches as you expertly change Ashton's diaper. Now, it's not hard to do, but you got to start by putting him down on that pad, on his back."

Shaking his head, Jimmy did just that. It was like flipping a switch, though, because Ashton immediately quieted down.

"Keep one hand on him, so he doesn't roll off the couch," Starrett directed. "You need three things from the bag. A fresh diaper, one of those little blanket things, and the wipes. Get 'em all out first, before you take the old diaper off. And then look and see how the diaper he's wearing is fastened. There's tape—you see how that works to hold it on?"

"Yeah," Jimmy said. Ash was grinning up at him, so he told the kid, "I think your father's related to Tom Sawyer, and that after this I'm going to be scrubbing the kitchen floor and thanking him for the opportunity."

"You're going to peel the tape back and take off the diaper," Sam instructed. "It's going to weigh about a ton, so don't be surprised. As soon as you get it off of him, use the little blanket to cover his package. Otherwise he's gonna piss in your face. It's not personal—it's just a baby-boy thing."

"It's not hard to do," Jimmy repeated Sam's earlier words, "except he might piss in my face."

"Wait until Tess sees you do this." Starrett pointed at him with the gleaming blade of a knife that looked suspiciously like a battle-ready KA-BAR. "You, my friend, are gonna get laid. Provided you follow through with step two."

"What? Feed Ash and put him to bed?" Jimmy asked. Man, the used diaper *was* ridiculously heavy. The baby seemed positively ecstatic with his diaper-free status, and he chortled and flailed, entertained by his own tiny feet, his shiny little butt in the air.

"Better cover—"

"Yeah, yeah," Jimmy said, but he covered the kid only loosely. It seemed a shame to weigh him down again.

"Step two," Sam lectured, as he continued to chop vegetables, "is all about what you do and say after you and Tess shut the door of your suite."

"I think I've got that part handled, thanks." Jimmy struggled to open the plastic container of wipes. What the hell was wrong with this thing?

"Yeah but, you're thinking of step three. You can definitely go from one to three, but it's two that's crucial if you really want to make it all work." He immediately backpedaled. "It's a crucial truth for *my* relationship—it may not be true for yours. But, see, we're both in a unique position, being connected to women who can kick most people's asses. As much as we might want them to stay out of harm's way, that's not in their nature. We love them because they're in the thick of it—so we've got to let them go be in the thick of it."

He paused as if waiting for Jimmy to respond, but when Jimmy didn't, he just kept talking.

"Early in my relationship with Alyssa," Sam continued as Jimmy finally got the container of wipes open and pulled one out, "she went overseas on a bodyguard assignment, and her helo was shot down. I had to sit at home and wait to find out if she'd lived or died. Let me tell you how much *that* sucked." He laughed. "When she came back, it was unbelievably hard for me when the time came for her to take another dangerous assignment. So I told her that. I said, *This is hard for me. I'm gonna need your help, because it's always going to be hard, and sometimes I'm gonna screw it up. And I need you to remember, when I do screw it up? That it's because I'm scared of the things I know are not in your control. It's not because I don't have faith in you.*"

Jimmy was silent as he wiped off the baby's belly—which seemed to be the only place Ash was even slightly wet. He looked at the new diaper, which was folded into a smallish square of plastic and God-knows-what.

"*This is hard for me* and *I'm gonna need your help,*" Sam repeated. "Those two little sentences can make a world of difference."

The diaper unfolded into something only slightly more recognizable—with elastic-edged leg-holes and a fairly obvious front and back.

"Other way," Sam directed. "It's a boy diaper, so the absorbent part's in the front."

Okay, so maybe the front/back thing wasn't so obvious. And who knew diapers had genders? Jimmy looked at Ash to try to figure out how to do this without picking him up.

Sam again came to the rescue—although not literally, since he stayed back behind that counter. Bastard. "Grab his feet and lift and slip it under his butt."

The baby laughed as Jimmy did just that. He replaced the piss shield with the front of the diaper and taped it all securely down. Well, hell. That *had* been easy. Now, what to do with the used diaper?

"Another thing," Sam said. "Just an FYI. If Tess is anything like Alyssa . . . If *you* start the conversation? Trust me, you can't buy her a better gift than that. It's what she wants. For you, you know, to affirm the fact that you're a team. You can also start by telling her something that's obvious. Tell her you're afraid that something you've done is going to harm her in some way—"

"In some way?" Jimmy had to interrupt. He covered the baby's tiny ears. "I'm fucking scared to death that those pricks from the Agency are going to reach out and touch me—through her. It's bad enough that we think they've already tapped Dave—"

"Whoa, don't tell me," Sam said. "Tell her. And if that's too hard to start with, then start with something else. Maybe, you know, that new scar she's got on her hand."

Jimmy looked up at him sharply.

"That's a hard one, too, huh?" Sam mused. "But to be honest, it's all gonna seem hard, so maybe it's best to start with the things that're getting between you."

Jimmy shook his head in disbelief. "What'd I do?" he asked. "Look at it too much while you were carrying me down the stairs today?"

"No," Sam said. "But I noticed it myself and figured it had to be bugging the hell out of you."

Tess had a scar on her right hand—both on her palm and on the back. A bullet had gone right through her, but she was unbelievably lucky—there had been minimum damage. It hadn't broken a single bone. She'd received the injury during the same incident in which Jimmy had nearly been killed.

He'd taken a bullet to the chest and had hit his head when he'd fallen—knocking himself out cold. Tess had been shot, too, but she'd crawled over to him and, trying to defend them both, she'd reached for the weapon he'd dropped—and gotten shot in the hand.

The scar was small, but it was still new and raw-looking. And every time Jimmy saw it—which was every minute of every day when she was with him—he was reminded of the fact that he hadn't been able to protect her.

And that the enemy they'd been up against then were amateurs compared to the people they were facing now.

Sam was quiet, still chopping tomatoes, just waiting for Jimmy to respond.

"I don't know what good talking about it is going to do," Jimmy finally said. "Except make her self-conscious—"

"I'd bet you a year's salary," Sam interrupted, "that that scar means something entirely different to Tess than what it means to you. And maybe if you start seeing it—and other things—through her eyes, it won't hurt so fricking much."

"Maybe it's supposed to hurt," Jimmy said.

"Ah," Sam said, putting down his knife. "Okay. Yeah. Here we go. It's supposed to hurt? What's supposed to hurt? *Life?*"

"I don't know," Jimmy said. "Yeah. It's hard. It's always so fucking hard."

"Well, okay then. Do me a favor, will you, and tell Ashton to quit laughing, because life is supposed to hurt and be hard."

"You're oversimplifying," Jimmy argued. "It's not supposed to hurt for him. He's a baby, and you're here, to protect him—"

"Like you're here to protect Tess?" Sam countered. "And how do we do that, exactly? And by the way, Lys and I agreed that we wouldn't say four-letter words in front of Ash, so watch your fucking mouth, dickhead. We also won't raise our voices in anger in front of him. And if one of us gets sick or injured, he's not going to know about it. Until he's old enough, we're going to be careful what he sees on TV and what we talk about in front of him, because as a four-year-old, he shouldn't have to worry about the fact that the world is going to hell in a handbasket. He's going to be dealing with the hurts he can handle—bullies on the playground, skinned knees, coping with wanting things that other kids have that we can't or won't give him. But you better believe, by the time that boy turns eighteen, we'll be treating him like an adult, because the rest of the world sure as hell will be treating him that way, too."

Jimmy attached the snaps that connected the T-shirt thing Ash was wearing, fastening it securely between his pudgy little legs. "You really think I treat Tess like a child."

"I think that's part of the problem, yeah. I think you might also want to try some alternative mission statements on for size. I mean, *maybe it's supposed to hurt?* How about *maybe it's okay if it feels good.* Not just a little good, sometimes, but *really* good, *most* of the time. Look at me." Starrett held out both hands, one of them still holding that deadly-looking knife. "I just got you to change my kid's diaper, and I know for a fact that before the month is out? You'll be doing the really ripe ones, too. See, I have faith in you, Jimbo. You're a very intelligent man, and you're going to recognize the correlation between action and reaction—as in Tess's reaction to you changing Ash's didee. So *that* happiness is hanging in *my* very bright future.

"As for right now? As I make this sauce, I'm enjoying a visit with my Uncle Walt, who loved me like the kind of father I'm trying to be to my kids. I might complain about having to cook, but it's only because I enjoy complaining—and because it makes Alyssa laugh. After this, I'm gonna fire up the grill, and while our dinner cooks—and it's gonna smell amazing—Ash and I are gonna take a swim in that pool. Then we're gonna eat. Walt was a genius and dinner will be a religious experience. Count on it. Oh, and sunset's going to be a gorgeous show tonight—I'm looking forward to that, too. Then it's bathtime for Ash, then storytime. It's Lys's turn to read, and the sound of her voice is . . . It just washes over you—it's even better than the barbecue.

"And then? After my beautiful son is finally asleep, I'm going to spend some time alone with my wife, which, appropriately enough, follows the pattern and will be about a million times better than listening to her read aloud. And, yeah, maybe later tonight, while I'm asleep, some of that hurt and ugliness that I know is out there in the world is going to creep inside of my head, but I also know that if I have a nightmare? I'll wake up and Alyssa will be there. And if I need to, we'll talk it through, and it'll fade away. So if it hurts, it only hurts for a very, *very* short while."

Sam finally fell quiet, the sound of his knife against the cutting board making a rhythmic thunking sound in the otherwise silent room.

Ash had latched onto his own tiny little thumb and was sucking it with enthusiasm.

So Jimmy cleared his throat. "You, uh, really tell Alyssa everything?"

"Hell, no," Sam said, putting down the blade and scooping his chopped tomatoes up and into a nearby bowl. "That shit's hard, although it does get easier. Each time you tell her something that you're afraid is gonna make you less of a hero in her eyes, but she looks at you like you've given her diamonds . . . ? That's a good thing. So yeah, it does get a little easier, but it's never gonna be a cakewalk. Remember the magic words of step two: *This is hard for me. I'm gonna need your help.* And don't be afraid to use sex as a reward. For *you,* I mean. You can go point-blank if you want. *Hey, sweet thing, here's my Big Happy List of Slightly Untraditional Yearnings. I really love you and want to move our relationship to the next level and talk about things that are . . . hard for me to talk about. I'm gonna need your help, and maybe a little incentive, so if you could just glance over the list and let me know how you feel about maybe trying number six. After we talk, of course, because see, I'm a little afraid that I might cry, and, well, number six will definitely cheer me up after . . ."*

Jimmy laughed. "I don't think anything's ever been hard for you, Starrett."

"That's because I've embraced the fact that step two leads not just to step three and the Big Happy List, but also to step four. Which is sit back and laugh your ass off as you enjoy the sometimes crazy but always interesting ride."

"What do you do about the nightmares on the nights Alyssa's not home?" Jimmy asked. "How do you deal with knowing that the next time her helicopter goes down, she might not come back? Not ever?"

Sam picked up his knife and began chopping again. "You enjoy today," he said quietly. "You live your life—right now. If you fill your heart with love, there's not a lot of room left for fear." He smiled. "That sage bit of advice is a direct quote from my Uncle Walt."

"I didn't have an Uncle Walt," Jimmy admitted. His father figure had been cut from a different mold entirely.

"Most people didn't," Sam agreed. "But you've got Tess. For now, anyway. The choice is yours—are you going to do the work you need to do to keep her, or are you going to let her walk away?"

It was the photos that pushed Dave over the edge.

The sight of the man who'd attacked him—identified as Liam Smith from County Cork, Ireland—with part of his face and the back of his head blown off, lying on the table in the morgue, didn't perturb him even half as much.

Sophia had to squint through her eyelashes and even turn away—it was that awful a sight. But Dave moved closer to the dead man.

"That's him," he told FBI agent Joe Hirabayashi. The two men's voices faded into an indistinct rumble as Sophia found a bench in the hallway and sat, just breathing, with her eyes closed and her head between her knees.

And then Dave was back, his hand warm on her shoulder as he painfully lowered himself down to sit beside her. "I'm so sorry."

"I think I might be coming down with something," she said. "I'm usually tougher than that."

"You shouldn't have to be." As usual, he was ready to take the blame. "I should've—"

"Do we need to wait here?" she interrupted him. "Or can we go?"

"We can go," Dave told her, as he helped her up. Or maybe she helped him. It was hard to tell which of them was steadier on their feet. "Yashi's going to keep me updated with any intel they find on Smith. He had a driver's license, but it's doubtful he lives at his listed address. Although, you never know."

"Does he have a connection to Anise Turiano?" she asked, aware that the woman's name was enough to make the muscles in Dave's arm tense.

"Not that we know of," he answered her evenly as he held open the door that led to the tiny alleyway parking area. "But we don't know much yet—aside from the fact that he's wanted in both the UK and Russia, as well as here in the States. He's got no apparent connection to anyone named Santucci, either. Although there's something up with that. Something Yashi's not telling me, which is . . ." Dave froze. And said a string of eyebrow-raising words that she'd never heard him so much as whisper before—certainly not in that particular order. "Sophia, get back inside."

The lot was empty. Nothing moved in the cold, gray, late-morning light. But then she saw it, too. A white packet, about the length and width of a paperback novel, had been placed on the windshield of their rental car, held in place by one of the wipers.

"*Now.*" Dave's words were a command, not a request, and he turned to open the door, to push her back into the building.

She wouldn't let go of him. "Not without you." She raised her voice, calling down the corridor, "Yashi! Joe! We need help!"

The FBI agent was one of the slowest-talking, least excitable men that Sophia had ever met. He must've had a resting pulse rate of fourteen, yet he now came running down the hall, quite possibly breaking the record for the twenty-yard dash, his sidearm already drawn as she pulled Dave back inside with her.

"There's something on the windshield of our car," she told Yashi, right over Dave, who was saying, "Yashi's *not* going out there—it could be a bomb!"

"Get back, away from the window," Yashi ordered, as Dave broke Sophia's hold on him and moved, nearly as quickly as Yashi had, not back, but toward the door.

"Dave!" Sophia and Yashi called his name in unison, but he didn't so much as break stride.

He went out the door first, as Yashi ordered Sophia, "Stay here," and followed.

"Dave, what is wrong with you?" Sophia shouted.

Through the glass door, she could see Dave quickly scanning the buildings that overlooked the alley, his gaze tracing the rooftops as he searched for a shooter and happily—she could tell from his body language—didn't find one. It was then he focused his attention on the white packet, slowing as he approached.

"Stay back," he ordered Yashi, who was several steps behind him.

"If it was a bomb," Yashi countered in a voice that held only a hint of his usual *I'm so bored* lethargy, "it'd be under the car, not in plain sight like that. It's gotta be a message."

Yashi tried to move past Dave as Sophia stepped through the door and onto the top step of the platform that led to the driveway.

"Get inside, God damn it!" Dave roared at her, even as he beat Yashi to the packet and snatched it up before the FBI agent could. "Are both of you crazy?"

"It's photos," Yashi called to Sophia. "It's a packet of pictures."

Whatever they were photos of, Dave got even more grim as he glanced through them. Yashi tried to take them, but Dave kept the packet out of the other man's reach and view, then headed purposefully toward Sophia. "Get," he said. "Inside. *Now.*"

She got, but only because he was coming back into the building, too. In fact, she held the door for him, which made him even angrier with her. If that was possible. Of course, she was pretty angry with him, too.

"If you thought it was a bomb, the correct procedure is to call the bomb squad and—"

Dave ignored her completely as he turned to Yashi, who again was right behind him. "We need a room with privacy." His voice was clipped, his eyes hard, his face that of a stranger as he took Sophia's arm none too gently. "And we need it now."


"If I tell you to do something," Dave told Sophia, his voice harsh and a little too loud even in his own ears, as Yashi closed the door to the interrogation room behind him, leaving to try to book them on the next available flight to California, "you do it. You don't ask why. You don't argue. You obey."

The little room had a single translucent, bar-covered window that didn't do much in terms of providing natural light. Fluorescent bulbs hung in two upside-down trays from the ceiling. One of the bars was spasming, the light flickering on and off intermittently, which only added to Dave's growing headache.

With pea-soup-green walls and a chipped industrial-tile floor, the room held little more than a scarred and pitted wooden table and two rickety chairs. There was an ancient sink with a decrepit faucet in the corner, a boxy metal paper-towel holder fused to the wall with that ugly-ass paint, a built-in bookshelf with a lone copy of the King James Bible.

It was a grim and awful room, except it now also held Sophia, who could make the most wretched shithole a place of beauty, just by her ethereal presence.

"Maybe you've forgotten," she said, her own voice louder than usual, too, as she glared back at him, "but I don't work for you, so as far as that *obey* thing goes—"

"No," he agreed. "You don't. You're my fiancée. Your . . . perjurious statement is now—without a doubt—part of an official CIA report—"

"*Perjurious?*" she repeated in disbelief, because, yeah, it was a pretty stupid word choice. She hadn't been under oath when she'd answered Bill Connell's questions.

Still, Dave wasn't in the right place to admit that, or to slow down. "Which means that the entire world now knows that if they want to hurt me," he continued, "and I'm talking *really* hurt me? All they have to do is go after *you*. So thanks a lot."

Her eyes filled with tears. "I was trying to . . . I didn't think . . ." She exhaled her frustration and started again. "I actually thought you'd like it if I . . ."

"Threw me a bone?" he finished for her because he was so god-damned angry, but not really at her—he was angry at himself. Okay, he *was* pretty mad at her, too—for scaring the crap out of him. And, yeah, he was also mad at her because she'd given him everything he'd ever wanted and then some. Which meant that now he was going to know *exactly* what he was missing when he gave her up.

And after seeing those photos, he knew damn well that he was going to have to give her up. God help him.

"What is wrong with you?" she whispered. "*You're* mad at *me*?!"

"What if there was a shooter on one of those rooftops," he shot back at her, "but there you are—standing there, arguing with me because I'm not enough of an action hero for you—"

"*What?!*"

"—so you ignore what I say—"

"I didn't *ignore* you! I didn't want *you* out there, either! You've already been injured, you're hardly . . ." She searched for the right word.

So he supplied it for her. "Decker."

Again Sophia exhaled her frustration, yet at the same time, she wouldn't meet his gaze. "That's not what I was going to say."

His stomach twisted at her words. She didn't say *that's not true.* Because it *was* true. "Yeah, but it's what you meant. I'm *not* Decker. But if I were? Well, we both know that if mighty Decker had told you to do something, God knows you'd not only listen, you'd have done it."

"That is *not* fair," she whispered, her eyes huge in a face that was lined and drawn. And still so beautiful, his very soul ached.

"I know," he admitted. God, he was a bastard, taking this out on her. This was his fault—all of it. He should have known, years ago, that this fiasco with Anise would follow him, wherever he went, forever and ever, amen. "I'm sorry." He choked the words out. "I'm going to have to call him. Decker. To ask for help."

Yashi had thought that was a good idea, suggesting they return to San Diego as quickly as possible. And Sophia, too, lit up at the mention of Decker's name.

"Good," she said. "Dave, that's a *good* thing. Because we *need* help, if we're going to find—"

He cut her off. "I have to put you someplace safe," he told her, because *they* weren't going to do anything. He was. He'd started this all those years ago, and he was going to end it. Or die trying. "With someone I can trust. And I absolutely trust Decker."

That is, he trusted Decker to keep Sophia safe. It was what would happen when she and Decker were locked together, for days, in a secure hotel room, that Dave didn't trust. Or maybe he did. Maybe he knew too well what would happen in that kind of forced intimacy.

They'd talk. And they'd talk. And they'd finally freaking *talk*—about all the things that mattered, the things that Sophia, for some reason, hadn't been able to talk about with anyone. They'd talk about the secrets that, in the darkest, loneliest, most fear-filled and jealous hours of the night, even when Sophia was sleeping beside him, Dave imagined that she was saving to whisper to Lawrence Decker.

And as for Deck's supposed relationship with Tess? Whatever it was right now, it couldn't possibly last. They might indeed have reached for each other, for comfort, to ease their mutual pain. Dave had seen it happen before. Two lonely, grief-stricken people, settling—in a way that was far different from how Sophia had settled for him.

It was different because James Nash, may his soul rest in peace, would be with them, his spirit lingering, forever. So Decker and Tess would, eventually, drift apart. If they hadn't already begun to do so. Dave honestly didn't know. He hadn't so much as spoken to either of them since the memorial service.

"*Put* me . . . ?" Sophia interrupted his thoughts. It was clear she didn't like that any more than she'd liked *obey*. But then she glanced over at the packet of photographs that he'd tossed onto the table. "I'm not sure I want to know what's in there."

As she looked into his eyes, Dave knew that she was imagining that those pictures were far more provocative than they truly were—at least seemingly so. He could only guess what she was thinking. Maybe that the photos were of the two of them, being intimate. Or maybe they were of him, catching gonorrhea from Kathy-slash-Anise.

Yeah, if someone had pictures of that, Dave absolutely wouldn't ask for doubles for his photo album. It was only recently, since he'd become Sophia's lover, that his memories of Kathy, laughing with him—in truth, her name was Anise and she was laughing *at* him—had finally begun to fade.

And he liked it far better that way.

Of course, maybe Sophia thought the photos in that packet were of him killing Anise, stepping back from the bloody mess as she grabbed the slit in her throat, gasping and gurgling, eyes staring, as her life slipped through her fingers. . . .

Sophia had said she believed him, that she didn't think he'd wielded the knife that had taken Anise's life. But her doubt still shone through.

"They're photos of you," Dave told her, as he turned to the table to push them from the packet, being careful to spread them out on the rough wooden surface with a pen he carried in his pocket. He did that even though he knew there'd be no fingerprints on them, no DNA—nothing at all to identify whoever had put them on the rental car.

She stepped closer, and he shifted to put the table between them as he watched her face, her eyes. He saw her realization that these pictures had been taken just last night. She'd been shot standing in the hospital lobby, through the big glass windows, while she'd waited for Dave to get the car.

She also knew—he could tell from her expression that she'd figured it out—that she could have been shot in a very different way. That camera could just as easily have been a sniper rifle. The photos were blurred slightly from the heavy rain, and taken from high above—no doubt from the roof of the building across the street.

"It's probable these photos were taken by the person or persons who hired Liam Smith to kill Barney Delarow and attack me," Dave told her.

"What do they want?" she asked, her eyes almost crystal clear as she looked over at him.

Dave shook his head. "If it were purely revenge, I'd already be lying next to Smith, here in the morgue." Or, Jesus Christ, maybe Sophia would. "If they wanted me dead, I'd be dead by now."

"How can you be so blasé—" she started.

"Because it's true. At the very least I'd still be in intensive care. If Smith had been told to kill me," he told her, "he would have. He got the best of me, Soph. If he wanted to, he could have sliced me into pieces—" He cut himself off as she turned away, her movement sudden, as she rushed toward the sink in the corner.

Damnit, he hadn't been thinking, and now she leaned over the chipped porcelain, eyes tightly closed, gripping the edges with knuckles that were white.

Just as she'd done last night.

Only this time it wasn't her bastard of a father who'd turned her stomach and made her physically ill—it was Dave.

Good work.

He touched her arm, her back, and she turned to look up at him, her eyes bright with unshed tears, her face almost shockingly pale. "I *don't want* this," she said through clenched teeth, her voice shaking.

"I know," Dave whispered, feeling his own eyes fill with tears. "I'm so sorry. I thought it was over. I thought . . ." He had to look away, had to wipe his eyes with the heel of his hand. "I was fooling myself. I think, deep down, I always knew it was going to come back and haunt me and . . . I should have told you, right from the start."

"But you did." Sophia was doing what he always did for her—defending him against himself. She would have reached for him, but he made himself take a step back, holding only her arm as he helped her over to the table and into a chair.

"No, I didn't tell you everything," Dave said quietly.

"You told me enough." She rested her head on the table, her forehead against her folded arms.

"Are you all right?" he asked—a stupid question, because it was clear that she wasn't.

Still, she nodded, head still down, eyes closed. *Yes.*

Right.

"You told me more than enough," she repeated.

"I left a lot out," he told her, "like the fact that there's a contingent over at the CIA still looking to prove that I'm guilty of murder and treason." He laughed—it came out sounding hollow as he sat, too. God, his side hurt, but it was nowhere near as bad as the ache in his heart. "And deviant sexual acts—let's not forget about that."

"Dave—" she started, lifting her head to look at him, but he cut her off.

"I also failed to mention to you that Turiano's killers were never caught. Or that I purposely let a former KGB operative believe I'd slit her throat because I naively thought that that would look good on my international 'résumé.'" He shook his head as he looked at the cracked tile on the floor—anywhere but into her eyes. "It's possible whoever hired Smith is a former colleague of Turiano's. Or even, I don't know, a family member. Looking for payback."

*What do they want?* Sophia had asked him.

It was possible that whoever was behind all of this wanted money. Or maybe they wanted nothing more than to put Dave through hell before they killed him.

"You really think, that after *all* this time . . . ?" Sophia asked now. "Just out of nowhere? Without instigation or provocation?"

He made himself meet her gaze. "That man you said set you up in Kazabek—the Frenchman, Michel Lartet. You once said you blamed him for Dimitri's death. Do you blame him still?"

His seeming change of subject had caught her off-guard. But then something shifted in her eyes, and it was clear she understood.

Dave knew that Lartet, a former friend of hers, had helped set up the meeting at which a Kazbekistani warlord named Padsha Bashir had killed Sophia's husband and, with Dimitri's blood still spattered on her clothes, had married her—to gain possession of her property and finances.

And her. In a society where women had no rights, Bashir had gained possession of Sophia, too.

After months of abuse and fear, she'd escaped from his palace during a devastating earthquake. That is, after running Bashir through with his own sword.

She hadn't killed him—although Dave suspected she'd wept at the news that he'd survived her attack. It hadn't been until some days later that she had, with the help of the Troubleshooters team, fired one of the guns that riddled him with bullets and ended his miserable life.

He knew that, at that time, she'd no doubt longed with all of her damaged heart to do the same to Michel Lartet.

Sophia answered Dave's question now with a nod. Yes, she still blamed him. "I'd cheer at the news of his death. But I wouldn't go after him. No. Even if I met him in a dark alley with a gun? I'd hold him there until the police came, and I would testify against him in court and Lord willing, help to lock him up forever. But I wouldn't . . ."

Kill him. She didn't say the words, but she didn't have to as Dave nodded his own understanding. He knew—because she'd told him, and also because he'd witnessed it—just how hard she'd worked, in the years since Dimitri's death, to put the past behind her. To move on. Time and distance had softened her need for violent revenge.

"But what if that earthquake had never happened?" Dave asked her.

"What if you'd spent all these years not in California, but locked in Bashir's palace?"

Had that happened, Sophia would, absolutely, *not* be the woman she was today. They both knew that.

"So you think that someone who'd been close to Turiano," Sophia asked, "was . . . in *prison* for all these years, and recently released?"

"That's one possibility," Dave admitted. "Or maybe they just found out that I was tied to her death. Hardly anyone is like you, Soph. Most people don't try to heal after trauma and loss. They don't seek help. They just live with it, and let it, I don't know, *fester*."

"Did you?" she asked.

He blinked at her.

"Did you let it fester?" she asked, even though he knew exactly what she'd meant.

Dave shook his head. "No."

"I say her name," Sophia said, "and you get . . . so tense."

"She broke my heart."

She was silent then, eyes down, her hands in her lap, fingers working nervously against what must've been a rough place on her fingernail. He wanted to still her fingers, to cover her hands with his own, but he didn't dare touch her—afraid he wouldn't be able to do what he had to do if this woman whom he loved so desperately was warm and soft in his arms.

"When I came back from Denver," she finally broke the silence to say. "Last week. You were away, on a trip."

Oh, shit. Dave understood what she was asking. "That had nothing to do with any of this," he told her.

"Are you sure—"

"Yes," he said. "Absolutely." She opened her mouth to speak again, and he stopped her. "Soph. Trust me. Please. My trip is not something we want to be talking about right now. We've got enough on our plate. Besides, it's completely irrelevant."

She was ready to argue—Dave saw it in her eyes—and he braced himself because, face it, saying *no* to her, for anything at all, wasn't among his strengths.

But he *was not* going to tell her anything about going back into Kazbekistan, and what he'd found out while there. Certainly not right now—although, now, it was quite possible that that was a conversation they would never have.

His intel, however, would not go to waste—he could share it with Decker.

"You said, back in the hospital," Sophia pointed out, "that if there was anything I wanted to know—"

"Anything about Anise Turiano. And I'm telling you that the trip I took has nothing to do with—"

"You said I could ask you about *anything*."

Dave grabbed his head, to try to stop the pounding in his temples. Because she was right—he had said that. She was right—but it didn't matter, because he wasn't going to talk about this. Not at a time when he needed to push her away. And yeah, the fact that he wasn't going to answer her questions was going to help to do just that, so . . .

"You said *just ask*," she reminded him, her heart in her eyes, "so I'm asking. If it's really irrelevant, why not just tell me and then I'll say, *Okay, yes, that is irrelevant—*"

Yashi saved him from her reasonable logic, knocking on that closed door.

"Come in," Dave called.

He felt Sophia's gaze on him as he turned to see the FBI agent push open the door and peek in. Yashi was clearly afraid of the conversation he was interrupting—his dark brown eyes were apologetic. No doubt their raised voices had been heard from the hallway.

"There were two seats on a nonstop to LAX out of Logan," he reported as he glanced from Dave to Sophia and back. "But we've got to leave for the airport, like, now. I'm going to drive you, 'cause we're keeping your rental, to go over it for prints."

Dave pushed himself to his feet. God, he ached all over. Except for his stitches, which stung. "You're not going to find anything."

"I know," Yashi agreed with a shrug as Sophia stood, too. "But it's procedure."

She seemed a little shaky, so Dave moved closer, watching her, ready to help her if she needed his support.

His physical support. He knew, because he knew her so well, that she wasn't just angry. She was hugely disappointed in him—which hurt.

But hey. The next few days were going to include pain the likes of which he'd never felt before. This was nothing compared to the shitstorm into which he knew he was heading.

Yashi nodded with his head toward the photos. "We'll want to hold on to those, too."

"Is there a ladies' room . . . ?" Sophia asked.

"Of course," Yashi said. "Down the hall. First door on the right."

He held the door open for her, but she didn't move. Instead she said, "Will you give us just one more minute, please?"

Dave looked to Yashi for help. "We really should—"

"A figurative minute, Dave," she said tightly. "Thirty seconds'll do it." She turned to Yashi. "Please."

And Yashi again closed the door tightly behind him.

Sophia looked at Dave. "I've said this before, and I'm going to say it again: I don't care what you did or didn't do to some . . . she-bitch who would've killed you if she'd had the chance. I don't care *why* you did *whatever* you did—and I don't care that you didn't tell me the details before now. We all have secrets. Believe me, I understand. But even if *you* don't think whatever it was you were doing last week somehow stirred this up or just, I don't know, made whatever is happening worse? You could be wrong."

"I'm not."

"You *could* be. Even you, David, *have* been wrong in the past. You're not perfect—"

"I'm well aware of that!"

"Someone tried to kill you, and now seems to be threatening me—"

"*There's* an understatement!"

"Is it?" she asked. "I don't know. All I know for certain is that right now, when you need to be forthcoming about *everything,* you suddenly won't talk to me!"

"What happened to *We all have secrets*?" It was a snarky thing to say, Dave knew it.

Sophia got in his face. "My secrets aren't going to get me killed. And you better believe if I thought, for one second, that my secrets put either one of us into danger? I'd be talking. And talking. And *talking.*"

She didn't let him respond, she didn't wait for him to rebut or even retort. She just marched out the door, slamming it shut behind her.

# CHAPTER
# SEVEN

Tracy was sitting much too close.

Especially considering the fact that just a few scant moments ago she'd told Decker she wanted to do him.

And yeah, okay, she was allegedly being sarcastic.

But she'd said the words, using the grittiest verb available, and Deck had felt his head snap back. And sure, she could pretend that she hadn't meant it, but there had been quite a moment there when their gazes had caught and held. It was obvious they both knew damn well, should they let it go that far, that there would be some serious heat between them.

Not that he would ever let it happen. He had better control than that.

Except now Tracy was sitting too damn close, the warmth of her thigh against his leg. She'd looped her arm around the back of the truck's bench seat, and rested her hand tentatively on his shoulder, which meant that his right arm brushed the softness of her left breast every time he took a left turn. Or a right. And okay, yeah—it happened every time he moved the steering wheel, and he was about to lose his goddamned mind.

It was just a charade meant to fool anyone who might be watching into thinking that Jo Heissman wasn't crouched and hiding on the cab floor at Tracy's feet. Although if someone from the Agency had followed the doctor to her office and seen her approach Decker's truck, then watched as the truck pulled out of the lot, they pretty much knew she was in here.

But Decker wanted her on the floor for a variety of reasons, most of them right out of the *Spy v. Spy* playbook. But some of his reasons weren't even *that* lofty—one being that he wanted Jo Heissman to be uncomfortable, and the other being that he wanted Tracy to have to sit that close.

Decker could feel her fingers, near the collar of his shirt, near the back of his neck. And Jesus, he was in a weird, *weird* place if he was sitting here, like some sixteen-year-old hard-on, thinking about the fact that if he braked a little too hard at the next red light, Tracy's hand might move and she might actually touch him, skin against skin.

He wanted to be touched like that so badly, it was embarrassing.

It was triple weird since all that petty, juvenile trash was running rampant through his brain, even as he listened to Jo Heissman tell her story.

"I was paid a visit," she was saying, "at four o'clock this morning, by a man who put a bag over my head—both to intimidate me and to conceal his identity. It was not a pleasant way to wake up."

"You must have been terrified." Tracy, again, was handling the conversational niceties—expressing sympathy, making the proper noises of support. Which was good, because if Decker had spoken he'd've given away the fact that he was skeptical—of the existence of both man and bag. "Are you all right?"

"I'm fine," Dr. Heissman said. "He didn't do more than threaten me."

"Thank goodness for that," Tracy said, which made him glance at her in the mirror. Who the hell said *Thank goodness* instead of *Thank God*?

Tracy did, apparently, because her response wasn't an act. Or was it? She seemed sincerely relieved, her full focus on the doctor, whom she appeared to believe with a naiveté that was sweetly charming. Which reminded Decker of the insult he'd hurled just before Dr. Heissman had made the scene. *You're a little girl.*

But there was no doubt about it. This was a full-grown woman sitting next to him.

"What did he want?" Tracy asked.

It was then that Jo Heissman hesitated, looking from Tracy to Deck. She wore expensive, rectangular-shaped glasses that added an additional level of elegant bookishness to her already intelligent eyes. She was closer to his own age than Tracy was, yet she was still a very good-looking woman. Her blue eyes and pale skin were a sharp contrast to her long, dark, yet-streaked-with-natural-gray hair. And her warrior-goddess attitude was not at all altered by the fact that he was making her sit, her knees up near her ears, on the grungy floor mat of his truck.

No doubt about it, he was a bastard for making her sit there, and he was a little surprised that she hadn't asked if she could join them on the bench seat, like a real person, now that they'd traveled several winding miles. But she didn't, so he let her stay where she was.

No one was following them—Deck was being careful—but that didn't mean a thing. The doctor could well be carrying—either intentionally or not—a GPS beacon which would reveal their location. In his current dour mood, he would bet she was carrying it intentionally.

"He said he was from the Agency's black ops division. And that he wanted information." Dr. Heissman spoke directly to Decker now. "About you."

This time when Decker glanced into the rearview, both to check the traffic pattern behind them—nope, they still weren't being followed—and to gauge Tracy's reaction, the receptionist was looking back at him.

Her eyes were blue, too, and just as sharply intelligent as the doctor's. The silent message she was sending him was clear—she was now leaving all responses and follow-up questions completely to him.

Yeah, he'd see how long that would last.

But for now, Deck cleared his throat. "What did he want to know?" he asked.

"Information concerning the last time I'd been in contact with you," Dr. Heissman answered. "He wanted dates, times . . . Methods—phone calls, e-mails, in-person meetings . . ."

Of which there had been exactly none.

"He was interested in the nature of our relationship," she continued. "Did I know you well?" She paused. "He asked where you were and what you did—on the night that Jim Nash died. We went over it in quite some detail. He was interested in minutiae."

Tracy chose that very moment to move her hand. Just slightly. But enough to touch Decker with her thumb, just on the bare skin side of his shirt collar.

It was not by accident. And it took everything in him not to react. But almost instantly he realized he should react—in some way—to the startling nature of Jo Heissman's news, so he said, "What the hell . . . ?" which also gave him a few extra seconds to push away the sudden images of sex that had jammed his brain waves: graphic and extremely visceral thoughts of slipping into welcoming arms and sliding into the slick, tight heat of any willing woman, not necessarily Tracy, although Tracy would certainly do.

And, Jesus, this was not what he should be thinking about when he'd just found out that the Agency—or someone saying they were with the Agency, which was not the same thing—was digging around, looking for more information, no doubt to verify that Nash was, indeed, dead.

Or still alive—in which case they would try to find him to reverse that condition. This was, Deck believed, absolutely in response to that DNA test on that bloody shirt of Nash's.

No, now was *not* the time for his body to decide it needed to challenge the long-held rules of his self-imposed celibacy. It happened from time to time—a petulant challenge—and usually at the most inopportune moments. Which this absolutely was. So, in truth, this latest uprising, so to speak, fit his ongoing pattern.

Apparently scones weren't the only thing on his predictable-behavior list.

"I don't know what's going on," Jo said, as he stared at the road, at the taillights of the car in front of him, and reminded himself of the disasters that always awaited him when he surrendered to his body's demands. Sophia was, as always, Exhibit A.

"But I tend to get uncooperative and downright cranky when people put bags over my head," she continued. "So I told him you were with me at the FBI headquarters in Sacramento for most of the evening that Jim Nash died. And that, since at that time I *was* your therapist, I told him I'd counseled you, extensively, when the news came down about Nash's death."

What the fuck?

Decker forced himself to focus on what the shrink had just said, which was that she'd lied to the alleged Agency operative who'd broken into her home. Decker *hadn't* been with Dr. Heissman for most of that evening— he'd been helping Jules Cassidy make arrangements for Nash's postoperative hospital care. Among other things. He'd purposely been far away from her when she'd received the news that Nash had died, because yes, she *had* briefly been his therapist.

He hadn't thought he'd be able to fool her, to feign real grief when he knew that Nash was still alive. But now she'd told the man—if there was a man—who'd bagged her—if there was a bag—that she'd been with Decker when he'd heard the tragic news.

"I admitted, when pressed," she added, "that you cried."

Decker *had* cried while in a session with her—the night before. But only to try to get the good doctor to reveal her connections to the Agency.

And yeah, Dr. Heissman wasn't the only liar sitting in his truck.

"Why would the Agency care where Deck was on the night that Jimmy Nash died?" Tracy asked, apparently unable to keep silent another moment, which was not unexpected. She put the exact right amount of confusion into the question, though, which was nice.

"I tried asking that very same thing," Heissman reported, "but my visitor was far more interested in being the interrogator."

"I'm supposed to believe, that with a bag over your head," Decker said, letting his disbelief ring in his voice, "you risked your life to provide the Agency with disinformation . . . ?"

"Believe it or not," she answered quietly, "that's exactly what I did."

Tracy moved her thumb against his neck—Jesus—even as he said, "I'm going to have to go with *not*. Because to believe that you lied to an operative from the very organization that you probably still work for—"

"What a surprise," the doctor said tartly. "You're still singing the same song you were the last time I saw you."

Which was early in the morning, on the day after Nash had, allegedly, died.

At that time, Decker had told her that he blamed the Agency in part for Nash's death, and he'd made it very clear to her that if he discovered she *was* still working for the Agency, if he found out she'd lied to him from the start?

He'd hunt her down and kill her.

He knew she was thinking of his threat as he glanced down past Tracy's perfect legs to where Jo was huddled. She met his gaze and held it, almost defiantly.

And because, apparently, his dick was in charge today, he found himself remembering kissing her—not because he'd particularly wanted to kiss her, but rather because she was there at a time when he'd needed someone to grab on to. And the grabbing had turned into a kiss. Which again fit his pattern. He'd kissed her on the same night that—Jesus—he'd broken down and cried. In looking back and analyzing, it was clear he'd reached some kind of emotional cliff that he'd launched himself off of.

Jo had said, at the time, that men in his profession often used sex as a substitute for emotional release, and that she didn't take that kiss person-ally—but that it wouldn't happen again.

So it hadn't. And in a matter of hours, they'd parted ways.

But it was entirely possible that the entire incident had freaked him out significantly more than it had her.

Because as he'd kissed her, the warrior goddess had given way to woman. Her body had been soft against his, clad only in a no-nonsense bathrobe over a silky pink nightgown. Which was completely out of char-acter. She was the sleep-in-flannel-pajamas type.

Or so he'd thought.

"I wasn't working for the Agency when I was at Troubleshooters," Jo told him now, her chin held high. "But as of four o'clock this morning, I'm apparently back on the payroll—and I don't want to be. I refuse to be. Which is why I came to find you. I thought, if anyone could help—if any-one would sympathize, after what Nash went through . . ."

Before he could ask exactly what she meant by that—*after what Nash went through*—Tracy spoke up again.

"We're going to help you," she told the doctor. "But it's going to be a difficult couple of days. Tess is coming to San Diego this evening . . ."

Decker looked at her sharply in the rearview, fearing that her naiveté had won and she not only believed Jo, but assumed they were all working toward the same goal, but he couldn't catch her gaze as she blithely continued.

" . . . and she and Deck are going to rent a boat and scatter Jimmy's ashes, at sunset. I'm afraid no one's at the top of their game right now."

And okay, maybe the naive-sounding concern hadn't been so naive but rather part of Tracy's amazing act, because she really did make effort-less lying seem like an art form. He almost believed her himself—even knowing that there were no real ashes to scatter.

Still, he wasn't happy because he very much didn't want Jo Heissman knowing that Tess was going to be in town.

Tracy glanced up, caught his look, managed to read his mind, and swore. Sort of. Along with *thank God*, apparently *shit* wasn't in her vocab-ulary either.

"*Shoot*. I shouldn't have told you that. Sorry," she said to Deck, even as she added to the doctor, "He's very protective of Tess."

It was beautiful—and almost made the fact that she'd revealed Tess's arrival worthwhile.

*Tracy* was beautiful—she was sexy, she was quick-witted, and he wanted to screw her. But that didn't mean shit, because he wanted to screw Jo Heissman, too. When he got like this, he'd unzip his pants for anybody. Again, Sophia was Exhibit A, and Jesus, he hated himself even more than usual today.

"What do you know about what Nash went through before he died?" Decker asked, referring back to what Dr. Heissman had just said. The words came out far more harshly than they should have, considering *he* was the person in this truck that he was most disgusted with.

She sighed wearily. "Nothing new. Only what I already told you." She looked up at Tracy, to tell her a story that Decker already knew. "I saw Nash once, at Agency headquarters. He was alone and he was going through a locked door that led to the black ops division."

"It had a keypad lock. He wouldn't have gotten through without the code, which he wouldn't have known if he wasn't a member of the black ops team," Deck explained, although she'd probably figured that out.

"Ghosts, we called them," Jo chimed in. "The operatives who worked for that division. There were rumors—never substantiated—that ghost operatives had a difficult time breaking ties with the Agency. They were always pressured to take one more mission, do one more job. And there were whispers, too, of methods of applying pressure that had overtones of blackmail. I have no proof, but I feel certain that Nash was subjected to this in the years following his severance from the Agency."

"So naturally, while it was going on, you looked the other way." Decker's words were rude, his voice sounded overly rough and a little too loud, even to his own ears, and he could feel Tracy's curiosity and concern as if it were radiating from her. She moved her hand again, this time to touch him more completely on his neck. Her fingers felt cool against the heat of his skin as she caressed him just a little—a minuscule version of a soothing embrace of support.

And, yeah, honey, thanks so much—that absolutely helped. Now, instead of thinking about how pissed he was about all of this—including the fact that Jo was completely messing up his plans: to drive Tracy to the safe house and, once there, to make sure they were never alone again—he was instead focusing on how badly he wanted those cool fingers touching a totally different part of his anatomy.

And now he was getting pissed at Tracy, too, because along with her concern, he was also picking up some curiosity and skepticism. Because despite what he'd told her earlier, it had to be beyond obvious that the animosity he felt toward Jo Heissman was personal. And knowing Tracy, she was no doubt thinking that he'd lied when he said he'd never slept with Jo, because in her world, sex was both the beginning and the end, and yet it also, paradoxically, just wasn't that big of a deal. If you were hungry, you ate. If you were horny, you screwed. And if the attraction was there, like a well-lit Burger King off a desolated stretch of highway at a time when everything else was closed, why the hell not get your rocks off, even though you knew that, like eating fast food, doing so was neither healthy nor smart?

So, if attraction existed between two people in Tracy's world, and they'd spent any time at all alone together, chances were strong that they'd gotten it on.

And since Decker was displaying bits of his deeply burning anger at Dr. Heissman, whom yes, he'd admit to finding attractive—even now, sitting near Tracy, who was desire personified—then according to the rules of Tracy's world, that anger surely had *some*thing to do with sex.

It wouldn't occur to Tracy that he was angry for other reasons, including the fact that during every single one of Decker's therapy sessions, Dr. Heissman had somehow managed to penetrate his expert defenses. She'd crawled around—unwelcome—in the densely murky shit that clogged up the inside of his head.

In those sessions, Deck had told the doctor things that he'd never told anyone. And, every now and then, when he was man enough to face the truth, he had to admit that the therapy—the talking—had actually helped him.

These days, he actually felt better about a lot of things that had haunted him for years. He'd finally started to recognize that even though he'd made mistakes in the past, his intentions had always been good and true.

He'd done the best he could, given the circumstances. His relatively new acceptance of that had brought him peace. Of sorts.

A fact which, ironically, pissed him off.

It pissed him off because he didn't trust Jo Heissman then, and he sure as double-fuck didn't trust her now, with her ridiculous bag-over-the-head story. *Help me*, his ass.

His bullshit meter was highly tuned and it was screaming. He trusted his instincts completely, and his gut told him that she'd been hiding something from him right from the start. He'd been aware of it during their so-called sessions, and he was aware of it now.

He didn't trust her, he didn't like her, but throw her a bang? Apparently today, his answer to that question was a hearty *hell, yeah.*

"I didn't look the other way." Dr. Heissman let some of her own anger show in her clipped words and in the flush that darkened her patrician cheekbones. "Not with Nash and not with any of the other operatives who were being—in my opinion—unfairly pressured to take on additional assignments. I filed reports and became very unpopular. When it became clear that my suspicions were being ignored, I resigned. Needless to say, no one pressured me to stay." She laughed her disgust. "Until now. In addition to last night's interrogation, I was given an assignment."

"Let me guess," Decker said. "You were told to contact me."

She nodded. "That's right."

"Which you're doing right now."

"I *wasn't* told to contact you and tell you everything that I've just told you," she pointed out, and it was clear he was pissing her off.

Tough shit.

"Which, incidentally, would've been the way I'd've done it, if I were you. Play both sides," Decker told her. "But go on. What else, pray tell, were you told to do?"

"To find out where you are, what you've been doing, where you go when you disappear. Apparently, you disappear quite often these days. He told me to persuade you to go back into therapy—"

"That's never going to happen."

"Obviously," Dr. Heissman said, with quite an edge to her normal dulcet voice. "I'm just letting you know what this man said. If you'd rather not know, then—"

"What did he threaten you with?" Decker asked.

"I had a bag over my head," she reminded him. "He said he had a gun, but—"

"No," he cut her off again. "I'm talking blackmail threat. He said *go gather this info,* you said *sorry, I no longer work for the Agency,* he said *oh yes you do* and *where shall I tell them to send your paycheck,* you said *no thank you,* and he said *you'll do this, or . . .* What? What was his threat?"

The flush was back on her cheeks. "I'd . . . rather not say."

Sex. It had to be sex. Cheating on taxes or some other kind of financial fraud generally didn't warrant that kind of a blush.

"Is it pictures they have, or a video?" Decker asked her.

She shook her head, as Tracy—eyes wide—wisely stay silent. "I refuse to be blackmailed," Jo decreed. "Which is why I came to you."

Maybe. It was also possible that everything she'd said was a scam to win his trust.

"I know how these things work," Deck said. "They don't just say *we have a video,* they give it to you. A copy, of course. I'm going to have to see it, first to verify that it exists, and second to weigh the blackmail material." He could see that neither Jo nor Tracy understood, so he explained. "If the video is of your son committing murder, there's a strong chance that you're going to do whatever your Agency master tells you to do, to keep it from going public. If it's you getting inside the head of one of your clients while he gets inside of—"

"It's neither of those things," she cut him off, rather sharply. Clearly it was a touchy subject. "And yes, it's photos. But it's really only a minor embarrassment—I've never done anything of which I'm ashamed."

"And yet you'd really rather not say," he reminded her.

"Because I value my privacy," she retorted. "I'm well aware that the choices I've made today—by coming to you—are going to result in the publication of those photos. I see no reason to endure the violation of my privacy before I absolutely have to."

"Honey, I just gave you a reason," Decker said. "Take it or leave it."

She made a sound that was part laughter, part disgusted exhale, part sigh of resignation, and said, "He was significantly younger and . . . He was my daughter's ex-boyfriend, okay?"

Well, here's to you, Dr. Heissman.

"It was an exclusive relationship," she said sharply, "that lasted several months, and didn't begin, might I add, until well after he and Ivy split up and she'd already moved in with her current partner. And the way you're looking at me right now? Coo-coo-ca-choo, right? *That's* why I didn't want to tell you. But it's a fact that having those pictures go public is only going to result in hurt feelings. It'll compound my already strained relationship with my daughter, which is unfortunate. But there'll be no damage to my career or my reputation. He wasn't a patient. He wasn't a student. He was a very attractive younger man with whom I spent a pleasant few months."

"Coo-coo-ca-choo?" Tracy asked.

"Mrs. Robinson. Simon and Garfunkel," Decker told her. "Theme song from *The Graduate*?"

"Got it," Tracy said. "These days us hep young'uns call it a cougar attack."

Jo actually winced at that. "His name was Peter. I'm planning to get back in touch with him, to warn him that these pictures have surfaced," she said.

Decker shook his head. "Don't."

"Well, I'm certainly not going to let him stumble over them on the Internet."

"When did the affair take place?" he asked her.

"It wasn't an *affair*. It was—"

"Before, during, or after your years at the Agency?"

She shut her mouth. Blinked. "During," she said. "It was close to the end."

"Huh," Decker said. Coincidental? He would bet that it wasn't. "Where were you when the photos were taken? Was it at your place or his?"

"A hotel," she answered. "We took a weekend and went to New York City. Do you honestly think that Peter had something to do with . . ." She shook her head in disbelief. Her obvious disappointment and hurt almost made him feel sorry for her.

Almost. Because he still wasn't convinced this wasn't part of an act. "I think you had a relationship with an attractive man at the end of your tenure with the Agency, and now these photos have turned up. It wouldn't surprise me a bit if the next thing they hit you with is 'proof' that this Peter *was* one of your patients."

"But he wasn't," she said.

"They're the Agency," he countered. "Whatever documents they provide will at the very least be realistic enough to create a controversy. Count on it."

Jo looked from Decker to Tracy and back.

"So what are you doing?" she asked. "Are you actually trying to frighten me into . . . What? Being their bitch?"

She'd surprised him with her slang, but his laughter didn't last longer than a short bark. "I'm suggesting," he told her, "that it's possible you're not being honest with us about the nature of the material they're holding over you."

She nodded, clearly upset. "I should have gone to the Troubleshooters office, to Tom Paoletti."

"Why didn't you?" Decker asked.

She met his eyes, and there it was again—that kiss. But she just shook her head. "Because I'm a fool." She laughed her disgust at herself. "And because, yes, they told me to contact *you.*"

"I believe her," Tracy said, but her words were punctuated by the poke of a fingernail into his shoulder. His ex-fiancée, Emily, had well-cared-for nails, too, and Jesus, he'd loved it when she'd dug in as he'd rode her, hard, as he'd sent her spinning into a freefall so intense that she often left scratches down his back and across his ass. She'd always been embarrassed and aghast in the aftermath, but he'd gotten off on it.

"Why are they so interested in you?" the doctor asked him. "What are they after?"

Decker just looked at her.

"Okay," she said. "You're right. It would be foolish to tell me anything. You've never trusted me. I know that. But I'm going to be contacted again. If I were you, I'd like to know what these people want and who they are." She paused. "Unless you already know."

"Why don't we just go to the Agency," Tracy chimed in. "Why don't we just show up and walk in the door and—"

"We need to be certain before we do that," Decker said, cutting her off. "Whether or not they're actually from the Agency, they've got access to Agency information. We go there, they'll know we've been there and . . ." He shook his head. "I'm not ready for that."

"Then, why don't we put Dr. Heissman somewhere safe," Tracy suggested. "Then *we* can go to her house, and wait for this man to come back, only, surprise, it's not her, it's me—and you, ready to kick his butt. We tie him up and fingerprint him, and presto, we have his identity."

We? "I'm sorry," Decker said, "but aren't you a *receptionist?*"

She actually rolled her eyes as she otherwise ignored him. "When is he contacting you again?" she asked Jo.

"He wasn't specific," she answered.

"No." Decker looked emphatically into the rearview mirror—which was the easiest way to meet Tracy's eyes. "You're not qualified, so no."

"You'd be there." She was actually arguing with him.

"But you won't be," he told her. "You're going to your friend's place, remember?"

"I can change my plans."

"No. And stop. You said you wanted to help? Start now."

Tracy closed her mouth at that, but he could see her protest in her eyes. It was killing her not to continue to argue.

Deck looked at Dr. Heissman. "I have several things to do tonight that take priority. If you're concerned for your safety, I'll help you access a secure location and—"

She was already shaking her head. "I'll be fine at home. Particularly if you give me something to tell him if—when—he comes back. It doesn't even have to be true. In fact, I'm happy to pass along disinformation if it'll get you to trust me."

Never gonna happen, hon. Aloud, he said, "Maybe we can get *them* to trust you—if you give them information that they probably already know, but that you couldn't have known without talking to me. Like, the fact that Tess and I are both currently under investigation by the FBI."

"What?" The doctor was genuinely surprised. "Why?"

"A former colleague of Nash's"—Decker told her the story that Tess, Nash and Jules Cassidy had come up with—"had a key to a sealed safe-deposit box, with instructions to open it only in the event of Nash's death. After he died, the seal was cracked and . . . Apparently Nash broke the black ops division's number one rule: Leave behind no evidence. He left a paper trail and some other souvenirs that tie him to several 'incidents,' some of them on an international scale. An investigation's under way to determine how much—if anything—Tess and I knew about any of this."

She shook her head. "That's ridiculous. You don't expect anyone to believe—"

"Believe it or not," he threw her own challenge-filled words back at her, "it's true. Your bag man will already know about it. I guarantee it. It's possible the Agency is working with the Bureau, but it's also possible that your man is collecting as much information as possible in a CYA move—because someone inside knows that the Agency is going to get looked at by the FBI next. You can let him know that Nash kept both Tess and me in the dark about all of this. And that, as far as we're concerned, we'd just as soon bury the truth with him. So if there's anything they can do on their side to quash the investigation, tell them to have at it." He'd driven in a big circle, and now pulled into the lot of a pizzeria and put the truck into park. "We're a block and a half from your office building. It'd be best if you walked back."

She didn't move. "You honestly expect anyone to believe that you want to *bury* the *truth*? I'm sorry, didn't you once tell me that if you found out I was still working for the Agency, you would *kill* me?" She looked at Tracy. "*Hunt me down and kill me,* I believe were his exact words."

Tracy looked at Decker in the rearview mirror as he shook his head.

"It's time to move on," he replied. "Isn't that what you shrinks are always encouraging us mere mortals to do? Well, I'm doing it. I don't want to know what kind of ugliness Jimmy invited into his life. He's gone and I've got Tess to think about now. I'll do whatever it takes to keep her safe. Including S-squared."

"Sit the ef down and shut the ef up," Tracy helpfully translated, as if the doctor—who'd worked extensively with spec op warriors—was unfamiliar with the expression.

Jo didn't even bother to glance at the younger woman, she just sat there, gazing up at Decker, a small smile on her lips. "I honestly can't tell if you're lying. I thought I could, but I can't. I mean, I *know* you are . . ." She shook her head. "We're on the same side here, Lawrence."

"There are no sides," Decker lied. "Because I don't want to turn this into a fight. The investigation will turn up nothing—there's nothing for the FBI to find, nothing for Tess and me to say. Nothing for the Agency to worry about."

She finally nodded. "I'll pass that message along. But if they're going to believe that I have access to you . . ."

"You're going to need to have access to me," Deck finished for her, aware that beside him, Tracy shifted in her seat. "You'll get it." He met the younger woman's eyes in the rearview and knew that she was thinking of a different kind of access. Or maybe he was the one who was thinking about it. "I think your problem with the Agency is going to go away when my problem with the FBI ends. If not, we'll deal with it. If you need me, I'll be staying at Tracy's place for the next few days."

"Upstairs from Tess," Jo verified.

He nodded again. "We should touch base tomorrow," he told her. "I'll want to see those photos."

She nodded, too. "Is your cell number the same?"

"Yeah, but my phone's not working. If you need to reach me before to-morrow, call Tracy, but keep in mind her line's not secure." He rattled off Tracy's number as Jo plugged it into her phone. She then started to hand him another one of her cards, but he shook his head, adding, "I still have yours in my phonebook."

That got him another glance from Tracy, who in about five seconds was going to slide all of her warmth and softness away from him. She'd al-ready taken her hand from his neck, a fact that made him feel far too bereft, considering.

"Do me a favor," Decker found himself saying to Jo, "and tell Tracy here that we never slept together—that there was nothing between us."

"We never slept together," the doctor repeated obediently, as she opened the door and climbed out. "But I wouldn't say that there was noth-ing between us."

And wasn't that just perfect?

As he shook his head, she closed the door and Tracy slid away. And Decker did the only thing he could do.

He put the truck in gear and drove.


"We need to bring more people on board."

Tess glanced over at Jules, who was driving the van. They'd just dropped off Robin and were now heading toward the low-rent part of town, where there was an entire strip of cheap motels—one of which they were going to pick as the place they'd meet up with Decker.

And Tracy Shapiro.

That was going to be weird—seeing Tracy again after accepting her condolences at Jimmy's memorial service. And Tess didn't even want to think about how awkward it was going to be when she and Deck went to the airport to pick up Sophia and Dave, later tonight.

Sophia *and* Dave. It was humbling to think about all that Decker had sacrificed to protect Jimmy.

"Yes, no, maybe?" Jules prompted, and she realized she hadn't answered him. What had he said? Something about bringing more people aboard—as in telling them Jimmy was alive, and asking for their help.

"I agree." Tess had the utmost respect for both Sam and Alyssa, and yet she couldn't help but feel anxious about leaving Jimmy without a bigger army to defend him, if need be.

"Decker's resisting," Jules told her. "And I totally get why he doesn't want to ask Dave for help, but we're running out of personnel."

She nodded. "I'll talk to him."

"I could call in some favors with SEAL Team Sixteen," Jules said. "But I'll run the names past you guys first."

"It's okay if we don't talk about this right now," Tess said. "I know you're freaking out about Robin. Unless it helps to talk . . ."

Troubleshooter Ric Alvarado had flown in from the Florida office, along with his extremely capable wife, Annie, to take over as head of Robin's security team, on and off the movie set. Ric's forte was in personal protection, but regardless of that, it hadn't been easy for Jules when Robin had gotten out of the van and into Ric's truck.

Tess knew that it hadn't helped that Robin hadn't kissed Jules goodbye. But he couldn't, because Jules was in disguise. The FBI agent had colored his hair—not drastically, but enough to make it look a naturally lighter shade of brown. He'd messed it up into a less conservative style, and with the goatee and mustache he'd grown over the past few weeks, Hawaiian shirt over a plain white beater, and drab green cargo shorts, he looked like a college student working a summer job driving a van.

The Hawaiian shirt hid his shoulder holster and sidearm as neatly as blue contact lenses and sunglasses hid the warmth of his soulful brown eyes.

He laughed now—a rueful chuckle. "I know Robin's safe with Ric and Annie," he said.

"But it's hard when you're not right there, with him," Tess countered. "Believe me, I'm dealing with that, too."

"We'll be back at the house before you know it," he reassured her.

Tess nodded. They would be—provided everything went as planned.

Except there already was a glitch. Deck's sat phone was having some kind of hardware failure and he'd yet to get his hands on a replacement. So they'd set up a plan for Jules and Tess to e-mail one of Deck's anonymous free-mail accounts with their location, upon their arrival.

They were going to a motel instead of meeting at the Troubleshooters office because Jimmy had requested they take extreme precautions. Keeping Tess's location secret was paramount. And the fact was, a hotel or motel room, with its single entrance, was always easier to guard and defend. True, there was no escape route, but if they found themselves under attack, they were the good guys. They could easily call 9-1-1 for backup from the local police.

After they connected, Tess was going to try to fix Deck's phone, but there were no guarantees she could get the job done before they left for the airport to pick up Sophia and Dave.

That was a meeting that, no doubt, wouldn't be fun for any of them. Tess would have to pretend that Jimmy was dead—something she hated doing—and that she and Decker were in a relationship. Decker would get an up close and personal look at Sophia and Dave—both of whom would have to deal with seeing Decker again.

Yes, it was going to be awkward all around, but there were a wide variety of reasons—both personal and professional—for them to not tell Sophia and Dave the truth. Everyone was in agreement about that. Well, everyone except for Jimmy, who'd wanted to bring Dave in, right from the start.

But now it was in Dave's best interest, wounded as he was, to stay out of the fight. And Tess knew Decker would be better off, too, if he knew Sophia was safe.

So she and Deck were going to have to sit down with Sophia and Dave and convince them that Dave's assault was connected to an investigation they were conducting, but that the details were *need to know*. And not only did Sophia and Dave not need to know, but lives could well be in danger if they *did* know what was going on.

They would then have to convince Dave and Sophia to get into a car and drive. And drive. Decker would bankroll them with a bag of cash and a series of bogus IDs. Which they'd use to pay for food and lodging—in order to stay under the radar. About a week in, Dave would be instructed to use his credit card—as if by mistake—in some distant city. It would keep the Agency busy, and would tie up God knows how many operators who would be sent to investigate.

Not that Sophia nor Dave would have a clue that any of this had anything to do with Jimmy.

Dave's long-term instructions would be to stay on the move, as iso-
lated as possible, until Decker or Tess contacted them and told them it was
safe to return.

Of course, they expected protest from Dave and Sophia—both of
whom would be unhappy at the thought of deserting Decker and Tess in
what surely was an hour of need.

But the plan was to divide and conquer.

Their first stop would be a hotel—different from the motel at which
they were meeting Decker and Tracy—where they'd set up Dave and
Sophia in an equally secure room, where they'd be able to talk.

It was likely that Dave and Sophia were being tailed, and that they'd
be followed from the airport. That was okay. It was good, in fact.

They'd openly provision the room with food and water—as if Sophia
and Dave were preparing to hunker down there for the next several
weeks—and put the DO NOT DISTURB sign on the door.

At which point, Tess and Deck would help Dave and Sophia slip out
of the hotel, undetected, so they could make their escape while their
enemy continued to watch a now-empty room.

Tess and Decker would then return to the motel where Jules was
babysitting Tracy—at which point they'd all head back to the safe house.

At least that *had* been their plan—before Dr. Heissman appeared on
the scene, going to Decker with her conveniently timed plea for help,
which would delay their return. Because they were running late and
there'd be no time to do it this evening, in the morning Tess and Deck
were going to have to pretend to release Jimmy's ashes into the ocean. And
wasn't *that* going to be fun?

"Why don't we just grab Jo Heissman," Tess said now, "put a gun to
her head, and make her tell us who her contacts are at the Agency."

Jules glanced at her.

"Don't respond to that," she said before he could even open his
mouth. "I know why we don't." That kind of coercion rarely worked. And
the information that came as a result of intimidation or even torture—it
was highly suspect and exceedingly faulty. "I'm just pissed off."

"We'll get more information by working with her," Jules reassured her.
"You've got to be patient, Tess. Because what if she's telling the truth? Or

what if she doesn't have a side—if she's just trying to protect herself, to stay alive . . . ? If we scare her or threaten her? She may decide that ours is not the side she wants to be on."

"I know." Tess sighed. "I'm sorry. I just want this to be over."

"I'm with you on that," Jules said, pulling into the potholed driveway of a run-down motel called the Seaside Heights.

It was neither seaside nor at a particularly elevated height. But it did have hourly rates, plus wireless—though only in the lobby.

Tess took her laptop with her as she followed Jules inside, the door screeching as it shut behind her. He went to the front desk as she put her computer on a coffee table that had seen better days, planting herself on an equally faded sofa.

The instructions for accessing the wireless were right there, on a little laminated card. Since her computer was already up and running, she followed the instructions and. . .

Bingo.

"What'dya say we splurge, sugar-pie, and get ourselves an entire night?" Jules asked her loudly, in a pitch-perfect imitation of Sam Starrett's Texas twang.

Tess laughed her surprise even as she double-checked that her computer's firewalls were in place. Zapping a quick e-mail with the motel's address to Decker's current free-mail account, she called back to Jules, "Absolutely, Pookie. And they say romance is dead."

# CHAPTER
# EIGHT

"You up for a walk on the beach?" Decker asked.

Tracy looked at him as they headed west, crossing the causeway into Coronado. After Dr. Heissman had gotten out at the pizzeria, she'd reached to turn on the signal jammer, but Decker had shaken his head. Which was weird, but okay. She was, as he was fond of pointing out, "only the receptionist." Maybe he had some secret-spy reason for wanting them to be listened in on.

Except now he was heading for the beach.

The Strand, with its miles of shoreline, comfortably uncrowded during a workday mid-afternoon, would be the perfect place to check themselves for any unwanted listening and/or tracking devices that Jo Heissman might've planted. And the windswept beach itself would be a good place to talk privately if they did find such a bug.

"Sure," she answered.

They rode in silence down past the Del, and then past the part of the beach where the Navy SEALs trained—the famed obstacle course visible over the top of the privacy fence. Which prompted her to say, "It would be nice, though, if we didn't run into anyone from Team Sixteen."

Deck glanced at her. "Don't worry. I happen to know that Zanella's out of the country."

Tracy actually gasped aloud. She heard herself do it, which is stupid. Because it was absurd to think that the story hadn't spread. Everyone in the Troubleshooters office surely knew about her intimate encounter with Navy SEAL Petty Officer Izzy Zanella. Or at least they knew the cheap, sordid, gossipy part where she'd gotten drunk and slept with him.

"You told me once that you and he . . . *collided*, was the word you used," Decker said to her now.

And okay. She *had* told him exactly that. In a phone conversation some months ago—that a mere mortal wouldn't have remembered so accurately. "You have an impressive memory."

He shrugged. "It's actually pretty average."

Or so he wanted people to believe. Which brought her to what *she* wanted people to believe. This was, without a doubt, her chance to set her record straight. The fact that the Agency might be listening in was a bonus. Maybe someone would write up a report and spread it throughout the SpecWar community. The heading, in bold font, would read: Tracy Shapiro Not a Total Slut. "I had revenge sex with him. With Izzy," she clarified, when she got another of those sunglass-shaded glances.

Deck drove a little faster, as if he couldn't wait to reach their destination. "You don't need to expl—"

"My fiancé cheated on me," she told him and whoever else was listening in. "*Ex*-fiancé. Lyle. He always used to say *believe it or not* when he was making up some excuse for why he was late. *Believe it or not, we had to submit the expense reports for the Fleegerwald case.* It took me a few years longer than it should have, but I finally learned that that was code for *Sorry I'm late, baby, but I had to stay at the office and get a blow job from one of the interns.*"

Deck glanced at her again, and she knew he was well aware that Dr. Heissman had said those very words to him. *Believe it or not . . .*

Tracy, too, was automatically in the "or not" camp.

"So in order to get back at Lyle, I got loaded and had my first—and last—one-night stand," she admitted, as he pulled into one of the beach lots. There were too many cars, so he pulled right out again and back onto the road. "I'll freely admit that it was not my finest hour. I compounded it not just by falling in love with Izzy, who was just pretending to be nice—but by *telling* him that I'd fallen for him. He ran away screaming, and . . . It was messy, and . . . Humiliating. Especially when he got married, like, fifteen minutes later, to someone else."

"To one of his teammate's sisters." Decker knew that factoid, too. "Word is he got her pregnant. At least you were smart enough to use protection."

"Yay for me." Tracy applauded, but then stopped. "Nope, it was still excruciatingly mortifying. And a crushing blow to the ego. Have you seen this girl? And *she*? *Is* a girl. She was practically wearing braces and a training bra. Okay, maybe not the training bra, but . . ."

"I've met her, but it wasn't under the best of circumstances," he confessed. "And yes, she did seem young."

"The good news was that—in the entire Charlie-Foxtrot? I finally broke off my engagement with that total man-ho, Lyle." She sighed. "The bad news is that everybody knows about my . . . collision with Izzy. And now they think that's my totally slutty MO."

"No they don't," he said, pulling into another lot. This one had only a few cars in it, and he headed for a distant, solitary corner.

"Yes they do," she countered. "*You* do."

"I assure you, I don't."

"Lawrence," she said, imitating Dr. Heissman's evenly modulated voice, "unlike some people, I *can* tell when you're lying."

He laughed as he put the truck into park and killed the engine. "Nice. You're wrong, I'm not lying, but that *was* very nice."

Tracy got out of the truck and stood, waiting, as he used the sweeper to check the vehicle, inside and out. And then he came toward her, his apology darn near dripping from him.

She held out her arms and spread her legs—in the classic Leonardo da Vinci pose that every air traveler had assumed at one time or another. He waved the wand slowly over her, being thorough as always.

And she felt herself start to sweat.

The sun was out, sure. And the day was fairly warm, despite the breeze off the ocean. But it was the fact that Decker was tracing the contours of her body with that device, careful not to touch her, that was really heating her up.

She knew, without a doubt, that he would not slip and touch her—and somehow that made it even worse.

"Can I just state for the record—" she started.

"No." He cut her off.

She turned to look at him in exasperation. "You have no idea what I was going to say."

"Yeah," he said, hunkering down to carefully run the wand over and around her sandals and feet. "I do. But let's not go there, okay? I'm having a tough enough day as it is."

"Go where?" she said, and then gasped as he stood up and, in one fluid motion, stepped—hard—into her personal space. So hard that she was pressed completely against him—stomach, hips, thighs—held in place by his hand at the curve of her waist, arm wrapped around her.

He was solid and warm and—holy Christmas—aroused enough for her to know it. There was no missing that fact—not a chance in heaven. He was sweating excessively, too. A trickle traveled down past his left ear and dripped with a plop onto her arm. His mouth was mere inches from hers, but she still couldn't see his eyes through his sunglasses. "Here," he said, his voice raspy. "Let's not go *here.*"

He released her as abruptly as he'd grabbed her, and she almost lost her balance. He immediately turned the device back on, rechecking where he'd held himself against her.

"Why not?" The words spilled out of Tracy before she could stop them. And then, since she'd already jumped into the deep end, she added, "If that was supposed to scare me off, well, sorry, but it pretty much did the opposite. I mean, *hello* . . ."

He laughed, but it wasn't a pleasant sound as he thrust the sweeper into her hands and assumed the stance, turning his back to her. "Didn't you just get through telling me that Zanella was allegedly your first *and last* one-night stand? Let's keep it that way."

"Allegedly?" She whacked him between the shoulder blades with the wand.

"Ow! What the hell?!"

"That's an insulting thing to say to someone who's just shared something painful with you. *Allegedly.* God." She was affronted. "There was nothing alleged about it. Of course, you only said that so I'd get mad at you and back off, because you, *Lawrence,* are a coward."

"Honey, trust me, I'm no coward. I'm just sane." He laughed, muttering as if to himself, "Most of the fucking time, anyway."

She moved around to skim the wand down his front, but he caught her wrist, and took it from her. "I got it from here, thanks."

She glared at him as she pointedly rubbed her wrist.

"I didn't hurt you," he told her. "So stop with the drama."

"*I'm* the drama queen?" she said, lacing her voice with heavy disbelief. "I'm not the one who just rubbed myself against you, and then acted as if it was . . . awful."

He laughed. "Awful. Yeah. If you don't like me calling you a little girl, then you really need to stop pretending to be one."

"Okay," she said. "Non *sequitur.*"

He shut off the sweeper and shoved it rather violently back behind the seat of the truck. "You know goddamn well that *awful* wasn't even close to what I was thinking and to pretend otherwise is beneath you. So knock it the hell off."

Tracy had to argue. "I didn't say I thought that *you thought* it was awful. I said you were *acting* as if—"

"Enough," he said. "Jesus Christ, no wonder Zanella ran screaming!"

Even as the words left Decker's lips, he regretted saying them. Even before he'd finished his sentence, he wished he could hit pause and rewind, and take it back.

It was as if he'd reached out and snuffed the fire that lit Tracy from within as she argued with him.

Jesus, who the hell ever argued with him? No one did—not besides Nash. Which was the reason that, despite their differences in personality and background, the two men were friends. Every-fucking-one else treated Deck as if he were some kind of demigod—with so much respect and even awe that it was impossible to have a relationship that wasn't mentor and trainee, teacher and student, or—Jesus help him—god and worshipful subject.

Every-fucking-one—except Tracy Shapiro. Who had the balls to argue with him, damn near constantly.

"I'm sorry," he said now. "I didn't mean that."

"Yes you did," she said, and the vulnerable hurt in her eyes made him inwardly let out a string of the foulest language he knew—with himself as the well-deserving recipient. "It's um . . . Well, it's not okay, because it, you know, was pretty mean. But . . . it's what you think and . . . It's good to know what people—men—think about you."

With all of her attitude stripped away, she looked tired and defeated, and he wanted to put it back—that light and life in her eyes.

"It's not what I think," he said quietly.

"Usually I don't find out," she told him, "until it's too late."

"What I think," he said, "is that Zanella's an asshole."

But Tracy was shaking her head. "I really *can* tell when you're lying, okay? At least some of the time. Like now. So, let's just leave our . . . non-relationship, for lack of a better term, exactly where it is. With an acknowledgment that the sex would be great, and that . . . everything that wasn't sex would suck. Is that fair enough for you?"

Decker couldn't do it. "I disagree," he said. "I enjoy your company very much, so . . ."

She was looking at him as if he were a moron. "I just pitched you a softball," she implored him. "How hard, exactly, would it have been to say, *Yes, Tracy, sex with you* would *be great*, which would make me feel better. Cheap and shallow, yes, but better. And then we could get into your truck and do whatever we have to do so that we can meet up with Tess."

"I like you too much," he admitted. "And the sex *would* be great. But I'm the one who screws up everything that isn't sex, so . . . It's not an option—you and me—as appealing as it sometimes—" he corrected himself "—frequently seems."

"Great." She was disgusted. "Now you have to go and be nice."

"I'm not nice," he told her. "I don't know why people think I am."

Tracy went around to the passenger side and opened the door to the truck. "Maybe it's because you keep yourself locked away from the rest of the world. Or up on a pedestal. Out of reach. People have to squint to see you, so most of them see you the way they want you to be. God knows I've been guilty of that myself."

Decker stood in the gravel of the parking lot as she climbed in and slammed the door behind her.

And then, when he didn't move right away, she reached over and hit the horn.

Which would have made him laugh, if he wasn't so pissed off—at himself, at Tracy, at Jo Heissman, at whoever those fuckers were who wanted Nash dead.

He climbed in behind the wheel. "Look, Tracy—"

"Shh," she said. "Don't talk. Unless it's to tell me where we're going."

Decker sighed. "Kinko's," he said as he put the truck into gear. "To use their computers to check my free-mail account."

"We don't have to go to Kinko's," Tracy told him, trying to be business-as-usual, but still obviously subdued and hurt by his verbal bludgeon. "I've got my laptop and one of those anywhere Internet jacks. If you want, I can get online right here."

Jules knew, as soon as he heard Alyssa's voice on the phone, that something had gone terribly, horribly wrong.

"Are you still in the van?" she said, instead of *Hello*, when he answered the call.

"No, we've reached our destination," he told her, purposely being vague despite the secure line. "We're waiting for contact." He glanced at his watch. Decker should have been here by now. "What's going on? Is everyone all right?"

Tess looked over at that. She was sitting on the other motel room bed, ankles crossed, surfing through the cable stations with the sound muted.

"Everyone here is fine," Alyssa said, and he repeated that for Tess's benefit.

"I'm putting you on speaker. Who's not there who's not fine?" Jules asked Alyssa, and sure enough, she hesitated, which told him volumes.

"The person I'm waiting for is late," Jules reported. "Is that—"

"No." Alyssa was absolute. "Deck's fine—at least as far as I know."

He made a noise that was at least part protest, and she added, "We're scrambling the hell out of this call. It's secure; we can talk openly. This isn't about Decker." She paused. "Jules, Max called and . . ."

What was it that was so difficult for her to tell him?

Max Bhagat was Jules's boss—and Alyssa's former boss—who worked out of the FBI's D.C. office. At one point, before Sam had gotten his shit together, Jules had been convinced that Alyssa and Max would be perfect together—romantically. He was wrong—that was before he understood that heartfelt imperfection was often better than logically perceived perfection.

"Max noticed," Alyssa told Jules as he gritted his teeth and waited for the virtual grand piano to drop on his recently highlighted head, "what he thought was a familiar name in a bizarre triple homicide case that came across his desk."

"Oh, crap," Jules said. *Familiar name* and *bizarre triple homicide* were two phrases he'd hoped never to hear in the same sentence.

"Sam wants me to make sure you understand that this isn't your fault," Alyssa said.

"Just tell me what's going on," Jules demanded, trying to quell the sick feeling in his stomach that came from knowing that his best friends were neither alarmists nor melodramatic. Whatever this was about, it was going to be bad.

"All three of the murders took place yesterday and last night," she informed him, crisp and businesslike as she conveyed the facts. "One in Annapolis, Maryland; one in Cincinnati, Ohio; and one in some little two-stoplight town called Biskin's River, Georgia. MO is identical—double-pop to the head. Ballistic tests haven't come back, but I've already checked the miles and airline flight times, and it's within the realm of possibility that the perp is the same person. It would've required some work to make all the flights, but . . . It's definitely do-able. Biskin's River's about a two-hour drive outside of Atlanta."

Tess had sat up on the edge of the bed as she listened, her pretty face somber, her eyes filled with questions as she gazed at Jules.

"Who are the victims?" Jules asked as he saw a reflection of his own guarded wariness and brace-for-it anxiety in Tess's eyes. "Will you please just tell me? Come on, do it like a Band-Aid—rip it off."

"The victims were all named John Wilson," Alyssa said.

What? John Who?

"Oh, my God," Tess breathed, and as Jules looked at her, he saw horror in her eyes. "Dr. John Wilson . . ."

And Jules remembered. Tess had helped him build an entire intricately detailed life for one extremely fictional John Wilson, the physician who'd "signed" Jim Nash's death certificate.

"I don't know how or why Max remembered Dr. Wilson's name," Alyssa continued, "but he did, and . . ."

"What the *fuck*?" Jules said. He'd purposely made their make-believe Dr. Wilson an older man, on the cusp of retirement, gotten him a passport and sent him "safely" overseas with his equally fictional wife.

"The three John Wilsons who were killed weren't doctors," Alyssa told him. "They were just civilians."

Jesus God, he was going to be sick, but he could tell from her voice that she hadn't told him the worst of it, though what could be worse than knowing that, two months ago, by choosing two common-enough American names — John and Wilson — entirely on a whim because he and Robin had recently rewatched Tom Hanks in *Cast Away*, Jules had condemned three innocent men to death.

"Jules," Alyssa said, all of the precise former-military-officer gone from her voice. Her words were thick with compassion. "One of the John Wilsons . . . He was only seven years old."

Jules closed his eyes. "Oh, dear God," he whispered.

"Alyssa, please, don't tell Jimmy," Tess implored. "Not until I get back. I need to be there —"

"Yeah," Alyssa said, regret heavy in her tone. "I'm afraid that horse has already left the barn. He walked in — rolled in, actually — on a conversation I was having with Sam and . . . Tess, I'm sorry, but we had to put him into lockdown."

"Oh, no," Tess said.

"Jules, you and Tess need to get out of there, ASAP."

"What kind of monsters would do something like this?" Jules asked. "Who *are* these people?" He stood up on legs that felt like they belonged to someone else. "God damn it, how many John Wilsons are there in this country? We need to issue some kind of warning, give them protection —"

"That's pretty standard in a case like this," Alyssa said. "Murders linked by a common name? Max told me they've already been in touch with all of the John Wilsons who file taxes —"

"Children don't file taxes," Jules pointed out.

"There'll be a press release issued. They'll get the story on the news."

"That's not good enough," Jules said. "We have to —"

"No." She was definite. "It's important that we let the FBI handle this. You need to stay far away from it. Don't even call Max — you're supposed to be on vacation. Communicate with him through me. This is another message that we've been sent — let's not react without thinking this through."

"*Thinking this through?*" Jules couldn't keep himself from shouting. "My God, Alyssa — I'm going to be thinking this through for the entire rest of my *life*!"

"You're upset," she said. "I know that. You have every right to be. I'm upset, too. I know what you're thinking and feeling and it's awful and it's *not* your fault, but I know you think it is, and I'm so, *so* sorry, but right now you and Tess *must* get back into the van. Quietly. Quickly. Just take your things and go."

"Jesus, I underestimated them," Jules said.

"We all did," Alyssa agreed. "You're not alone in that."

"Yeah, but I'm in charge," he countered. "I'm responsible for—"

"Right now, you're responsible for getting yourself and Tess to safety," she cut him off, that Navy-Lieutenant edge back in her voice. "Jules, I need you to recognize that you're probably not thinking clearly here. I need you to step down and let me make the decisions right now. Just temporarily, until we regroup."

Jules laughed. "You think I'm not thinking clearly? I'm thinking a little too clearly—"

"And I'm telling you, sir, that I know that you're not—that you can't be," she interrupted him again. "I need you to trust me."

It was the *sir* that got to him. Alyssa never *sir'ed* him unless she was dead serious.

"I trust you," he said on an exhale.

"Then put me in charge."

"You're in charge."

"Good," she said. "Now follow my orders, and get yourself and Tess into the van, because you *are* in danger. This message was directed at *you*, Jules. Whoever they are, they know you were on the scene when Jim Nash died—"

"Oh, my God," he said. "Robin—"

"I've already called him in," Alyssa told him. "I was having trouble reaching you, so I anticipated—"

"It's fine," Jules said. "Just tell me he's safe."

"He's safe. Ric and Annie are with him. They've arranged for helicopter transport—the goal is to get all of you back here as quickly as possible. They're going to call in with a rendezvous point. You're going to head back in with Robin and Tess, while Ric and Annie bring the van—"

"Robin starts filming tomorrow," Jules said, and as the words left his lips he realized how inane they were.

"No, he's not going to do that." Alyssa was patient with him. "It's not safe. I'm making the code red call, Jules. This is no longer your choice, it's mine. We're using the back-in-rehab cover."

"Oh, crap, no," Jules said. They'd created a Plan B, before embarking on this dangerous mission, that would allow them to pull Robin—a recovering alcoholic—off the movie set and get him to safety, by pretending that he needed to go back into rehab. The story was going to be all over the TV entertainment "news," as well as the Internet—it was probably already posted on TMZ.com.

"Robin was completely on board," Alyssa told him. "He's worried about you and Tess. He wants you to get in the van and get out of there. So do it. Get into the van."

Tess was already gathering their things—packing up the book that she'd brought and tying her sweatshirt around her waist by its sleeves.

"Jules," Alyssa said again. "This is *all* you have to do right now, okay? One step at a time. Just get in the van and get Tess and yourself to safety."

"What about Decker?" Jules asked.

"I'll keep trying to contact him," Alyssa said. "He'll work out a way to get in touch with Dave and Sophia."

Jules exhaled, hard. "Jesus, Lys," he said. "Seven years old . . . Haley's almost seven." Haley Starrett, Sam's daughter from his first disastrous marriage, was funny and sweet and smart, and God, someone had delivered a double-pop to a seven-year-old's head.

"I know," Alyssa said quietly. "Get back here, Jules. The people who did this are running scared. Which means they've probably already made a mistake. We're going to find them, we're going to track them down, and when we do?" Her voice turned hard as steel. "We're going to put them down like the rabid dogs that they are."

The flight to LAX was full, which was frustrating because it meant that they probably wouldn't talk.

Not that Dave was ready to say anything—in fact, Sophia could tell he was relieved that they'd had absolutely zero privacy since she'd slammed her way out of the interrogation room at the morgue.

She closed her eyes as the plane took off, as gravity punched her back in her seat—she hated flying, she always had, but today her stomach roiled and she had to grit her teeth against the nausea.

But then Dave reached over and took her hand, lacing their fingers together, giving her a squeeze of reassurance. She knew she must've felt like ice to him, because he surrounded her hand with both of his, trying to warm her.

She kept her eyes closed against the sudden rush of tears.

She wanted, so badly, to go home.

No, what she wanted was to go back in time to Sunday morning. She wanted to put her fingers into her ears so that she wouldn't hear Dave tell her that Maureen had called. She wanted to *not* go to Boston, *not* see her father, *not* get that crazy phone call from Dave while she stood in the hospital lobby . . .

And *not* take that unwelcome step back into a world filled with violence and death. She'd had enough of both—she'd realized it with a jolt in the hospital—during the first thirtysomething years of her life.

And it wasn't death like her father's impending demise with which she had the problem. His passing was natural. It was part of the circle of life, and he was more than ready to move on.

The nurse had told Sophia that she wouldn't be surprised if he died within the next few days—especially now that he'd seen her, his only daughter. Especially now that she'd given him the forgiveness that he'd wanted for so long.

Her granting that forgiveness had further lightened her own soul, too.

For twenty minutes. She'd felt absolutely great about where she was in her life, and where she was going—for the twenty minutes from the time that she'd left her father's bedside, until she'd run out of the hospital to find Dave, soaked and bleeding in the parking lot.

There'd been *so* much blood.

And the truth was that she hadn't stepped back into a violence-filled world. The truth was that, by working at Troubleshooters Incorporated, she had never really left it.

Dave spoke softly, his voice low so that the woman sitting beside her, in the aisle seat, wouldn't overhear. "I'm so sorry."

Too often, when people said they were sorry, they didn't mean it. Dave, however, was completely sincere. Sophia didn't doubt that. She never had.

"What if we leave?" she asked quietly, too. She opened her eyes to look at him. "What if we just . . . go somewhere. Far away. Out of the country. We can hide."

He was silent for a long time, just gazing at her. And she realized, as she looked back at him, that she had absolutely no clue what he was thinking right now—or how he would respond. A muscle was jumping in the side of his face as he clenched his jaw. The Dave she could read so well had been replaced by this expressionless near-stranger.

He finally spoke. "Forever?" he asked her.

Sophia nodded, searching for the man who was so good at making her laugh, but not finding him in these somber eyes. "If we have to, yes."

"You don't mean that," he said quietly. "And even if you did, I would never do that to you. Take you away from your friends, your job, your entire life?"

"I don't care," she insisted.

"Yeah," he said, "you do. And even if we did it, Soph, even if we ran? We'd spend the rest of our lives looking over our shoulders and—" He broke off, shaking his head. "No." His eyes got even harder, his face and his voice now stony, too. "This has to end. It's going to end."

"How?" she asked him, a flood of tears rushing to her eyes. "With you dying? Because I don't want it to end that way."

"It won't," he whispered. He never could stand to see her cry.

"You can't promise that," she accused him.

And he nodded his agreement, his mouth a grim line. "I know."

*I want my Dave—the real Dave—back*, she was tempted to say, but the woman sitting next to her had taken off the earphones to her iPod. The plane had reached what seemed to be cruising altitude, and the need for Sophia to cling so desperately to Dave's hands had passed.

So she let him go.

Just as she let go of her fantasies. Because this *was* the real Dave—this tight-jawed operative sitting beside her now. The truth of the matter was that this man had been one of the CIA's top field agents long before she'd met him.

And for the past few months, she'd just been playing at normal. For the past few months, she'd been fooling herself. She'd wanted a home and a family—not another grave to tend. And the really stupid part? It was that she'd seen Dave in action, plenty of times. He'd helped save her life more than once through the years—including that very first night they'd made love.

But the fact that he was comfortable not just toting a submachine gun but also using it had somehow always seemed the exception rather than the rule. Yes, he regularly went out on overseas assignments, but to Sophia, he'd always seemed so much more at home sitting in an office, at a computer.

But he hadn't resigned from his job with the CIA by choice—he'd left under a cloud of suspicion and shame. He'd told her as much, months ago, but until now, she hadn't given any thought to what that really meant—and how it surely had affected him.

With his hair a mess, bleary-eyed from doing research on his computer, coffee mug in hand, slightly overweight and out of shape, dressed down in cargo shorts and a T-shirt touting the name of some ancient rock band—his favorite was The Ramones—he'd often kept his desk between himself and the rest of the world. But that hadn't been the real Dave—Sophia knew this now. That had been a slapped-down, heartbroken, eating-too-much-chocolate-to-make-himself-feel-better, subdued version of David Malkoff, CIA operative extraordinaire.

And the hard truth was that one of the main reasons Sophia had chosen him—and moving their relationship from friends to lovers *had* been her choice—was because she wanted to feel safe. Because she didn't want extraordinary.

"I don't know what we're doing here," she said to him now, regardless of the iPod woman's astonishingly overt curiosity. "If you won't talk to me. . . ."

Dave nodded, as if he'd been waiting for her to say those very words. "I'm sorry," he said again, and again, it was clear that he was sincere. He was extremely sorry.

It was then that the flight attendant came by, selling snacks and drinks. They both shook their heads, but the attendant stayed in the aisle to serve the iPod lady a coffee.

Until the cart was gone, they sat in a somewhat awkward silence.

Sophia finally broke it. "I get that you don't want to talk to me," she said. "Will you talk to Decker or—" She stopped herself. Gave a laugh that came out sounding far more like a sob. "I was actually going to say Jimmy Nash. I must be more exhausted than I thought."

There was a flash of real pain mixed with the sympathy in Dave's eyes. "I forget that he's gone sometimes, too." He exhaled hard. "I wish I *could* talk to him. We were closer than most people think."

She nodded, swallowing past the lump in her throat. "I know. He told me—more than once—how much he admired you." She was silent for a moment—they both were; he'd turned slightly away—and then she said, "I understand why you wouldn't be eager to talk to Deck. . . ."

Her voice trailed off because Dave turned to look at her, and tears were shining in his eyes. "Life can be tough," he whispered, "and we don't always get what we want. God knows Tess and Nash didn't. And I know you didn't—with your father and mother and . . . with Dimitri's murder."

She didn't argue—she couldn't.

"We're both so tired," he continued as he pushed up the armrest that was between them, making sure it was securely out of the way. He turned off the overhead lights and pulled down the window shade. "Can we just table this discussion for now? Please? Just come here. You're freezing."

He put his arm around her and pulled her close so she was as comfortable as possible, with her head on his shoulder. Then he put a blanket around them both. Taking care of her—as always.

"If you want, we can fight about this more tomorrow," he said wearily. "But close your eyes and rest for now, okay?"

She *was* chilled, and he was so warm. So Dave. So much so that she almost started to cry. Instead she pulled his head down and kissed him.

To hell with the curious iPod lady.

He hadn't shaved while in the hospital, and his chin rasped against her as he hesitated only slightly before accepting her kiss, just as he always did. He returned it as something longer, deeper, hotter—again, as he always did.

And when he finally pulled back, she was breathless and dizzy. And as surprised by it as she always was.

"I'm going to make things right," he whispered. "Whatever happens, you're going to be safe, I promise you that."

He kissed her again, and she knew in that instant what her real problem was. She'd gotten into this relationship with Dave, thinking that she was settling for someone nice enough. Someone who loved her and would never hurt her. Someone who would be a good husband and a loving father to her children as they sailed through life on an easy, even keel.

Her problem really wasn't that there were mysteries unsolved, questions unanswered—that seemingly transparent Dave did, in fact, have secrets that he kept from her, from everybody.

Her real problem was that, after all the sorrow and loss in her life, she desperately *didn't* want to be in a relationship with someone she absolutely couldn't bear to live without.

And yet here she was, with the same fear she'd felt last night, as she'd followed Dave into the hospital, welling up in her throat whenever she so much as *thought* about his putting himself in danger.

*Don't leave me,* she'd said.

*Never,* he'd answered, but she'd learned, the hard way, that that was a promise no one could keep.

# CHAPTER NINE

"Ahead, on the left," Tracy announced, as she spotted the sign with the stylized ocean waves for the Seaside Heights Motor Lodge a fraction of a second before Decker did. The neon lights were faded and dull in the still of the early evening, and most of the letters were missing—it said only SSD HGTS. The road was divided and they had to pass the place and U-turn to get to its parking lot.

"Somebody needs to buy a vowel, and wow, *hourly* rates?" Tracy craned her neck to look at the place as they went past. "Very classy. My mother would be so proud."

Decker glanced at her. She'd been quiet for most of the trip from the beach—even during the endless crawl in hellishly heavy traffic that had made the forty-minute drive take nearly an hour and a half. Of course, they'd stopped to pick up sandwiches, which had tacked on thirty additional grueling minutes.

"Not that I'm going to tell her. I mean, even if I did, she would just look at me as if I were certifiable." Now that she'd started talking, it was clear she didn't know how to fall silent again, because she just kept the babble going. "She thinks I'm overqualified, and that Troubleshooters is just a fancy name for the local Rent-A-Cop company. She doesn't get why I'm not sending out my résumé to every doctor and his dentist brother in Southern California. She actually e-mailed me a list that was called something like 'Eligible Men in the Medical Profession Across the United States,' and I'm like, *Why stop there, Mom? Why not send me the 'Fifty-Two*

*Years Old and Unhappily Married'* list, while you're at it. As long as I'm marrying for mercenary reasons, why not be a home wrecker, too." She exhaled her disgust. "When she's not pushing the receptionist-marries-the-doctor plan, she's trying to get me back together with Lyle. My ex. She's like, *All men cheat, Tracy. That's just the way they're wired—*"

"It's okay if we don't talk," Decker finally cut her off as he braked to a stop behind a line of traffic sitting at a light, waiting to make the turn. "I know you're still upset with me."

"I'm not," she lied, and he looked at her again. "I'm not," she insisted. "I do think you're a total loser, but at the same time I feel sorry for you, because you're obviously going to spend your life alone and pathetic." She paused for maybe a sixteenth of a second before adding, "Of course, when I walk into this flea-ridden, no-sleep-all-sleaze motel with you, the forty private investigators hiding in the parking lot, staking the place out, are going to think that we're here to get it on, and maybe that's enough for you—having people think that—"

"Your mother's wrong," Decker changed the subject, because getting it on with Tracy was a topic he wanted to avoid. Especially when she was right. Anyone who saw him approach the motel with Tracy *was* going to think that he was one lucky, *lucky* son of a bitch. And he could be, with just a small amount of effort. Still. Even now. Even after his thoughtlessly cruel comment about Zanella running away screaming.

He paused to see if she'd shut up, and what d'you know? She had. She was waiting for him to continue, although he could tell from her eyes that she had at least several more paragraphs of opinion to impart. So he changed the subject more completely, by saying, "All men aren't wired to cheat."

"I know that," she said, but then she asked, "Did you?" The look of stunned surprise he shot her must've held some confusion, because she felt compelled to be more specific. "Ever cheat on what's-her-name? Your former fiancée. Emily?"

Jesus. What an intensely personal question to ask anyone, let alone a co-worker. Especially since he couldn't recall ever discussing with Tracy the fact that he so much as *had* a former fiancée, let alone that her name was Emily.

But apparently she didn't care that her question was also an admittance of the fact that she'd been gossiping about him with someone in the office, because she simply sat there, looking back at him, as if she expected him to answer. So he did.

"Yeah," he said, as the light turned green and the cars in front of him started to move.

Tracy reacted as violently as if he'd reached out and smacked her, sitting back in the seat and all but gasping at his confession. "Seriously?"

"I cheated on her," he confirmed. "After she cheated on me. It was . . ." What had Tracy called it? "Revenge sex. But I think the ultimate revenge was Em's, because . . ." Tracy was still watching him, waiting for the end of his sentence. So he gave it to her. "I knew it didn't matter what I did. I knew she wouldn't care. She hadn't moved out yet, but inside of her head, she was already gone. There was nothing I could do or say to change that. And the sex—cheating on her to *do unto her*, you know . . . ? It only made me feel like a bigger piece of shit."

"I'm sorry," she said quietly, but then surprised him by adding, "but that's such total male crap. *There was nothing I could do or say to change that.*" She mocked him, pitching her voice ridiculously low. "Of *course* there was something you could've done, you just didn't want to make the investment."

He laughed his disgust as he made the U-turn far too fast, on tires that squealed their protest. "I didn't make the *investment*? *I'm* sorry, but *that's* total *female* crap. She didn't want *me*—if she did, she wouldn't've had a problem with my being gone so often. I was a chief with the SEAL teams, for God's sake. I invested in everything but the reality—which was that we were doomed from the start—because she was investing all of *her* time and effort into trying to turn me into someone that I fucking wasn't!"

Jesus Christ, what was it about Tracy Shapiro that caused him to lose his shit so quickly? He made a point never to raise his voice, and yet here he was, damn near shouting at her again, peppering his speech with a word that he'd noticed she very rarely used. In fact, the only time he'd heard her say it was when she'd used it as a verb. "Excuse me," he appended. "I'm . . . sorry."

She was thinking close to the same thing. "You know, I can always tell when you're not really angry, because you get loud and you swear a lot. When the anger's real, you're quiet and it's way more scary."

He didn't slow down enough as he pulled into the potholed parking lot for the motel, and the truck bounced crazily, gravel spraying as he hit the brakes too hard. There was a too-small spot between two badly parked sedans, and he zipped the truck in, still going too fast, because the asshole in him wanted to make her squeak with alarm.

Which she did, making him feel like an even bigger asshole.

"I'm not angry," he agreed as he put the truck into park. "I'm incredulous that you would have the audacity to argue with me about a relationship that you know *nothing* about."

"I wasn't arguing."

Jesus, was she really going to argue about *this* now, too?

She continued before he could laugh in her face. "I was challenging your version of the truth. Every story has two sides, and I'm pretty positive Emily's is different than yours. Did you love her?"

Her question again caught him by surprise. "What does that have to do with—"

Tracy cut him off. "Everything," she said in a voice laden with an unspoken *you moron*. "It has everything to do with . . . *everything*."

"Yes," he answered her honestly, because why the hell not? "I did, okay? Very much. But not enough to throw my own self away to turn into her fucking—freaking—Stepford Husband."

Tracy nodded. "She was wrong to want you to change. She should have loved you enough to . . . Well, I mean, who did *she* love, really? You? Or someone else—someone that she wanted you to be?"

Decker blinked at her. Neither one of them made a move to leave the truck, and they both just sat there in the flickering light from the neon sign. "So now, what? You're suddenly on my side?"

She nodded, unperturbed. "Yeah, because you were right. If she was trying to change you . . . ? I mean, sure, you've got a nasty streak—which, yes, is probably why I find you so attractive—but most of the time you're a pretty sweet guy. And she just throws something like that away? I'm betting she wasn't all that bright."

"She was plenty bright," he said. "But she didn't understand what she was getting into. And I didn't make it any easier for her. And then when—"

He stopped himself abruptly, clenched his teeth and jaw against the words that had almost come out. *And then when Andy died, I checked out for a while. For too long. Hell, I left the scene permanently. Em left me, yeah, but the cold truth is, I left her first.*

"When . . . what?" Tracy prompted, almost gently.

Decker took the keys out of the ignition and opened his door. It clunked against a blue sedan that had too many dents and dings for him to worry about one more. So he didn't. "I don't know how long Tess and I are going to be at the airport. You might be waiting here at the motel for a while. Which of your massively huge bags do you want me to bring inside for you?"

She hesitated only briefly at his pointed change of subject and ignored his dig. "I'll just take my laptop case," she told him as she opened her door, too. "I've got some books in there. As long as I've got something to read, I'll be fine."

"Don't sign online under any of your own e-mail accounts," he reminded her as he got out of the truck's cab, grabbing the bag of sandwiches that they'd stopped and picked up. "Let's be extra safe."

"You must think I'm a slow learner," she said, slamming her door shut behind her. "I mean, we had this exact same conversation just a few hours ago."

"Let's continue to be extra safe," he amended.

As they met at the front of his truck, he reached to take the computer case from her, but she put the strap up over her head, so its weight was across her chest. It was a solid *I don't need your effing help, loserman,* so he backed off.

He wasn't surprised—he was learning that, with Tracy, there was no telling what she'd do or say next—when she looked him in the eye and said, "If you ever want to talk about it—the fact that Emily cheated on you—I've been there, done that. I walked in on Lyle and one of his bitch paralegals. Heather Something. He screwed her in our bed." She cleared her throat. "I still feel hurt and, yeah, really angry, just thinking about it. And I really am just talking about talking. You've made it very clear that . . . But that doesn't mean we can't be friends."

Friends. Decker stood there, looking into Tracy's blue eyes, trying to remember the last time he'd wanted to kiss someone as badly as he wanted to kiss her. Last woman he'd kissed had been Jo Heissman, and he really hadn't kissed *her*. He'd just reached out, blindly, and she'd been there on the other end of his mouth. Before that had been Caroline, Andy's twin sister. But their hookups had been few and far between. The first time had been on one of the crushingly awful anniversaries of Andy's death, right after her divorce and many months after Em had moved out. It had been about comfort in the face of that still-gaping loss—tinged with far too much sorrow ever to turn into anything real and lasting.

He'd last gone to see Caro about a year ago—his first visit post the disaster that had been his Kazbekistan encounter with Sophia. He'd gone looking for God knows what, but when he'd tried to turn her kiss hello into a trip into her bedroom, Caro had pulled back. And told him she'd been meaning to call him—that she was getting remarried, to some professor at the university, at the end of the month.

She'd told him that she'd thought long and hard about it, but had decided it would be best not to invite him, since it had been so long since they'd even so much as spoken on the phone. Subtext: You total piece of shit—using me for sex and then sending flowers, as if that would make up for the subsequent zero-contact for well over a year.

And maybe that hadn't been Caroline's subtext, but was instead the subtext Deck himself had interjected. Because, Christ, it *had* been a long time since he'd so much as given a single thought to her.

"Okay," Tracy said now. "No response. So, that's a big negative on the friendship thing. Maybe I *am* a slow learner." She turned to the motel—a 1950s-era two-story building that looked as if its most recent renovation was the new roof someone had slapped on, back in 1978. "Room 114 is . . ." She squinted at the numbered doors in the deepening twilight, and pointed past the empty swimming pool. "Looks like it's over this way." She started down the cracked concrete path, walking with her usual attitude.

And that far end of the motel exploded in a roaring ball of heat, noise, and flames.

The force flung Decker back and he jettisoned the bag of sandwiches he was carrying in order to grab for Tracy. He tried to catch her, to take her down to the ground and cover her, to protect her against the flying debris. But as he wrapped his arms around her, her laptop bag caught him hard in the chest and he went down like a bowling pin, losing control of his feet, his head hitting the concrete with a crunch—hard enough to scramble his brain. Still, he didn't let go of her and together they bounced and scraped across the dusty yard, with him beneath her, like a human sled, even as he coldly, logically assessed the situation.

Bomb.

If they hadn't been caught in traffic, if they hadn't lingered in the truck, they'd both be dead right now.

No one in that part of the hotel—certainly no one in Room 114—could possibly have survived a blast of that magnitude.

Which meant that Tess and Jules were dead.

They'd been vaporized. Decker knew that with a stab more painful than any blistering heat could ever be. Still, he found himself turning his head as he held tightly to Tracy, as he tried to regain at least a little control, to roll with her toward the parking lot, toward his truck. He turned his head so as to best be able to gauge the height of the flames and the direction of the wind—to use his years of expertise with explosives to figure out the best way into that holocaust, so he could search for survivors.

But Deck well knew from the size of those flames, from the roiling cloud of dark smoke in the early-evening sky, even as he heard his own voice shouting—"No!"—he knew there would be no survivors. Tess and Jules were dead. And Nash, too, was as good as dead. He wouldn't—couldn't—survive losing Tess this way. It would prove to be too much, too awful. As it would be for Robin, left without Jules.

Jesus Christ.

They'd gambled and lost. Lost hard, lost big.

And even knowing all of those things, Decker dug his elbow into the ground so that they finally skidded to a stop. He made sure Tracy was conscious and alert, pulling her chin so that he could see her face. It was smudged with dirt, but her eyes—although conveying her shock—were clear.

"Dial 9-1-1," he shouted over the ringing in his ears, and she nodded, reaching into her handbag.

He pushed himself to his feet—Jesus, he'd rug-burned his entire upper back—and headed toward blazing rubble.

Which was when he was shot.

He felt the slap in the side of his arm, and actually saw the bullet as it left his body with a surreal, almost beautiful fountain of blood. And he turned, spinning, crouching, zig-zagging back to Tracy as he heard the retort of a sniper rifle and then another and another.

Was it one shooter or two? He couldn't tell. But the bullet that had hit him had come from behind them, probably from across the street, from the roof of the Rings of Saturn Motel, another crumbling flophouse. Unlike the Seaside Heights, it was a whopping three stories, which wasn't great, but it was far better than the ten-story Holiday Inn a quarter mile down the road. Ten stories gave a shooter a high enough altitude to pick his targets off like fish in a barrel. Three stories was the equivalent of squirrels in the backyard. Hell of a lot harder to hit. Provided the squirrels didn't do something stupid, like stand still.

Decker grabbed Tracy and dragged her to the truck as his back window shattered. He threw her inside anyway, reaching for his keys with an arm that didn't work as well as it should have. But he had two arms, and he jammed the keys into the ignition with his left hand even as he used his right knee to put the truck into reverse. He stood on the gas, all the way out to the road, shouting, "Help me. Tracy! Put it into drive when I say now—Now!"

Tracy was shouting—he could see her mouth moving—but she did exactly as he asked.

"Good girl—get down now—keep your *head down!*"

With a squeal of tires, as she scrambled onto the floor where Jo Heissman had so recently sat, Deck, too, scrunched down and rocketed east, driving hard and fast, zigging through the still-heavy traffic, taking a right turn from the left lane as the horns of disgruntled drivers blared behind them.

He sat up a little then, looking into the rearview. No one had followed them onto the side street. Still, he wasn't going to take any chances. As he took a bridge that crossed the 5, he saw that traffic was finally moving, and he took a left, heading for the nearest entrance onto the freeway.

"I can't find my phone," Tracy was saying, her words muffled as she dug frantically through her oversized bag. "I can't find it—"

"It's okay," he said as he got onto the 5 and NASCARed his way into the left lane. His own voice sounded distant, tinny, but his ears were surely fucked up from the blast. The world also had a weird, surreal quality to it that came from the fact that he, and he alone, knew that Tess and Jules were dead. The entire population of the planet should have been down on their knees, out in the street, screaming their outrage to the sky. But that wasn't happening. Even he himself was still driving, still talking, still moving, still living. "I was just giving you something to do," he told Tracy.

He could feel his heartbeat pulsing in his injured arm, and it occurred to him that the strangeness he was experiencing might be due to a loss of blood.

"I have to call Tess," Tracy told him, her head practically inside of her bag, as he steered with his knees so he could reach around to touch his upper arm.

His hand came away drenched with his blood. He wiped it on his jeans as he took hold of the wheel and exited the freeway at the last split second, again pissing off commuters who were no doubt already pissed off enough about having to work late, people who had no idea what did or didn't matter.

Tracy looked up at him. "I have to make sure she got out of—"

"She didn't," Decker said quietly.

"Don't say that! We don't know that!"

She was fierce in her hope, so he let her keep it as he scanned for police cruisers before running the red light at the end of the ramp.

He had to get to a place where he could stop his bleeding and check Tracy—make sure she wasn't in too much shock to realize that she, too, had been shot.

"I need to find my phone," she insisted. "You used it last and . . ." Her voice trailed off, and as he slowed to take a left onto a smaller, less traveled street, he glanced over and down to see her poking her finger through a hole in the top flap of her leather computer bag. "Was it possible that someone was shooting at us?"

"Me," Decker said as he almost missed the right turn into the little residential neighborhood. Yeah, this was the right place. He hadn't been here that often, so he was feeling his way. "They were shooting at me. You just happened to be standing too close."

Small but well-maintained houses, most of them brightly lit, lined a quiet street. No one was out—everyone was inside, eating dinner. Which was good, because a truck with its back window shot out was likely to draw a second glance, and maybe even inspire a phone call to the police. And while Decker wasn't paranoid enough to believe that any of the local officers were on the Agency's payroll, he was certain that whoever had just killed Tess and Jules had access to the SDPD's computer system.

"Oh, my God," Tracy breathed, her search for her phone finally abandoned. "Decker, you're bleeding! Oh, my *God!*" He took a left as Tracy poked her head up so she could see out the windows. "Where are you going? We need to get to a hospital!"

"We can't," he told her. "We walk into an ER, and we're as good as dead."

"If you bleed to death," she pointed out, "you're not just as *good* as dead, you actually *are* dead." She moved up on the seat to get closer to him, never mind the fact that she was now sitting in a growing pool of his blood. "And I, for one, am not going to let you die."

"Honey," he told her, "I'm already dead. My goal right now is to keep *you* among the living."

"You need to stop the truck," she insisted as she reached to look beneath the sleeve of his overshirt. "Oh, my God, Deck. You really need to let me apply pressure."

"Ow," he said. "Don't! We're almost there." And there it was.

"Isn't this . . . ?" Tracy peered out the window into the rapidly darkening night as he pulled into the drive.

"Sam and Alyssa's," he told her.

"It doesn't look like they're home."

"They're not."

"Then why—"

"Tracy." He cut her off. "I need you to help me. See the keypad next to the garage?"

She peered out the front windshield again at the standard two-bay garage, and he turned on the truck's brights. "Over to the right."

She nodded. "Yes."

"I have the alarm code."

She understood what he needed. "Tell me and I'll do it." She opened the door, but he stopped her.

"Wait. We need to get this truck into the garage and close the door behind us—as quickly as possible, but . . . We can't leave any blood on the driveway."

She looked at him. Looked at herself. They were both a mess, but at least she wasn't bleeding—at least that he knew of. Without a word, and without his having to ask, she kicked off her sandals and unfastened her belt. "What's the code?"

He told her as she shimmied out of her bloodstained pants, giving him an eyeful of smooth, tanned thighs and panties that were gleamingly, virginally white. She perched on the end of the bench seat, where his blood hadn't yet spread, as she reached again for the door handle, repeating the string of numbers he'd told her.

She did a quick check of the neighborhood, making sure no one was watching, then opened the door and crossed the driveway as quickly as possible, hopping as she stepped on a stone with her bare feet.

And okay. So much for virginal, because her panties were thongs. He lowered his brights, because it was obvious that she didn't sunbathe in the nude.

And yeah, the cure for his out-of-control libido was to witness the death of Tess Bailey, the woman his best friend loved more than life.

He was sitting here, staring at Tracy Shapiro's near-perfect—if cavefish white—ass, and it was his arm that was throbbing. His dick was numb. All he felt was sick with misery.

And dizzy. Jesus.

As the garage door went up, Tracy turned to give him a thumbs-up for victory, her hair and breasts bouncing like some starlet in a horror movie, and he focused hard and put the truck back in gear with his left hand.

He was in luck—he didn't have to back up. Both sides of the double bay were empty, and he could pull right in. Tracy followed as he did, and—good girl—she quickly found the button so that the door lowered behind them.

Decker cut the motor and killed the lights.

A cell phone ringtone, on a very quiet setting, ran up and down and up and down a scale. He searched for Tracy's missing phone—it had to be hers—cursing as he jarred his injured arm by reaching under the seat. Jesus, the pain almost made him black out, and as he retrieved the phone, he sat for a moment with his eyes closed, seeing stars and willing himself to remain conscious.

He had to get a message to Dave and Sophia—he wasn't going to be able to meet them at the airport. And Jesus, he had to contact Alyssa and tell her about Jules and Tess.

Tracy opened the driver's-side door, and her voice seemed to come from a long way away as she said, "That's my text message ring."

Decker looked down at the phone in his hand and saw on its screen that Tracy had indeed received a text message.

"9-1-1." Tracy leaned closer to read the message aloud. "*Head for home STAT. Trying 2 reach U.*" She laughed, taking it from him. "It's from Tess. She sent it less than a minute ago. My phone's regular ring was set on silent—I have twenty missed calls, from her and Jules both." She looked up at him, joy on her beautiful face. "Deck—I was right. They're alive!"

Decker reached for Tracy's cell phone, no doubt needing to see Tess's text message with his own two eyes.

Which would've been fine with Tracy, except that his eyes very literally rolled back in his head and, if she hadn't dropped the phone and caught him, he would've face-planted on the concrete floor of the garage.

"Oh, my God," she said. "Decker! *Deck!*"

But he didn't rouse. He was completely limp and much heavier than he looked and she sank under his weight—dead weight. God, no. She tried to lower him down without hurting him, or at least not hurting him worse than he already was.

"Decker," Tracy kept saying, "Deck!" She bumped into something hard—his gun in a shoulder holster—as she wrapped her arms around him. Gravity won and she fell backwards, smacking her butt on the cold floor, as his head lolled and one of his booted feet caught on the running board of the truck.

And oh, merciful God, as she cradled his head, she felt a huge lump already formed in the back, beneath his hair, and yes, her hand came away smeared with blood. It fact, it seemed possible that most of the blood on his clothes and in the truck cab had come from that cut on his head. "No," she heard herself saying. "No, no . . ."

She was almost entirely underneath him, and as she shifted to get him onto the floor without letting go of his poor battered head, her elbow burned. She dismissed the pain as she gently lowered him to the concrete.

His face was slack, his eyes open a small but frightening slit as, kneeling beside him, she felt for his pulse. Both his neck and her fingers were slippery with blood, and it had been a long time since she'd checked another person for a pulse. It was vastly different from monitoring her own heartbeat during an aerobic workout at the gym, and she couldn't find it, and panic surged.

"Please don't be dead, don't you *dare* be dead—"

And the overhead light went out, plunging them both into darkness.

The fixture must've been set on a timer, hooked up to the opening garage door, rigged to shut back off after a limited amount of time.

But before she could react, before she could even start to wrap her brain around what to do next, she felt it.

*Bump. Bump. Bump.* Decker's heart was beating—steady and even strong beneath her fingers—and her relief almost knocked her over. "Thank you, thank you!"

The pitch darkness was disorienting, and she knew that the door to the truck was hanging open, somewhere over her shoulder. The last thing she needed was to smack into it and knock herself unconscious, too.

She used Deck's prone body as a frame of reference, turning, intending to follow his leg—his foot was still hooked into the cab—to the open door of the truck, where she could turn on the headlights, and jeez, this wouldn't be a problem if, like normal people, he'd set his interior light to go on whenever the door was open and. . .

Okay, *that* wasn't his thigh beneath her outstretched, exploring hands. "Sorry," she told him, even though he would never know that she'd groped him in the darkness. As embarrassing as it would've been, she desperately wished he was conscious and alert and talking to her.

*Honey, it's all right. I know you didn't grab my junk on purpose. Just be careful of that open door, turn on the headlights, and then I'll tell you where Sam and Alyssa hide their extra key so we can get into the house, get cleaned up, and figure out how to contact Tess and Jules so they don't think* we're dead.

His actual leg was solid, and she followed it all the way to his foot. She had no idea where the switch for the lights was, but she felt her way to the usual places in the dashboard. Nope, that was the windshield wipers. Nope, those were the emergency flashers. Okay, the flashing was obnoxious, but they provided just enough intermittent yellow light for her to find and turn on the headlights—thank goodness—before she switched them back off.

She had to slide Deck forward slightly to unhook his foot. She lowered it to the ground—his boots weighed about four tons; no wonder he was buff, walking around all day in them—and then scrambled to the door that obviously led into the house, and found and flipped the switch for the overhead lights and swiftly looked around.

As far as garages went, it was neat and clean. Orderly. Everything was hanging on the walls, from work tools to bicycles—except for a pint-sized pink bike with streamers at the end of the handlebars and a license plate saying "Haley," no doubt ready for use by Sam's daughter when she came to visit. It was parked near a lawn mower and a weed wacker and it was all so suburban-normal that it gave Tracy pause. Or it would have given her pause if the unconscious man on the garage floor hadn't been potentially bleeding to death from a gunshot wound.

In truth, she'd imagined an arsenal of weaponry hanging on the walls. A collection of swords and knives, stakes and beheading tools. Alyssa always made her think of Buffy the Vampire Slayer, and Sam . . . Former SEAL Sam Starrett made Tracy think of perfect sex—the kind that ended with her unbelievably handsome lover smiling into her eyes and saying in his adorable Texas accent, *Darlin', I'm going to love and cherish you forever, but please, right now? Would you let me clean your refrigerator while I do your laundry? It would make me the happiest man in the world.*

She hurried back to Decker, stopping to scoop up her cell phone. The battery had come out when it had hit the concrete—she had no idea if it was broken or simply dead from temporary lack of power. Either way, she knew she couldn't use it. Deck had warned her, repeatedly, back when they were on the beach, that it wasn't secure.

Still, she *would* use it—to call for help—if it looked as if Decker were going to die.

She knelt beside him, gingerly pulling back the open front of his overshirt to take a look at his gunshot wound. But she couldn't get it over his shoulder, so she tried instead to pull up the short sleeve and . . .

Oh, jeez, oh, no. There was what looked like a furrow, about three inches long, in the side of his upper arm. It looked raw and painful and it was still oozing blood—but at least it wasn't pouring out of him. That was good, wasn't it?

Still, she looked around for something relatively clean to use to apply pressure.

Sam and Alyssa's washer and dryer were out here in the garage—along with one of those utility sinks—and Tracy headed for the dryer, praying for a load of towels or sheets. But it was empty, which wasn't really a surprise, knowing Alyssa, who was too perfect to leave a load of anything anywhere before she left her house.

Tracy's pants—only partially bloody—were still in the front of the truck, and she grabbed them and returned to Decker, wrapping them as tightly as she dared around his upper arm, tying the pants legs together.

She realized that she had to check him for additional gunshot wounds—for all she knew he'd been hit more than once. His jeans were sodden with blood, mostly on his right side, which could've come from his injured arm or that cut on the back of his head. But it was impossible to tell whether or not he'd been hit in the leg, too. She tried running her hands across the denim, checking for holes—little tears like the one in her computer bag and. . .

Computer!

She had her computer, and her plug-in-anywhere Internet access. She could e-mail Tess and Alyssa and Jules—at least let them know she and Deck were alive.

She yanked the case from the front seat and brought it back over to Decker. She took the computer out and set it on the floor and—she hadn't turned it off after leaving the beach. It had only been hibernating, so it sprang immediately to life.

Tracy quickly accessed her address book, found Tess's, Jules's, Alyssa's, and Sam's e-mail addresses, and typed a short, quick note, fingers flying over the keyboard. *Alive. Need help. Gunshot and poss head injury. Phone not secure. We're in garage. Key?*

She didn't want to be more specific than that, and it really wasn't going to be that hard for them to figure out. Tess didn't have a garage—their apartment building had a carport. And Jules didn't live in San Diego, which left Alyssa and Sam.

Before she hit send, she added *Can't help D&S—please provide backup,* because there was no way Decker was going to make it to the airport to pick up Dave and Sophia. Even if he miraculously came to right now, his truck was missing its back window. Not to mention the fact that there were an unknown number of mad bombers and gunmen scouring the city, quite probably looking for them.

Tracy also zapped a quick e-mail to Lindsey, her best friend at Troubleshooters—petite, Asian American, and a former detective with the LAPD. *You home?! 9-1-1—need help now.*

She turned up the computer's volume so that she'd hear when a response entered her inbox.

And then she turned back to Decker—who may or may not have been bleeding to death from a second gunshot wound in his leg.

She didn't have a choice; she just had to do it. She took a deep breath, exhaled hard, and unfastened Decker's belt. Silently apologizing to him, she unbuttoned and unzipped his pants, then pulled them down to his knees.

His thighs were like tree trunks—well, okay, maybe not redwoods, but still . . . For a man of Decker's size and seemingly slender build, he looked as if he ran marathons in his spare time. She knew he didn't—she would've heard about it by now, in the office, over coffee. Wouldn't she have? Maybe not from Decker himself, but from someone.

His legs were tan, with crisp, springy man-hair that, on his right side, was damp and matted with blood, but beautifully uninjured. Except— shit—his tightie-whities were dark red, again on his right side, and Tracy took another deep breath and pulled them down, too, freeing—eek!—an extremely impressive package that she had no business looking at, so she didn't, except God, it was *right* there, flopping about as she made sure he hadn't been shot in that vulnerable juncture between leg and groin.

She tried to be businesslike, tried to think in medical terms as she then tipped him onto his side to make sure he hadn't been shot in the gluteus maximus. He hadn't been. *Nice* gluteus maximus. Okay, wrong, *wrong*— that was another inappropriate thought, and she shouldn't be thinking it, except it was true. It was a simple fact. A completely no-ulterior-motive, emotion- and attraction-free observation—nice glutes—and yes, maybe later she could attempt to sell herself the Brooklyn Bridge.

She pulled up his overshirt and T-shirt, and his back was smooth and tan and muscular and unmarred, save for what looked like a terrible rasp- berry all across his shoulder blades—no doubt from sliding in the dirt, pushed back by the explosion as he'd tried to shield her from harm. She had several similar rug-burn-like scrapes on various parts of her own body, she was sure, but none as bad as that one.

Tracy lowered him back down as gently as she could, and there were his man-parts again—which she was really only looking at because she was trying to decide whether or not to pull his blood-soaked briefs back up, or find him a clean pair from his luggage in the back of the truck, when she realized . . .

His eyelids were fluttering.

"Oh, my God," Tracy said, her heart leaping into her throat as she leaned over him. "Decker! Deck!"

She pushed his hair back from his face, touched the rasp of unshaven beard on his lean cheeks, and he opened his eyes.

He opened his eyes!

And he looked straight at her, frowned slightly, and said, "Tracy. What the hell . . . ?"

And Tracy couldn't stop herself. "Thank God you're all right," she said, and burst into tears, which was stupid—she knew it was stupid—and foolish and girly and all those things she tried so hard not to be. Tried and nearly always failed.

But it hadn't just been the threat of his bleeding to death that had scared her. That bump on his head had also been a terrifying prospect.

Sam Starrett liked to tell a story about their boss, Tom Paoletti, who'd once been his commanding officer when they were both back in the SEAL teams. Tom had received a near-fatal head injury while out on an op, in the middle of some godforsaken desert. Sam occasionally did an imitation of Tom walking around and giving orders—and then gingerly lowering himself to the ground and saying, "Tunnel vision's getting worse. Sorry to be such a motherfucking pain in the ass, men, but I'm checking out now. Goddamn *son* of a—"

Everyone always laughed when Sam did his impression, closing his eyes and going limp mid-sentence. Tracy had always assumed that Tom's walking and talking right up to falling unconscious was an exaggeration— part of the good-natured mocking and ribbing that happened daily in the office, but Tom had told her, no. Even with a head injury bad enough to put someone into a next-step-is-death coma, there was often a stretch of time called the "lucid interval." And it could end rather abruptly.

It seemed unlikely that, if the drive from the motel to Sam and Alyssa's house had been Decker's lucid interval, he would rouse from a coma without extensive medical intervention.

So it was far more likely that his head injury wasn't all that massive. And for that, Tracy sobbed her relief. She wanted to grab him and hold on to him, but she was afraid to jar his injured arm, and—oh, yeah, don't grab him *there*—he was naked from the waist down. Well, not totally, since his boots were still on and his pants and briefs were around his knees. It not only looked really awkward, it *was* really awkward. And embarrassing.

"Good news! You weren't shot in the butt," she wanted to tell him, but she couldn't get the words out, she was crying too hard.

And he didn't seem to care, because he started to sit up, wincing as he put weight on his injured arm, but then lowering himself back down. "Whoa. Light-headed . . . I'm . . . Jesus . . ." Still, he reached up to touch her, to push her stringy, straggly hair back from her face so he could better see her. "Are you hurt?"

She couldn't answer. She just shook her head no, as she tried—and failed—to stop crying.

"You sure?" He looked like he was going to give sitting up another try, light-headedness be damned, so she put her hand on his chest, to keep him lying down. He touched her arm with a hand that was warm, with fingers that were slightly rough against her bare skin.

And she forced some words out. "I'm sure. I'm fine. But you're not."

"What the hell happened?" He winced again as he shifted his injured arm, checking the makeshift bandage she'd applied—and she realized he was still foggy.

"You were shot," she said. "You also hit your head when the bomb went off. At the motel . . . ?"

As she watched, his memory came stuttering back. She could see his growing awareness—coupled with confusion—in his eyes.

She helped him along by telling him, "We're hiding in Sam and Alyssa's garage. We're safe. You made sure we weren't followed."

And suddenly he *did* sit up, banishing his light-headedness with sheer will as he grabbed both of her arms, his face suddenly fierce. "Did we really get a text from Tess? She and Jules are alive? God, please say yes."

She nodded. Said it. "Yes."

It was quite possibly both the craziest and the most beautiful thing she'd ever seen. It was certainly the last thing she'd expected, but as Lawrence Decker gazed at her, his eyes filled with tears. "They're alive," he whispered, not exactly a question, but not an absolute statement, either—as if he couldn't quite believe it.

Tracy nodded, laughing even as she, once again, began to cry.

Decker laughed, too. "Thank you, *thank* you, sweet Jesus," he breathed. And out of all the solemn and self-proclaimed-holy religious services Tracy had attended back when she still lived with her parents and they made her go both to temple and to church, his six barely voiced words were *the* most heartfelt and sincere prayer of thanks she'd ever heard in her life.

He pulled her against him in a crushing embrace that was probably no more than a dodge to keep her from watching him fight to push his tears away, but Tracy didn't care. He was warm and he was solid and he was *alive*, and she wrapped her arms around him, too. She held on tightly as she sobbed shamelessly into his shirt, nearly overcome by her own relief.

She wasn't relieved—as he obviously was—about Tess and Jules, because she'd never truly believed that they were dead. No, her relief was all about this man with his beautiful never-the-same-color eyes. They'd been mostly green in this light—or maybe it was the sheen of tears that had made them look so exotic.

"It's okay," he murmured, his arms tight around her, his hand in her hair, stroking down her back—warm and soothing and solid. "It's going to be okay, thank God." His voice was a rich rumble in his chest, but she felt it catch, felt his body shake, and she knew he was fighting like hell to keep himself from crying the way she was, and it didn't seem fair.

"It *is* okay," she pulled back to tell him, but then there he was—his face, those eyes, that usually tight, grim mouth—mere inches from her.

Which was when he kissed her.

And again, she knew instantly as his mouth crushed down on hers—demanding and hard—that his motive was purely about not letting her see him cry. Or maybe he was kissing her so that he wouldn't cry. Maybe it was a substitute release that would keep those tears that brimmed in his eyes from overflowing.

But then, God, it didn't matter *why* he was kissing her—only that he *was*. Because kissing Decker was nothing like she'd expected. She'd imagined that locking lips with him would be not unlike surfing the lava spilling out of a volcano. But she was wrong—it was a thousand times more extreme. He was rough, he was hungry, and he was completely in charge. No hesitation, no *May I?* No *maybe* about it. No hidden sweetness beneath the maelstrom. Just pure unadulterated, passionate sex, laced with ownership and domination as he took total possession of her mouth with his tongue, with his lips, with his *teeth*, and it should have turned her off, feminist that she was, but it didn't.

It only made her want more.

Which he gave her by touching her, his hands sweeping down her back to cover her bare butt, pulling her closer, massaging her—fingers slipping beneath the silk back of her thong, even as his other hand claimed her breast. There was nothing even remotely gentle about his touch as he found and caught her nipple between thumb and forefinger, and she heard herself moan as she kissed him and kissed him, as the heat she'd been fighting for seemingly *years* now pooled, liquid and hot, between her legs.

Which was when he pulled back. "Where the *fuck* are my pants?!"

# CHAPTER
# TEN

Tracy was breathing as hard as Decker, who stared at her. She was, no doubt, as wild-eyed as he was.

"Yes. That. It wasn't . . ." Her voice came out sounding breathless and thin as she felt her face flush. "I didn't . . . Your shorts were covered with blood and I was afraid. . . . So I looked . . ."

She shifted, to move back even farther from him, and her arm brushed against him—against *him*—and oh, dear God. That was fast. Fast and furious, so to speak.

"Sorry," she said, even as he said it too.

"Sorry, I'm . . . Adrenaline can really . . . you know. Ramp things up."

"Really?" The word left her mouth even as she realized that the right thing to do was to not keep talking about it, but to kiss him again.

Except he was giving her the body-language equivalent of *stay back*. Which meant that the *real* right thing to do was to turn away and count the ridiculous number of life vests Sam and Alyssa had hanging on their garage wall—as if they were prepped and ready for the next big flood.

Instead, like an idiot, she actually stupidly glanced down and . . .

He'd tried to pull the tail of his shirt over himself, but it hadn't really done the trick.

"Wow," she said—again, her mouth went off in advance of her brain, so she added, "Sorry. *Sorry*." Although she wasn't quite sure what she was doubly sorry for. Kissing him back and *ramping things up*? Heck, those kisses had ramped things up for her, too, although her ramped-up things weren't as obvious as his.

His tears—if there had even been any—were long gone. His eyes now brimmed with embarrassment as he reached for his briefs—apparently preferring them on, despite their blood-soaked condition. And yes, he was actually blushing, too—a thin line of flush beneath his tan, right along his cheekbones.

"It's, you know, physiological," he told her. "Adrenaline kicks in and. . . . It, um, can be inconvenient."

"Not for your girlfriend," Tracy pointed out. "I mean, *Good-bye, honey. Have a nice day. Hope someone tries to kill you again because last night was amazing. . . .*"

It was supposed to be a joke, but he didn't laugh.

His briefs were stuck on his right knee, and she tried to help him, which in hindsight was a stupid thing to do, because he really didn't want her help, especially with her own pants-free rear in his face. He said, "I got it, thanks," in a voice that brooked no argument, which made her instantly let go.

He efficiently packed himself in, like some kind of dream male under-wear model, to tightie-whities that were extra tight and no longer white.

"I can see why you were, uh, concerned," he said as he reached down to untie his boots. "I'm a mess."

He obviously wasn't going to attempt to pull his blood-soaked jeans back up so Tracy said, "If you want, I can throw them into the washing ma-chine."

"Yes," he said, "that would be good. Thanks. I could really use a shower."

"There's a wash sink out here," Tracy said. It was surreal how polite they were being after licking the insides of each other's mouths. "Unless you know where the key to the house is . . . ?"

"No," he said, "but I don't need it. Just give me a sec." He got his sec-ond boot off, but then took a moment, closing his eyes and holding his forehead.

"Are you all right?" Tracy asked, her concern instantly back.

"Yeah," he said. "Yes."

"No tunnel vision, double vision, blurred vision . . . ?"

"I'm fine." His words were countered when he reached up to touch the back of his head, and swore.

"Seriously, Decker," she told him, helping him pull his jeans off his muscular calves, but keeping her distance this time, staying down by his feet. "It looks to me like you hit your head pretty hard. You've got to tell me—right away—if you start experiencing any symptoms of head injury. I mean, any symptoms in addition to falling out of your truck, unconscious . . . ?"

He shook his head gingerly. "That wasn't . . . I'm okay. It was . . ."

"Adrenaline?" she asked, as she yanked his pants free, impatient with his *I'm too macho to accept the truth about a potentially fatal injury* attitude. That, combined with her embarrassment over that kiss, sparked some seriously confused anger. He'd kissed *her*, hadn't he? Although it was entirely possible that she had jumped him. But even if she had, he'd definitely kissed her back with enthusiasm. "Too much blood rushing to your—"

"I fainted," he said, cutting her off, shooting her a hard look. "All right?" His blush was back—he was clearly embarrassed to have admitted that. "I'm fine. I have a very hard skull. I've hit my head plenty of times, much harder than this. But I lost some blood, and when I got the news about Tess and Jules . . . I passed out. Okay? Relief can do that."

"Adrenaline and blood loss and relief," she countered, methodically emptying his pockets onto the floor, then carrying his jeans to the washing machine. She threw them in and turned the dial to a heavy-duty wash cycle, small load. Hah. This man was giant when it came to loads. She rinsed her hands in the water that poured into the machine. "You've got your medical issues all figured out. Great. I'm happy *you're* convinced you're okay—that your fainting wasn't a big deal. As long as you tell me—immediately—if you start experiencing any other symptoms of head injury."

He laughed as she shook her hands as dry as she could before opening an overhead cabinet where she found a bottle of laundry soap. She didn't bother measuring it, she just eyeballed it as she poured it in on top of water that was turning an upsetting shade of pink.

"Not a big deal?" he asked. "Believe me, I'd prefer a fractured skull over having to admit that I fainted like some little old lady." He exhaled his disgust, and as she turned back to look at him, she saw that he'd pushed himself to his feet, but then crouched back down, all the way to his hands and knees. *"Fuck."*

"Well, *that's* just stupid," Tracy said, dropping the lid of the machine with a metallic *boing* and hurrying back to him. "You'd rather be in a coma?"

"I'm okay," he said, waving her off.

So she stepped back, but stayed close enough to catch him if she needed to. "And you didn't faint like any little old lady that I've ever met. I mean, how would you know anyway? You fainted. I was there, and you did it the same way you do everything. With a truckload of testosterone." He still hadn't moved. His head was down, his eyes closed, so she inched even closer. "Will you please let me help you?"

"Don't," he said. "Don't—I'm trying hard not to puke."

"Oh. My. God. And that's not a symptom?" she asked, kneeling beside him. "Of, like, what? Concussion? Or yes, even a fractured skull! Maybe you got your freaking wish! Haven't you read *The Secret*?"

Decker opened his eyes and looked directly at her. "Are you fucking kidding me?" He laughed in her face. "Yeah, I've read *The Secret*—or enough of it to know it's crap. Like I really wished myself here, with a gunshot wound. That's the stupidest shit I ever heard."

"Well, *I wished* Tess and Jules alive," she retorted. "I believed it with *all* my heart—so how stupid is it now?" She felt tears spring into her eyes. God, no, don't let her cry again—not over this.

"Then you better stop believing that I have a concussion," he shot back at her. He rested his forehead on the garage floor. "Jesus, I'm gonna be sick."

Tracy looked around—there was a collection of brightly colored sand toys in a mesh bag, hanging near a pair of skimboards. She went to it, quickly unhooked the bag, and pulled out a yellow plastic pail in the shape of SpongeBob SquarePants and brought it back to Decker.

"Here," she said, crouching beside him and putting the pail on the floor next to his head. She took his arm. "Come on. Sit up. Or do you want to lie back down again?"

She pushed his hair from his face, feeling to see if his forehead was warm. There was no way he could've gotten an infection from that gunshot wound so quickly, was there?

But she knew from working at Troubleshooters that operatives going into the field always brought antibiotics with them in case of injury, specifically to avoid infection. Maybe it did happen fast. Bullets had to be horrendously dirty, and one of them had cut that furrow in Decker's arm.

He opened his eyes and looked up at her. "It doesn't work," he said, and at first she didn't follow, but then she realized he was still talking about *The Secret*. "Because I keep wishing—Jesus—that you'll just please, *please* stop touching me."

Tracy pulled her hand back so fast she almost smacked herself in the face with it. "I'm just trying to help," she said, as her stinging hurt morphed into indignant anger. "God, you're arrogant. Do you honestly think I'm here going, *Oh, goody, he thinks he might throw up. I think I'll kiss him again. Yum.* You suck and you're stupidly closed-minded, too. Because you didn't read far enough in the book," she informed him. "You have to think about the thing you *want* to have happen. If you put it in a negative form, if you focus on what you *don't* want, it not only doesn't work, but it gives you the exact opposite of what you really do want. You can't say, like, *I don't want it to rain, I don't want it to rain.* Because the universe doesn't hear the *don't*. It just hears *want rain*. You have to say, *I want the sun to shine*."

"You use *The Secret* to control the weather?" he said, painfully pushing himself into a sitting position. She practically had to sit on her hands not to reach to help him. "Honey, if you can do that, you definitely need to ask Tommy for a raise."

She made a sound of exasperation as he made sure that his overshirt covered his still-obvious symptom of too much adrenaline. "That was just an example," she said. "A simple one. Easy to understand—even for those of us who are *blockheads*. It wasn't supposed to—"

"How about if I don't just wish it or think it?" he cut her off. "How about I actually say it? No fricking secret, just right on the table. Don't. Touch me. I'm human, okay? And it's too much for me right now. I shouldn't have kissed you, it was wrong, and if I could, God damn it, I'd take it back."

She didn't know what to say to that, so she just sat there as the washing machine finally finished filling with water and the wash cycle kicked on.

"And Jesus, *please*. Don't look at me like that," he added, saying again, more quietly this time, "It's too much."

Tracy nodded as she looked away. She pushed herself back to her feet, hyper-aware that she was wearing only a pair of thong panties with a tank top that was now dirty and torn. She tried to keep her front to him as she went to the back of the truck, where she had two "massively huge" suitcases of clothes. She opened the truck bed's hard plastic cover, unzipped one of her bags, and found a pair of jeans and a T-shirt. But then she pulled out a second T-shirt, because after she washed up in the sink, she was going to need to use something to dry herself off.

She'd brought soap—organic and chemical-free—and she dug for that, too, because the alternative was to use Sam and Alyssa's laundry detergent, which would dry her skin. Last thing she needed was a rash that wasn't figurative.

"I'm not looking at you," she informed Decker as she marched past him to the sink, carrying her clean clothes, careful not to hold them against her. She had streaks of his blood pretty much all over her, mixed in with some of her own, too. Her elbow was a mess. "Now it's up to you to not look at *me* while I wash up and get dressed."

"I'll get the door open so you can use the shower in the house," he said, back on his hands and knees. He was pretending he was in that position on purpose, as he searched through the rubble of items she'd removed from his pants pockets, looking for God knows what.

"Yeah, well, I kind of need it to happen in *this* lifetime," she said, turning on the water in the sink and waiting for it to warm up, "so I'm just going to—"

"Okay," Decker cut her off, removing several small metal tools from a small leather packet. "All right. You win. Help me. Over to the stairs so I can get the freaking door open. We'll get inside, we'll both get cleaned up. I can do this."

She set her clean clothes down atop the dryer as he made it all the way to his feet. He spread his legs in an attempt not to sway, but she wasn't fooled.

"I *win*?" she asked as she stalked over to him and looped his arm around her shoulders, putting her own arm around his trim and annoyingly attractive waist. "I'm sorry. The blast from the bomb that nearly *killed* us must still be interfering with my ability to hear clearly, because I could've sworn I just heard you say that I *win*. What exactly do I win? Besides this fabulous chance to look at you and touch you without being frantically warded off by the sign of the cross?"

They made it over to the stairs and up them, but none of it was easy for him, considering his current shade of green. He inserted the little metal instrument into the lock, and . . .

The door didn't open.

Decker swore under his breath. "Hold still," he ordered.

"I'm not the one who's about to fall on his head," she retorted. "Again." But she tried to brace him more absolutely, which unfortunately required more physical contact. She put her left leg around behind him, so that he was standing on the step between her feet.

Between her legs.

Don't think that. Don't go there. He wanted to take back that mistake of a kiss, and Tracy now believed—absolutely—that even if they got into the house, even if the people who'd set the bomb and shot Decker surrendered to the authorities, even if the planets aligned and choirs of angels sang their blessing, that she and this man were never, not in a million years ever, going to finish what they'd started.

*Never say never* was a popular adage at Troubleshooters Inc., but right now *never gonna happen* was written all over Decker's every move, his every bit of body language, his every expression on his not-particularly-handsome-yet-still-gorgeous face. Which was his loss.

Unfortunately, it was Tracy's loss, too.

She tried to steady him even more by clinging to the door frame with her left hand—there was no banister—and she finally gave up and just wrapped her right arm around his waist, her front pressed solidly against his back. "I've got you," she said. "Just concentrate on the lock. You can do this with your eyes closed. We both know that."

In the past, she'd witnessed him getting past far more difficult locks— like the one on her motel room door, on that near-deadly training mission in New Hampshire, back when she'd first started working for Troubleshooters. Tracy had been in the shower, and he'd let himself into the room she was sharing with Sophia. He'd been looking for clothes to bring to the tiny blond woman who'd fallen into some kind of pond, out in below-freezing weather.

For Decker, it always came back to Sophia. It was good to remember that, especially while experiencing this kind of warm and sweaty full-body contact. God, he was ripped—the six-pack beneath her hand was hard-muscled and tight and sexy as hell.

So Tracy told him, "I sent an e-mail to Alyssa, letting her know that you won't be able to pick up Dave and Sophia at the airport."

"Damn it," he swore. "I forgot about them."

"That's okay," she said. "I didn't."

He glanced back at her, over his shoulder—his eyes a flash of color in his grimly pale face. "It's not okay."

"Yeah, Deck, you know what? It actually is." She exhaled her disgust. "Didn't you just finish telling me that you're human? Well, congratulations, you really are. Fortunately, you're not alone tonight. I'm here to help you, and I did. *Thank you, Tracy. Why, you're welcome, Deck.*"

The muscles in his entire body strained and tightened even more as he did something with that little metal lockpick. And, yes! The door finally popped open.

"See?" Tracy said. "I knew you could do it."

"Don't tell me you visualized it, because I won't be able to keep from throwing up."

"Fine," she sniffed. "I won't tell you, then."

The security alarm started to beep its warning. They had only a short time—maybe thirty seconds—to input the code before it started to wail.

Decker moved to go into the house, but Tracy stopped him. "Let me. I'm moving faster." She made sure, though, that he was steady before she let go of him and slipped through the door into Sam and Alyssa's shadow-filled kitchen.

"Code's the same as for the garage." Decker started to recite the numbers, but she cut him off.

"I remember it." The alarm control box was identical to the one that provided electronic security at the office. Tracy punched in the code, and the light stopped flashing, and turned from red to green.

They were in.

"Did Alyssa e-mail you back?" Decker asked, holding on to both sides of the frame as he came through the door, as Tracy quickly checked to make sure all the blinds were down before she tried the various light switches and found one that lit the kitchen.

There was a set of hooks holding raincoats—slickers—in a little mudroom that led directly to the backyard. She took one and covered her backside, tying it by the long, yellow arms around her waist as she answered him. "Not yet. Not that I know of."

He still looked as if keeling over were an option, and she reached for him—but apparently he'd used up all his asking-for-help cards. He was back to waving her off as he sat down heavily at the kitchen table. "I'm okay."

She quickly went into the garage and got both her computer and her clean clothes. She set her laptop down on the counter and shook her head as Decker looked at her.

"Still no response from anyone. And by the way, if you're dizzy from loss of blood instead of oh, say, a fractured skull," she pointed out, "it'll help if you have a cookie and some orange juice—you know, like when you go to the bloodmobile?"

"I don't give blood," he told her. "Too many inoculations from trips overseas."

"Well, I do," she said, as she searched through the kitchen cabinets, "and they give you a cookie and some juice if you feel like you're going to faint."

"I really don't want a cookie," Decker said. "Or juice."

"You're doing it again," Tracy pointed out as she found a box of cookies—chocolate chips—and a jar of organic apple-pomegranate juice. She tried to open the lid of the juice, but it was stuck. "Remember, the universe doesn't hear *don't*."

He made it all the way over to the counter and reached to take the jar out of her hands. "I don't want any juice," he said quietly. "Go take a shower."

She looked at him. "Careful. You're awfully close. I might touch you."

"I'm sorry I . . . said what I said," he apologized—even as he put some additional distance between them. "It's not your fault."

"It's not my fault, what?" she countered, as she opened the package of chocolate chips. "That I make you *feel* something—other than miserable?"

He just stood there looking at her.

So she held out a cookie. "Sorry it's not a scone."


Tom Paoletti met them at the airport.

Tom, not Decker.

Dave saw him standing there before Sophia did—he was at the bottom of the escalator in the baggage claim area. His arms were crossed and his legs were spread in that fucking obnoxious Navy SEAL stance that Dave had come both to hate and to love—equally passionately. Sometimes it seemed as if everyone he knew at TS Inc. had at one time been a Navy SEAL. Or else they were currently a Navy SEAL.

Everyone except for him.

Which pissed him off because he knew that, in their eyes, it made him subpar.

And at the same time, as infuriatingly cocky as SEALs could be, he loved having them around, *watching his six,* as they called it.

They could never call anything what it really was—watching his back—when there was a way to say it with either military or nautical jargon. Tom himself was the least obnoxious of the bunch, and he still called the bathroom the *head* and the floor the *deck.* Walls were *bulkheads* and terrorists were *tangos* and Dave knew from experience that if his boss was in a room with another SEAL, the NavySpeak would fly.

"Paoletti dead ahead," he murmured to Sophia, who still looked exhausted despite the fact that she'd slept seemingly soundly, almost to the very moment the plane touched down here in California.

"I thought Decker was meeting us," she said.

Dave nodded, unable to look at her, for fear his sudden wave of jealousy was evident on his face. Fucking Decker. "Yeah, I thought so, too," he said—far more tightly than he'd intended.

Her patience was fraying, because she exhaled her obvious disgust with him. "I didn't say that I *hoped* he was meeting us," she countered, "only that I *thought* he was. God, Dave."

Tom was approaching so he couldn't respond with, *God, Dave what?* or explain that she'd misinterpreted his unhappiness as being somehow linked to Decker, and yes, okay, it was, but only to some degree. The rest of it had to do with Tom—and why their boss himself had chosen to meet them at the airport, rather than sending someone else.

Someone lower down the chain of command.

"Where's your wheelchair, Malkoff?" Tom asked, stepping forward to take Dave's bag off his shoulder. Normally easygoing, the taller man wasn't bothering to hide his displeasure.

"I don't need one, sir," Dave answered. "And obviously you didn't think I needed one, either, or you'd've been standing in front of the elevators."

"I was," Tom informed him, pointing over Sophia's shoulder. "You've been out of the hospital, what is it? Ten hours?"

"I'm fine," Dave lied, as he turned and . . .

Yes, all right. Tom *had* had a clean shot of the lift from where he'd been standing.

Sophia answered the boss's question, "Nine and a half hours. I'm sorry, sir," she added. "I tried to talk him into using a wheelchair, but . . . I have to confess that I didn't try very hard. It's been a long couple of days and one can only keep hitting one's head against a wall for a limited amount of time."

"But I'm fine," Dave argued, "and we'd've had to wait for them to bring the chair."

Tom had turned his attention to Sophia, no doubt taking note of the lines around her mouth and the haunted look in her eyes. It used to be her standard affect—that *gone to hell and not quite sure she was back yet* expression—and Dave hated that he'd been the one to cause its reappearance.

"You okay?" Tom asked as he took her bag, too, and she nodded. Forced a smile. "How's your father?"

"Doing his best," she said, "to make amends before he—Oh my God, *Dave!*"

She was looking at him in horror, and he looked down and realized that he'd bled through both his bandage and his shirt. "I must've pulled some stitches getting my bag from the overhead rack," he said as he drew his jacket closed. "It's nothing." He hoped. It hurt—more than it should have.

"I've got a car at the curb," Tom informed them. "Let's go. We can do a damage assessment in the car. If you've got checked luggage, I suggest we don't wait for it—"

"We don't," Sophia said tersely as she put her arm around Dave's waist—as if he needed her support. And God help him, maybe he did. Ow.

"Where's Decker?" he asked Tom as they moved swiftly—as swiftly as he could manage—toward the door.

"He's been delayed."

"What's going on?" Dave asked.

"I don't know," Tom reported as the glass doors to the passenger pickup area opened with a *snick*. "I got a call from Alyssa, asking me to meet your plane. She said it was urgent. She told me about your attack, told me that the plan was to set you up in a secure hotel room—make sure you're safe." He glanced at Dave again. "She specifically said to make sure *both* of you are safe."

"That's a very good idea," Sophia said.

Dave knew that now was not the right time to disagree. Besides, he needed about twenty hours of injury-healing sleep—which wasn't going to happen without his complete faith in the fact that Sophia was secure and protected. So he'd go wherever Tom was taking them, and he'd sleep, and when the time came to leave, to hunt down and neutralize the threat, he'd leave—knowing Sophia was in capable hands.

But . . . great. Dave's heart sank as he saw that one of Tom's SEAL friends—a chief by the name of Ken Karmody—was behind the wheel of the car that was waiting for them.

And it was quite a car. Instead of Tom's usual SUV, he'd brought one of the low, sleek, black sedans that were used by the company to pick up high-profile clients.

Dave had realized that there would be a driver—since Tom had been waiting for them inside—but he'd hoped their boss had brought along one of the other Troubleshooters operatives: Lindsey or PJ or, hell, even Tracy Shapiro.

While he appreciated Chief Karmody's particular skill set—SEALs were quite the talented drivers—Dave wasn't happy about having him for an audience. The conversation that he knew was coming was going to be hard enough.

Tom was going to ask for Dave's resignation. Dave didn't blame him. Anise Turiano's unsolved murder had raised its ugly head, and the whispers about Dave were going to start up again. Tom didn't need that. He'd worked hard establishing Troubleshooters' pristine reputation, and would—rightly—not want this ugliness to tarnish it.

"The Card was over for a cookout when Alyssa called," Tom explained as he tossed their bags into the trunk. Ken's nickname was WildCard, which of course got shortened even further. What was it with SEALs and nicknames?

Sophia helped Dave into the backseat, and climbed in after him.

Tom got in, and "The Card" put the car in gear and moved them, swiftly and steadily, into the stream of traffic heading out of the airport. "I've filled him in on the situation," Tom continued. "He's done short-term assignments for Troubleshooters before—he knows how to be discreet."

"Sorry to pull you—both of you—from the party," Dave said.

"It's nice to see you, Ken," Sophia chimed in, even as she opened Dave's jacket and pulled up his shirt to look at his bandaged wound.

The SEAL glanced into the rearview mirror, at Sophia and then Dave, before nodding. "Always glad to help Tommy. It was either me or the senior, and since Teri's about to pop . . ."

"How *is* Teri?" Sophia continued the small talk, as she peeled the adhesive part of the bandage from Dave's side. He gritted his teeth. "We must be getting close to her due date."

"Yeah, it was three days ago," Kenny reported. "The senior's about to have an aneurism. It's kinda fun to watch."

Tom's good friends, Senior Chief Stan Wolchonok and his wife, Teri, were having a baby. They were one of many couples who were expecting—in fact, the entire SoCal SpecWar community was having something of a baby boom these days.

"Teri's going in for daily checkups," Ken continued. "But everyone's healthy, so no one's too worried. It's a watch-and-wait thing."

"That's wonderful," Sophia said, and she meant it. And yet there was a wistfulness in her words that Dave knew he wasn't imagining. "How's Savannah?"

As Ken told Sophia about his own wife, Dave recalled hearing through the grapevine—possibly from Sophia herself—that Teri Wolchonok had had at least one miscarriage. As had Sophia, back when she was married to Dimitri.

No doubt about it, life could certainly suck a giant cosmic ass.

"We might need to stop at a hospital," Sophia said, and Dave realized that she was frowning as she looked at his stitches. "Sir, I'm going to need you to look at this."

Dave pulled his shirt up even higher so he could see what had caused her alarm. As he'd suspected, he'd pulled several of the stitches, and it was oozing blood. And yes, it looked a little inflamed. "It's not that bad. We're not stopping. We can't."

"I wasn't talking to you," she told him.

Tom had turned to look over his shoulder at them, squinting to see Dave's injury. "Did they give him antibiotics?"

Sophia nodded, as she looked at Dave. "Are you taking them?"

"Yes, I am," he said as he looked at Tom. "Sir, this is probably a good time to let you know that I intend to have a letter of resignation on your desk—as soon as I find some paper and a pen."

Sophia was now looking at him as if he'd crapped on the floor of the Oval Office.

Tom, however, surprised him by shaking his head. "That's not necessary."

"We both know that it is," Dave countered. "You don't actually think I'd let both your and Troubleshooters' good names be tarnished by—"

"You didn't do anything wrong, Dave," Tom cut him off. "I'm standing behind you. We had this conversation when I hired you. Nothing's changed."

"Are you kidding? Everything's changed," Dave argued. At his interview, years ago, they *had* had a completely open conversation about why he'd left the CIA, and Dave had expressed concern about the fledgling personal security firm's reputation. But Tom had had a serious manpower shortage, and had hired him anyway. "You're no longer shorthanded. You don't need—"

"I didn't hire you because I was shorthanded," Tom cut him off. "I hired you because I trust you. Like I said, nothing's changed."

The emotion that hit Dave lodged squarely in the center of his chest. It joined forces with his fatigue and made him ache. If he'd been alone, he would've curled into a ball and wept. But he wasn't alone.

"With all due respect, sir"—Dave had to work to get the words out evenly—"you need to reconsider. This could get ugly and—ow!"

Sophia was applying a new bandage—she had supplies in her purse— with too much force. "I'm pretty sure Dave gave me a letter of resignation today, too." She looked at him, her anger simmering in her eyes. "That's what that was, right? You actually got me to say *I don't know what we're doing here*, which is a precursor to *I need some time to think*, which leads to *This isn't working out*, which is what you wanted me to say, isn't it?" She didn't give him time to respond. She just yanked his shirt down over the fresh bandage and turned to Tom. "Did Dave go out on an overseas assignment for you last week?"

Ah, hell. "Soph," Dave started. "I told you it's irrelevant—"

"Shh," she spoke over him. "I'm asking Tom."

"I went overseas," Dave told her, "yes. But no, it wasn't for Tom, okay?"

"So he requested some days off," Sophia persisted, talking directly to their boss, purposely not looking at or acknowledging Dave. "Did he tell you where he was going?"

"Sir," Dave reminded him, "I told you my plans in confidence."

"And I told you," Tom countered evenly, "that I wouldn't lie if Sophia—or anyone—asked me about your trip. That's always been my policy." He nodded to her. "Yes, he did tell me."

"Please," Dave begged, because her next question was going to be more direct. "Sir. This is the last thing she needs right now—"

"What Sophia needs," his boss came back, about as sharply as Dave had ever heard him speak to anyone, "is for you pack of imbeciles to stop treating her like damaged goods, and respect her enough to let her make her own decisions about what it is that she does or doesn't need."

Beside him, Sophia actually started to applaud. "Thank you *so* much, sir," she said.

Behind the wheel, WildCard started to laugh, like the SEAL asshole that he was.

"Why is this so important to you?" Dave had to ask her. "Because at this point, when you find out where I went—"

"It's important," she shot back at him, "because I'd like to know how many other people are going to try to kill you this week!"

"Ah, Soph . . ." She wasn't kidding. She was terribly upset with him—and had been since the attack—and he couldn't really blame her. He exhaled hard. "It wasn't that kind of . . . It was . . . intelligence, okay? I was gathering intelligence. It wasn't dangerous." He caught himself in what was a rather intense understatement, especially when Tom helped him out by pointedly clearing his throat. "It wasn't the kind of dangerous that could possibly follow me home. And"—he finished his earlier thought—"when you find out where I went? It's going to be tremendously anticlimactic and actually kind of funny."

"Good," she fired back, "because right now I've got your blood under my fingernails again, and I could use a good laugh."

Ah, God.

"He went to Kazabek," WildCard told her, shrugging as he met Dave's eyes in the rearview mirror. "I didn't make you any promises and, even sitting up here? This conversation is excruciating. I'm just speeding things along."

Dave was incredulous as he turned to Tom, who was sighing heavily and shaking his head at the younger SEAL. "You *told* Karmody . . . ?"

"Yeah," WildCard said, "he told me. *You* can say that your trip was irrelevant and assume it had absolutely nothing to do with your taking a knife to the gut in Boston. But Tommy's not about to assume anything—which is why he runs TS Inc., while *you* work for *him*."

Dave could feel Sophia staring at him in stunned horror. "I'm not laughing," she whispered.

Yeah, he couldn't help but notice that.

"You went to *Kazabek*?" she continued, getting louder as she went on. "By *choice*?"

"Yes," he copped to it. "I did. And it has nothing, whatsoever, to do with Anise Turiano."

"Unless whoever you pissed off over in K-stan is using the Turiano thing to smack you down, after you did whatever you did to piss 'em off," WildCard suggested helpfully from the front seat.

"I didn't piss anyone off," Dave said, as Sophia stared at him as if she couldn't recognize him and was trying to figure out where on earth they'd previously met.

"That you know of," WildCard interjected, which was when Dave lost it.

"Will you *shut* the fuck *up*?!"

"I'm pretty sure he said what we were all thinking," Tom turned around to say, that edge back in his usually mild voice. "Before I brought the chief into a potentially dangerous situation, I had to be upfront with him about all possible threats, and face it, Malkoff, we don't know enough about this situation to assume anything. You know as well as I do that when we take on a case—"

"This isn't a case," Dave interrupted him. "You're not taking on anything other than providing protection for Sophia."

"*And* you," Tom countered. "I want to know who might try to kick down your hotel room door. I want to know all theories, all possibilities. I want to hear about your crazy cousin who hasn't spoken to you since your grandmother died and left you her favorite rocking chair. You *don't* get to assume *anything* when we're standing between you and the bullets, and you damn well know it."

"I am *not* a client," Dave said hotly, "and you're not going to be protecting me. I'll stay far away from you, so that—"

"Intelligence," Sophia interrupted, repeating the word he'd used. "You went back to Kazabek because of . . . *me*?"

Her words stopped the argument dead, as both Tom and the SEAL chief tried to become invisible in the front seat.

Dave didn't answer her—he couldn't figure out how to explain without saying things that he knew she wouldn't want said in front of an audience. But as another mile sped by, he knew she was capable of waiting forever for his answer, so he finally said, "I thought it would be easier—for you. To talk about some of the abuse that you lived through. I thought if I knew . . . If I could find out what happened to you, then . . . So, I . . ."

"Oh, my God," Sophia breathed, her eyes filled with horror. "I was wrong. What I said to you before. My secrets *could* have gotten you killed."

"No," he said, even though everyone in the car knew that he was lying. "Soph, no. I was never in danger."

"This could be my fault," she whispered, stricken. "One of Bashir's nephews, looking for payback . . ."

"No, Sophia—"

"You don't know that," she said. "Oh, my God. Ken, please, pull over! Please! Right now! I'm going to be sick!"

# CHAPTER
# ELEVEN

Jimmy was sitting on the floor of the panic room when Tess unlocked the door.

His shirt was torn—as was one of the knees of his jeans. His lip was swollen and his cheek looked as if he were going to develop a terrible bruise.

He didn't stand up. He didn't even try. He just sat there, looking up at Tess, with his relief solid in his eyes. Of course, there was wariness mixed in there, too. He knew that she was angry.

No, *angry* was too simple a word for this emotion she was feeling.

"Where, exactly," she asked him, miraculously able to keep her voice from shaking, "were you going to go? Barely able to walk, let alone run?"

"I can run," he told her.

"For what?" she scoffed. "Five steps?"

"It took two Navy SEALs to get me down here."

"Alyssa's not a SEAL."

"Well, she should be. She's tougher than any SEAL I've ever met. She kicked my ass."

"Thank God. And lucky for me," Tess said sharply, "there were *two* people on guard, so you didn't go . . . where, Jimmy?"

She knew where. She just wanted to hear him say it—that his intention was to sacrifice himself, so that this dire threat would vanish. God damn it. Her mouth trembled—she couldn't stop it, but she pressed her lips tightly together so that it wouldn't be as obvious.

He looked as if he might start to cry, too—but she knew better. He wouldn't let himself. Not in here, with the lights on. Not so that she could see. He would lock everything inside, the way he always did, the way she knew he'd already done with that terrible, soul-wrenching news about the three dead innocents, all named John Wilson.

"I wanted to make sure you were safe," he admitted, and she noted the careful wording. Not *I wanted to find you.*

"Which I wouldn't have been, the moment you'd set foot outside this house and virtually announced to the world that, yes, you are still alive. Unless you were thinking you could *buy* my safety . . ."

He looked away.

"Right now they're just guessing," she told him, this time unable to keep her voice from shaking. "But they're doing a damn good job. They found us, by the way, in San Diego."

She could practically hear the sound of his surprise and fear as his head snapped up.

"Yeah," Tess said. "The dead John Wilsons saved our lives—Jules's and mine. Alyssa called a code red at the news and pulled us in, so we weren't at the motel when they blew it up. Whoever the hell *they* are."

"Jesus Christ," he breathed. "Are you all right?"

Tess nodded. "Decker and Tracy were lucky, too. They got knocked around and Deck hit his head. But they're secure. Lindsey's going to go pick them up. We'll work out a way to get them back here."

"Tracy *Shapiro*?" he asked.

"She somehow figured out you were still alive. Deck thought it would be a good idea to contain her, so he was bringing her back here." Tess left the door wide open as she came to sit several feet away from him, leaning back, as he was, against the wall. She gestured toward the hallway. "If you're going to go, you should just do it now."

His gaze flicked from her face to the door to the row of monitors that nearly covered one entire wall of the room. She glanced up at it, too. There was movement on only a few of the screens—those showing the big main living room from three different utilitarian angles.

Jules was sitting on the couch, looking as if he'd been hit by an emotional bus. He'd taken the news about the three dead John Wilsons extremely hard. He'd barely said a word to anyone in the helicopter—instead retreating to that uncommunicative, stony-faced place where so many men in the SpecWar world went, rather than deal honestly with their anger and grief.

Robin was now sitting close to him, one arm around his shoulders, his other hand on Jules's knee, while Sam stood and Alyssa sat across from them. Alyssa was leaning forward, talking intently—the microphones weren't on, so they couldn't hear what she was saying. Whatever she was telling Jules, he just kept shaking his head. No.

"No one's going to stop you," Tess told Jimmy. "This isn't going to work—none of it will—if we have to hold you here against your will."

"I know that." He nodded, unable to hold her gaze, still watching the monitors, where Robin now put both arms around Jules, who made no move to embrace him in return—locked as he was in the tough-guy land of numbness. But then, in the solid warmth of Robin's arms, he crumpled.

Tess saw Jules's anguished expression for only a split second before he grabbed hold of Robin and buried his face against the taller man's neck and shoulder. But it was such an exact representation of what they all were feeling, she almost started to cry, too.

There was movement then from another monitor—Sam and Alyssa had gone into the hallway, heading purposefully toward the little room where Ash was fast asleep in his crib.

"I just . . . ," Jimmy started.

Tess waited. She always did. Because hope sprang eternal. And every now and then, like the other night when he talked about his dream, he actually threw her a crumb.

Except it wasn't like that. Not really. He didn't withhold intentionally. He was who he was, and Tess had known that going into this relationship. She knew from the start that it wasn't going to be easy, but she'd never dreamed it would be this hard. Still, it was what it was, too. And she?

She loved this man. Completely. She told him that now. It was so simple, those three little words, and so absolute—her voice clear in the stillness of the basement room.

Jimmy stood up, and for one split second she actually thought he was going to do it—he was going to walk out the door.

But he only moved over to the panel that controlled the monitors, where he turned off the switches that shut down the cameras in the living room, granting Jules and Robin privacy.

And there he stood, just staring at the other monitors, scanning the

ones that showed the quiet peacefulness of the night out along the driveway and down by the gate and the fence that surrounded this property.

"I think it's safe to assume," Tess told Jimmy, "that at this point? They
know you're alive. And we've *all* been marked for removal. Deck and me,
at least. Probably Jules, too."

He nodded without turning to face her, as the silence stretched on.

It was only when she mentally started gathering herself up—to go upstairs and put some food in her too-empty stomach, to rinse off the dirt
from the road—that Jimmy spoke.

"I can't imagine . . . how fucked up you've got to be," he said haltingly, with his back still to Tess, "to intentionally hit a kid."

At first his words didn't make sense. Her first thought was that Jimmy
had somehow hurt little Ashton in his struggle with Sam and Alyssa. But
then he turned to face her, and she realized from the look in his eyes that
he was using the verb *to hit* as a synonym for *to delete*. Which was the accepted Agency euphemism for *to kill*.

As if hitting a kid wasn't bad enough in the common-usage sense of
the word.

"The seven-year-old John Wilson," she realized. Was he really talking
to her about this?

Jimmy nodded. "You've got to be . . . beyond evil . . . A psychopath.
Two John Wilsons would have done the trick. Two would have caught our
attention. The third, the child . . . That was . . . beyond twisted. It was
sick."

"This isn't your fault," she said. "You understand that, right? If you
really had died, they would've gone after the doctor who signed your death
certificate. They would have found him and tortured him and killed him,
too."

"They know how to hurt me," he spoke over her. "Whoever they are,
they know things about me, about—" He stopped, but it wasn't to fall into
one of his excruciatingly long silences. It was to start over. "It was right
after I started working for the Agency. Before I was partnered with Decker.
Before I even met him. Way before 9/11. It was a black op and I was in the
field. Right place, right time—and I was tapped to delete a terrorist we'd
been hunting for years. The Merchant. You know him."

It wasn't a question, but Tess nodded. Everyone in the counterterrorist community knew of the man known as the Merchant. He'd been ruth-

less in the attacks he'd planned against the West. He was notorious for bombing schools and hospitals. He'd also expanded upon the concept of the human shield—always surrounding himself with children. He didn't climb into a truck or SUV unless it was packed with kids.

Sure, most of them were there because their parents were his supporters, but that didn't make the idea of using a surgical strike to take out his vehicle any less unpleasant.

Jimmy painfully, carefully lowered himself down again on the floor. "Our intel came from a reliable source. We knew the Merchant was in Turkey, in a little town in the mountains near Armenia. I was . . . nearby. In range. It was purely coincidental, but . . . I was in place."

Tess knew what was coming. "Oh, God, Jimmy."

He glanced at her only briefly, his face twisted in a grimace. "I fucking hate thinking about this shit. What's done is done, and I can't change it."

*Intentionally* hit a kid, he'd said. "Whatever you did," she told him, "it wasn't the same as—"

"It was worse," he told her, his eyes dark with self-loathing. "What I did was worse. I was set up to take the shot. I had maybe forty seconds while the target walked along a footbridge—it was the only way in or out of this church that was on an island, surrounded on all sides by a river. I knew he'd be wearing body armor, and I knew he'd have children with him, so I'm ready to take a head shot, which is hard enough for me under normal conditions."

Tess nodded. She knew that much about him, at least. The sniper rifle had never been Jimmy's weapon of choice.

His silence stretched on as he stared at the floor between his feet, his gaze unfocused, his mind both miles and years away. God only knew what he was really seeing, thinking, feeling. . . .

Tess tried to bring him back, tried to help. "I know you didn't kill him." The Merchant hadn't been taken out until August of 2000— ironically, it was Alyssa Locke who'd fired the sniper shot that had ended his miserable life.

Jimmy looked up at her, his mouth grim, his eyes rimmed in red. "No," he agreed. "I didn't. But I should've."

"What happened?" she asked, as gently as she could.

And this time, although he didn't answer right away, he held her gaze.

And when he finally spoke, his words surprised her. "Sam told me I should say. . . . that I should tell you . . . that this is . . . hard for me." He whispered the last words, but then laughed his disgust. "Christ, that's an understatement."

"You talked to Sam about. . ." She couldn't keep her disbelief from her voice. It seemed so unlikely, so unlike Jimmy to talk to anyone about anything.

But he nodded. "He talked to me. At me. He told me that . . . I'm going to. . ." He choked the words out. "Lose you—"

"He's wrong," she interrupted him. "Look at me, Jimmy. I'm right here. I'm *right* here."

He turned away—but not before she saw the sudden sheen of tears that filled his eyes.

Tess spoke through the lump that ached in her throat. "It's okay if you don't want to tell me. It really is. But if you think our enemy knows how to hurt you, then you need to tell *some*one. Jules or . . . Sam. It's okay, Jimmy, if it's easier for you to talk to Sam—"

"What are the odds?" he asked.

She didn't understand. "What do you mean?"

"You risk so much, for such crazy odds," he told her. "I look at that scar on your hand and . . . You reached for that gun, but . . . what were the odds that you'd get shot in the hand instead of in your head?"

He was talking about that awful day, just a few short months ago, that they'd both been shot when a squad of heavily armed men had surrounded them and the people they'd been guarding.

They'd been distracted right before the attack—arguing about Jimmy's refusal to talk to her, to ask for help. She'd told him that day that she could handle his silence, but what she couldn't deal with was his lies.

Yet at the same time, on a certain level—when she stepped back and looked at it objectively—she understood. When Jimmy had worked for the Agency, his job had been to lie, and to lie both well and often. His very life had depended upon it.

So it made sense that, even years after his split from that organization, he should still struggle to be forthcoming.

Tess had been telling him that, two months ago. She'd told him that she was willing to cut him some slack, but that this grace period was not going to last forever. There would come a time—and it was fast approaching—that his lying would end their relationship.

Which was when their attackers had opened fire, hitting first Tess and then Jimmy. His injury had been far worse than hers. And he was right. She *had* been willing to risk anything to save him. So she'd reached for a gun.

She now shook her head. "They shot me in the hand because they wanted hostages—"

"But you didn't know that at the time. You could've been killed. You *should* have been killed."

"I thought you were going to die." She brought it down to the bottom line. "You were bleeding, you were unconscious—"

"So you thought you might as well die, too?" He honestly didn't understand.

Tess pushed herself to her feet. "I thought that I could save you," she said. "I thought if I could just get that gun, then maybe—"

"A .22." He interrupted her. "It was a .22-caliber handgun, and you were surrounded by . . . Was it one or *two* dozen men with submachine guns? Damnit, I *know* you're not an idiot, Tess—"

"*We* were surrounded," she reminded him. "And you were dying. So, yes, I took what I thought was our only chance."

"A chance doesn't involve miraculous divine intervention," he pointed out. "It has better odds than one in, Christ, seven *trillion!*"

She knew that, yet she'd reached for that weapon anyway—and had gotten a bullet through her hand. Seconds later, she'd been knocked unconscious by a really ugly man who jammed the butt of his rifle against her head. Oh yeah, and then she was dragged off as a hostage.

Left for dead, Jimmy had roused and rallied and, even though he was bleeding badly, he'd tried to connect a severed phone line to call for help.

Not for himself, but for *her.*

"I wasn't going to let you die without a fight," she told him, her voice shaking as she moved closer, getting right in his face. "You know before . . . ? When I said that you should just walk out of here—if you're so intent on leaving? I was bluffing. If you'd actually gone, I would have grabbed you and tied you down. Because I am not giving up on you—on *us.* Not without a fight. To *hell* with the odds."

"If I go," he told her quietly, "it'll be because it's the only way—"

"No." Tess cut him off. "The *only* way we're going to get through this is together. All of us. You already tried to do this alone, and you failed, Jimmy. It's time to go after these sons of bitches as a team."

"And if we still fail . . . ?" he whispered.

"We won't." She was absolute. "Not a chance."

He took her hand, looking down at her scar, brushing it almost tenderly with his thumb. "Such crazy odds," he said again.

"Maybe not," Tess told him. "Alyssa's convinced we're closer to finding them than we think." She squeezed his hand, desperate for him to believe that this battle they were fighting wasn't hopeless. "They hurt us with the John Wilsons. And yes, it was sheer luck that got us out of that motel. But we're not going to let this second chance go to waste. We're going to figure out who these people are. And then we're going to get them."

"And live happily ever after," he said.

"Are you mocking me?"

"Never," he said. "No. It just seems like more crazy odds."

Tess searched his eyes, but all she could see was resignation and despair.

"Do you love me?" she asked him.

Jimmy didn't answer right away, and when he did, his voice was a whisper. "With all my heart."

"Then we fight," she told him. "Together. As a team. Regardless of the odds."

Jimmy pulled her close and kissed her. His mouth was so sweet, so familiar. As she melted into it, into him, she was aware of how long it had been since he'd kissed her like this—and since she'd kissed him back with equal passion.

God, it had been months since her desire for him hadn't been trumped by her worry over his injury and her frustration over his reticence and lies.

When he ended the kiss, the tears were back in his eyes.

"The Merchant," he said. "The botched assassination. Whoever it was who killed that kid yesterday? I'm certain that he knows about it."

"I'll tell Jules and Alyssa," Tess promised.

"There's more," Jimmy told her, but it was clear that he didn't know where or how to begin.

Tess tugged him over to the sofa, and he gingerly lowered himself down. She sat beside him, still holding his hand.

As his silence stretched on.

"I'll recap what I know," Tess suggested quietly. "Correct me if I'm wrong, okay?"

Jimmy nodded.

"You got called to Turkey where the Merchant was visiting a church on an island," she told him. "You were out there, alone, in position to take him out via sniper rifle, and you knew it was going to have to be done with a single shot to the head."

It was the help he'd needed, because he spoke. "I wasn't out there alone. I was connected by radio headset to a situation room, probably deep in the Agency's main HQ."

"What?" Tess was stunned. And indignant. That had made the op at least ten times more dangerous for him. Field operatives kept radio silence because radio waves could be intercepted—and traced.

"I was new," he said. "Untested. They still didn't trust me."

"Did they ever?" she asked.

"Yeah," Jimmy told her. "I think they did. Although trust is probably the wrong . . . Let's just say that they got to a point where they could bank on my patterns of behavior."

"Who was there?" she asked. "In the sitch room?"

"My contact was Doug Brendon," he said.

"Oh, my God," she said.

"Yup."

This was long before Brendon was appointed head of the entire Agency.

"Jack Finch was there," Jimmy reported. "And Doc Ryan, who ran the psych group. Oh, and the idiot who led support back then. What the fuck was his name?" He squinted to remember. "Matt Hallfield. What an asshole. We used to call him Matt-hole. He had his second in command with him—Russ Stafford."

"Why does that name sound familiar?" Tess squinted her brain, but nothing came forth.

Jimmy shook his head. "I don't think you ever met him. He never actually said much—although it couldn't have been easy to get a word in edgewise with Matt-hole around. I think Stafford left right around the same time that Hallfield died. Around 2001, I think. Yeah. It was right after 9/11. Although maybe he went into admin and we just never crossed paths again."

"That's easy enough to find out." The Agency's records were hacker-proof—unless the hacker had previously worked in the Agency's support division as a computer specialist, the way Tess had. "Ryan and Hallfield were just before my time," Tess told him. "But people were still talking about Hallfield."

Apparently the former head of the Agency's support team had had terminal cancer and committed suicide—which had really shaken up the entire organization. The tragedy had prompted then-director Finch to put even more emphasis on the mental health department, making psych evaluations mandatory, even for support staff.

"So Finch and Hallfield and Brendon and the others are talking in your ear," Tess prompted Jimmy, who'd fallen silent again.

"Yeah," he said. "They were watching images—both from satellites and from a minicam I was wired with." He met her eyes. "That was the last time I did a job like that. After that, I managed to break the equipment that they gave me when they sent me out. Eventually, they just stopped giving it to me. But I was too green at the time to . . . I should've. . ."

"So they're watching, too," Tess encouraged him, interrupting his recriminations, "as the Merchant comes out of the church."

Jimmy nodded. "He's got these kids surrounding him—no big surprise there. Their heads come up to his waist—which is strategic."

Tess knew what he meant. Body armor—at least the kind most readily available back in the early 1990s—ended roughly at the waist. Really paranoid people might also wear protective shorts, but at the time, it would've been a two-piece ensemble. A sniper trying to take out a body armor–protected target had a shot at getting the job done by aiming for the juncture at the waist, and hoping there was a muffin-top induced gap.

"There's another kid," Jimmy continued, closing his eyes, "maybe a little younger than the others. He's sitting on this bastard's shoulders, pretty much wrapped around his head. And I can't do it, Tess. I can't take the shot, not at that range, with the weapon that I had. Any bullet I fired would go through the man's head and blast a hole in that kid, too. So I reported that."

She braced for what she knew was coming.

"But the order comes down, direct from Finch. *Do it anyway*," Jimmy whispered. "And then Hallfield comes on. And he tells me it's okay. His team has identified the kid as being the son of Fariq al-Qasim, one of the Merchant's top henchmen. And I look through my scope at this little boy, and he's smiling and laughing, like he's enjoying the ride, and I . . . I can't do it. Time's running out, the target's got maybe ten more seconds before he reaches the safety of his car. And Brendon comes back on, and he's cursing and screaming—*Do it, God damn it!* And he tells me if I don't, all of those children will die, because he's going to order an airstrike on that vehicle. And I'm a fucking idiot, because I believed him. So I shoot, but I aim for the man's chest, because maybe he's not wearing any body armor at all, you know? I hit him—it's a clear shot, nowhere near any of the kids, and he falls, and I'm out of there. I'm gone."

But the Merchant *had* been wearing body armor. He'd survived the attack.

"The threat of the airstrike was just a bluff," Jimmy said quietly. "I didn't know it then, but no way were we going to risk photos of dead children in every newspaper in the country—and around the world. That was back when the press wasn't entirely run by corporations, when we still cared about shit like that, when public opinion polls mattered. So no harm, no foul—except because I took the shot instead of calling off the mission and fading into the mountains? The motherfucker knew that we'd tried for him. And two days later, he blows up Fariq al-Qasim's son's school bus, as if to say *Fuck you. See how strong I am, and how weak you are?* Thirty-one children died, including the one whose life I was unable— unwilling—to take."

"You aren't weak," Tess argued.

"The kid was going to die anyway," Jimmy told her. "If I could go back, have a do-over, I'd take the shot and kill the kid. Save thirty others. Plus all the other people that motherfucker killed in terrorist attacks between then and the time he really was deleted."

"You didn't know that back then," Tess told him. "You didn't see numbers. You saw a little boy."

"A seven-year-old boy," Jimmy said. "And now another seven-year-old boy is dead because of me."

"No." She was absolute. "He's dead because there are people out there who are evil, who know that if you're still alive, you have the power to bring them down. And I agree," she added. "Whoever killed the John Wilsons knew that you were unable to cross that line all those years ago and intentionally kill al-Qasim's son."

They also no doubt knew that Jimmy had agonized over the choice that he'd made, after he'd found out about that bus. Tess frowned. Wait a minute.

"Who handled your psych evaluations?" she asked.

Jimmy shook his head. "I didn't have psych evaluations back then," he told her. "Not really. I mean, I did on paper. Dr. Ryan signed off on the re-ports. But nobody wasted any time on me."

She stared at him. "You're not kidding, are you?"

He smiled tightly at her disbelief. "I think they liked me—exactly the way they'd found me. Why change perfection, you know?"

"So you never sat down with—"

"Nope. There was this one time, when an outside mental health orga-nization came in, and Ryan's office cribbed me the answers for the written test. Told me what to say in the interview, too. I kept it in my repertoire—kind of like Christmas carols. You dust 'em off and sing a rousing chorus once a year."

"That's not the way it's supposed to work. Finch and Brendon—"

"Weren't interested in my mental health," Jimmy finished for her. "I don't think they expected me to live long enough to need it. I don't think they *wanted* me to live long enough to. . . ."

"Do you think they're behind—"

"Finch is dead," he told her. "And Brendon . . . He just wasn't that smart."

"He was smart enough to become head of the entire Agency."

"He was a political appointee," Jimmy pointed out.

Right. "What happened to Dr. Ryan?" Tess asked. "Didn't he have a heart attack, right in his office? He didn't come back from that, did he?"

"No. He died, I don't know, maybe a few months later?"

"When was that?" she asked.

Jimmy shook his head. "Honestly? I tried to stay as far from Ryan's de-partment as possible."

It wouldn't be hard to find out that date. "It just seems weird," she said, "that almost everyone in a leadership position in that situation room is now dead."

"I have no clue what happened to Russ Stafford."

"I wonder if he went down into the black ops sector."

"No." Jimmy dismissed the idea. "I would have seen him there."

Tess had to look away, because that one little sentence held so much information. Jimmy had performed so many black ops for the Agency, he'd known everyone in black ops support.

"I think," she said carefully, "that you should make a list of everyone you came into contact with at the Agency. And as many as you can remember of the ops that you performed."

"I've done that," he said. "I gave it to Cassidy."

"You already . . . wow." She was surprised. "You did it while I was . . . in San Diego?"

Something flickered in his eyes, and he opened his mouth, and she knew with a heart-aching sense of dread that the next thing he said to her was going to be a lie. But then he closed his eyes and exhaled, hard, and said, "Please don't be mad. But I made the lists back when I was in the hospital."

"What?" she said. "When?"

"Whenever you went to shower, or get coffee," he admitted, an apology in his eyes.

"I'm not mad," she said. And she wasn't. The wobble in her voice was from her relief—and disbelief—that he'd actually told her the truth. "I'm a little confused. You could barely hold a pen. I could've helped."

"I didn't want you to," he said quietly. "I didn't want you to see it. The ops list. I didn't want. . ." He shook his head. "I told Cassidy that I thought it would upset you, but the truth is, I didn't want you to find out all the really awful shit I've done."

"I've seen your Agency files," she reminded him.

"This is different. Black ops . . ."

"Jimmy." She squeezed the words out past her heart, which was again lodged securely in her throat. "You know me better than that."

"But I could see it," he confessed, "in Cassidy's eyes. He looked at the list, and then he looked at me differently." He closed his eyes and rubbed his forehead, as if he had a terrible headache. "I don't want you to look at me like that."

"I won't."

"You might."

"But if I don't see the list," she gently pointed out, "won't you always wonder?"

Jimmy looked at her then. "I'd rather wonder with you, than know without you."

"You're going to have to trust me," Tess told him, and there they sat.

"Is it okay," he finally asked, "if I show you the list in the morning?"

Tess nodded. "Yeah." It had been a long day—for both of them. And if Jimmy were going to continue to heal, he needed to get his rest. She, however, still had work to do.

"I love you," she reminded him as she got to her feet, as she held out a hand to help him up, too. "I'm not going to love you any less tomorrow."

Jimmy nodded, but she could tell from his eyes that, although he desperately wanted to, he didn't believe her.


"Sorry it's not a scone."

Decker stood in Sam Starrett's kitchen, on legs that were still way too unsteady, staring at Tracy Shapiro, who'd just offered him a cookie.

No, *offer* was too gentle a word. She was forcing the fucking thing on him. And damn it, he watched himself reach out and take it from her hand. His fingers brushed against hers by accident—or maybe not—and he wanted . . .

He wanted to kiss her again, and not stop this time. He wanted to back her up against the cabinets and lift her onto the counter and spread her long, gorgeous legs. He wasn't quite tall enough, and he'd have to stand on his toes as he pushed himself inside of her, as he made her come.

Himself, too. This wasn't complete altruism he was feeling here.

Feeling.

Yeah.

She was right when she'd said that she was making him feel something other than his usual misery. He'd been far from miserable while he was kissing her.

It was only afterwards that he'd been fully submerged in a steaming pit of despair.

But Jesus, she was beautiful, even with her hair a mess and her face smudged with dirt and blood. With her classically beautiful, almost perfectly proportioned features, with those big expressive eyes and her flaw-

lessly perfect skin, she was a knockout—and that was before looking south-
ward at her stammer-inducing, brain-freezing, incredibly female curves.
Her breast had nearly overflowed his hand—and he had big hands.

He'd also liked the force with which she'd kissed him back—as if she'd
seen his bet and raised him the limit, as if she were ready and willing to es-
calate from that not-very-gentle kiss to full body-slamming, heart-
stoppingly rough-and-tumble sex in a single heartbeat.

The woman had no fear—which was a real problem, since Deck too
often scared the shit out of himself. If she didn't stop him, then who the
hell would?

And the really stupid thing? It was that if his jeans hadn't already been
down around his knees, he wouldn't have stopped kissing her. Which
would have ultimately resulted in his jeans *getting* pulled down to his
knees as she straddled him and he slammed himself inside of her.

Yeah, if he hadn't gotten injured and bled all over his clothes, she'd be
fucking him blind right now, on the cold concrete floor of their co-
workers' garage.

So, no. He didn't want a goddamned cookie.

He put it down on the kitchen counter, and Tracy opened her mouth
to protest, of course.

Decker spoke over her. "You need to wash out that elbow," he told
her—and she bent her arm and tried to see it, which never worked, but
gave him a better look at the scrape. It was a real mess, with ground-in dirt
that would hurt like a bitch to clean. "Why don't you shower, and after
you're dressed, I'll help you with it."

"You've got a scrape on your back that's way worse than this," she
countered.

"I doubt it," he said. His shoulders felt rug-burned and raw, true, but
there'd be no pieces of dirt to pick from his skin because his shirt was in-
tact. He didn't have to see it to know that.

Tracy, of course, was indignant. "It is," she informed him. "It's—"

"Why," he interrupted her, "is everything always an argument or a
contest with you?"

She made a sound of exasperation and total disgust, and he realized
he should have kept a count of how many times, today alone, he'd pro-
voked that particular noise from her. It was probably well into double dig-
its.

"Since when is informing you of a fact an argument?" she asked. "As for contest? You win. Okay? I concede any and all contests. Congratulations—you're the biggest idiot in the room."

She pushed her hair back from her face, and left behind a streak of soot above her eyebrow.

*Soot?*

Jesus.

He'd had no idea they'd been that close to the smoke and flames from the explosion, and he had to hang on to the counter as relief flooded him again. He was incredibly lucky that they weren't both dead. Doubly lucky, considering someone had been lying in wait for them with a sniper rifle.

"Are you all right?" Concern softened Tracy's eyes as she reached for him. But she didn't make contact—she didn't let herself.

Which was simultaneously a blessing and a shame.

"I'm fine," he said.

His nausea had evened out quite a bit once they'd gotten inside the house. He was feeling less as if he were going to hurl any second— although now that the ringing in his ears was fading and the dizziness was departing, he felt every stinging scrape and battered bruise. His arm was throbbing in unison with his heartbeat. Among other things.

"I really don't want to leave you alone out here," she said. "Why don't we find the bathroom. You can shower while I'm in there. The bathroom," she added quickly. "Not the shower. You get to shower alone. Unless you need help . . ."

Her words inspired images of her head tipped back as water cascaded down her face, her throat, her magnificent breasts as she *helped* him as only a naked woman in his shower could. . . .

"Not *that* kind of help," she chastised him. "Even I'm not pathetic enough to suggest that we . . . God."

"I knew what you meant," he defended himself. "You're there if I fall down. Which I'm not going to do."

"If you knew what I meant, then you shouldn't have been thinking—"

"You can't possibly know what I was thinking," he interrupted.

Tracy exhaled her disgust. "Oh, please. You're a man. What is that statistic? Men think about sex something like four thousand times a minute. You were thinking it. I could see that you were thinking it."

"Is four thousand times a minute even possible—"

"It's the equivalent of constantly," Tracy shot back. "Even for someone who's as much of a prude as you are."

"I'm a prude," he repeated. "Yet I think about sex constantly?"

"That's usually how it works," she told him. "You're so bottled up, your head's going to explode."

"Your analysis of me"—he was incredulous—"comes from what? The fact that I haven't tried to fuck you by now?"

She flinched at his harshness, but didn't back down. "No," she retorted, and took a breath, about to launch into what was sure to be an infuriating counterattack.

"It's called restraint," he shot at her before she could begin. "You should try it sometime."

It made her sputter, and say, "I had no idea restraint was a synonym for cowardice."

Oh, no. No.

"You know, *you* kissed me," she continued.

"You took off my pants." The words came out of his mouth before he could stop. He knew, damn well, that her intent hadn't been at all salacious.

But she blushed, even as she defended herself. "To make sure you weren't going to die! Do me a favor? If I'm ever lying on the ground, unconscious and covered in blood? Undress me. I'd rather not die simply to protect your pious and distorted sense of decorum."

"I won't have to undress you," he told her. "You barely wear any clothes as it is."

"Oh!" she said. "My! God! You just proved my point. You sound like my grandfather! My pants are wrapped around your wounded arm—in case you didn't notice."

"I'm not talking about your lack of pants," he pointed out, aware as hell that he, too, wasn't wearing any. "I'm talking about. . ."

"The way I dress when I've got pants on," she finished for him. "I know. Which makes you a misogynist as well as a prude. *Women didn't dress that way when your Oma was young.* No, Opa, they did. Oma just didn't have any boobs after spending four years on rations in London—and giving most of her share of the food to Uncle Paul."

"The jeans you were wearing last night were not your grandmother's." Why was he arguing? There was no way he could win this.

"Why can't you just admit that you're hot for me, and stop blaming me for it, like it's something I intentionally did—like I chose to be born with big-boob genes. It's not like I've been doing stripper aerobics or . . . or pole dancing in front of you. Last time I looked in the mirror, the neckline of my shirt wasn't cut down to my navel. I'm covered completely. Or maybe you think because I actually have breasts instead of mosquito-bite boobs like the women you see on TV, I should wear a burka."

"I don't think you should wear a burka," he said, reeling slightly from the idea of Tracy doing stripper aerobics. Talk about incentive to go to the gym. "You're overreacting."

"No." She got in his face. "Overreacting is what jerk men do if women don't wear a bra that's padded enough. Forget comfort. I have to make sure my bra doesn't let even the slightest hint of nipple show—"

Nipple. She actually said the word *nipple*, and Decker had to work to keep his gaze from moving below her neck. He found himself, instead, watching her mouth.

"—because some stupid man will think I'm giving him some kind of body-language green light," she continued, "when in truth I'm just cold."

The lipstick she'd had on earlier was gone. It was likely that he'd kissed it off her, but the truth was, she didn't need it. Her lips were smooth and pink and full.

"You *so* want to kiss me again," she accused him.

Deck jerked his gaze back up to her eyes, and for a moment, they stood there in silence, just looking at each other. He didn't breathe—he couldn't breathe.

He could see his desire reflected in her beautiful eyes. It was more than just sexual attraction and heat, it was a wistful longing for something more, an awareness that their seemingly constant bickering—and his too-harsh words—kept them both from having to acknowledge the truth. Which was that he liked her—more with each passing hour.

More, even, because she'd called him on the fact that he wanted, again, to kiss her.

So he answered honestly. "Yes. I do. But I won't. Again, it's called restraint."

He took advantage of the fact that he'd surprised her with the truth, and beat a retreat from the kitchen. It was definitely time to put even more space between them, so he headed down the hall, looking for the god-damn bathroom.

But Tracy followed him—the arms of that ridiculous yellow rain slicker that she'd tied around her waist flapping about the tops of her thighs. "Oh, good," she said. "Run away. You just proved my point."

The first bathroom he found was only a half—no shower—so he kept going, taking the stairs to the second floor, jarring his injured arm with each stupid step.

Tracy, meanwhile, felt the need to continue talking at him. "I'm going to say it again: What you call restraint is *cowardice*. And it's not just sex you run from, in case you haven't noticed. It's intimacy."

And there was the bathroom, on the right, door open, tile floor, large walk-in shower stall.

"I've seen you run away from conversations with Jimmy Nash," Tracy continued "He's supposed to be your best friend—"

"Men don't have best friends," Decker said, as he flipped on the light and pulled back the shower curtain with a *screeee*. "Only little girls do." As the words left his mouth, he knew they would serve to incite her further—which was probably why he'd said it.

"Oh," she said, attitude practically steaming from her ears as he turned on the water to let it heat. "Nice. But wrong. Again. *People* have friends—and some of those friends become special. You can mock it all you want, but Nash loves you. And whether you man up to it or not, I *know* that you love him. You're willing to die for him. Would it really kill you to have a meaningful conversation with him?"

A linen closet held a stack of neatly folded towels. He took out two, putting them on the counter of the sink before turning back to Tracy. "You know nothing about my friendship with Nash."

"I've known you both for years now," she countered, hands on her hips. "I know enough."

"He's been 'dead' for two months," Decker found himself responding, despite the fact that he knew—*knew*—that engaging in this conversation wasn't going to lead to anything good. "You have no idea how many or what kind of conversations I've had with him—"

"I would bet a million dollars," Tracy proclaimed, "that not one of those conversations started with you going, *How are you feeling about this being-dead thing? Or I'm freaked out by having to put my hands all over your fiancée, and it's particularly difficult to deal with, since Sophia's—"*

"Jesus," Decker said, looking toward the ceiling.

"*—hooked up with Dave.*"

Something snapped. He felt it go, in his forehead, right over his left eye. "I am *not* in love with her," he said. "I have never *been* in love with her. I had sex with her. One time. A hundred fucking years ago, on the other side of the world. It was abusive. And wrong. She was afraid of me, and I knew it, and I let her go down on me because I told myself that she had information I needed, and that it was life or death that I find out what she knew, but what I really wanted was a blow job, and it didn't fucking matter whose mouth it was. Is that all right with you?"

Tracy stood there—he'd silenced her at last—as the water finally turned hot and started steaming up the bathroom mirror.

But then she blinked. And said, "Men turn into idiots when sex is involved. I mean, how was she supposed to give you any information when she's using her mouth to—"

"Why is it you always feel compelled to comment?" Decker asked, his voice actually cracking. "I didn't say, *She gave me a blow job, please discuss.*"

"Well, what did you *think* I would do after you tell me something like that?" Tracy looked at him as if he were mentally defective. "Run away? Or faint, like . . . like an old lady? A *blow job! Oh, no!* I've met a lot of men in my life, Sparky, and I'm pretty certain nearly all of them have, at one time or another, been the recipient of a blow job, given to them by a person with whom they didn't end up living happily ever after. Two of them I'm absolutely certain about, having participated in the blow job in question. Although I think I prefer the phrase *hummer.* It sounds more fun—less like work. Blow *job*, you know."

Decker just stared at her.

"I was right," she told him. "You *are* a total prude. Is this *really* what you've been making such a big deal about for *all* these *years*?"

He didn't answer her—he couldn't.

And being Tracy, she couldn't shut up. "How do you reconcile your boatloads of guilt with the fact that Sophia has seemed—for *years*—to be desperate to get with you again? You know, I know her. Not well, but well enough. She's not crazy. Okay, she's maybe a *little* damaged, but really, who isn't?"

And still he just stood there, with the water pounding down behind him, gurgling down the shower's drain. Tracy took a tentative step closer, and he couldn't back away—there was nowhere to go in the little room. Besides, the anger in her eyes had changed to something softer and warmer. Compassion. And genuine concern.

"Is your guilt from the fact that you liked it?" she asked. "You should give yourself a break. You were single. She was willing and, rumor has it, it *can* feel pretty good."

Willing? "You have no idea what Sophia's been through."

"I kinda do," Tracy said. "She's talked to me about the months that she was a prisoner in Padsha Bashir's palace. I've seen her scars. She's let it go, she's moved on. You know, I actually think that one of the hardest things for her has been the fact that *you* haven't—let it go."

"So, what are you saying?" Decker asked, his voice rough, even to his own ears. "I should transform myself into someone I'm not? I should change who I am and what I feel—just to make Sophia's life easier? Jesus, if I wasn't going to do it for Em—"

"No," she countered. "Letting go isn't the same as—"

"I don't love Sophia," he said again. "I didn't even like her—not at first. But, yes, I really liked the sex. Way too much, considering that she tried to kill me while she—"

He shut his mouth on the truth that had almost escaped—the fact that he had never climaxed the way he had that night long ago, not before and certainly not after.

And there they stood, in that bathroom, his half-confession sitting there, awkwardly, between them. He could feel his face heat with his embarrassment, and he didn't dare look into Tracy's eyes. He didn't want to see the growing awareness as she realized exactly what he'd just told her.

And he had told her—even though he'd stopped himself. But Tracy was extremely smart. She was going to figure it out.

"Just wait outside," he said quietly. "Please. I'll shower first—"

"There's nothing wrong with rough sex," she said. "You know that, right? I've only kissed you once, and I'm pretty sure that if we were going to get it on? You'd eat me alive. I mean, as opposed to slowly licking me all over with the very tip of your tongue. Which . . . could really work, too."

Decker laughed. At least he meant to laugh, but it came out as more of an "Unh." As if someone had punched him in the stomach and air escaped.

"It makes sense—sort of—that you would feel an . . . elevated sense of . . . urgency from a . . . perceived threat," she told him.

"It wasn't *perceived*," he found himself telling her. "She tried to shoot me."

"*While* she was . . . ?" Tracy ingested that information. "And you . . . got off on it. Okay, that's . . . maybe a little weird. But, hey. Only a little. Normal is a very wide spectrum. And maybe it wasn't the threat of violence that revved you up. Maybe it was Sophia."

"I hardly knew her, and I didn't trust her," Decker pointed out.

"As obviously you shouldn't have," Tracy agreed. "But she's very pretty."

"It wasn't the *threat* of violence. It *was* violence."

"The violence toward *you*, you mean, right? I mean, you're not, like, into—"

"Yes," he said. "Violence toward me. Jesus. I'm not *that* fucked up. Please, just let me take a shower—"

"So maybe your ultimate perfect girlfriend is a cross between a librarian and Kato from *The Pink Panther*," Tracy surmised. "Out in public, she's all buttoned-to-the-neck and proper. But at home, she's jumping out at you, dressed like a dominatrix in leather and stilettos, shaking out her hair and taking off her glasses as she takes you to the ground and pins you down and. . ."

Jesus.

"That's actually kind of hot," she mused.

She was serious. The heat she was speaking of was evident in her eyes and time hung, for a very odd moment, as he looked back at her. He knew she was thinking about being dressed all in leather and pinning him to the floor, her arm jammed up under his chin, pressure on his throat, as she unfastened his pants with her other hand and . . .

Yeah. It was outrageously hot. He could overpower her in a heartbeat—but he wouldn't.

He looked away first.

"I'm thinking Emily might've had a problem with the role-playing, though," Tracy added. "I'm thinking she leaned a little too much—in reality—toward the stereotypical-librarian end of the fantasy. Was this, maybe, one of the things she wanted to change about you?"

Decker shook his head. "I'm not talking about her—or about this."

She ignored him and kept right on talking about it. "There's nothing wrong with you," she told him. "Everyone's into *something*. These days bondage and discipline is practically mainstream."

"I'm not into—" Decker stopped himself. "Just because I . . ." He shook his head. "I've never . . ."

"Maybe you should," she said. "You know. Experiment."

He looked at her.

She looked back.

He could picture her, dressed only in high heels, as she lit, one by one, all of the candles in her bedroom, as he lay naked and prone on her bed, his hands tied to her bed frame with silk scarves.

"I'm not having sex with you," Decker said again, but this time the words seemed less forceful and certain. This time they rang with doubt. Because, Jesus. Tracy knew the truth—or at least part of it—and she wasn't running away. "You work for me."

"No, actually, I work for Tom Paoletti."

"But you take orders from me, too."

"So what? Sam takes orders from Alyssa. Big deal. Besides, it sounds like what you want is someone to *give* you orders. I think I might be really good at that."

Holy shit.

And Jesus, were they really talking about this? Some of what he'd just told Tracy were things he'd never admitted before, not to anyone. He'd barely even admitted them to himself.

"It makes sense now," she told him, and the electric heat in her eyes changed to the more even warmth of compassion, "that you would keep your distance from Sophia. She probably doesn't share many of those kinds of fantasies. And even if she once did, she probably doesn't anymore. And if you did let yourself fall in love with her? You'd be right back where you were with Emily. Trying to be someone that you're not. Like you said—having to be so careful—"

"Why don't you shower first," Decker said. She blocked his path to the door, but he moved toward her, intending to lift her, bodily, out of his way, if need be.

But she backed out into the hall with him, talking as she went. "And that's not even taking into consideration the fact that whenever you're with her, you probably feel like a deviant, even though everything she endured is apples to your oranges. Sophia *wasn't* a willing participant. You're looking for someone who is."

She stopped moving, so he did, too, and they just stood there.

"I'm not looking for anyone," Deck told her, but God, he was lying. And when she started moving toward him, try as he might, he couldn't back away from her.

So he stayed where he was as she got closer. And closer.

"There's nothing wrong with you," Tracy said again. "Except for the fact that your inner prude has been shouting at you for years, telling you that you're screwed up. You've got to bring the logical part of your brain into the mix. Because how can there be a right or a wrong way to have sex? I mean, psycho-killers aside, there's just *not*. The only question that you need to be worried about is *Honey, do you like it when I do that?* If the answer's yes, game on."

# CHAPTER
# TWELVE

S ophia sat on the floor in the bathroom at the hotel and tried not to cry.

"Soph?" Dave knocked softly on the door. "Can I come in?"

"It's unlocked," she called, swiftly wiping her eyes and running both hands down her face.

He opened the door and poked his head in first. "You all right?"

"Yeah," she said. "I'm feeling much better."

"You think it was something you ate?"

She just shook her head, because she didn't know what to say or how to say it.

"Next time, please, don't shut me out," he said.

"I'm sorry," Sophia said. "I just needed . . . a little space."

When they'd first arrived at the hotel and she'd rushed into this bathroom, she'd actually been surprised that Dave had left her alone, despite her insistence.

He'd used the time, though, to change out of his bloodstained shirt and into one of his faded T-shirts, which was good. Bloodstains made her queasy during the best of times.

She was also glad he'd changed because with his T-shirt, jeans, and sneakers, with his hair a mess from running his hands through it, he looked like the Dave she'd known for years—like a guy who worked in tech support. A com-spesh, or even a hardware dweeb. Or maybe a technical writer—hammering out his first angst-filled novel during his lunches and coffee breaks.

He certainly didn't look like a super-spy compatriot of 007's.

"I don't know what I'm most upset about," she told him now as he came all the way into the room. "The fact that you went to Kazabek, or the fact that you thought going there was no big deal. I guess when it's said and done, though, it's pretty much the same thing."

Dave leaned back out into the hotel suite and said, "I'm sorry, sir. I know this is an imposition, but could I ask you and Karmody to sit out in the hall?"

There was a murmur of voices, after which Dave said, "Thank you, sir," and then she heard the sound of the heavy hotel room door closing.

He turned back to her, closing the bathroom door behind him even though he'd emptied out their hotel suite. "I'm sorry I upset you," he said as he sat near her, on the edge of the bathtub. He lowered himself down carefully, gingerly, and she knew he wasn't taking the painkillers the doctor had prescribed for him.

"But you're not sorry that you went," she inferred.

"No," he said quietly. "I'm not. Tom's job is to be overly cautious, and rightly so, but he wasn't in Kazabek with me, so he doesn't know—"

"I'm aware of that, yes," she said. "That you went in there alone—"

"I'm good at what I do," he tried to reassure her. "I know when I've been compromised, and I wasn't. There are now four people on this planet who know where I was last week, and they're all right here, in this hotel. I went in using a different name, a completely different identity."

"And the people you talked to, while you were there . . . ? Didn't they know you?"

"No."

She sat there for a moment, ingesting that information before she asked, "Who, exactly, did you talk to?"

"Does it really matter?" he countered.

Did it? Probably not. Still . . . "Was it anyone I know?"

"Maybe, but probably not. I didn't get any names, but they were all servants—women—who worked in Bashir's palace," he said quietly, "during the time you were held prisoner there. They did laundry and . . . cleaning. They washed the floors and . . . other things."

Sophia had to look away from him. Her stomach was churning again, even though it was empty. It had to be empty—she'd thrown up so much already, both on the side of the road and here in this bathroom, too.

"What did they tell you?" she asked.

He was silent for so long, she finally looked up. And she found him still watching her, his elbows on his knees, hands loosely clasped together.

God, how many times had he sat exactly like that as they'd talked—sometimes well into the night. This man was her best friend, and had been for years. Good old reliable Dave, always there when she'd needed a shoulder to cry on. Or someone to have sex with after years of zero intimate contact due to terrible prior emotional and physical trauma.

Sophia had always loved Dave's smile, but he wasn't smiling now. His mouth was tight and the muscle was jumping on the side of his jaw. The hardness in his eyes and on his face—the edge that she'd seen repeatedly since he'd been knifed—was back. And she realized it wasn't so much an air of danger as it was determination and self-confidence—or perhaps more correctly, a *lack* of his previous uncertainty and self-doubt.

For years, she hadn't thought of him as being particularly attractive, but he was. It was true, he wasn't the most handsome man on the planet—his face was a little too long, the bags under his eyes too pronounced, making him look, always, just a little bit sad. But the bright intelligence and gleam of humor that shone in his eyes was tremendously appealing—although there wasn't much humor there now, as he finally answered her.

"Everything," he whispered. "They told me everything, Soph. So now you don't have to. Because now I know."

She laughed. It was that or start to cry. "And that's why you risked your life," she said again. "To find out something that I could have told you—that I *would* have told you, if you'd asked? *What happened, Sophia, after that bastard killed your husband and claimed possession of you and everything you owned? What exactly did he do to make the experience even more of a nightmare?* I would have told you *everything.* But no. You had to go to *Kazabek* and maybe get yourself killed."

"I've been back there," he said. "Dozens of times since—"

"Oh!" she cut him off. "God! Is that supposed to make it okay?"

"It is what it is," Dave pointed out. "It's not like you didn't know." He faltered. "You *did* know, didn't you? That I've gone there on assignment?"

And there they sat, staring at each other, as Sophia realized the problem. *Her* problem—because it was entirely hers. Her eyes ached with a renewed rush of unshed tears, and she fought to keep them from falling.

"No," she said. "Actually, I didn't."

"Jesus." Dave was aghast. "Really? I mean, I know I didn't talk about
it. Not with you, because, you know, Kazabek. Not your favorite place in
the world, but . . . I thought. . ." He shook his head. "I'm so sorry. I
didn't—"

"You're not supposed to go to Kazabek," she interrupted him. "You're
also not supposed to get stabbed in a parking lot."

"Well, yeah," he said. "That's kind of a given, across the board."

"No," she said. "*You're* not. You. Dave."

It was clear that he didn't understand.

"It's my fault," Sophia told him. "Entirely. So don't you dare apologize
again. I don't know what I was thinking, but I *was* thinking it—"

"Thinking?" he repeated. "Soph, you lost me."

She tried to explain. "Like, I wanted the biggest excitement in our
lives to come from . . . from . . . deciding what color tile to use when we
re-do the bathroom. From, I don't know, having the toilet clog. From out-
smarting the coyotes to keep them out of the trash. I didn't want to be
here—worrying if you're going to get an infection from being *stabbed*—let
alone worrying about who's going to stab you next. Or shoot you.
Or . . . God only knows what they're going to do next! I didn't realize I was
signing on for that."

He misunderstood. "I know. And I should have told you more extensively about the situation with Anise—"

"This isn't about Anise freakin' Turiano!" She cut him off. "It's about
who you really are. *What* you really are. Please, *please* don't get me wrong,
I'm not saying that you deceived me, because you didn't. *I'm* the one who
lied. To myself. About you. Because you're not the man I thought you
were." Dear Lord, she was completely messing this up, and that last bit in
particular had come out totally wrong. "The man I thought I knew."

That wasn't right, either. And Dave couldn't have looked more devastated and wounded if she'd taken out a gun and shot him point-blank.

"How can you say something like that?" he whispered, before she
could even attempt to try again, "and then claim it's not about Anise?"

"It's not," she said, desperate now to explain that which she hadn't even completely figured out for herself. Her head was filled with so much noise, so much chaos, and her stomach churned and boiled. "What I *meant* was . . ." She stopped for a moment, trying to organize her thoughts, to find the right words. "When we first got together—" She defined it more specifically: "When we became lovers, it was because I wanted to be with the man I had lunch with for all those years. The . . . the *Dave* who has to watch his weight and forgets to get his hair cut. The Dave who would rather talk to me on the phone for hours in his Las Vegas hotel room than hit the tables in the casino. I didn't want trips to Kazabek, and death threats and knife wounds. I didn't want James Bond. I wanted . . . to feel safe. I wanted a relationship with someone who's . . . I don't know . . ."

"Boring?" He supplied the word.

"No," Sophia said. "Well, *yes*, but in a *good* way. Normal, Dave. I wanted *normal*."

And great. Her explanation had made him feel even worse.

"And in a company filled with exceptional men," he said quietly, "I guess I fit that bill. Wow. Okay. That answers a lot of questions, like what exactly is someone like you doing with a guy like me."

"No," she said. "Don't you see? I thought you *were* the exception."

He didn't say it, but she knew what he was thinking. He was the exception—by being, in her eyes, unexceptional.

"For the record, I'm hardly James Bond."

"I'm sorry," she said sharply. "Did I misunderstand you just a few minutes ago when you reassured me that your going to Kazabek was no big thing and—"

"So what does this mean?" It was typical of Dave, to bulldoze right to the bottom line. His eyes were dark with his hurt, and with something else, too. Anger. "You don't want James Bond, and apparently you feel I'm enough like James Bond to warrant this discussion, so . . . What are saying, Soph?"

"I don't know," she said.

"Are you breaking up with me?" he asked. "Because. . ." He struggled to compose himself, as he nodded his head. "That's probably a good idea."

"No," she said, closing her eyes. "That's not—"

"If these people are after me, then—"

"I'm just trying to be honest with you, while I wrap my head around the reality, which is different from what I'd imagined—"

"It's better if we're not together," Dave said.

"I *don't* want to break *up*!" she said. "I love you!"

"Do you?" he asked quietly.

"Yes." God, she was going to be sick again. She had to close her eyes and grit her teeth.

"Because it sounds like you're not sure you really know me. It sounds like you think I'm a little too much like Decker, and if you're going to be with a Decker, you might as well go for the real one—"

"Oh, my God!" she said. "How could someone so smart be so *stupid*? This has nothing to do with Decker and even if it did? He's made it very clear that he doesn't want me!"

Oh, wrong, wrong, *wrong* thing to say, as true a statement as it was.

"I'm sorry." She said it right away, but it was too late. The damage was done.

Dave was already standing up. "Hokay," he said. "That's great."

"Dave, please, wait. I'm *so* sorry—"

"No," he said. "I think we better end this conversation before . . . I'm exhausted. I didn't sleep on the plane and you're ill, and we're clearly not—"

"I don't want Decker," she told him as the tears she could no longer hold back slid down her face. "I want you."

"Lunch me," he reminded her. "Fat me. *Boring* me. I get it, Soph. I do. But I'm not the man you thought I was, and frankly? This current version of me is not sure how to give you what you want. So I'm going to go for what *I* want. Which is you, safe, while I find and neutralize the threat. If that's too James Bond for you? So be it." He opened the door, but then, instead of walking out, he came back over to her, in a move that was classic Dave. "Come on. Let's get you into bed. You'll be more comfortable. I'll move the trash can close, in case you need to. . ." He was so gentle, his hands so warm as he helped her to her feet, helped her out of the bathroom and over to the bed. "I'll sleep out on the couch."

"You don't have to—"

"Yeah, I do," he said, then used the words she'd said to him earlier. "I, uh, need some space, too."

He was lying. Sophia knew that what he really needed was the ability to wake up before she did, and leave—on some crazy mission that wouldn't just neutralize the threat but would probably get himself neutralized as well.

It was now or quite possibly never—and he had to know before he left. So as he took most of the throw pillows off the big bed, as he pulled back the covers so she could climb in, Sophia blurted it out with absolutely no lead-in, no setup, no warning. "I need to tell you that . . . I'm pretty sure I'm pregnant."

Even after their hellish day, Tracy Shapiro still smelled incredibly good.

Decker stood there, in the hall of Sam and Alyssa's house, as she got closer. And closer.

She spoke, firmly, decisively, clearly, concisely. "Go into the bathroom, take off your clothes, and get into the shower."

"This is hardly the time or place—"

"I'm willing to bet that with you, it's *never* the time or place," she countered, "which makes here and now as good as any. I'll get my computer. And my phone. We'll hear if Jules or Alyssa contacts us. Until then, all we're doing is waiting. And getting cleaned up. So go on. Get cleaned up. Leave the door open."

"I'm not—"

"I *didn't* say you could talk."

When he opened his mouth to speak again, she reached between them—they were standing so close she didn't have to reach too far. She grabbed his entire set of equipment, with a grip that wasn't exactly gentle, but wasn't exactly not. Regardless, he nearly went through the ceiling.

Jesus! He just managed to bite back the word as he reached down and caught her wrist.

But Tracy said, just as sharply, "And I *certainly* didn't say you could touch me."

It was the moment of truth—he knew it as well as she did. Whatever was going to happen—or not happen—depended upon what he said or did next.

But then she stood on her toes and kissed him—just a brief, delicate flutter of her soft lips against his. "Shhh," she whispered. "It's okay."

So he let go of her wrist and just stood there, silently, hands at his sides, breathing hard, as her tear-his-balls-off grip turned into something else, something far more like a caress, yet still absolutely possessive. He closed his eyes as she touched him, cupped him, stroked him.

"Do you like this?" she whispered, and when he opened his eyes to look at her, he saw that she was smiling just a little—the corners of her mouth quirking up. Probably because she'd just asked him a question, yet had told him not to speak.

He nodded—one short jerk of his head—as he held her gaze.

"Me too," she murmured. "Go figure. So go ahead—into the bathroom. Take off your clothes and get into the shower."

Decker hesitated, because it meant he'd have to pull away from her. And his response to her question—did he like this?—had been an understatement. *Like* was hardly the right word. It was possible he'd never before been this overwhelmingly hard for anyone—not in his entire life.

"Do it. Now," Tracy said in that take-no-shit, commanding-officer tone, and he moved, pulling free from her grasp, which left him feeling cold and almost bereft.

But she was right behind him, and he could feel her watching him from the doorway as he unfastened the makeshift bandage around his arm and shrugged out of his overshirt. His shoulder holster and sidearm hit the floor with a thud as he wasn't quite careful enough with it, in his haste to pull off his T-shirt.

The pain as he raised his arm made his eyes water, but he didn't give a shit. He just pushed it aside—both the pain and his analysis of whether or not it heightened his completely fucked-up sense of pleasure. At other times, he would've been way too far inside of his own head, but not now.

He was completely present, here in this little room, and he hesitated only slightly before he lifted the elastic waist of his shorts over his raging hard-on and slipped them down and off his legs.

He was doing what she'd told him to, and he looked up at her as she made a little sound of approval—a little "Mmm," as if he were something being wheeled in on a dessert cart.

He loved the way she was looking at him, but the fact that he loved it made him feel self-conscious, so he turned and stepped into the shower. The water was too hot, and he adjusted it before he turned back to reach for the shower curtain.

"Leave it open."

He put his arm back down, as she added, "Do *not* move. I'll be right back."

Tracy vanished—he could hear her heading swiftly down the stairs. She was going to get her computer and her phone, as she promised. Jesus, with her out of the room, he was suddenly shaking, his knees actually weak. He knew he should shut the curtain—that doing so would further break the spell, but he didn't move. He didn't want to move.

He knew, also, that he should take himself in hand, literally—and remove sex from the table. But he didn't do that, either.

Instead he stood there, as the warm water ran down his face, down his body. His head and shoulders and arm stung, as did dozens of other little scrapes and cuts all over him, but he didn't care. He just wanted to get clean so that Tracy would touch him again.

Please Jesus, let her come back and touch him again.

His arm screamed as he pushed the water out of his face, squeegeeing it back through his hair.

"I said *don't move.*"

She was back, putting her computer on the lid of the toilet, then closing the bathroom door behind her.

As he watched, she opened the mirrored medicine cabinet to peruse its contents, then rifled through both the closet and the cabinet under the sink. Whatever she was looking for, she didn't seem to find it. She didn't seem particularly perturbed, though, as she then took off her shirt and untied the rain jacket from her waist, leaving herself clad only in her underwear. And yes, her bra was, just as she'd described it, a relatively sturdy piece of equipment—white, like her panties—but sexy just the same.

Of course, Tracy Shapiro would've been sexy in a burlap sack.

The clasp of her bra was in the front, between her perfect breasts, and she reached as if to unfasten it as he watched, transfixed, as water pounded on his back.

"Don't look at me."

He obeyed, averting his gaze, but . . . "Permission to speak." His voice sounded rough and almost unfamiliar to his ears. He didn't wait for her to grant her permission, because he was afraid she might say no. "That doesn't work for me. The not looking . . ."

She changed her directive. "I agree. *Don't* stop looking at me and . . . Wash yourself."

He found the soap by feel as she held his gaze, her own hands still on that front clasp. She waited to open it until he was lathering himself, and then there she was, in her incredible, full-breasted glory, her nipples tightly peaked, a rosy shade of dark pink on triangles of pale that were shaped like a bikini top—a contrast to her lightly tanned arms, stomach, and chest.

She smiled then—probably at the gone-to-heaven expression on his face—but then immediately wiped it away as she got back into this role that she was so obviously enjoying playing.

But that moment of reality was jarring. What in hell was he doing here?

This was not a casual hookup with some beautiful stranger. This woman worked with him. *For* him, really, although she'd argued against that point rather persuasively.

He'd always liked her.

And after the past few days, he really, *really* liked her.

He liked her point-blank, in-his-face opinions and questions. He liked her seemingly mindless chatter—because it wasn't mindless. She always had a point, even if it took her a while to get there. He liked her quicksilver smile and her melodic laughter. He liked the way she rolled her eyes and waved off the many things she considered inconsequential.

And he loved her matter-of-fact adventurousness when it came to sex. It shouldn't have surprised him that she'd be into something like this, but it did.

The way she looked naked was mere icing on the cake. Outrageously delicious and perfect icing, sure, but a total bonus.

But icing or no, it seemed unlikely that this was going to end well. How were they going to be able to look at each other when they next went into the office? How—

"Stop thinking," she ordered him curtly. "I can tell that you're having second thoughts, so just stop it." She stepped out of her panties and into the shower with him, closing the curtain behind her, cocooning them into what felt like a warm and completely private world.

She pushed her way under the water, gasping as she let it run down her face and her incredible body, as she reached up to push her fingers through her now-wet hair.

"I don't think I can do this," he said, as he tried to shift back. But there was nowhere to go and his ass bumped the cold tile.

She pushed the water from her face, as if surfacing from a swimming pool, and blinked at him with long, dark eyelashes that were matted and glistening, making her look like a mermaid, escaped from the sea.

"I'm sorry," she said, one elegant eyebrow raised. "Did I give you permission to speak?"

"May I have permission to speak?"

"No," she said, holding out the soap to him. "Wash me. And don't stop until I tell you to."

Wash her.

It was then he heard it. The sound of a motor—a low rumble, way in the background.

In a flash, Decker dropped the soap and shut off the water, pushing Tracy back against the wall, one hand up and over her mouth. "Shhh," he warned her as she clung to him to keep her balance, as he used his body to trap her more securely against the tile wall.

She was soft, she was slick, and his leg was pressed tightly between her thighs, and Jesus, he was right—the sound that he'd heard was that of the electric garage door going up.

Tracy's eyes were wide as she stared at him over the top of his hand as she heard it, too.

He scrambled out of the shower and grabbed his sidearm, yanking it free from its holster. He had no pants—although he probably wouldn't have taken the time to pull them on, even if he had a pair.

He turned off the bathroom light, listening at the door before throwing it open, and checking the hall in both directions.

It was empty. He sensed Tracy behind him—she'd wrapped herself in a towel. There was silence, but it was brief before the rumble started again—this time no doubt the door was going back down.

"Get your clothes and follow me," he told Tracy nearly silently, and she swiftly gathered them up before following him down the stairs. "Get ready to run. I'm going to—"

"I'm not going anywhere without you!"

"Yes, you are," he countered. "It's my turn to give the orders. You're going out the back door—"

"Tracy?" A female voice called from the kitchen.

"Oh, my God," Tracy said. "Linds?"

And yes, it was indeed Troubleshooters operative Lindsey Jenkins who came around the corner, her weapon drawn. She immediately raised her hands at the sight of Decker's.

"Whoops," Lindsey said, her eyes widening even more as she realized he was naked. "Holy shit! Sorry. *Sorry!*" She started to laugh—and disguised it as a cough as she respectfully averted her eyes, and then turned around. "I'm guessing you didn't get the message that we were on our way over . . . ?"

"Obviously not," Tracy said. "Shoot, Deck, you're bleeding again." Apparently she'd missed Lindsey's use of the plural pronoun, because she whipped off her towel and tried to use it to stanch the flow.

And, damnit, blood *was* dripping from his elbow onto the carpet runner on the stairs. Starrett was going to be pissed. Still, it wasn't as bad as it had been.

"Why don't you get some clothes from the truck and throw your jeans into the dryer," Tracy told him. "I'll see if there are any bandages in the bathroom. If not, we'll improvise. I'm going to finish getting cleaned up and—"

She gasped as she caught sight of the man standing in the shadows, just behind Lindsey. It wasn't Mark Jenkins, but rather one of his SEAL friends. The quiet one. Jay Lopez.

"Oh, good. Hi, Jay," Tracy said, holding her clothes up in an attempt to cover herself. It didn't work. Deck tried to hand the towel back to her, but she didn't take it. She turned and ran upstairs.

"Hey, Tracy. I'll, uh, do another perimeter check of the house," Lopez said.

"Good plan," Lindsey said briskly. "I'll make a quick sweep of the second floor and—"

Deck tucked the towel around his waist, because his arm really wasn't bleeding all that much, and . . . Jesus, this looked bad—because it looked like exactly what it was.

"Help Tracy," he ordered Lindsey. "Lopez, don't go far. I want to get out of here as quickly as possible. Meet me in the garage."

Lopez nodded and vanished.

Lindsey paused as she passed him on the stairs, stopping two steps up from him, so that they were eye level. "I *really* am sorry. But for the record? Tracy's a friend of mine. If you're taking advantage of her? I *will* kick your ass."

"Help. Tracy." He said it again, more clearly this time.

She nodded. "I'm going to say the same thing to her, because you're my friend, too. But for what it's worth, Chief?" She smiled, and her eyes sparkled, not just with amusement but with genuine approval. "Hoo-*yah*."

Sophia was pregnant.

Dave stared at her, and she stared back at him as she sat on the bed in the hotel suite, chin held high and defiant. She was crying, but she was wiping her tears away as fast as they fell.

"I'm not sorry," she said. "You're looking at me as if I should say that I'm sorry, but I'm not."

"How . . . ?" he breathed.

She tilted her head slightly and gave him a look, and he laughed—he couldn't help it. Sophia was *pregnant.*

"Okay," Dave said. "Yeah. I know *that* how, but . . . you're on the pill." Even as he said the words, he remembered their first time, that first night. "But you skipped a day."

She nodded. "I didn't think it would matter. And even if it did . . . I thought . . ."

Dave nodded, too. That very first night, at the bar in the hotel in Sacramento, they'd talked about the fact that they both wanted children.

Someday.

Of course that was before Anise Turiano roared back to life, like an apparition from hell. That was back when he'd foolishly believed he had a future.

He'd found his own little piece of heaven that night, in Sophia's arms, in her kisses, in her touch. She'd pulled him back onto a hotel room bed very much like this one, where they'd made love for that very first time.

He'd been so careful about making sure he didn't pin her down, even though he was on top. He'd been careful to pay attention to everything she said and did, every sound she made. He'd been careful—except for the part where he completely forgot to put on a condom.

"I remember," Sophia whispered now, "that night so clearly."

Dave remembered, too. Time had seemed to stand still as he'd kissed her, touched her, loved her. He'd moved almost excruciatingly slowly, with long, deep thrusts and equally languorous withdrawals. He could close his eyes and still see, burned into his brain, an image of Sophia's beautiful face, her eyes closed and her lips slightly parted in ecstasy. He'd kissed her throat and the smooth softness of the underside of her chin, tasting her with his tongue as she spread her legs wider to take more of him, all of him.

He'd redefined pleasure that night as she'd come around him, clinging to him and kissing him, her mouth so hungry, so sweet, as her release seemed to shake her to her soul. He'd come, too, practically in unison with her, in a powerful rush, in slow motion as the entire world as he knew it was torn in half, as colors flashed behind his eyelids, as a full freaking choir of angels sang their hearts out.

He'd told her that he loved her, the words damn near ripped from his throat, as he crashed into her, inside of her—no barriers between them.

And then? After the fireworks were over, as he'd tried to gather up and re-form his brain from the shards that had exploded across the universe, Sophia had sighed and breathed his name. "Oh, Dave . . ."

And any lingering doubts that he may have had about entering a relationship wherein he knew, up-front, that he was his lover's second choice . . . ?

Completely obliterated.

He'd had no idea at the time that he and Sophia would have such a lasting souvenir from that evening. But it seemed somehow fitting and, yes, even perfect and sweet that they had.

And okay, maybe he *had* had an idea—when he'd realized that he'd failed to protect her. His panic had lasted about two seconds, before she'd reassured him that she was taking birth control pills to regulate her periods. She'd missed a day, yes—hard to keep up with a prescription regimen while being held hostage by crazed neo-Nazis—but it would be, she'd told him, no big deal.

Oops.

"And it's not bad for the . . ." He couldn't say the word *baby*—he was afraid he might burst into tears. "For everyone's health? That you've kept taking the pills even though you're pregnant?"

She shook her head. "The insert—the information—that comes with the prescription recommends testing for pregnancy if you don't get your period when you're supposed to and . . . We should probably get one of those home tests to be absolutely sure but . . . Dave, I'm pretty convinced."

Dave nodded. "I'll get one. There's a drugstore across the street."

"I've been pregnant before," she reminded him. "The morning sickness started at about eight weeks then, too. And it's really morning, noon, and night sickness."

Morning sickness. Holy shit. For some reason, the mention of morning sickness drove home the fact that Sophia was, right this very moment, carrying a little piece of him around inside of her. It seemed so surreal.

"What can I get for you?" he asked her. "How can I make you feel better?"

She shook her head. "You can't, and . . . I'm fine."

"Don't pregnant women eat a lot of crackers?" he asked.

She smiled, but it was wan. "Crackers would be good. For later. Right now, I'm . . . But, thank you."

And there they sat.

Dave broke the silence. "It was really great sex," he said. "I feel good about the fact that it was really, *really* great sex. I don't know why I should feel so good about that, but I do."

Sophia laughed. "You're not going to be one of those guys who parades me around going *look what I did*, are you?" Her laughter faded, and she added, "I mean, depending on whether or not we decide to stay together."

Ah, yes. That. Also depending upon whether or not Dave survived these next few days or even weeks.

Dear God. He'd been resolute before, but now it was beyond imperative to keep Sophia safe. If he'd been afraid that she was a target as his so-called fiancée, she was now, literally, twice the target.

He took a deep breath. "Please don't take this the wrong way, but it's important that you don't tell anyone about . . . the baby."

He felt himself laugh as he said the word, even as he felt a rush of tears to his eyes. Everything he was feeling, including the hurt from finding out that she'd wanted him only because she thought he was normal, i.e., *boring*—it was all tangled up in a ball of chaos and confusion, with one fact front and center: that there were people out there looking for him, who wanted him to suffer before they ended his life.

And he could not—he *would not*—let them get anywhere near Sophia and their child.

"God, I want this," he whispered. "So much. But I don't know how—"

Sophia kissed him.

She kissed him the way she always did—with a sweetness that turned almost instantly to fire. Which was probably his fault. He couldn't get enough of her and could never keep himself from revving it up, instantly, whether they were out in public or in the privacy of a hotel room.

She pulled back, breathless. "Please don't sleep on the couch."

Dave reached to tuck a stray strand of hair behind her ear, as he continued to fight the urge to cry. "I don't know," he said. "Lumpy couch versus king-sized bed. Alone versus the woman of my dreams in my arms . . ." He put his hand on her stomach. "With our baby right here, handily nearby—in case I need to start her in utero calculus classes."

Sophia laughed. "Calculus. At seven and a half weeks? I don't think she has more than a brain stem yet, although I could be wrong." She started to cry again. "Dave, I'm so sorry about—"

"Hey, it's all right," he said, pulling her close and kissing her. His throat felt unnaturally tight. "She'll grow a real brain. Give her time."

"How can you be so okay with all of this?" she asked.

He sighed. "Because life's not perfect, Soph. You do the best you can with the cards you're dealt. And my hand is pretty freaking great. I've loved you for forever, and now you're having my baby. God, I finally understand that terrible, *terrible* song, because right now I just want to sing it to you. I won't, though, because, you know. Like I said, I love you, and don't want to subject you to that torture."

She laughed, but it didn't slow her tears.

"There's also a part of me," Dave continued, "that's too scared to sing. It's that part of me that's trying to figure out how I'm going to protect you— and our incredible, brilliant, beautiful baby. I don't know how I'm going to do it, but I am. And I'm sorry if that sounds too James Bond, but it's only temporary, okay? I'm going to take care of this problem, and then I'm going to come back, and I'm going to marry you, and I'm going to retire from Troubleshooters and get a job in an auto repair shop, only fixing dents in left front fenders of Subarus—or something equally boring."

"Dave, I don't want you to—"

"Shhh," he told her, silencing her with a kiss. "That's for the future, okay? Right now, let's just show our baby how much her daddy loves her mommy."

And with that, Dave kissed her again—because when he was kissing Sophia, he allowed himself to believe not only that she loved him, but that everything was going to work out. And that they were going to live, perhaps not happily, but *contentedly* ever after—which absolutely *was* good enough for him.

# Chapter Thirteen

Decker didn't want her to ride with him.

Tracy sat in the backseat of Navy SEAL Jay Lopez's unassuming little hybrid car and tried to be invisible as they followed Decker through a vaguely industrial part of the city, where he was intending to ditch his poor battered truck.

He'd told Lindsey and Lopez that he didn't want to leave it in Sam and Alyssa's garage. It was entirely possible, even though they'd swept the vehicle carefully, that Jo Heissman *had* left behind some kind of tracking device.

It would have to be something cutting-edge, that didn't yet register on standard bug-sweeping equipment. But technology frequently played leap frog. Tracy had learned about that when, as Troubleshooters' field equipment supervisor, she'd come across a purchase order for new equipment—a mere two weeks after they'd received brand-new state-of-the-art bug sweepers. She'd thought it was an error, and had brought it to the boss's attention. But Tom had explained that, over those scant few weeks, there'd been a technology bump in which their new equipment had become instantly obsolete.

The tech world moved at lightning speed. Someone would invent a new, undetectable tracking device, Tom had explained, and everyone else would work feverishly on a way to detect it. Once they did, it wouldn't be long before someone else invented a newer, undetectable device—and on and on it went.

So, yes, it was not just possible but entirely likely that Dr. Heissman had slipped a tracking device into Deck's truck. How else could they have been followed to the Seaside Heights Motor Lodge?

Except something wasn't right about that. The timing. It seemed wrong. If the bad guys had followed Deck and Tracy to the motel, when exactly did they have time to plant that bomb?

She and Decker had sat in his truck in the parking lot for several minutes, it was true. But she for one hadn't seen any movement in the motel courtyard.

Although, it was possible that whoever planted the bomb had gone around the back. It was possible the bomb could have been planted outside of the building. Surely forensics or explosion experts could tell that sort of thing.

Tracy wished Decker were there so she could ask him about that.

Yeah. *That* was why she wished Decker were there. Right.

Except the backseat of this little car was not designed for people who were more than three and a half feet tall. She was sharing it, too, with a pizza box. Apparently Jay Lopez had been sitting down to dinner when Lindsey had called, looking for backup. The box was, alas, empty. Her stomach growled, and she dug through her handbag for a PowerBar and came up empty-handed.

"Mark's OCONUS again," Lindsey said from the front seat.

Tracy realized that she wasn't talking to Lopez, who of course, would have already been aware of the fact that Lindsey's SEAL husband was out of the country.

"He was supposed to be back tomorrow," Lindsey continued, "but . . . Looks like they're keeping 'em around awhile longer."

"Iraq?" Tracy asked, focusing on her friend. It was a good way to avoid obsessing over the way Decker hadn't been able to look at her when she'd come—showered and fully dressed—into the garage. He'd given her zero eye contact as he'd briskly announced that she should go with Lindsey and Lopez, and that he was taking his truck.

"Nope. Afghanistan," Lindsey reported.

"I was hoping you'd say Germany," Tracy said.

"I wish." Lindsey sighed. "It's bad over there."

"He's going to be okay," Tracy told her friend. "Mark's good at what he does."

Lindsey shifted in her seat to better face Tracy. "So . . . You want to tell me what's going on with the bomb at the motel and the back window of Deck's truck shot out?"

Tracy sighed. "I can't. Not without Decker's permission." And okay. The word made her blush, even though Lindsey and Lopez couldn't possibly know what had gone on in that bathroom before they'd arrived.

*Did I say you could talk?* Here in the quiet of Lopez's car it seemed absurd not only that those words had come out of her mouth, but that Decker had been on board enough to obey her.

Holy crap, he was one nicely put together man. No doubt about it, Lawrence Decker was the reason God had invented nakedness. And even though Tracy's experience with living, breathing, in-the-flesh naked men was seriously limited, she'd seen a statue or two in her time, as well as more than a few male bodies on film—that is, if you could call the adult-cable-channel porn Lyle used to watch "film." Deck put them all to shame, with the kind of hard muscles that a man couldn't get from merely going to the gym.

"Then . . . you want to tell me what's going on with you and Deck?" Lindsey asked.

"Nothing's going on," Tracy started to say, but changed it to a simple, "No." Lindsey, after all, wasn't an idiot. Naked plus naked equaled something, not nothing. "Not in front of Lopez. No offense, Jay."

"I'm not listening," he said.

"And you didn't see me naked either, right?" Tracy asked.

"Sorry, no," he said. "I definitely saw you naked." He glanced at her in the rearview mirror. "I have an appreciation of fine art, and I recognize what an honor it was to be one of a rare few who've been granted a private viewing of one of God's own masterpieces."

Tracy stared at him. "How could you possibly be friends with Izzy Zanella? That was . . . Thank you." *Rare few*, he'd said, which was both respectful and sweet, despite the Tracy-is-a-slut rumors that were surely swirling in the SpecWar community.

"He's hitting on you," Lindsey reported. "You may not recognize it, because he's so polite, but this is Jay's way of saying, *Yo, hot mama.* Consider yourself warned."

"You decide that Chief Decker's too old or grumpy for you," Lopez told Tracy with a smile that could have melted butter, "you know where to find me."

And okay. *He* probably looked really good naked, too. And he was closer to her own age than Deck was. *And* he was about a billion times less grim and bottled up.

*Friend of Izzy Zanella* went into the con column though, along with what was, Tracy realized, a total deal-breaker. He was *Not Lawrence Decker.*

God, when had *that* happened? They hadn't had sex—not even close. Well, all right, maybe a *little* close. But still. Deck had kissed her—once. One time. She'd grabbed his junk, okay, and then ordered him around a little bit. They'd both gotten naked and stared at each other a whole lot.

He'd also told her what had happened between Sophia and him—and why he'd been so utterly unable and unwilling to bring their rather odd, strained relationship to the next level.

And yeah. There it was. *That* was what had happened. Decker's confession had been the emotional equivalent of full-penetration sex. The intimacy hadn't been physical, but that didn't make it any less powerful and, well, intimate. In fact, everything they'd said and done over the past few hours—including almost dying—felt *far* more intimate than any sexual act Tracy had ever performed with her rather pathetic line-up of exes.

And God help her, true to her pattern, she was well on her way to falling for Deck. All she could think about was getting him alone again—so she could spend about four hundred more hours gazing into his crazy-beautiful eyes.

And yes, okay, she also wanted to hook up with him. Badly enough to chase him down the street, if need be.

Which, ironically, she was pretty much doing, since Lopez was currently following Decker's truck. Although, right this second, both truck and car had stopped at a railroad crossing, where lights were flashing and flimsy wooden barriers were coming down.

"What the . . . ?" Lopez hit his horn.

"*What* is he doing?" Lindsey asked, disbelief in her voice.

Tracy sat forward to see Decker pull his truck into the oncoming lane, and—avoiding the barriers—gun it, tires squealing, across the tracks.

"Hold on!" Lopez shouted as he yanked the wheel hard left to follow, but the train was nearly on top of them. He hit the brakes as Tracy screamed, and they skidded to a stop on the non-Decker side of the tracks.

"Are you insane?" Lindsey shouted as the train roared past, hardly more than a foot from the front of the car.

"SEAL," Lopez said with a shrug.

Lindsey turned to Tracy. "Where is he going?"

"I don't know," she said. Decker still didn't have a functioning phone—they couldn't even call him to ask.

"You don't know." Lindsey clearly didn't believe her.

Tracy shook her head, fighting a rush of tears.

"You have no idea why he would want to lose us?" Lindsey persisted as the train kept on coming. It was a freight, with no end in sight. "Because that's what that crazy psycho just did. He freaking lost us."

"Maybe he didn't realize how close the train was," Tracy said, but she didn't need the disbelieving looks that either Lindsey or Lopez sent her from the front seat to recognize how stupid that sounded.

"After the train passes," Lopez said, "and the gates go back up? Decker is *not* going to be waiting for us."

"I know," Tracy said. Had he really been in that much of a hurry to get away from her? Or . . .

Wait a minute. *Wait* a minute.

"Alyssa told me to get you and Decker to the helo pickup point." Lindsey was as pissed as Tracy had ever seen her. "She doesn't want to tell me the details about what's going on? That's fine. The assignment's easy enough. Oh, but be sure to bring Lopez, she says, just in case, because apparently someone tried to blow both Decker and Tracy to Kingdom Come at some sleazoid motel in the suck-ass part of town. And for the record, I *really* don't want to know why you were going there."

"Jo Heissman," Tracy said. "Oh, *shit.*"

But Lindsey was on a full-blown rant and didn't hear her. "But okay, it really is fine," she continued, "because I'm down with *need to know.* I respect that. But what would've been *nice* to have been told is that Decker, despite a bullet wound in his freaking arm, won't particularly *want* to go to the helo pickup point. A little warning that we'd have to strong-arm Chief Crazy Pants would've been helpful."

Lopez, however, had been paying attention. "Joe *who?*"

"Josephine Heissman," Tracy said again, as the freight train's caboose sped past—and sure enough, with the sudden unobstructed view across the tracks, Decker's truck wasn't anywhere in sight. No doubt about it, he was long gone. "That's where Decker went. Probably to her house."

Lindsey blinked at her. "*Dr.* Heissman?" she asked. "The shrink?"

"She lives out on Coronado," Tracy told them, as she unzipped her computer bag and opened her laptop. Since Jo was a former Troubleshooters employee, Tracy still had her personal information—including her home address—in the company database. "Go," she ordered Lopez as she looked up the address. "Drive. West. Hurry. Because if Decker did go to her house? He may well have gone to follow through on a threat he made—to kill her."

Dr. Heissman was sitting in her living room. She was curled up, one foot tucked beneath her, in an oversized, overstuffed chair, reading a paperback novel.

She didn't hear Decker come in, and he stood there for quite a few minutes before she noticed him—she was that engrossed.

It was as if she'd prepared for him—or someone—to pay her a visit. The drapes were closed, shades were drawn—no one could see into the house from the street.

She'd changed out of her business clothes, into pink sweatpants and a T-shirt, and her hair was up in a ponytail.

Pink. Huh. It still surprised him that she would wear that girlishly pale color.

Her feet were bare, and she'd poured herself a glass of wine, which sat with her cell phone on the end table beside her, ignored, as she was clearly caught up in her book. The only sound was that of her turning pages—and the quiet ticking of the clock on the mantel of her fireplace.

Her home was nice. It was one of those antique cottages that peppered the area—built shortly after the turn of the twentieth century. The architectural style was called Arts and Crafts—and the only reason Decker knew that was because SEAL Team Sixteen's Senior Chief Stan Wolchonok's house was from the same quaint era. Although the senior'd preserved the original rich, dark woodwork in his house. The doctor's had long been painted over, which was a shame.

Her walls were soothing—tans and beiges and a shade of mustard that was surprisingly nice, with occasional splashes of color from abstract modern artwork: not his favorite, by a long shot. He was a landscape man. Give him a good seashore. Sand dunes. A sailboat on the horizon. But a splotch of colors, arranged in a vaguely sexual scramble? Maybe he was fucked up, but when he looked at art like that, he rarely saw anything besides female genitals and the occasional scrotum. Or he saw absolutely nothing at all—which was somehow worse. It was as if everyone in the world was laughing at a joke that he didn't get. And that made him uncomfortable—like it was additional proof that there was something seriously wrong with him.

Besides, if he was going to think about uncomfortable things, he might as well take a well-measured moment and acknowledge the fact that he wished, with all of his frozen and jaded heart, that Lindsey and Lopez had shown up at Starrett's just a *few* minutes later than they had.

The truth of the matter was that he'd wanted Tracy to touch him again, as they stood together in that shower.

Although, if she *had* touched him, then he'd probably be standing here wishing that Lindsey and Lopez had shown up *twenty* minutes later and . . . Bottom line was that Deck knew that even if he'd fucked her, he'd be standing here now wishing he'd had the chance to fuck her again. Of course, if he'd fucked her twice, he'd want a month with her, and then a year, and then an entire goddamn decade. . . .

Jesus, he could use a solid decade with Tracy's fire and life and laughter—and yes, particularly her *there's nothing wrong with you, Sparky,* anything-goes attitude toward sex.

But really, and far more reasonably than wishing for a full decade, he would've gladly taken just a few more minutes of her looking at him like she was going to enjoy eating him alive.

If there *was* something wrong with him? It was wrong with her, too, and . . . There was absolutely nothing wrong with her. *Absolutely* nothing.

Except for the fact they worked for the same company, that she was just a little too young, *and* that he didn't have enough room in his life for a full-time, high-maintenance girlfriend. And anything he started with Tracy would be full-time and highest maintenance, he did not doubt that.

Although the fact that he was more than likely going to die in the near future countered all of those arguments—at least it did if he were thinking selfishly. It added to them if he was thinking about Tracy, who'd be left behind to bury him.

That was something he never wanted to lay on anyone, having buried his share of friends. Damn, but thinking about that made his battered head ache.

It was then that he must have sighed—heavily enough to make Jo

Heissman look up. She saw him and gasped, leaping to her feet and knocking over that long-stemmed glass of wine.

Decker didn't move. He just dispassionately watched it go down—a dark red splash of liquid on the pale-colored rug.

She put her book spine up on the arm of her chair, her voice an accusation. "You startled me." It was clear she was on the verge of bustling into the kitchen to get a towel to blot at the spill, so he shifted slightly to block her.

"Leave it," he said, and she stopped and looked at him. Really looked this time.

"What's wrong?" she asked, perceptive as always.

"You honestly don't know?"

She shook her head, her eyes narrowing as she noticed the bandage on his arm. "You've been hurt. Are you all right?"

"You and your friends . . ." He gave his performance everything he had in him, calling up every ounce of pain he'd felt on that hellish ride from the motel to Starrett's—before Tracy had found the text messages that proved that there was, indeed, a God. Or that there truly was power to *The Secret*. Still, it didn't take much effort to bring it back—the emptiness, the despair, the howling, impotent, yet still-vicious rage. He couldn't do more than whisper. "You and your friends killed Tess."

Jo Heissman's reaction to his words was physical. She blanched as she took a step backwards, actually lurching and nearly falling down. "Oh, merciful God," she said as she caught herself and sank into her chair. "Oh, no. Oh, Deck, I'm so, *so* sorry."

Her concern and distress—and surprise—were genuine. But then he saw it dawn in her eyes—the realization that he blamed her and that he'd come there to follow through on that threat he'd made two months ago. He saw her glance toward her cell phone, saw her look at her front door. He saw her weigh her options—call for help, run. . . .

Instead, she chose surrender as she stayed where she was and clasped her shaking hands together in her lap. "Well, I guess it's now or never as far as your trusting me. Which I know that you don't. But I do. I trust *you*."

He took her phone off the table, and pocketed it. "Did they tell you to plant a tracking device in my truck?"

"No! I didn't—I *wouldn't*. I would have told you. Lawrence, please, sit down and talk to me."

He shook his head. "I'm not really in the mood for a therapy session right now, thanks."

She apparently didn't care, because she pushed on. "Not only do I trust you, but I also have faith in you. I know you're distressed, and you have every right to be, but you're not a killer—as much as you'd like other people to believe that you are."

"You're wrong," he said, which was stupid, because he knew that she was trying to engage him. What he needed to do was keep his mouth shut, unholster his sidearm, and scare her into silence. Last thing he needed was her crawling around inside of his head—and maybe bumping into Tracy while she was in there.

No, wait. It wasn't Tracy, it was *Nash* that he was worried the doctor would find out about.

Tracy—Jesus. What was he doing, thinking about her right now?

"No, I'm not," Dr. Heissman was saying. "You've killed. I understand that. You're a soldier in a bloody and awful war. Of course you've taken lives. But not like this. Never an . . . execution." She met his eyes with a gaze that was steady and absolute, despite her trembling hands. "Not without sufficient proof—and as angry as I know you are, you don't have that. You can't—because the proof you need doesn't exist. And even if you somehow had enough . . . circumstantial evidence to convince yourself . . . Well, you didn't kill the man who was directly responsible for Jim Nash's death. You brought *him* in alive."

Decker wanted to applaud—she was playing both the shrink and logic cards with perfection. "I'm not the same man I was back then," he said, which was, oddly enough, a truth.

"No," she agreed, "you're not. You're still plenty angry, yes, I can see that. And rightfully so. I know how much you loved them—both Jim and Tess. God, I'm so sorry. But . . . your anger is different. It's . . . *You're* different than you were in our therapy sessions. I can see it in you. You're at peace. Somehow. It's. . ." She shook her head. "You *are* different. And you're lying about . . . something." Her voice caught. "God, please tell me you're lying to me about Tess."

She was just guessing. She had to be. She'd told him earlier that day that she had trouble reading him, that she couldn't tell when he was lying. And yet . . .

She paused only momentarily and when he didn't respond, when he didn't so much as blink, she kept talking. Her words of reason were her only available defense, and she wielded them expertly. "I know you want to see the blackmail photos before you make any decisions in terms of . . . what you intend to do with me."

"Nah," he said, "I really don't. I'm just going to shoot you. At the very least it'll shut you the hell up."

She was no idiot, so she lowered her head and finally kept her mouth shut as he crossed the room and sat down on her leather sofa. It was nice. Distressed and soft, it was the yellow-brown color of a well-worn pair of cowboy boots. "But okay, you're right. I'm lying. I'm pretty sure I'm not going to shoot you. At least not tonight. And Tess isn't really dead."

Her head came up, her eyes wide. "Thank God. Is she"—her gaze flicked to the bandage on his arm—"all right?"

"Yeah. They did try to kill her, though," he told her. "Your friends tried to take all of us out with a bomb. I got a little shot in the aftermath, but everyone's fine."

"A *little* shot . . . ?" she said.

"It happens."

"Whoever did that—they're not my friends." She didn't bother accusing him of being an asshole for telling her that Tess was dead. She knew damn well why he'd done it—to try to see what she knew, if anything, about the attempted hit.

What she knew was jackshit, and he actually believed her when she'd said she hadn't planted a tracking device. It still didn't mean she wasn't in league with whoever had set that bomb—although he was starting to believe that less and less.

"Don't get too excited," Decker warned her. "I might decide to kill you anyway, just because you piss me off."

"How could you joke about . . . any of this?" She cut herself off. "Don't bother answering that. I do understand how difficult this must be, and in order to cope, it's natural to—"

"I'm not joking," he said. "Where are those photos?"

She stood up, and he did, too.

"Stay in your seat, please," he said. "Just tell me where I can find them."

Dr. Heissman nodded. "On the kitchen table," she said, as she slowly sat back down in her chair. "I was expecting you to ask for them. I had them ready—to send to you, if that was what you wanted."

Yeah, like he was going to give her the mailing address for the safe house. Dream on.

She watched as he went into the dining area and through the open door into her little kitchen. The cottage was so small, she could see him clearly from where she sat—and vice versa. She had one of those old-fashioned refrigerators with the rounded top and front, and a gas stove that had a griddle in the middle. It was cozy, like he'd stepped into a time warp back to his Grandma Lillian's kitchen in New Jersey—with everything neat and tidy, and with its homey and simple white curtains covering both the window over the sink and the panes of glass in the back door.

A small, two-seat table was over against the wall, and on it lay one of those cardboard USPS priority mailers, with his name already printed in block letters on the front. It was unsealed, and he looked in to find another envelope—plain, brown, and taped shut. He pulled it out.

"I was hoping," she said, her voice faltering for the first time, which made him glance up to see that she'd gone another shade paler, "that you wouldn't have to look at them while I was here."

"Sorry," he said as he tore open the envelope and dumped the photos—half a dozen eight-by-ten glossies—onto the table. "You're not going anywhere. I've recently acquired this strange new attachment to not dying."

In the other room, Jo Heissman silently sat back in her chair and closed her eyes.

The first few photos were pretty traditional blackmail shots. In them she was having missionary-position sex with a dark-haired young man, his tattooed ass gleaming. He covered most of the doctor's body as she lay on a bed in an opulent hotel room. Her face was clearly visible, though— there was no question it was her. And that she was enjoying herself thoroughly.

Deck spread the others out on the table and . . . Hello, Dr. Heissman. And okay, he'd be pale and blushing, too, if he knew she were looking at similar photos of him, taken during what should have been private moments.

Oddly enough, the pictures did absolutely nothing for him. Or to him. In fact, he couldn't remember a time when he'd wanted to get with this woman less than he did right now. That was kind of weird. He flipped through the photos again.

In all six of the shots, her face was in sharp focus.

Not so much for her lover, though. In fact . . . "None of these photos show your boyfriend's face."

"Is that unusual?" she asked from her chair in the living room, her voice tight. "I've never been blackmailed before, so . . ."

"It goes along with my theory," Deck told her. "That your boyfriend here helped set up the blackmail. That it was insurance—part of the Agency plan to keep former employees compliant. Glad to see you used condoms, because if that's the case, your boyfriend was far from exclusive—he was running the same scam on other women, although definitely not in your department, and probably not even in the Agency's D.C. branch. What did he tell you his name was again?"

"Peter," she said. "Olivetti. I'm sorry, I just can't wrap my mind around it. He dated my daughter for . . . it was at least two months. That seems like such a huge investment of time."

"He dated her in order to meet you," Decker pointed out. "Two months is nothing for this kind of long con. Did he tell you he traveled for work—was he frequently out of town?"

"More often than not." She nodded. "I'm a fool."

"No," he said. "Just human. He's . . . certainly attractive enough, and . . . I'm sure he made a point to be everything you wanted him to be."

"Sometimes I think it's worse to deal with you when you're being nice," she said.

He had to laugh. Tracy had said almost exactly that earlier. "As opposed to when I'm threatening to kill you? That's a little twisted—that you like that better, Doc."

"I'm human, remember?" she said. "A *little twisted* comes with the territory."

"Do you have any photographs of Olivetti featuring his face?" Deck asked.

"I do," she said. "On my computer. May I?"

She gestured to a corner of the dining room where she'd tucked a small desk. Upon it was a laptop, plugged into a modem.

"Please," he said. Their manners were impeccable, even though there probably wasn't a chapter in any etiquette book on "How to Converse with Your Former Therapist While Holding Blackmail Photos of Her with Her Legs Spread." *Please* and *thank you*, however, had universal appeal. He left the photos out on the kitchen table as he joined her in the dining room.

"They're from the same trip to New York," she told him as she slipped into the chair. She manipulated the mouse and accessed her pictures file as he moved to look over her shoulder—making sure she wasn't taking the opportunity to e-mail anyone who might want to kill him.

"We took one of those Circle Line Cruises," she continued, glancing up at him. "I wanted to see the Statue of Liberty again, and . . ." She frowned, and rearranged the contents of the folder so that it was a list instead of icons. She scanned it. "That's funny."

"File's gone, huh?" He'd expected as much.

"It was here," Jo said, clicking back to her pictures file, "in my vacations folder. But there were others. He sent me a download of himself when he went to San Antonio—outside of the Alamo." She accessed a file called "Downloads," which was neatly organized in subfolders, one of which was labeled Friends. She clicked on it and . . . "That's gone, too." She looked up at Decker. "*Son* of a bitch."

Olivetti—or whatever his name really was—had erased himself from her computer. "Any hard-copy photos?" Deck asked, expecting the answer he got.

"No. *Son* of a *bitch.*"

"How about any kind of backup? A flashdrive or—"

"No," she said. "Not for the photos. I mean, yes, for important ones. My kids, my parents, but . . . Peter wasn't exactly a keeper."

*Bang, bang, bang!*

Shit—someone was hammering on the front door.

They both jumped. Dr. H. leaped to her feet and then flinched, and Decker realized that he'd drawn his sidearm even as he'd grabbed her arm. He pushed her farther into the corner, out of line of the door.

"Pizza delivery!" came a male voice as whoever was out there found the buzzer and leaned on it. *Enhhhhhhhhhhh.*

Decker looked at Jo, who shook her head. She hadn't ordered pizza.

But then the person at the door lowered their voice. "Chief. It's Lopez. Pretend you don't know me when you open the door. There's no sign of surveillance, but that doesn't mean they're not out there." He raised his voice again. "Angelo's Pizza!"

"Who's Lopez?" Dr. Heissman asked, her eyes wide.

"A friend," Decker told her. Somehow he and Lindsey and Tracy had followed him here. Somehow? Yeah, right. Tracy Shapiro was too fricking smart for her own good.

"Come on, Chief, open up," Lopez was back to whispering. "I know you're in there. Nothing good is going to come from hurting the doctor—"

What the fuck had Tracy told him?

But as Deck headed toward the door, the sound of shattering glass came from the kitchen.

This was not good. This was very, *very* not good. That was the sound of one of the panes of glass in the back door being broken—end result being that whoever was out there could reach in and release the deadbolt and lock.

Like Lopez, Decker had seen no sign of surveillance when he'd pulled up. But he'd purposely parked out front—with hopes that whoever had followed him and Tracy to the Seaside Heights motel would likewise follow him here and strike again. At which point, his plan was to charge the attack. It was one surefire way to find out who was attacking.

But his intention had been to do it *without* Tracy as a potential target. It made him sweat—knowing that she was currently out there, with Lindsey, no doubt waiting in Lopez's car.

"Go into the bathroom," Decker ordered, pushing Jo down the hall as he dug her cell phone out of his pocket and thrust it at her. "Lock the door. Call 9-1-1."

He didn't wait to see if she obeyed him. He ran to the front door as he took out his backup weapon—a .22 that he'd taken from the lockup in his truck and tucked into the back of his pants before breaking into the doctor's house. He flung the door open and tossed the .22 to Lopez, who dropped the pizza box in order to catch it. "I need backup, now!"

Lopez was on Deck's heels as he charged the kitchen, prepared to shoot the motherfucker who was breaking in, if need be. He could identify the body after the fact.

But whoever was out there was astonishingly inept when it came to breaking and entering. Sure enough, shards of glass glittered on the kitchen's tile floor. And if that weren't proof enough of an attempted illegal entry, a hand was reaching through the broken panel of glass, gingerly feeling for the lock.

"Don't move!" Deck shouted as he knocked aside the hand and . . .
"Oh, *shit!*"

That was Tracy's hand. It was *Tracy* who was on the other side of the kitchen door. Decker realized it a mere fraction of a second too late. He'd already yanked open the door, and the momentum pulled her into the kitchen, knocking her onto her knees right on the broken glass, her arm still caught in the window panel.

"Stand down," he ordered Lopez, who immediately backed off.

"Ow," she said. *"Ow!"*

Her arm had been forced down onto the glass that edged the broken window, scraping her badly enough to draw blood.

"Goddamnit," Deck said as he helped untangle her from the door, cutting himself in his attempt to keep her from getting cut again. "What the hell were you doing?"

"Is she all right?" Tracy asked, ignoring the fact that blood was dripping down her fingers and onto the floor. She pushed herself to her feet, brushing the glass from the knees of her jeans. "Ow! Decker, where's Jo Heissman?"

"She's right here," Lopez reported. "She's all right."

"Oh, thank God," Tracy breathed.

"I was calling 9-1-1, but I'm on hold. Should I hang up?" the doctor asked, as Decker caught Tracy's injured arm and tried to look at it.

*"Ow!"*

"Yes," Decker told Dr. Heissman, adding, "Sorry," to Tracy.

"Everything all right in here?" Lindsey came in through the still-open front door, her sidearm at ready.

"Get that door closed," Decker ordered as he pulled Tracy toward the sink. "Lindsey, relieve Dr. Heissman of her cell phone. Take her upstairs and help her pack a bag. We're going to move her someplace more secure. Lopez. Do what you can to get this mess on the floor cleaned up. And let's call someone to come board up the broken window."

"I'm on it, Chief."

"Ooh!" Tracy drew in her breath in a hiss. She looked at her uninjured hand. "I think I've got . . ."

Decker looked closely. Sure enough, she had a nasty splinter of glass lodged in her palm, just below her thumb. "Hold still." He was able to grab hold of it and pull it out, but not without—"Fuck!"—sticking himself with the damn thing.

"Sorry," she said.

"Next time use your brain," Deck told her brusquely as he ran the water in the sink and held her arm under the flow. He had to wash off the blood in order to get a better look at her collection of cuts and scrapes. God *damn* it, he'd done this to her. "Never brush yourself off with your hand when you've got broken glass on you. But you won't have to remember *that* if you apply the *never* rule to breaking into someone's house. You suck at it, by the way."

The worst of her scrapes looked to be only superficial, thank God, because she'd taken the time to carefully clear out most of the jagged edges of glass left in the panel before she'd reached through. None of her cuts were deep enough to require stitches. Still, it no doubt hurt like hell. It hurt him just to look at it.

Decker became aware of the fact that he was touching her—her hand, her arm—as she shifted slightly, toward him. She pressed the entire length of her leg against his in a move that was deliberate. Had to be. No way could that've been accidental. Particularly since she kept it there.

Funny how it was suddenly hard for him to breathe.

"*You* suck for running away," she murmured, glancing up at him.

"Yeah," he said, just as quietly, his gaze carefully focused on her arm. He did not, however, move. He could have shifted to the right and put some space between them, but he didn't. He didn't want to. "I know." He reached for the soap and pumped himself a small handful. "This is going to sting."

"Ow!" she said.

Decker looked at her in disbelief and laughed. "I haven't done anything yet."

"It's the anticipation," she said. "It's killing me. Just do it already, will you?"

He did, rubbing the soap as gently as he could into her arm. She made that sound again—air drawn in between her teeth—and he murmured, "Sorry."

"No, it's good," she said. "It means it's getting clean, right?"

"I think it just means that it hurts."

"Well, I like to think it means it's getting clean, so don't stop."

*Wash me. And don't stop until I tell you to. . . .*

Decker froze, but only for the merest fraction of a second, as an echo of her words reverberated in his head.

She felt his hesitation and looked up at him, a question in her eyes. A question and the answer—it was clear that she knew exactly what he was thinking. And yes. There it was again. That oxygen-sucked-out-of-the-room sensation.

He changed the subject—to the next volatile topic.

"Did you really think I'd hurt her?" he found himself asking. "Dr. Heissman?"

Tracy answered honestly. "I didn't know what to think," she admitted. "I mean, I came here ready to . . . I don't know. Talk you off the ledge. If I had to. You were so angry with her, in the Starbucks, I just . . ."

"Much of what I do and say . . . It's an act," he told her.

"I know that," she said. "And I'm usually pretty good at telling the difference, but . . . I think I was afraid that we'd, I don't know, maybe . . . opened some doors."

She was talking about what had gone down between them in Starrett's upstairs bathroom. Silly him, for assuming that she wouldn't bring it up.

"You seemed a little—" She stopped herself. Corrected herself. "You seemed *extremely* freaked out. And I know I mocked you for it, but I do know that you're *not* a coward, so—"

"Maybe I am," Decker whispered. "You scare me to death."

It was obviously not what she'd expected him to say, and she laughed, but then jumped and turned to look as, over by the door, Lopez loudly cleared his throat. He was using a dustpan to sweep up the glass.

"Sorry to interrupt. I just wanted to make sure you knew I was in here," the SEAL said, as Decker finally finished rinsing the soap from Tracy's arm and turned off the water.

"You're not interrupting anything." Deck stepped back from her—and instantly missed her softness and warmth.

It was pretty remarkable. He'd always considered himself to be a man with relatively few needs. Some of the other Troubleshooters operatives often bitched and moaned about their hotel accommodations or other travel inconveniences. But Decker rarely gave a flying shit. He needed clothes to cover him, and food to eat, and a safe place to sleep—what kind of bed and whether or not it was or wasn't firm enough just didn't play into it.

It had always seemed ridiculous to him, but for the first time, he understood why people complained. Because as impractical as it was, the idea of going through his day with Tracy glued, soft and warm, to his side—or maybe sitting on his lap—was remarkably appealing. It would, without a doubt, improve his quality of life on a scale that he'd never before imagined possible.

And it wasn't even about sex, it was about physical contact. Connection. Jesus, he couldn't remember the last time anyone—*anyone*—had so much as touched him, let alone given him a hug.

He reached to pull several sheets off a roll of paper towels and used them to blot both water and blood from Tracy's arm—and as an excuse to touch her again.

She knew it, too, and she shifted closer, so that her shoulder brushed his. She looked up at him, and their gazes caught and held.

And held . . .

"As long as I have your attention, Chief," Lopez said, dumping the glass into the trash. "Looks like there're some photos on the table that, uh, might want to get put away?"

What? Oh, *shit*. "Yeah," Decker said, letting go of Tracy, fast, and turning toward the table in question. "Thanks. Sorry, that you, um . . ."

"I'm not complaining," Lopez said. "It's just a little . . . Okay. A lot unusual. I guess maybe it's just my day to see everyone I know naked."

"Oh, my *God*," Tracy said as she looked to see what he was talking about. Her mouth dropped open as Deck quickly scooped up the pictures and grabbed the envelope. "Decker, wait."

But he covered the photos, lowered his voice. "I think it's safe to say that the doctor's being blackmailed. You don't need to see these."

"I figured that's what that was," Lopez said. "Sorry—they were hard not to notice."

"Please." Tracy reached out and caught Deck's arm. "I'm not trying to be cute or freaky or . . . This has nothing to do with me and you, and me wanting to . . ." She closed her eyes, exhaled, and started over. "May I please see that top picture again? Because those tattoos. . . . ? I think that might be my ex, Michael."

# CHAPTER
# FOURTEEN

Unable to sleep, Jules found his way into the kitchen, looking for God knows what.

Only the dimmest of lights was on, but Sam was sitting on one of the four stools at the big center island counter, dressed down in cut-off sweats and a well-worn T-shirt, big bare feet hooked in the rungs. Cold cuts and bread were spread out in front of him as he ate a sandwich.

"Hey," he greeted Jules through a mouthful of turkey and Swiss on what looked like marble rye.

"Hey." Jules opened the refrigerator and stared at the contents. It was well-stocked—with absolutely nothing that he wanted. Because he didn't really want anything to eat.

What he *wanted* was for three innocent people—one of them a child—to not be dead.

But his stomach churned and burbled and he knew he had to put something into it. He wasn't going to be able to hunt down the killer if he made himself sick.

As opposed to heartsick, which he already was.

"How about I make you a sandwich?" Sam asked. It wasn't really a question, because he was already doing it—taking a couple of slices of bread from the bag and plopping them onto the same plate he was using.

Jules closed the fridge with a sigh. "Sure, why not?" He sat on the stool down at the end, leaving one empty between them. "Thanks."

"You should probably stay off the Internet for a few days," the former

SEAL advised him as he squeezed a generous amount of spicy brown mustard onto the bread. "Robin is getting reamed by all of the celebrity gossip sites. It's not going to help your blood pressure to see that circus."

Jules laughed, even though he wanted to cry. "You know what Robin told me?"

"Nope. What did Robin tell you?" Sam used up the rest of the turkey and started opening the other packs of meat.

"Hey."

They both looked up to see Jimmy Nash, leaning on a cane for support as he hobbled his way into the kitchen. His dark hair was a mess and he was wearing his plaid pajama pants with a T-shirt.

"Look at you," Jules said. "Up and about like a big boy."

"Barely," Nash said.

"You know," Jules said, "when you get the doctor's approval to begin physical therapy, it generally means you can *begin* physical therapy. Which means that you still spend a certain amount of time taking it slow and using a wheelchair and okay, I can see that you've already tuned me out. I'm talking to myself, aren't I? Yes, I am."

"I'm making sandwiches," Sam told Nash. "You want one?"

"Thanks." Nash planted himself on the stool on the other side of Sam. "Ham and cheese."

"Is this just a sandwich?" Sam asked. "Or is this a *sandwich*?"

Nash didn't look at either of them. He clearly knew of Sam's theory that the perfect post-sex food was, hands down, the sandwich. "None of your business."

"You're right," Sam said. "It's not, but . . . I'm just one of those guys who're in love with love. Just tell me this. The diaper thing? Thumbs-up or thumbs-down?"

"Are you drunk?" Nash asked.

"Nope," Sam said. "No alcohol in *this* house. I am, however, celebrating a milestone. Ash said *da-da* tonight," he reported. "And okay, he actually said *da-da-da-da-da*, but who's counting? He was looking right at me. Boy's a genius." He glanced at Jules. "It helped bring balance to a bad-news day. But it's not always so obvious. Sometimes you've got to look for it, you know? It's there—the little things, the people who love you. Sometimes you've got to resist the urge to put up a wall, or create distance. You've got to draw people close, not push 'em away."

"You think I'm pushing Robin away," Jules surmised.

Sam shrugged. "I think that you're here, talking to me, instead of talking to the Boy Wonder. Which brings us back to what you were saying."

Jules squinted, trying to remember. "What was I saying?"

"You said, *You know what Robin told me?*" Sam repeated. "I said, *What?*"

"Right," Jules said. "He said, *Oh, well.*" He imitated Robin's melodic voice. "He said, *Hey, babe, it's going to be all right. If I don't do this movie, there're going to be others. And if there aren't, fuck it. I'll do theater. It'll be fun.* Fun. I'm ruining his career. Everyone's always saying that Robin ruined *my* career, but look what I'm doing to his."

Sam used a deadly-looking knife to cut the towering sandwich in two and pushed the plate in front of Jules. "He *did* ruin your career. You're wasting your time in Boston, and you know it."

"Fuck you," Jules said. "I love Boston. And what is wrong with you? There's no way I can eat all of that. Even if I was hungry. It's not a sandwich, it's a freaking deli counter." He leaned forward to talk across Sam. "Nash, do you want—"

"He wants ham and cheese," Sam answered for him. "Besides, I was counting on an appearance from The Little Engine That Could." He gestured with his head to the doorway where, indeed, Robin was coming into the kitchen. He'd thrown on his bathrobe, and it hung open over a pair of boxers. "Oh, to be twenty-something and be able to eat from dawn to dusk."

Jules looked at him. "What are you talking about? You eat all the time."

"Yeah, but I work it, hard, to keep my girlish figure." Sam pointed his knife at Robin. "'Bout time you got down here, B.W."

"Yeah, well, if no one bothers to wake me up when they can't sleep . . ." Robin shuffled over to the refrigerator and opened it. Like Jules had done, he stared, squinting, into the brightly lit and well-stocked shelves, and closed the door without taking anything out.

"You were so tired," Jules told him.

Robin turned to face him, leaning back against the far counter, arms crossed. "Really? And of course, you're *never* tired when I wake you up if I'm having a nightmare." He narrowed his eyes at Jules "Or, oh, say, when I can't sleep because my brain's going too fast and some nasty little voice in my head starts whispering about how easy it would be to take that edge off, just by having a drink—reminding me what it would taste like, what it would *feel* like—"

"No," Jules said. "No—"

"We're a team," Robin told him. "That's what you always say when I wake *you* up. So tell me, *are* we a team, or is that just—"

"I get it," Jules said.

"Do you?"

He nodded. "I do. You're right—I should have woken you."

Robin *was* right. Their relationship wouldn't work if it wasn't two-way, if it was all about Jules taking care of Robin, with nothing in return. And, frankly? The last thing either of them needed was for Robin to feel as if he couldn't wake Jules in the middle of the night.

"I am sorry," Jules said again. "But it's making me crazy that on top of a dead child—as if that weren't bad enough—I'm fucking up your career."

"Do you hear me complaining?" Robin asked.

"No," Jules said. "But you should be."

"Let me get this straight," Robin said. "I should be upset because *you think* I should be upset? Should I also check with you to find out if I'm hungry?"

"You're hungry," Sam chimed in. "He's always hungry," he told Nash.

"Okay," Jules said. "You're right again. I'm being an idiot. A great, big, wrong-about-everything idiot."

Robin came over, grabbed Jules by the front of his T-shirt, and kissed him. "But a really cute one." He sat down on the empty stool between Jules and Sam, and aimed his next words at Sam and Nash. "Any word about . . . anything?"

Sam added lettuce to Nash's sandwich. "You mean besides your long-time heroin habit?"

"Seriously? Like being an alcoholic doesn't give the story enough teeth?" Robin started to laugh, but he tried to stifle it as he turned to Jules. "Sorry, babe, I know you don't think this is funny."

"It's not. Comedy equals tragedy plus *time*," Jules pointed out as Sam cut Nash's sandwich and pushed over the plate.

"Thanks," Nash said.

"Where's the tragedy?" Robin asked, helping himself to half of Jules's sandwich, just as Sam had predicted he would. Predicted and planned for—typical SEAL. "I just don't see it. You and Tess aren't dead. You could've been killed," he said with his mouth full. "Instead, you get to wake up tomorrow—which is really great. Personally? I'm enjoying the idea of you waking up the day after tomorrow, too. So let the tabloids say I've sprouted gills and can breathe underwater. You're alive and I'm alive, too. Everything else is bullshit, babe. *Everything* else."

Jules nodded as he let himself get lost in Robin's eyes.

"That's better," Robin murmured. "At least you're looking at me now. Did you know you cut almost all eye contact when you're jammed up too far inside your own head?"

"No, I don't," Jules said. "Do I?"

"Did Starrett tell you about the meth lab at the Seaside Heights motel?" Nash asked, as Robin and Sam both nodded.

"Meth lab," Jules repeated, leaning forward to look past Robin. "As in crystal meth?"

"It's highly flammable," Nash said.

"No shit," Jules said.

"The police report," Sam explained, "has a meth lab as the cause of the explosion. It was, apparently, in the room next to yours. The evening desk clerk was killed in the blast. He was believed to have been cooking meth in there for months."

Robin looked from Jules to Sam to Nash. "We don't actually believe that, do we?" he asked. "I mean, that it was a coincidence? That Jules and Tess just happened to pick the motel with the meth lab, and get the room next to it?"

"Right now we believe that whoever engineered the blast wants the police to think it was a meth lab explosion," Sam told him. "We, however, know it was not."

"This was another message," Nash said tightly. "To me. It was supposed to be a bloody one, with a body count."

"It'll be easy enough to prove," Jules said. "I mean, that there really *wasn't* a meth lab there before today." If the motel had been used to cook drugs for any length of time, toxic by-products would be on the grounds and in the structure itself. "I'll request a chemical analysis of the area."

"Two people—a man and a woman—fled the scene in a truck," Nash said. "That was in the police report, too."

"Decker and Tracy," Sam said.

"Anyone report shots fired?" Jules asked.

"Only Deck and Tracy," Nash confirmed.

"Best guess?" Sam said. "Is that the shooter mistook Tracy for Tess."

"Or maybe they didn't really care who they killed," Nash pointed out grimly. "As long it was someone who knew me."

"Any word on when they'll be back here?" Jules asked. "Deck and Tracy?"

"Not yet," Sam said. "But with any luck, they'll be here soon."

They sat there, then, in silence, just eating their sandwiches.

"I was thinking," Nash said. "About Robin. Rumor going around is that he's in rehab again. But he's not. He's right here. And he's clean. You're clean, right?"

"Squeaky," Robin said. .

"When this is over—and it's going to be over soon, one way or another," Nash said. "But when it's over, if you still care what anyone thinks? Make a statement. You weren't in rehab, but you knew there'd be rumors, so you took a drug test every day, and here are the results. Clean, clean, and clean."

Robin looked at Jules, who felt himself look away. He closed his eyes and stopped himself, and made himself look back at this man whom he'd loved enough to marry. "I hate that you have to do that," Jules told him.

Robin nodded as he touched Jules's foot with his on the rung of the stool. His toes were cold. Jules had bought him slippers, but he never wore them. Even when he was cold.

Correction—even when Jules thought he was cold.

"I know," Robin said quietly. "But it's a good idea, so I'll do it. It's just part of, you know." He shrugged. "The bullshit that doesn't matter." He slipped off the stool and held out his hand to Jules. "Let's go see if I can't get you to fall asleep."

"You want me to call you when we hear from Decker?" Sam asked.

"Nope," Robin said.

"Yes," Jules answered, squeezing Robin's hand. "Please."

"Hey, Cassidy," Nash said, and Jules turned back from the doorway to look at him. "Tess wants to see that list that I, uh, wrote. Will you get me a copy of that in the morning?"

Jules came back into the kitchen. "Yeah," he said. Nash was referring to a lengthy and detail-filled list that he'd drawn up, chronicling the black op missions—including deletions—he'd undertaken for the Agency, from

the beginning of his career, right up until a few months ago. He'd specifically requested that Jules not share it with Tess. Apparently, he'd changed
his mind. "You want me to, um, be there when you show it to her?"

Nash didn't answer right away. He looked at Jules, but then his gaze
flickered over to the doorway, where Robin was standing.

"No," he told Jules quietly. "Thank you, but . . . I gotta do this one
alone." He smiled wryly. "Well, not exactly alone. I mean, I'll be with Tess.
She says we're a team, too. It's funny, she used that same word." He nodded. "I guess I'm going to find out if she means it."

"She does," Robin said, and Jules turned to look at him. He was standing there looking like the movie star that he was, with his casually covered
muscles and that almost too-beautiful face that still often graced magazine
covers. "She loves you, Jim. Unconditionally. I know because . . ."—he
smiled at Jules—"I've got someone who loves me like that, too."

Jules looked at Sam, who was shaking his head.

"You know, Rob, you are sometimes just so fucking gay," he said.
"Ow!"

Nash had smacked Sam with the back of his hand, as Jules rolled his
eyes and pulled Robin down the hall.

"What the fuck?" he heard Sam say, laughter in his voice, as he followed Robin up the stairs that led to their third-floor suite.

"That was nice." Nash's voice carried, too. "What he said. It was . . .
really nice."

"I was kidding," Sam protested. "They know I was . . ." He raised his
voice. "Hey, you guys know I was kidding, right?"

"Good night, Sam," Jules called, as Robin pulled him into the darkness of their bedroom, and shut the door behind them.

And then Jules closed his eyes as he lost himself in the sweetness and
fire of Robin's kiss.


"We need to get out of here," Decker said with his usual quiet-yet-staccato
grim. "And we need to do it now."

"At least let me check my laptap," Tracy persisted, following him into
the kitchen, where Lopez had nailed a piece of wood over the window
she'd broken. The SEAL locked the door and nodded to Deck. "To see if
the pictures—"

Lopez spoke over her. "It's as secure as it's going to get, Chief."

"Good enough. Let's go." Deck took Tracy's arm and moved her back into the main part of the little house. "Your pictures of Michael aren't going to be there," he told her.

It was clear that he believed Tracy absolutely—that it was, indeed, the man she'd met at the rock climbing gym, who told her his name was Michael Peterson, in those photos with Jo.

Michael *Peterson*. He hadn't even bothered to give himself a completely new name—probably because he thought Tracy was lacking in the logic and reasoning department. And oh, my God. Big giant *ew*. The idea that she and Jo both had sex with the same sleazoid con artist was humiliating.

Although Tracy had to admit that her own humiliation wasn't quite as awful as the doctor's. At least there weren't graphic photos out there of Tracy and Michael getting it on, with Tracy looking at him with that same, adoring *what did I do to deserve a stud-muffin like you* look on her obviously sex-starved face. At least she hoped there weren't photos.

Oh, please God, don't let there be photos.

"But shouldn't we see?" Tracy asked Decker again. "If we've got a picture of this man, of his *face*—"

"Let's not waste time," Decker dismissed her again. "We've already been here too long."

"What's the plan, boss?" Lindsey was by the front door, with Jo Heissman standing beside her. The older woman was carrying a small bag and was clearly ready to go. She, too, was watching Decker with great interest—no doubt waiting for him to save the world, or maybe just to save her.

"We should at least *check* my computer," Tracy said, digging in her heels. "For all we know, *that's* where the tracking device is. And we're, like, carrying it around. *Hello, come and get us. We're too stupid to live.*"

Decker nodded. *"That's* the plan," he said. "In fact, we should take Dr. Heissman's laptop, too."

*"What?"*

"Whoever these people are," Deck told her, told all of them, "they gained access to Dr. Heissman's computer—and probably yours, too. There's a solid chance they left behind a cyber-fingerprint. If they did, Tess'll find it. And with luck, it'll help us find *them*."

Tracy alone argued as Lopez grabbed Jo's laptop, and with the doctor's help packed it up. "Tess didn't find it before." All of the computers that came and went from the Troubleshooters office were regularly checked for this type of security breach. Tess herself had checked Tracy's laptop a number of times, post-Michael.

Deck was undaunted. "Yeah, well, now she'll know what she's looking for."

"What *is* she looking for?" Tracy asked. "A tracking device doesn't make sense."

"He didn't put a tracking device in your computer," Decker agreed. "They didn't use a tracking device to follow us to the motel—"

"Because I used my traitorous computer to access that e-mail from Tess," Tracy finished for him, "which had the motel's address. *Hello, we're too stupid to live—come blow us up.*"

The bomb at the Seaside Heights Motor Lodge *had* been set in advance of their arrival. Except . . .

"That e-mail from Tess came into your e-mail account, not mine," Tracy argued.

"That's right," Deck said. "Which means when Tess looks, she'll search for some kind of spyware or virus that gives the user access to *all* computer activity. You'll have an opportunity to talk directly to her, if you want, with any ideas or suggestions. But right now my priority is to get you and Dr. Heissman to a secure location."

"*Me* and Dr. Heissman?" Tracy repeated.

Decker nodded as he gazed steadily into her eyes. "They made a mistake," he told her. "And they know it. You and Jo Heissman were never supposed to meet. She's not working with the Agency, the way I thought. In fact, she never was."

Over by the door, Jo inhaled sharply. "You really believe that?" she asked.

Decker gave her only the briefest of glances. "Yes, I do. I owe you my apology, Doctor." He turned his complete focus back to Tracy. "The fact that the doctor was hired by Tom, to work with us at Troubleshooters . . . ? That was a coincidence. One that's working now in our favor."

"I don't understand," Tracy said.

"They used *you*, honey," he told her. "To monitor Nash. You kept everyone's schedule on your computer. They didn't need Dr. Heissman to do what you were already doing for them."

"Oh, my God," she said.

"Your relationship with Michael started back in January?"

She nodded. "It ended in January, too. He broke up with me just a few days after he . . ."—she had to look away from him—" . . . spent the night at my place."

"Where he had access to your laptop," Decker said, his eyes and voice gentle.

"He didn't," she insisted. "I have password protection. I'm careful about not letting anyone use my—"

Lindsey chimed in. "Was there ever a time when you weren't with him, maybe while you were sleeping?"

"He had access to your laptop," Decker said again, in that way he had of making a statement sound absolute.

And Tracy had to face it—it *was* absolute. She exhaled her frustration. "I'm such an idiot."

"It wasn't your fault."

"Yes it was," she said. "I should have known he was too good to be true."

"Live and learn."

"Right," she said. "Great. But I still don't get how any of this connects to Jo. Other than it's backwards proof that she wasn't there in the office to spy on Jimmy Nash because, like you said, she didn't have to."

"These are not people who make mistakes," Decker explained, "these people we're up against. I don't believe they would knowingly attempt to blackmail Dr. Heissman with photos that include pictures of a man you had an intimate relationship with, if they thought you were going to get anywhere near either Dr. Heissman or these photos."

Tracy agreed. "It seems sloppy at least."

"Yes, it does." He nodded. "That tells us one of two things," he said. "That they're either desperate enough to take that risk, or they didn't count on your connection to . . . me."

He meant Nash. Didn't he? Maybe he didn't. Tracy liked—too much—the fact that Decker thought she had a connection to him. God, she *was* an idiot. There was no way this thing that had sprung to life between them could end with anything even remotely close to the words *and they lived happily ever after.*

"Either way, they've made a mistake," Deck continued. "They've given us the man known as both Michael Peterson and Peter Olivetti. We don't need a photo of him, Tracy. I'm going to call a police sketch artist and have the two of you describe him. We can do it over the phone, via computer. We'll get something that's close enough—see if we can't ID him from that. But step one is to get you and Dr. Heissman somewhere secure. Because whoever was shooting at us outside of the motel . . . ? Honey, I'm now certain that they were trying to kill *you*."

"Me," Tracy heard herself squeak.

Decker nodded. "I thought I was their target, or that maybe they thought you were Tess, but . . . Killing you—and probably Dr. Heissman now, too—is a priority for them. They know you have information that can hurt them. You can both sit in a witness stand and point a finger at the man you knew as Olivetti or Peterson. We're all in danger—that's very clear— but you're at the top of their hit list."

She felt the blood drain from her face. "Oh, my God," she said. "Oh, my *God*."

"I'm not going to let them hurt you," Decker said, in that manner he had of making her believe he could change the orbit of the earth if he wanted to.

Tracy nodded. "I know. I'm just . . . Okay. I'm okay. I'm not happy about this, but . . . I'm okay." She drew in a deep breath and exhaled hard. These terribly dangerous killers—who had absolutely no problem murdering innocent people—saw her as their prime threat. She made herself focus. "Okay," she said again. "So where, then, are we going? Because I definitely don't think we should go . . . to the place where we were originally going." She didn't want even to mention the safe house. "Because if they're after me? Well, let's absolutely not lead them *there*."

"I agree." Deck included Lindsey, Lopez, and Dr. Heissman in his next words—which were really just a series of letters. "TS HQ."

TS, Troubleshooters. HQ, headquarters. They were going into the office where they worked—which wasn't just an office. It was a highly secure, well-fortified building where there was not only a cache of weapons, but a vast array of high-tech equipment. Good plan. *Good* plan.

"Let's do it," Decker said. "Lindsey, with the doctor. Tracy, you're with me."

Words to warm her heart. He cared about her enough to want to protect her himself.

"Lopez called for backup—those are the headlights you're going to see out there, so don't be scared," Deck continued. "There're four additional vehicles—Lindsey, you and Jo are going in Silverman's SUV. You know Bill Silverman?"

Lindsey nodded.

"Have him take the bridge to Harbor Drive," Deck continued. "Stay off the 5."

"Roger that," she said.

"Junior and Fred'll be your escort—one in front, one in back. But they're going to drop you and go," Decker told her. "So when you get to the office? I want every security system on and running at full alert."

"Yes, sir."

Decker wasn't done. "Lopez, glue yourself to my rear bumper—I want Warner right behind you. Targets—I want you on the floor, heads down. Let's do this—let's go."

Tracy did exactly as she was told—she ran across the lawn, bent in half, then scrambled quickly into Decker's truck, keeping her head down.

She was silent, too. But that didn't last for long.

"Are they SEALs?" she asked. "Warner and the others?"

"Silverman and Junior are with Team Sixteen," Deck told her as he started the engine of his truck. "Warner and Fred drive the team's delivery vehicles."

To his surprise, she knew exactly what he was referring to. "From the Special Boat Squadron. They're SWCCs. Special Warfare Combatant-Craft Crewmen."

"Very impressive." She even pronounced it right. *Swicks.*

"I dated a SWCC once," she told him, then immediately recanted. "It wasn't a real date. It was as a favor to Lindsey and Mark. This guy Bob was trying to get this waitress named Jeanne to take him seriously, so we went to dinner to, I don't know, make her jealous or something."

If she was frightened, it wasn't evident from her voice. It didn't wobble or break. But she did seem to want to keep talking.

"Believe me when I say I now know everything there is to know about MK-Vs and SWCCs," Tracy continued. "*And* Jeanne."

So Deck kept the conversation going. "Did it work?" He put the truck into gear, waiting as half of the vehicles peeled off, leaving to follow Lindsey and Dr. Heissman in Silverman's car.

"Like a charm," Tracy said, adding, "Chief."

"Lopez shouldn't call me that," Decker said as she tried to make herself more comfortable down on the floor. She was still holding that paper towel around the cuts on her arm. "It's been a long time since I've been a SEAL."

"Jay Lopez isn't the only one," Tracy said. "I've heard Tom call you *Chief*. More than once. Sam Starrett, too. In fact, all of the operatives who are former SEALs do it. The non-military operatives—like Dave Malkoff—call you *sir*."

He glanced down at her as he backed into a neighbor's driveway and turned his truck around. She was looking at him, hard, as if trying to see inside of his head.

"So why *did* you leave the teams?" she asked.

Deck didn't have to answer her. He didn't have *time* to answer her. He needed his full attention on the street in front of him. He needed to watch for the attack—which was coming. He knew it was coming. It was just a matter of where and when. And it was his utmost priority to get Tracy out of his truck before it happened. Jesus, what he would've given for ten or fifteen trucks and SUVs filled with SEALs and SWCCs—even someone who was desperate would've backed off from that.

Still, as he pulled out onto the main road, with Lopez and Warner right behind him, he found himself telling Tracy why he'd left the teams. "You ever hear of the Khobar Towers bombing?" he asked her.

"Of course," she said, as if she were insulted that he would think she was that utterly ignorant. She went on to give him the *Headline News* version of the story—probably as proof that she knew her recent American history. "It happened in Saudi Arabia, at a military apartment complex at the airbase near Dhahran. Terrorists took out an entire building, severely damaged a second one. It was . . . way before 9/11. Pre–USS *Cole*, too. I want to say, ooh. . ." She squinted as she thought about it. "1997?"

"Close. '96," he corrected her. Jesus, had it really been twelve years? "It was kind of a tipping point for me. I was due to reup right after—it happened in late June and . . . Up to then, I was career Navy, but after the terrorist attack, I got out. We weren't doing enough—at least my team wasn't, not directly. We couldn't—I understood that, but . . . Then I got tapped by the Agency. It was a chance for me to go into some of the countries where terrorists lived and trained—something we couldn't do with impunity in the military. That changed some after 9/11, but back then?" He shook his head. "I needed to *do* something, and the Agency had very few rules. It was a good fit—at least at the beginning."

"Were you in Al Khobar?" she asked. "During the attack?"

"No," Decker told her. "But I was there a few days after. A good friend of mine was stationed there."

He glanced at her, and he could see her watching him from the darkness, her somber face intermittently lit by street lamps. She was doing the math—and he saw that she figured it out. So he said it. "I went to bring what was left of his body home."

"I'm so sorry," she said quietly. "That must've been devastating."

"It was hard," he agreed.

The Surfside Plaza was as good a place as any, and he pulled into the strip mall's parking lot without signaling or slowing down. Lopez, good man, was right behind him, following him over the crumbling driveway, back behind the auto parts store, where the dumpster sat, out of view from the street.

"When I tell you to," Decker told Tracy, "get out, stay low, and get into the backseat of Lopez's car."

"What!?" She said it as if he'd asked her to build a sandcastle out of horse manure.

"Don't argue," he said as he braked to a stop on the far side of the dumpster. "Not with me, not with him. And whatever happens? Do exactly what he says."

"Decker, what are you planning?"

"Trust me," he said, reaching down to touch her face, his thumb against the softness of her cheek. "Do you trust me?"

She hesitated only briefly before she nodded, her heart completely in her eyes, right there, laid bare for him to see. It should have been terrifying, knowing that somehow, someway, this spark between them wasn't just about sex anymore—at least not for Tracy. Somehow, someway, he'd started to matter—he'd become significant to her. And being Tracy, she wasn't afraid to let him know it.

But then she said, "Don't you dare get anything important shot off before we finish what we started."

And Decker laughed. He couldn't help himself, and he leaned over and kissed her. He caught her off-guard and he didn't give her time to kiss him back, which was a good thing, because she had to get moving. Her life depended on it. "Game on," he told her. "Go. *Now.*"

"I'll see you over there," she said, and she was gone.

# CHAPTER
# FIFTEEN

Tracy sat in the conference room, in the Troubleshooters office, verifying that, indeed, all of her photos of Michael Peterson had been wiped from her laptop computer.

It was weird being back here. It seemed bizarre that it had only been yesterday that she'd told Tom she was leaving for the day, and locked the door behind her as she'd headed for the bus stop.

It felt like a lifetime ago.

Of course, the past hour alone seemed like *four* lifetimes—arriving here, and finding out that Decker was nowhere to be found. They'd split up after she'd gotten into Lopez's car.

Lopez had told her it was like a version of a shell game, with her as the shiny but elusive prize. He'd taken back roads to the office, while Decker, apparently, had dangled himself like bait along the main drag, hoping that whoever was trying to kill her—and him, too—would go after him.

At which point, apparently, Decker's plan was to do a high-speed U-turn, and start chasing the chasers.

Sometimes, Lopez had told her with a perfectly straight face—he was actually serious—you gained more from running *toward* an attacker than running away.

So here Tracy sat, worried that Decker was lying in some street somewhere, bleeding—again. And maybe, this time, bleeding to death.

Lindsey had come in, trying to engage Tracy in a conversation, now that Lopez wasn't listening in. "So. I had no idea you and Decker were . . . you know. Friends in a naked way."

For someone who had jumped her now-husband's bones mere days after being introduced, Lindsey could be pretty disapproving of sexual activity that she considered inappropriate.

"I'm not having this conversation," Tracy told her friend. "You know, the one where you tell me I don't respect myself enough. Because I do. I respect myself. Very much."

"I just want to make sure you know what you're doing," Lindsey said. "You guys work together. It could be awkward and . . . I mean, okay, I didn't really expect his thing with Tess to go anywhere. But then, of course, there's Sophia."

Of course, there *was* Sophia. Whom Tracy was convinced was just dallying with Dave, while carrying a torch for Deck.

But Lindsey surprised Tracy then. "To be honest, I never really saw *that* working out either—Sophia and Decker. Her baggage and his baggage . . . Bad match."

"What baggage does he have?" Tracy found herself asking, like a pathetic eighth-grader in the cafeteria. "I mean, in your opinion?"

"Well," Lindsey said, as she sat down next to her at the table. "I'm not completely sure—and that's part of it. He doesn't talk. About anything. To anyone. Ever. Like—just as an example—when we all go out for a beer at the Ladybug Lounge. I've watched him and he stands off to the side. I've seen it more times than I can count."

"Did you ever ask him to sit with you?" Tracy asked.

Lindsey looked surprised, but then laughed. "No," she said. "But he's *Decker*. He doesn't want to sit with lowly me. If he did, all he'd have to do is ask."

Tracy just raised her eyebrow and looked at her friend.

As she watched, Lindsey thought about what she'd said and nodded, her brown eyes filled with chagrin. "I really suck," she said.

As a team leader, Decker would never ask to sit with any of his subordinates, for fear they would feel obliged to say yes. And as for the other team leaders? Dave usually grabbed a booth with Sophia, whom Decker wouldn't go near, for reasons that Tracy now understood. And Tom, Sam,

and Alyssa—all fellow team leaders—had also all been former naval officers. As a former Navy chief—an enlisted man—it made sense that
Decker wouldn't be completely comfortable hanging with them, either.
And his partner and best friend—Nash—was in an intense, still-new romantic relationship with Tess. Joining them, time after time, would have
made Decker feel extremely third-wheel.

"He stands off to the side because we put him there," Tracy told Lindsey. "I did it, too. I never really thought he was human. But he is." She
shrugged. "So here I am. And you know what?"

Lindsey shook her head.

"I think it's possible I've never respected myself more."

And Tracy's best friend in the world, whom she admired more than
any other woman she'd ever met in her entire thirty-something years of
life, smiled at her.

"Good," Lindsey said. "And you look like you're not freaking out because he went off the radar—which is good, too. Because Deck? He goes
off radar a lot. You want to do this? Hook up with him for any length of
time? You better get used to waiting and wondering."

Tracy nodded. "I know. I'm freaking out inside," she confessed. "I
wish he would get back here already."

"That's normal," Lindsey said. "To wish that. And it's okay, too, if you
freak out when you're with me." She glanced over her shoulder. "When
the door's closed. But for the record? Deck's very good at what he does.
He'll be back soon."

Tracy had to smile. Those were words she herself told Lindsey, repeatedly, when her husband, Mark, was overseas with his SEAL team. Lindsey
recognized that, too, and grinned. "Also for the record," she said, "reunion
sex? Always extremely great."

Tracy felt her cheeks heat. "I honestly don't know how this is going to
play out," she told her friend. "I mean, I know what I want, and I'm pretty
sure I know what *he* wants—right now. But what he wants tomorrow . . . ?"
She shrugged. "I'm trying to . . . be reasonable."

"Who are you," Lindsey mocked her, "and what have you done with
my too-impetuous friend Tracy?"

She had to laugh. "Shut. Up."

Lindsey laughed, too, and stood.

But Tracy caught her arm. "Hey, change of subject?" she said. "Michael Peterson."

Lindsey nodded and sat back down. She knew the name well.

"Do you remember," Tracy said, "when we did a girls' night out back in January? It was a Thursday, so we had a wine-free dinner." The Troubleshooters office was open Thursday evenings, so they'd all had to go back to work. "That's wine without an H."

Lindsey nodded. "You, me, Sophia was in town, and . . . I think . . . Didn't we invite Tess, too?"

"Yeah, and it was weird because she and Jimmy were fighting," Tracy said. "That's the night. I went out with Michael the evening before and . . ."

"You brought him home with you," Lindsey remembered. "I remember thinking that you were insane. What was it, your second date?"

"Yeah, I've beaten myself up enough over the past six months, thank you very much," Tracy said. During their date—their second date ever, yes—Michael—if that was his name—had started talking about getting married. He'd stopped himself, and looked mortified, as if he were embarrassed and afraid that she would think it was too soon. Tracy had played it so cool, like, *we really do need to get to know each other,* although inwardly she'd started shopping for a dress. He was smart and funny and sweet and pulse-stoppingly handsome. He was perfect, and he *loved* her. Or so he'd said, with tears in his evil, lying eyes.

"Sorry," Lindsey said.

"Live and learn," Tracy repeated Decker's words to her. It *was* a good motto. She was going to pin the words to the wall of her workstation. "But here's my question. After we got back to the office, I wanted to show you his picture, and I had one on my phone, but it was so small, so I downloaded it onto my computer. Or was that *your* computer? Wasn't that when you just got your Mac?"

During the past year, Lindsey had become one of those obnoxious PowerBook users. Anytime anyone had trouble opening or downloading a file using their PC, Lindsey would nod and say, "That wouldn't happen with *my* computer."

She now stood up. "I *think* it was mine. Let me check."

"It was months ago," Tracy said, following her into the hallway, trying not to get too excited at the possibility. "You probably deleted the file."

"Nah," Lindsey said as she led Tracy into her office. "My hard drive's massive. And I've been busy. And lazy." She sat behind her desk and woke up her laptop. "Michael wiped your phone, too, huh?"

Tracy nodded. "It freaks me out. Thinking that he came back into my apartment to do that. I mean, I remember looking at his picture in February." On Valentine's Day—she was such a loser. "So sometime between then and now . . ." It had to be either while she was sleeping or in the shower. "That gives me the creeps."

"Okay, January, huh . . . ?" Lindsey frowned at her computer screen and started flipping through picture files. "Lemme see. . . ."

And then, like magic, there it was. The photo of Michael that Tracy had taken while he was talking on his cell phone, leaning against the front hood of his car. "Yes!" Tracy leaned closer to look, and Lindsey hit print.

"Would you look at that?" her friend, a former LAPD detective, said. "We've got his face—and his license plate numbers."

"Those won't be his plate numbers," Tracy said.

"You never know," Lindsey told her. "If he thought you were easy—" She winced. "Not you—the job. You've got no military or law enforcement training. You're a receptionist, not an operative. That kind of easy. This may actually be his car."

Her computer had printed the photo on regular paper, so it wasn't very high quality, but it was still good enough.

Tracy followed Lindsey as she took the picture down the hall to the lobby, where Jo Heissman was being babysat by Lopez. Lindsey handed the older woman the printout.

Jo laughed grimly, and looked up at Lindsey and then Tracy. "That's him," she confirmed. "Peter Olivetti."

It was stupid, but part of Tracy had hoped both she and Jo were wrong. Of course, it was only relatively recently that her twenty-year-long hope that someday her prince would come had been fully dashed.

"AKA Michael Peterson." Tracy turned to Lindsey. "Is there a secure way—completely secure—to send this photo to Alyssa?"

"I'll call her," Lindsey said.

"Tess is with her," Tracy said. "Tess would know."

"I'm on it." Lindsey disappeared down the hall.

Jo stood up. "When do we get to find out what's going on—what this is all about?"

"I'm not at liberty to say," Tracy told her, told Lopez, who'd also gotten to his feet.

"Is Jim Nash still alive?" Jo asked. She had a way of looking at people as if she could read their minds.

So Tracy thought about Decker, about how badly she wanted him to walk through that door. Please, God, she wanted to know that he was safe. And then, she wanted him to take her by the hand, and lead her back with him to his office, where he'd close the door. Only, as soon as the door shut, it wouldn't be his office anymore, it would be a hotel room. In Paris. With roses—hundreds of them—in vases around the room, surrounding a pillow-covered bed. And on any surface where there weren't vases of roses, there would be lit candles, smelling faintly of vanilla.

Outside of the window would be cobblestone streets and the most beautiful sunset, with an accordion playing a haunting, romantic tune— way in the distance.

Decker would look at her, and she'd smile and say *Game on*, and he would smile, too, and then with heat in his beautiful eyes, he'd kiss her and . . .

"God, I wish," Tracy told Jo, through a throat that ached with longing. She didn't wait to see if Jo believed her as she followed Lindsey down the hall.


Decker's intention was to stop in at the Troubleshooters office and pick up the secure satellite phone that Lindsey had left there earlier.

His intention was to call Jimmy Nash while he drove over to the hotel where Tom and one of his SEAL friends were standing guard outside of Dave's—and Sophia's—suite. Because it was time—and he hoped Nash would agree—to tell Dave—and Sophia—the truth.

But when he walked in, Jo Heissman, who was hanging in the lobby with Lopez, sat up and called, "Tracy! Decker's back!"

Jo had been curled up and dozing on one of the couches, near where Lopez was using a laptop computer to monitor all of the security cameras that were positioned outside of the building. The SEAL was both guarding Jo and standing sentry—with no risk of mosquito bites.

"Okay," Lopez said, "I didn't see your truck enter the parking lot, and that's a problem."

Decker leaned over the screen. Pointed. "My truck's there now."

Lindsey appeared in the hallway, and she, too, shouted for Tracy. "Tracy, Deck's here."

"So it is." Lopez looked up at him, embarrassment and chagrin in his brown eyes. "Sorry, Chief. I don't know how I missed that."

"Have some coffee," Deck told him. "Stay alert."

It was then that Tracy came flying down the hall, past Lindsey, and he braced himself because it seemed inevitable that she would launch herself into his arms. But she didn't. She stopped short, and just stood there, looking at him. And there it was again. Her heart, in her beautiful, intelligent eyes.

"Are you all right?" she asked, as behind her Lindsey faded into her office.

"They didn't come after me," Deck said as he gazed back at her, admittedly a little disappointed. It had been a long time since a woman had been so happy to see him that she'd flung herself at him. Emily had never been the flinging type. In fact, toward the end, she'd gotten so passive-aggressive about the time he spent away, she'd made a point never to be home to greet him when he returned.

Ranger was always home, though. And Ranger always damn near knocked him over in delight, whether Deck was gone for two hours or two months.

Decker hadn't realized how much he'd missed that.

"You say that like it's a bad thing," Tracy said. "Like you're unhappy that you weren't attacked."

"I am," he admitted. "I want this over and done."

Tracy nodded. "I think it's safe to say that we all do."

Damn, but she was beautiful, even with no makeup on. Especially with no makeup on. She'd washed it off in the shower. Her hair was wavier than it usually was—probably because she'd done nothing to it or with it. She'd gotten into his truck, several hours ago, with it still damp.

From the shower.

And yeah, guess what *he* couldn't stop thinking about.

She was wearing those jeans that he liked, with a campaign T-shirt saying "Got hope?" and those cute pink and white sneakers on her feet. She looked unbelievably good, although admittedly not as good as she'd looked when she was naked and holding out her hand to him.

In the shower.

She held out her hand to him now, but it wasn't to pull him down the hall and into his office, where she'd kick the door shut and unfasten his pants. No such luck. She was holding out her hand because she was giving him a sat phone.

"I programmed it with your number," she told him. "I think it's secure, but you should double-check that with Alyssa or Tess before you use it."

"Thank you," he said. Their fingers touched only briefly before she pulled her hand away. "That's, um . . ." He looked at it, flipped it on, flipped it shut. "What I came back for. That's great that you, uh, thought to have this ready for me. I appreciate that."

Jesus Christ, he sounded like a moron. *I appreciate that?* What the fuck was his problem? If he wanted to drag her into his office and kiss the hell out of her, he should just goddamn do it.

"I'm in charge of equipment," Tracy was saying. "I figured you'd want to have it. I mean, okay, *I* wanted you to have it. It was driving me crazy that you were out there without a phone. But you should definitely check with Tess—on a line that we know is secure—to make sure that I set it up right. It's too important not to, and . . . I won't be insulted. Not at all."

Decker looked at her standing there. She was nervous as hell, and so clearly trying hard to be a professional. She turned, her body language indicating that she wanted to walk with him back down the hall—probably to his office where he could access that secure landline.

And kiss the hell out of her.

He glanced back at Jo Heissman and Jay Lopez, both of whom were watching them. It was clear, from where they were sitting, that no one was willing to let the doctor roam free. Which was a good thing. Just because *he* didn't think she'd maintained her Agency ties didn't mean he wasn't wrong. And if the doctor really wasn't on the side of the bad guys, she wouldn't mind their precaution.

Of course, she was a cougar, so maybe she was just enjoying Jay Lopez's low-key but enormously attractive undivided attention.

And okay, that was harsh. And Deck had to confess that one of the reasons he didn't like his former therapist was because she knew too much about him. Including the fact that he would never, *never* kiss Tracy here in the lobby of the company office.

Never.

And Jo Heissman also knew that odds were he wouldn't do it, even in the privacy of his office, with his door shut.

She was shaking her head at him—just slightly—the smallest of smiles curving her lips. Yeah, she'd noted all the body language and whispered conversations between him and Tracy, back at her house, and she knew damn well what was up. And as Decker met her eyes, she actually flashed him an L—for loser.

"You're allowed to be happy," she said, adding, "Shortest therapy session ever."

That made him laugh and shake his own head as he turned—and lengthened his stride to catch up with Tracy, who was nearly halfway down the hall.

"You need to call Tess and Alyssa anyway," Tracy was saying, "because I found a picture of Michael or Peter or whoever he really is."

"Really?" he said, instantly back in step. "A picture of his face?"

"No, of his elbow." Tracy shot him a look of disdain as she stopped at his office door. "Yes, of his face. And of his license plate, too. Go, me."

And really, that was all it took. Ballsy Tracy was back, kicking nervous Tracy to the curb. Nervous Tracy made Decker think too much about fraternization, and how, for years, he'd had a self-imposed zero tolerance rule when it came to sexual relationships with fellow employees. Nervous Tracy made him nervous, too, but he knew exactly what to do with ballsy Tracy. He grabbed her by the arm—the one that he hadn't scraped the shit out of with Jo Heissman's back door—and yanked her into his office.

She slammed against him, but the full-body contact didn't faze her. On the contrary, she had her arms around his neck, her hands in his hair, and her lips locked on his before the door that he'd kicked shut hit and locked into its frame.

Her mouth was soft and sweet, and Jesus, so eager.

It was a replay of that kiss they'd shared in Sam and Alyssa's garage, except he was neither dizzy nor nauseous nor without his pants—which, this time around, was a crying shame. He was none of those things, *and* he was also no longer aghast at the idea of where this might go.

In fact, Deck knew *exactly* where it was going, and he couldn't fucking wait to get there. But it couldn't happen now. Not here. Okay, maybe here, but definitely not right now.

He pulled free. From her mouth only. The rest of her he held on to—tightly. She was soft and warm and pliant—as if she'd melted against him. She was breathing as hard as he was, and looking at him as if she could not believe he'd stopped kissing her. He understood her amazement. He could barely believe it himself.

"This was what I came back for," he told her, his voice barely more than a whisper. "Not the phone. I just wanted to make that clear."

She pulled his head down and kissed him again. And yeah, it was even harder to stop kissing her this time, because his hands were on her incredible ass and God save him, he'd wanted his hands there for what felt like a lifetime, and he didn't want to move them to a place more suitable for a serious conversation. So instead, he kept kissing her as he pulled her even closer, and merciful Jesus, she sat up on his desk and opened herself to him, and yeah, there he was, a real hero—dry-humping her, because he could . . . not . . . stop. . . .

It was Tracy, then, who pulled away. "You have to make that phone call," she breathed. "We both have work to do."

Decker nodded. And kissed her again.

She was laughing as she pulled away again. "I am *not* going to risk getting you mad at me for distracting you when you should be saving the world."

Deck nodded again. And kissed her again.

And this time, instead of pulling away, she pulled him closer. "Unless," she whispered. "You're okay with our first time being a quickie . . . ?"

Decker had to laugh. "I'm stopping," he said.

But he kissed her throat, her neck, breathing in the sweet scent of her hair, and she clung to him more tightly. "Sixty seconds," she breathed into his ear. "I'll set the alarm on my phone. When it goes off? We're done."

Decker caught her mouth with his own. Mmm. "I'm pretty sure at this point we've been talking about it for more than sixty seconds."

"My point exactly," she said. "I take longer bathroom breaks in the middle of a workday. Even in the middle of a crisis."

He stopped what he was doing and looked into her eyes. "You're serious."

Tracy laughed and shook her head as she pushed him away from her—well out of kissing range. She straightened her clothes and slid down off the desk. "I would hate it if someone was hurt or killed while we were getting busy. Even for sixty seconds. And I know you'd be thinking about it the entire time, which wouldn't be fun for you. I mean, I know you're already freaking out because we're in your office, not to mention the fact that I'm me—that I work *for you*"—she made quote marks in the air— "which is not true, but I know you don't think so, and knowing you it'd probably be a problem if it was only that I worked *with* you. So no, I'm not serious."

As she continued speaking she crossed over to the couch that he usually kept cluttered with files and boxes and papers and books. She'd cleared it off—it was obvious that while he was gone, she'd been camping out here, in his office. She'd brought in a fleece blanket—one of those little ones that people took to evening football games—a pile of new legal pads, and some kind of computer printout.

"Okay, I'm probably a little serious," she said as she picked up the printout and held it out to him. "Because I really love the way you kiss me and I want very much to do that again. At a time when we both feel as if we *can* take a break. Maybe even . . ." She paused dramatically, a sparkle of humor in her eyes. "For five or yes, even ten minutes."

Decker laughed.

"I know," she said. "It's almost too exciting to imagine. And considering the way you kiss me . . . ? I'm going *big* in terms of imagination. FYI, I'm using *The Secret*, too," she teased. *"The best ten-minute break I've ever taken in my entire life is in my very near future.* But right now, Sparky, we need to get to work."

Deck saw that the list she was holding contained personnel information for everyone who worked both out of this office and out of the Troubleshooters' Florida office. And he knew that she'd anticipated—exactly—his next move, and was preparing to contact everyone who was on their employee roster.

He nodded, and picked up his desk phone, punching in access to the company's secure landline.

Tracy gathered up all of her things. "I'll get you a cup of coffee," she told him. "And that picture of Michael Peterson–Peter Olivetti—who, by

the way, has the same middle name, which is *Asshole,* agreed upon mutu-
ally by his conned ex-girlfriends everywhere."

And with that she left the room, closing his door tightly behind her.


Jimmy was awake when his phone rang. He tried to answer it quickly, because Tess had fallen asleep, curled up next to her computer and a variety
of photos and papers that she'd spread across the plush carpeting of the
bedroom floor.

He saw from the incoming number that it was Decker—about fucking
time. "What's going on?"

"It's time," Deck said.

"I figured as much," Jimmy agreed as he watched Tess push herself up
so that she was sitting. She swept her hair back from her face and looked
at him questioningly, so he repeated Deck's words and embellished. "It's
time to bring the entire Troubleshooters team on board—let 'em know I'm
alive, tell 'em what's going on." It was extremely likely that their enemy
would also realize that he was alive, but so be it. It was time to protect their
friends—as well as ask for their help.

She nodded, and Jimmy told Decker, "Tess agrees."

"Where is he?" Tess asked.

"Where are you?" Jimmy repeated into his phone. "I'm putting you on
speaker."

"TS HQ," Deck told them both. "I'm with Lindsey and Lopez. And
Tracy. We're babysitting Dr. Heissman—you got my message about her,
right?"

"That you no longer think she's Satan?" Jimmy said. "Please bear in
mind that I'm not yet convinced."

"No worries—we're not letting her run free."

"But you're undermanned over there," Jimmy pointed out. "Lopez is
adorable, don't get me wrong, but he's no Lindsey—"

"We're in lockdown," Decker said. "The building's secure. Don't even
*think* about coming out here. Tracy's already started calling people in—
we'll have backup ASAP."

Jimmy glanced at Tess, who looked pointedly back at him. "I'm not
going anywhere," he promised them both.

"Besides," Decker continued, "I need you working the *what the fuck* angle. Everything these motherfuckers are doing now? It's drenched in panic. We need to figure out what it is that they know that we know. Jesus, I'm tired. Did I just make any sense at all?"

"They, as in the motherfuckers," Tess translated, "appear to know, absolutely, that we, as in the collective we currently participating in this phone call, have information that will, again absolutely, serve to identify them, thus resulting in their going to jail for a long, long time."

"They're not afraid of jail," Jimmy interjected. They were afraid of him—and they were right to be.

But Tess wasn't done. "However, we haven't yet figured out what it is that we, collectively, know. So really, the best thing we can do right now isn't to hunt for them in order to shoot it out, but instead to hunker down, do research, and crunch facts and information. I think when we put it together, we *will* know who they are."

"Exactly," Deck said. But then he paused. "I understand why you're not eager to share that list that you made, but—"

"No," Jimmy interrupted him. "I'm doing it. In fact, I'll call Cassidy right after I hang up. He's got a copy for Tess. I'll have him get a copy to you, too. Just . . ." He sighed. "Shit."

"I won't leave it lying around," Decker said.

"No." Jimmy tried to explain. "It's just . . . Christ, this is hard to say, when I don't even fucking know what I *want* to say—"

"How about that we've *both* done things that we never would've done, except we thought we were working for the good guys," Decker said quietly. "We found out, the hard way, that the end really *doesn't* justify the means. Because if you believe that it does, then you shoot the seven-year-old in order to kill the terrorist, and you don't fucking blink. Am I right?"

Jimmy looked at Tess, who'd clearly spoken to Deck at some point over the past few hours. But she shook her head. She *hadn't* talked to him. This was something he'd figured out on his own.

"And then? Eventually? You just shoot the seven-year-old," Decker continued. "Unless, sometime, long before you hit that point, you admit you got it wrong, and you walk away. You walked away, Jim. We both did."

Jimmy felt himself nodding, even though Decker couldn't see him. "It's just that those things on that list—"

"Are in the past," Decker finished for him. "It's over and done."

"I'm just," Jimmy said. "I'm . . ." Afraid. He, who'd spent most of his life fearless, was afraid that the two people who mattered most to him in the world were going to turn away from him when they found out the truth.

"Jimmy," Decker said quietly. "I know you. I *know* you. And Tess does, too. The list is . . . It's not nothing, because I see that it matters to you, but there's so much more to you than some list of past transgressions."

Tess had pulled her knees in tightly to her chest, and was sitting there on the floor—with tears in her eyes—nodding.

"Okay?" Deck asked.

"I hear you," Jimmy said. What he really wanted to say was *I want to hear you say that—later.* But he didn't. Because he was too afraid of what he might hear from Decker later.

"Tom Paoletti's over at the Hilton, with Dave," Deck said. He added, "And Sophia," almost as an afterthought. "I was gonna go over there—"

"*Not* a good idea," Tess spoke up.

"If anyone should be told in person, face-to-face . . ." Deck said.

"I agree," Tess said. "It should be Tom. And Dave and Sophia. But you're talking about putting yourself at risk in order to do that. As well as risking the safety of everyone who's currently at the office."

"I think I should call him," Jimmy interjected. "Dave. Tom, too. I want to call them. Is that okay with you?"

Deck was silent on the other end of the phone. "Fair enough," he finally said. "But do let them know that the sooner they get over here, the easier I'll breathe."

"I'll pass that along," Jimmy told his friend. "Keep us posted if anything comes up."

"Will do," Decker said. "Oh, yeah. The picture. Tracy's photo of Michael Peterson–Peter Olivetti. Let's crop his car and his plate numbers out before we float it out there. It's a long shot that those numbers will lead us to a current address, but let's play that card close for now, all right?"

"Agreed," Tess said. "I'll tell Jules and Alyssa to dig for an address under the radar. We'll let you know what they come up with."

"Thanks," Deck said, and cut the connection.

Jimmy turned off his speaker and dialed Jules Cassidy's cell.

The FBI agent took three rings to answer it, which meant that Robin had made good on his promise to help him sleep. "Everything okay?" Jules asked.

"Yeah," Jimmy said. "Sorry to wake you, but I just spoke to Deck. I've got some info I want to pass along, plus . . . I'm ready to show Tess the list, so as soon as you can . . ."

"I'm on my way," Jules said.

Jimmy hung up the phone to find Tess looking at him. "Well, here we go," he said.

But she shook her head. "I'm not going anywhere."

He nodded, but he wasn't going to hold her to that.

He reached for his phone again, because he had to call Tom and Dave—give 'em the "good news."

Although, ultimately, when Dave realized the implications of Jimmy's not being dead? He was *not* going to be thrilled.


Dave rewrote his will, longhand.

He also made a list of all of his various bank accounts. His years of frugal living would make it possible for Sophia to never have to work again, provided she lived modestly and the kid went to state schools and . . .

Dear God, he didn't want to die.

But he had to be ready to. And knowing that he could take care of Sophia, even after death, was going to help him be ready for anything.

He'd used up all the paper in the room, and had sent SEAL Chief Ken Karmody down to the front desk for more. And then, finally, for envelopes.

"Anything else I can get you, master?" Ken asked. "Maybe a snack from the kitchen, a bottle of wine, a foot massage . . . ?"

"No, thank you," Dave said as he wrote Decker's name on the outside of one of the envelopes. He'd written a note—well, a report-sized note—telling Decker everything he'd found out on his recent trip to Kazabek, about Sophia's husband Dimitri's death. He put the note inside and sealed the envelope.

"Yeah, see, I was kidding," Ken was saying as across the room, Tom Paoletti's phone rang. "And . . . Just . . . Never mind."

"Don't go far," Dave said, looking up to add, "Please? I'm sorry if I seem rude or abrupt, but . . . I'm trying to do this while Sophia is sleeping. I need you to witness this, to make it legal." Tom had already signed it, while Ken was downstairs.

Ken realized what Dave was doing, and sat down on the other side of the writing desk. "I'll sign whatever you want," he said, "but it's not necessary, because we're not going to let anything bad happen to you."

Dave looked at the SEAL. "You mean, you're going to *try* not to—"

"*Star Wars* fan," Ken said, shrugging expansively. "I can't use the word *try* without my mental Yoda kicking in. So . . . we're *not* going to let anything bad happen to you."

"Holy shit," Tom said from the other side of the room. He was talking on his phone. He said it again, laughing this time. "Holy *shit.*"

"Well, in my experience, there are no guarantees in this line of work, so in case using the Force doesn't get the job done . . ." Dave handed Ken his pen, spinning the document to face him.

"I think I know what you're thinking," Ken told him as he painstakingly printed his full name. "One of the most beautiful women in the entire world is in your bed. The universe doesn't randomly do shit like that, you know, the beauty falling for the geek, so your death *must* be imminent."

Dave nodded. "It's a *little* more complicated than that."

Ken nodded as he put the pen down on top of the paper and pushed it all back across the desk. "Of course it is. It always is. But sometimes you've just got to bring it down to the bottom line." He leaned forward and spoke in a stage whisper. "There's a gorgeous woman in your bed, Dave. Right now. And you're out here, talking to me. What is wrong with this picture?"

Dave just shook his head as he sealed his will in a second envelope, which was when Ken noticed the first one.

"Aren't you going to write *Open only in the event of my death* on this?" he asked as he tapped on the envelope.

"I was going to," Dave answered evenly, "but I thought it would be too dorky, even for me."

"What if Deck opens it and you're *not* dead? That could be embarrassing."

"I'll be happy," Dave said, "to be embarrassed, which means I won't be dead."

"Good point." Ken nodded, but then said, "Well, I'd write it, but, hey, I'm a dork."

"You're a SEAL," Dave reminded him.

"And a dork. One is not exclusive of the other. It's not like they give you your budweiser pin with one hand and take away your laminated Battle-star Galactica Fan Club card with the other."

"Yeah, well," Dave said, "I'm not a SEAL, so people don't think it's cute when I'm a dork."

"So what if you're not a SEAL," Ken scoffed. "You're a legend in the SpecWar community. Anyone who knows anything knows you could breeze through BUD/S with one hand tied behind your back. And the fact that you're capable of fooling people into thinking you're too geeky to tie your own shoes? That's money in the bank. Being underestimated has saved *my* ass a time or twelve. I know you know what I'm saying."

Dave did know.

"You want me to hold on to those for you?" Ken asked, pointing at Dave's two pristine envelopes.

Dave nodded. "I'd appreciate that."

"No problem-o." Ken folded and smashed both envelopes in half and stashed them in one of the many pockets in his cargo pants. "I look forward to giving them back to you," he said. "Now, go into that bedroom, wrap your arms around that woman o' yours, and get your ass to sleep."

Dave stood up, the pain in his knife wound making him press his hand against his side. Something wasn't right with it. An infection was setting in that the antibiotic he'd been given wasn't able to kick out of his system. Either that, or some little piece of dirt or fabric hadn't been removed. He needed a return trip to the hospital—which wasn't going to happen in the near-future.

The SEAL however, didn't miss anything. "You okay?"

"I think I might need an upgrade in my antibiotic."

Ken got out his phone. "You want me to call Kelly?"

Tom Paoletti's wife, Kelly, was a doctor. "No," Dave said, "it can wait. Until morning."

"You sure?"

"Yeah, thanks," he said. "And thank you, too, for saying what you said about BUD/S."

The SEAL held out his hand for a fist bump. "I speak the truth, my brother. Besides, it's good when we brainiacs stick together. You and I are living proof that the hottest of the hot blond chicks? They loves it when their men be super-smart. We catch their attention with our ability to use complicated physics and/or calculus to save the world from destruction, and we seal the deal with our uniquely dorky but endearing charm."

Dave had to smile. "If only that were true."

"Malkoff." He looked up to find Tom Paoletti coming toward him. "Phone call."

Tom was holding out his sat phone, as if Dave should take it.

So he did. "Who is it?" he asked Tom.

"It's the answers to a lot of questions," Tom told him.

It wasn't like his boss to be so cryptic or evasive. Or annoying because he was being cryptic and evasive. Dave reminded himself that both Tom and Ken were doing him a huge favor as he dutifully put the phone to his ear, and said, "Malkoff."

"Hey, Dave," came a familiar voice. "It's Jimmy Nash. I'm kind of not dead."

# CHAPTER
# SIXTEEN

C alling the Troubleshooters staff was a two-step process.

Step one was a phone call to a potentially non-secure line. The message, whether delivered to an answering machine, voice mail, or an actual human, contained code that would give the operative the heads-up that a) the situation was urgent and their response was needed immediately (9-1-1); b) the return phone call should be made on a secure line (call when you get to Grandma's); and c) the situation was dire enough that said operative should get him- or herself, and his or her family if applicable, to immediate safety (red alert); and d) if available, they should come in (we need help).

Tracy had written a brief script that included all of those phrases, and had left messages, not just across the country, but around the world. "Hi, PJ, this is Tracy, with a 9-1-1 red alert. Auntie had a little accident and we need your help. Please call when you get to Grandma's."

Tom currently had forty-three operatives on staff, most of whom were part-time employees. Many of them lived overseas. There were only about twenty who operated, full-time, out of either the San Diego or Sarasota offices.

Of course, the roster grew considerably if all of the SEALs, both officers and enlisted, who'd given up a day or even a week off to "do Tommy a favor" were added to that list.

But Decker was working that military angle, making phone call after phone call to the Coronado Navy Base from his desk.

Lindsey was fielding the incoming calls and breaking the news that Nash wasn't dead.

By three A.M., Tracy was done, and she knocked on Decker's half-open door. She could see him at his desk, still on the phone, but he waved her in.

She'd brought him another cup of coffee, and as she came forward to set it on his desk, he reached out and, with a touch of a single button on his keyboard, he wiped his computer screen clean.

"Thank you, sir," he said into his phone, nodding his thanks for the coffee. "I'll have Commander Paoletti give you a call as soon as . . . Yes, sir. I will, sir." The phone rattled as he tossed it back into its cradle and he exhaled hard, running both of his hands down his face. "I don't know how Tommy does this. He calls in favors all the time. It's like walking a tightrope—how much ass-kissing is too much, because you don't want to do that, but God forbid you don't pucker up enough."

"Well, I think it's relative," Tracy said as she sat in one of the chairs positioned in front of his desk. "Whose ass it is you're kissing? I mean, it makes sense that, same way there are some asses that you want to kiss completely non-figuratively, there're also bound to be some people for whom you can pony up the right amount of respect and figurative smooches, so that it's not really ass-kissing, per se."

He laughed. "I must be tired, because that just made sense."

She narrowed her eyes at him. "Damn straight it made sense. I was serious."

"The people whose asses I want to kiss," he told her, "both figuratively and literally, are few and far between."

Zing. There it was, that electric current between them, as Decker told her very clearly, with his eyes and with the implication in his silence, that Tracy was on his short list.

That silence stretched on, so she filled it. "Do you always watch porn when you talk on the phone?"

"Porn." He was surprised, and he laughed again as he realized she was referring to his screen wipe. "No, honey, that wasn't porn."

"I know," she said. "I just like making you smile."

It was clear that he didn't know what to say to that, so he didn't say anything. He did, however, look at the door—as if he wished she'd shut it. Or maybe as if he wished she hadn't come in.

"There's not a lot to smile about right now," he finally said.

"Was that Nash's list you were looking at?" Tracy asked.

"Yeah," he said. "I'm sorry, but you can't see it."

"I wasn't asking to," she said. "I was just . . . Are you . . . all right?"

Decker nodded. "Thank you for asking," he said. "But yes, I'm fine." She thought he was going to leave it there, but to her surprise, he didn't. "I've been living in this . . . crazy world a long time. There's not much out there that can still shock me. Besides, I knew a lot of this—I'd figured most of it out. I mean, Jim would disappear for a few days. Or even longer. Then I'd watch the news on TV, and . . . Two plus two is usually four."

"Still," she said. "It must be strange to have it all verified."

He smiled at that. "What's strange is seeing it in print. You live in this world for long enough, and you stop leaving a paper trail—for anything. And here's this lengthy document with all this information that. . . . I keep wanting to hit delete." He shook his head. "You should've seen me after my first in-country assignment for Troubleshooters. I'm supposed to write up an expense report, right? Only I've shredded all my receipts. I went on autopilot and . . . Tommy paid me back, on faith." He changed the subject. "How's your arm?"

"It's fine," she said. "How's yours?"

"Fine."

"I've got the weirdest buzzing in my ears."

He nodded. "Residual ringing from the blast," he said. "Plus fatigue. It's been a long day. You should . . ." He stopped himself from saying it, and laughed.

So she said it for him. But first she reached behind her and pushed the door shut. It closed with a very loud click.

"I should take a break," she said. "You should, too. Wanna get naked? Or should we just sit and talk, and then both go entertain ourselves individually, in our respective bathrooms?"

This time, when he laughed, the weariness on his face dissolved. The heat in his eyes also softened into amusement and a different kind of warmth. "You do say exactly what you're thinking, don't you."

"What's wrong with that?" she asked.

Decker shook his head. "Absolutely nothing."

"I didn't always," she told him. "Say what I mean. I know you think self-help books are stupid, but I've learned a lot from them, like, how do you expect someone to know what you want if you talk in code? Like it's up to them to go and find a secret decoder ring?"

"I don't think *all* self-help books are stupid," he said.

"I started to listen to some of the things I said to people — mostly men," Tracy told him, "and I know I sometimes — often — take ten minutes to say something I could say in four seconds, and I'm working on that, too. But I noticed that I'm pretty good at communicating, except when it comes to things that are really important, and then I screw it up because I don't come right out and say what I want. So in case I haven't made it clear yet? I want you. Not just to have sex with, although for the sake of full disclosure, I will, without hesitation, choose sex in any position imaginable over playing gin rummy right now. Although gin rummy would be fun for those times when I wear you out."

She truly did love making him laugh. But she loved it even more when he surrendered and let himself look at her with that smoldering fire in his eyes.

"Please note I'm keeping your desk between us," Tracy continued. "I've sensed a certain . . . volatile element when we're in close proximity. And yet . . ." She reached out her hand, sliding it across the cluttered surface of his desk. "I can't seem . . . to stop myself from . . ."

Holding her gaze, he reached out and interlaced her fingers with his. But then he looked down at their hands on his desk, and he turned her arm over, so he could examine the cuts and scratches she'd gotten from trying to break into Jo Heissman's kitchen.

"I'm so sorry about this," he murmured as he brushed his thumb gently across her wrist.

"I'm not," she said. "I was trying to save you. It was silly, I know, but . . . I'd do it again, in a heartbeat."

And there they sat, just holding hands, as Decker's fatigue once again hardened his face into an expression that was oddly part wistful and part grim.

His hand was warm and large, with big, blunt fingers that were tough and callused. He was holding on to her only loosely, and she ran her own fingers between his and across his broad palm, loving the contact, as innocent and sweet as it was. It wasn't hard to imagine, though, what it would be like for him to touch her in far less innocent places with those big hands.

He sighed, and Tracy knew he was trying to figure out what to say, and how to say it, so she reluctantly let him go. He didn't try to hold on to her, which wasn't a surprise.

She sat back in her chair and just looked at him as he sighed for a second time. So she said it for him.

"I know that you can't do this," she told him quietly. "Not here, not like this. I know it's so far outside of your comfort zone that . . . I wouldn't do that to you, Deck. I'm just teasing when I . . ." She shook her head. "It's just another game. You know, pretending that we might actually get busy in here."

He nodded. "I can't," he said. "I'm only halfway through Nash's list and—"

"I know," she told him. "And it really is okay." She forced a smile, tried to lighten what she was saying. "It was very motivating, though. It will continue to be motivating. Let's figure out who we're up against, take them out as quickly as humanly possible—and then have dinner. At my place. Without the dinner. Unless you want to lick it from my naked body. Because that would totally work for me."

Decker laughed. He closed his eyes and shook his head, and when he looked at her, it was—again—with that soul-melting heat. "You're hurting me," he said.

"Honey"—she purposely used his standard term of endearment for any and all women—"it cuts both ways. And please note that when I said I understood and that it was okay? I didn't say I'd stop teasing you," she told him. "But only when the door's closed and no one else can hear." She stood up to open it, but first leaned slightly across his desk and lowered her voice. "Do let me know, though, if your comfort zone starts . . . expanding."

He laughed again, and she couldn't help herself. She reached out and lightly touched his face, her fingers sliding against the smooth warmth of his skin, then rasping against his growth of beard. "This is outrageously sexy," she said as she caressed his chin, "but for that dinner thing . . . ? I think I'll make you shave."

Decker laughed again, but he was definitely sounding choked— which was nice—as she turned and opened the door.

And got back to business. "We should meet with Lindsey," she told him briskly. A glance at the clock on Deck's desk told her that they'd taken that full ten minutes — it just hadn't been as satisfying as she'd imagined, back when she'd first confused the pretending with reality. Back before she hadn't given much thought to exactly how noisy it would get inside of Decker's head if they actually *did* have sex, here in his office. "We need to coordinate who's arriving where, when." She stuck her head into the hall and raised her voice. "Hey, Linds? You got a sec?"

"Hey, where've you been?"

As Dave sat down on the edge of the bed, Sophia pushed her hair back out of her face.

"Surreal-land," he said as he looked at her. The light was on in the bathroom, the door open a crack. Nobody was supposed to look good in fluorescent light, but Sophia did. She looked soft and warm and still half-asleep. "I'm kinda still there."

She thought he was still freaked out by the news of her pregnancy. "I'm sorry that I blindsided you—"

"No," Dave said. "Soph, this is . . . I just got off the phone with James Nash."

Sophia looked at him and as he looked back at her, she woke up. She sat up. "What? How?"

He told her, all of it, the whole long story that Nash has given him over the phone, and she cried, and okay, he even cried a little, too. But then he told her that Nash, Alyssa, Jules Cassidy, and Decker all believed that the knife attack and subsequent framing of Dave for Barney Delarow's murder had nothing to do with Anise Turiano, and everything to do with Nash.

"It was a test," Dave said, "to see if I knew whether Nash was really dead or still alive. The apparent thought being that if I knew Nash was alive, I would've contacted him after being attacked. Santucci, by the way? Nash's name before he became Nash."

"Oh, my God," Sophia breathed.

"Nash said he wanted to tell me," Dave told her, "right from the start, but . . ." He cleared his throat and said it. "Decker wanted distance. From me. And you."

She nodded and, unable to hold his gaze, looked down at her hands, clasped tightly in her lap. "Please, can we not have a fight about Decker right now?"

"He's at the Troubleshooters office," Dave told her. "He wants us to come there. He says we'll be safer, and I agree. We should pack up and go. As soon as Tom gets back, if you're up for it." Their boss had gone to make sure his family was safe. After he brought Kelly and Charlie to the office, he would be back to help Ken escort Dave and Sophia over there.

"Are you up for it?" she asked. "Did you sleep? Because I know you're not going to sleep once you get to the office."

"I'm fine," he said, and stood up to get his things from the bathroom.

But Sophia stopped him with a hand on his arm. "We probably won't have a chance to talk after we get over there, and I know I said some things before that hurt you—"

"You don't have to explain," he said.

"But I do—"

"No," he said, gently shaking her free and turning on the light on the bedside table. His cell phone was there, plugged into the base of the lamp, and he unplugged it and slipped it into his pocket. "I know I said that I'd change, that I'd be whoever, whatever you want me to be, but that's insane. And stupid. You know me. You *know* me. I'm the same man I've always been. And you either want me or you don't. You either love me or you don't. I can't make you love me—"

"But you did," she said. She'd followed him to the edge of the bed, and knelt there, pillow in her lap. "Somehow, you did. That night in Sacramento, I told myself I was having sex with a friend. A dear friend, who loved me. That was what I wanted. To be loved. But then you kissed me, and . . . God, Dave. And I thought, okay, maybe it was just because I hadn't had sex in a long time, and I pretended for a while that it was just about that—the sex. And I convinced myself that you were exactly what I needed because you were safe, because you would never, ever leave me—and even if you did, it would be okay because I didn't love you the same way I loved Dimitri."

Dave stood there, wishing he were sitting down, unwilling to press his hand against his side because then she'd know he was hurting, as he waited for her to finish. God, he was too tired and in too much pain to cry.

"I know this," he said quietly, "I know. I don't expect you to love me the way you loved Dimitri. Or even Decker. I would never assume that you—"

"But I do," she said. "You're not listening to me. I *do* love you. I love you *more* than I ever loved Dimitri, more than I ever loved Decker, because I wasn't friends with either of them, Dave. Not the way I am with you."

He struggled to understand—as well as to stay standing.

"You're my best friend," Sophia told him, and he focused on her face, on that gracefully shaped mouth that he loved to see curving up into a smile, "and you're my lover—you're my everything, including the father of my child. You're my *life*, Dave. And when I saw you in that parking lot, and you were bleeding and I thought that I might lose you, it scared me to death. Because I wasn't supposed to care. I wasn't supposed to love you that much." The tears that she'd been fighting escaped, flowing down her face, as she whispered, "But I do. That's what I'm trying to tell you. I *do*."

"Wow," Dave heard himself say, as if from a million miles away. "This is a really, really good dream."

And the world went black.


Tracy slept on Decker's couch.

He'd turned off the overhead light when she'd first dozed off, then spread a blanket over her when she went into a deeper REM cycle.

He sat now, in the circle of light thrown from his desk lamp, listening to her quiet, steady breathing, working his way through the list of black op assignments that Nash had done in the name of the Agency and the United States of America.

It was unlikely he was going to find anything. It was probably Tess who held the key.

Because, along with names, locations, and a brief description of the assignment, Nash had also marked the dates of those ops during which, even if he hadn't been overtly attacked, he'd barely escaped with his life.

The first time had been just shortly after Tess and Nash announced their engagement to be married.

It was probably pathetic that Decker remembered that date so clearly. But the news had left him—while happy for Nash—feeling oddly depressed. He'd indulged and bought himself a new truck. So yeah. He remembered the date.

And was it a coincidence that Nash's first attack had come so closely on the heels of his engagement to Tess? Deck didn't think so. He thought it was far more likely that Tess, with her years of working at the Agency as support staff, knew something that, combined with Nash's knowledge — gained from crawling through Agency mud — was enough to make their enemy sweat.

Which didn't mean Decker didn't finish going over that list with a fine-tooth comb. He did, and then he went through it again.

When he finished that second time, the office was silent.

Lindsey was probably napping.

Or she was in the lobby with Jo Heissman, who had actually wept at the news that Nash was alive. They'd put her to work making a list of all of the Agency operatives she knew who worked for the black ops division during her own tenure there.

At the very least, it was keeping her busy.

In a few hours, Lopez was going to be relieved by two other SEALs from Team Sixteen — the result of Decker's epic ass-kissing. Cosmo Richter would take over his babysitting duties, while Bill Silverman prowled the perimeter of the office building.

Despite all of Tracy's SOS messages, no one else was scheduled to arrive until late morning, at best.

Ric Alvarado, the head of the Florida office, and his wife Annie had flown in to run security for Robin Cassidy while the actor was on set. When the news came down about the motel blast and the three dead John Wilsons, they'd tossed Robin onto a helo and flown his ass back to safety.

When Tracy called, Ric and Annie had been halfway to the safe house themselves, via van. Instead of turning around, they were continuing on to their destination. Both Alyssa and Jules wanted them out there, Tracy had reported. "It frees them up to come down here, if they need to."

"Frees *who* up?" Decker had asked.

"Not Jimmy," Tracy had assured him. They'd all agreed that Nash should remain at the safe house. "Everyone's on the same page about that. At least everyone but Jimmy."

Deck's smile was tight. "I bet."

"Jones is in Atlanta," Lindsey had reported. "With Martell Griffin. They're catching the next flight out here." She checked the list she was carrying. "The rest of the Florida contingent is already on the red-eye. Ric anticipated needing them. They'll head for the safe house, too, which'll free up Sam and even Tess."

"No," Deck said. "I want Tess with Nash. Please tell Alyssa. And Jules. That's important. Nash won't stay put unless she's there."

"Will do," Lindsey said.

"How about you?" Tracy asked. "Did your ass-kissing give you anything other than a pair of SEALs and some badly chapped lips?"

Decker smiled. "Nice."

"Thank you."

"It did, actually," Decker told them. "I called in all the favors that I could. We'll have most of the SWCC team back here, but not until early afternoon. I tried, but I couldn't talk Commander Koehl into rescheduling their morning training op. But I did manage to convince him to let us keep Lopez for a while longer." He looked at Lindsey. "Mark—and the rest of Team Sixteen—won't be back until the end of the month."

Lindsey tried her best not to get tense. "Is there a problem I should know about?" she asked.

"Not that I know of," Deck said. "Koehl sounded pissed about the delay, but not too pissed."

"I'm going to bank on my faith in you, boss," Lindsey said. "I'm going to trust that you *will* tell me if there is a real problem, okay?"

"Count on it," Decker promised quietly.

"So is that it?" Lindsey asked. "Cosmo, Silverman, Lopez, and a bunch of SWCC-boys?"

"We'll get Gillman, too—at about the same time we get the *men* from the Special Boat Squadron," Deck corrected her. "Until then it looks like we're in wait mode."

Lindsey nodded as she headed for the door. "I'll tell Lopez not to go anywhere."

"Take a break, while you're at it."

"With all due respect," Lindsey said, "you're looking like you could use a break first. I'm good for a few more hours. And I know Lopez is—"

"Lopez is off his game," Decker told her. "He didn't see me drive up."

"Really." Lindsey frowned. "I'll make sure he takes a nap when Cosmo gets here. But like you said, we're in wait mode. So with all due respect—"

"I have more reading to do," Decker said, careful to not look at Tracy.

Lindsey nodded. "If you say so, Chief. I hope you'll reconsider, though. I know I don't have to remind you that you've had a recent gunshot wound. And the fact is, all hell *could* break loose in the very near future, so—"

"Thank you." He dismissed her.

And with that, she was gone, closing the door—tightly—behind her.

Decker turned to look at Tracy, and they just sat there for a long moment, in silence.

Then she stood up. "I'll get out of your way, too."

"Don't," he said. "Please? Stay. Just . . . Keep me company?"

Tracy didn't hesitate. She also didn't try, in the slightest, to make it be about sex. Because she knew that it wasn't. "Of course," she said.

But now she stirred, and Decker looked over to find her awake and watching him from his couch.

"Hi," he said.

"Hi," she said. "The blanket fairy made a special delivery while I was sleeping."

Deck smiled at her. "I've been called a lot of things, but never that."

"I'd like to see you in sparkly wings." She stretched beneath the blanket. "I think I'll add that to my list of things I'm going to make you do. It's about number twenty below shaving, though, which goes right above making you lick me all over."

"Making me," he said, through a throat that was suddenly tight. "Why do you suppose that's so appealing. To me?"

She somehow knew that he was dead serious, and her flirty tone instantly evaporated. "Why should it matter?" she asked quietly, seriously. "If you like it, Deck, you like it. Why should there be a wrong way or a right way to have sex? And if there is, who gets to define right? The Pope? Your mother? *My* mother—kill me now? As long as everyone's a consenting adult—that should really be the only rule. If I say yes, and you say yes . . . ?" She laughed. "We're not talking about having sex on the front lawn. We're being private. If we're someplace safe and we've closed and locked our door . . . ? Let's please not bring my mother—or anyone else's mother or father—into the bedroom with us."

Tracy wasn't done. "Because what feels good is subjective. Telling someone how to have sex is as absurd as telling them what kind of ice cream they should like best, when there's a world of flavors out there." She sat up. "I know you don't like to talk about Emily, but I find myself wondering what it was that she said or did to you—"

"It wasn't her fault," Deck interrupted. "She said nothing. She didn't . . . know. We never talked about . . . sex."

Tracy was surprised. "Never? Like, not even, *Hey, hon, you want to do that thing where you do that thing . . . ?*"

"We didn't really talk about . . . anything," he admitted. "And then when Andy died, she tried for a while to . . . But . . . I just pushed her farther away."

"Andy," Tracy said. "Your friend who was killed in the Khobar Towers attack."

Decker nodded.

"Was he a SEAL?"

"Air Force. Pilot. He flew F-15s."

"Huh," she said. "How did an enlisted SEAL manage to become friends with an Air Force officer?"

"Past life," he told her, but it was clear that she didn't understand. Probably because that expression was just something Andy used to say. *This is my buddy Larry. We were friends in our past life, pre-ROTC.* So he explained. "We were tight since fifth grade. Andy Klein was the funniest kid in Ms. Bergeron's class at Oakmont Elementary."

"That's amazing you stayed friends all that time."

"Doubly amazing," he concurred, "since I was a Navy brat. That was the longest we ever lived anywhere. My dad was stationed in Korea and my mother didn't want to go, so . . ." He shrugged. "We lived with my grandmother in Jersey, for three glorious years. And no, I'm not being sarcastic. It was great not to move every six months. And even when we did move— summer after seventh grade—we still visited regularly. Andy and Caroline—he had a twin. They lived across the street from my gram, so . . . I spent a lot of summers with them both. Right up through high school graduation."

"Are you still friends with Caroline?" Tracy asked.

Deck laughed. Figured she'd pick up on his mention of Caro. "Not so much, no. Andy always thought I'd marry her, but . . . After he died, I couldn't look her in the eye." He looked Tracy in the eye and confessed, "And that was *before* I slept with her and then didn't call her for about two years."

She winced. "Ouch."

"It was not my finest hour."

"I meant *ouch* for you," Tracy told him. "Because you lost her, too."

They sat for a moment, just gazing at each other, and then Tracy asked, "How come you couldn't look her in the eye?"

It was time to change the subject. This was where, the few times Deck had actually spoken to anyone about Andy's death, he'd led the conversation elsewhere. But as he looked back at Tracy, as he looked into her warm and sympathetic eyes, he found himself saying words that he'd never before uttered. "He was still alive when I got to the hospital at the airbase."

She blinked. And leaned forward slightly. "*Andy* was? But I thought you went there to bring his body home."

"That's what I told everyone," Deck admitted, having to whisper because he'd never before said any of this aloud. "A mutual friend, a captain, was a doctor there, and she called me. She knew Andy wasn't going to live. His wife, Becca, had just miscarried and she couldn't travel — the captain knew that and so she called me."

"Oh, my God," Tracy said. "Oh, Deck . . ."

"When I saw Andy, I . . ." He couldn't look at her so he looked at the wall, the floor, the wood grain of his desktop. "The injuries and burns he sustained were . . ."

"He must've been in terrible pain," she murmured. "Burns can be—"

"Agony," he agreed, losing himself for a moment in the warmth of her eyes. But then he looked away again, unable to tell her that most of Andy's legs had been gone, as well as his hands. He'd sat with his friend, but there'd been nothing to hold on to, so he'd put his hand on top of Andy's head, where somehow, miraculously, he hadn't been burned.

"The doctor told me he wouldn't last the night, but . . . I stayed with him for seventy-three hours. I talked to him. And I promised him—he insisted—that I'd tell his mother and Becca and Caro that he'd died right away. The captain backdated Andy's death certificate, and I made up some bullshit story about how he was missing, but then someone thought they saw him, but then they finally found his body in the rubble and . . . I brought him home and we buried him, and everyone cried and hugged each other and nodded and said, *At least he didn't suffer.* And I nodded, too.

"And Emily knew something was wrong, but I couldn't tell her," Deck continued quietly. "No, that's not fair to her. I could've, but I didn't. Instead, I let it get between us and drive us even farther apart."

"She should have tackled you to the ground." Tracy was determined to defend him. "I would have. I would have *made* you tell me."

He looked at her, sitting there, with her hair disheveled and her hopeful T-shirt twisted around her, the top button of her jeans undone, as if she'd tried to get more comfortable while under the cover of the blanket. Her chin was up as she gazed at him, as if she expected him to challenge her statement.

But he agreed with her. "Yeah, I think you probably would've."

And then, after getting him to confess, Tracy would've completely rocked his world with the kind of physical sex that was meant to exhaust—to wear out and wear down. At which point she also would have convinced him beyond a shadow of a doubt that it was not just okay but *necessary* for a man to cry over the painful, horrible death of his best friend in the entire fucking world.

"I keep thinking *the hell with it*," Decker whispered now, as he looked at Tracy sitting there, looking back at him with such love in her eyes. "I keep thinking, if I die tomorrow, which will I remember more fondly, in those last seconds of my life? The fact that I had some unbreakable rule about appropriate behavior in the office? Or the fact that I jettisoned my rule and took the best ten-minute break in the history of the world?"

Tracy laughed her surprise as she realized he'd changed the subject. "Wow, talk about pressure."

"Come here and kiss me," Decker ordered her. His voice sounded like someone else's to his own ears. "If you just kiss me for ten minutes, it'll rate."

But she didn't move. "What if you live?" she asked him quietly. "Tomorrow?"

It was a damn good question.

"I've been thinking about that, too," he admitted. "About the fact that I'd actually like, very much, to, well, live. Which sounds crazy, because most people generally want to? But it's been a long time since I've given a shit."

It was hard to see her face completely clearly in the dimness—his circle of light didn't extend out to where she was sitting. But he was pretty sure that there was a sudden sheen of tears in her eyes.

Which, for some reason, didn't scare him. It had always scared him when Emily cried.

But Tracy *didn't* cry. She cleared her throat, and said, "Then maybe, since you *do* give a shit, it's not entirely inappropriate if we actually, you know . . ." Her voice trailed off, and Decker waited, curious to see what her word choice would be. If they *had sex, fucked, made love* . . . ? He knew, with a flash of clarity, which words he would have used.

But she didn't finish her sentence. She started over.

"Maybe it's not breaking the rule. Maybe it's just discarding an old rule and creating a new one." She paused. "If I tell you a secret, will you promise not to tell anyone?"

He had to smile at that, considering the magnitude of the secret he'd just told her. "I promise."

"Not even Nash?"

He pretended to think about it. "Okay, not even Nash."

That made her smile, as he'd hoped it would. "Don't be a jerk." She took a deep breath and said, "I once saw Tom and Kelly come out of the supply closet. The one right outside the conference room?"

Her upward inflection at the end of her statement implied that she wanted some sort of response, so he said, "I'm not sure this is something I want to know."

"It is," Tracy insisted. "Try not to be a prude for a second, will you?"

"I'm not a prude."

"Shh," she said, "we can argue about that in a minute. Listen to what I'm saying, okay? I was collating a report. I was in there—in the conference room—for at least forty minutes. I was facing the door, but I didn't see them go into that closet. Which means they were in there for *more than* forty minutes. And they were *not* counting rubber bands."

"I don't know," Deck said. "I go in there myself, sometimes, just to count rubber bands. We have somewhere around four hundred thousand. It takes at least three hours to count 'em all."

Tracy laughed as she threw one of the couch pillows at him. "Fine," she said. "*Be* a jerk. But for the record? Sam and Alyssa have sex in Alyssa's office all the time, too."

"I don't want to know that," he said, but then asked, "How exactly *do* you know that?"

She looked at him, and imitated Sam's Texas drawl, "*Tracy, hold all of Lys's calls. We're having an important lunch meetin'.*" She rolled her eyes. "Hello. Obvious. And when she was pregnant? He used to pretend he was giving her a massage during lunch. *Her back is actin' up—Tracy, hold her calls.* There was definitely massaging going on. Sam just left out the part where there was a happy ending for *everyone.*"

"Tom and Kelly, Sam and Alyssa," Decker pointed out. "They're married."

"To someone they work with."

"Kelly doesn't work here," he countered.

"Yeah, right," Tracy scoffed. "Tell *her* that, when one of the operatives needs a house call from a doctor in the middle of the night. Look me in the eye and tell me she's never treated you in a pinch."

Decker looked her in the eye, but then shook his head. "Can't."

And there they sat, again, in silence.

"Can I just say something more?" Tracy asked. "Because it's important to me that you understand I'm not looking for sex for the sake of sex. Although the sex *would* be incredibly great. I know that. But I also know that I'm . . . reckless, when it comes to relationships. And I know that you said—and maybe this was just something you said but you didn't mean— that you didn't want a one-night stand—"

"I don't," he said.

"Good," she said. "That's good. I also know that you've got this kind of weird, deep connection to Sophia"—he opened his mouth to speak, but she silenced him—"shush, let me finish."

Decker gestured, *Go on.*

"I know she's with Dave right now, but that's just right now," she said earnestly. "And of course, there's Emily, whom you still talk about with a certain wistfulness. She clearly meant a lot to you."

He shook his head. *Wistfulness?* Was she kidding?

"And now I find out about Caroline—"

He couldn't keep his mouth shut any longer. "She and her husband just had their second daughter."

"Okay," Tracy said. "I'll put her in the *nothing lasts forever* column with Sophia. As opposed to Jo Heissman, who's here in the *could be fun* column with me."

"I'm sorry," he said, laughing. "Jo Heissman would *not* be fun." Of course, that hadn't been what he was thinking just yesterday—Jesus, was that really less than twenty-four hours ago? It had been a long, *long* day.

"My point is," Tracy told him, "that I know I'm not the only woman in your life—and these are just the women I know about. Tess. I didn't think of Tess."

"Please don't," Deck said.

"My point," she said again, because apparently she hadn't yet made it, "is that there's a world of options between one night and, you know, the illusion of forever. Shades of gray," she told him. "We could go into this believing that we're going to just be together until we're not together anymore. It doesn't have to be the beginning and the end, Deck. It doesn't have to be perfection. It could just be what it is."

He didn't say anything, he didn't move—because he was trying to find the words to tell her that, whatever this was, it felt big, and that scared him. Although now it scared him even more to think that it might not feel as big to her.

"Your turn to talk," she said. "I mean, I could keep babbling if you want, but I'd rather know what you think. About that."

"I think," he said slowly, "that we've covered it all. We could live, I could die—I'm not going to let you die. That's not an option. I'm tired, I'm hungry, I'm not in love with Sophia, and if I never see Emily again it would be too soon. I'm over-caffeinated, my arm hurts, my back stings, I'm pretty sure I smell bad, and all I can think about is how much I want to kiss you. Probably because I know damn well that if I do kiss you, we're not going to stop there. And I *am* going to kiss you, I'm definitely going to kiss you and yeah, that scares me—a lot—because I've never wanted anyone as much as I want you. Right now. Right here. To hell with right or wrong. To hell with everything except me and you. What do *you* think? About that?"

Tracy stared at him, her eyes wide, for several long, silent seconds. But then she stood up. In three long strides, she was locking the door. As she turned to face him, she said, "I think, *Game on.*"


Decker kissed her.

Tracy didn't see him move, but somehow he was around his desk—maybe he'd gone up and over the top—and he'd slammed himself against her and was, God, yes, kissing her.

It was crazy and breathtaking—like a dream that suddenly went from her weeding her garden in the placid late-summer sunlight, to full-power, heart-pounding, gonna-come-any-second-now intercourse.

Except they still had their clothes on—and God, she wanted them off.

But she loved kissing this man too much to stop. He kissed her as if he owned her, as if he would never, ever let her go. She loved the feel of him, too, so solid—both his chest, which she was plastered against, and his back, which she'd wrapped her arms around because being plastered against him wasn't enough. She wanted to be even closer.

His hands weren't gentle as he touched her, as he tried to pull her closer, too, as he pushed the solidness of his thigh between her legs as if he wanted to crawl inside of her.

She wanted that, too. Desperately.

*Condom.* She wanted to stop kissing him just for the nanoseconds necessary to tell him that she'd pocketed some condoms from the equipment locker—they were allegedly used to protect the more sensitive weapon muzzles from rain and water—and yet at the same time, she didn't want to stop kissing him.

Her desire to not stop won out—until she realized he had her shirt half off. She stopped kissing him then, to help him pull it over her head, and while she was doing that, he unfastened her bra.

"Shh," he said, "*shhh!*" and she realized that she was laughing, but she couldn't stop. She was giddy and she tried to unfasten both her pants and his at the same time, but gave up when he kissed her again, his hand on her breast, hot and so possessive.

He hiked her up so that she was sitting on his desk, and she pulled free from his mouth in alarm—but she didn't knock anything off, which was good, because Lindsey and Lopez would've come running at the clatter. She realized then, as he pushed her back, as he yanked her jeans down her legs, that she hadn't knocked anything off his desk because he'd cleared it completely, probably while she'd been sleeping.

He'd shaved, too, Tracy realized with a jolt.

This wasn't some spur-of-the-moment, impetuous decision he'd made as the result of fatigue and caffeine and hormones gone awry. He'd cleared off his desk and he'd shaved—he'd planned to be right here, right now—because he'd made up his mind that this was what he wanted.

*She* was what he wanted.

Tracy grabbed for the back pocket of her jeans just in time, just before they were out of her reach—and pulled free the foil-wrapped accordion line of condoms that she'd snagged from the closet for exactly this purpose.

But Decker had gotten some of his own—and he'd not only managed to unfasten his pants while he'd undressed her, but he was almost done covering himself, too.

For several seconds, time seemed to hang as she looked at him, as he gazed back at her as she lay there, naked and sprawled across his desk, propped up on her elbows, hair wild around her shoulders, legs spread as she waited for him.

He still had most of his clothes on, but he took off his shirt, since it got in the way, leaving him bare-chested with his jeans unzipped.

The devil in her made her stop him before he took that last step toward her. "Wait," she said. "This is a big deal for me. I mean, you're not green."

It took him a second to understand what she meant, but by then she'd reached between them and taken hold of him—holy God, he put George to shame—both wrapping her fingers around the whole wonderful, solid, living length of him, and rubbing him against her because even though she'd told him to do just that, she couldn't wait.

He was laughing now, too—she was the one telling him to "Shh!" as she pushed him just a little bit inside of her—and it felt so good—using him as she used George, to touch herself in . . . exactly . . . the right . . . place.

"Tracy," he breathed, his eyes hot, his mouth still wet from those long, deep kisses they'd just shared, and although he grabbed her wrist, he didn't pull her hand away from him, so she didn't stop what she was doing.

"I just want to . . ." Her voice came out sounding breathless as she pushed him even farther inside of her.

He wasn't laughing anymore as he said, "Honey, I gotta . . ."

"Oh, yeah," she said as he reached for her, his hands hot on her bare skin even as she locked her legs around his waist. He claimed her mouth again—the man could kiss—as he pulled her hips toward him and filled her with him—with *all* of him.

"Hunh," he exhaled, as she said, "Ohh," even as she pushed him deeper, still deeper.

She loved the way he was holding her, loved the way he was kissing her, his talented tongue filling her mouth, and she really loved the way he was moving, with her, against her, driving himself inside of her, as if he could not and would never get enough of her.

She came much too soon, exploding as she clenched her teeth around the sounds she wanted to make as she tried to be quiet. It was just as good, because *I love you, God, I love you,* was back there, in her throat, and if they'd been in her bedroom or even in her kitchen—she wanted to do this again, on her kitchen table; and okay, to be honest she wanted to do this on every table on the entire planet—she could well have said it, sung it, screamed it aloud.

Instead she swallowed the words as she felt him, too, buck and rock against her as he came and came and please, God, let it be the greatest sex ever in his entire life so that he wouldn't . . .

Run.

Screaming.

Tracy couldn't help herself, she started to cry, because there was no way that this man, this incredible, amazing, wonderful, brilliant, funny, sexy-as-hell man could ever, in a million years, love someone as average as she was.

"Hey," he breathed in her ear. He was breathing hard and she could feel his arms, his entire body shaking as he held her there, still held her close, their bodies still joined. "Where'd you go?"

"I'm right here," she whispered back.

"I didn't hurt you, did I?" He was actually worried—he pulled back to look at her, to look into her eyes. Which, of course, meant that he saw that she was crying.

She made herself laugh, willing her tears to dry up as she wiped her eyes. "I'm just . . ." She shook her head as she pushed slightly against him, which made him pull back, pull away, pull out.

Leaving her feeling cold and vulnerable. And a little too naked.

"Seriously," he said as she slipped off his desk and began searching for her underwear. It took him far less time to discard the condom and fasten his pants. "You're going to stop with the honesty?" he continued. "You're going to stop saying exactly what you're thinking, *now?*"

Tracy couldn't find her panties, so she pulled on her jeans without them as she answered, "You're not going to like what I'm thinking."

Decker stood there, looking at her. Without his shirt, and despite the bandage around his arm—or maybe because of it—he looked like he was ready to pose for some kind of super-sexy, rough-and-tumble *Men of the SpecWar Community* beefcake calendar. Except for the consternation on his face. "Try me."

She couldn't find her bra or her shirt, so she wrapped the blanket around her shoulders—the one that he'd brought her while she was sleeping—and she sat down wearily on the couch. "I lied," she said, "about not wanting forever." She closed her eyes. "I do the same thing with every new guy. I have sex, and I fall in love, only this time I fell in love with you *before* we had sex, and I don't know, I thought maybe that meant when we *did* have sex, I would have some sort of clarity, I guess, about what I really wanted, but all I want is you. And right now? Forever doesn't seem long enough." She laughed—to hide the fact that she was crying again. "Commence the running and screaming. Join the club and move to Maine."

She felt him sit down next to her, heard him sigh. "Tracy," he said. "For the record? Whatever I do, screaming or not, I seem to end up running, full speed, toward you."

"Is that a compliment or an insult?" She looked at him. He was so tired, he looked as if he were having trouble focusing his eyes.

Still, he managed to smile at her. "Just a confirmation that the universe doesn't seem to recognize *don't.*"

Tracy laughed—for real this time.

But then his smile faded as he reached over and took her hand. "I don't just want," he told her. "I want you. I got clarity." He paused. "Good word. *Clarity.* It's a good thing to have, too. I recommend it. Along with a nap. Which now I *really* need."

She looked at him. "Are you telling me that . . . ? I mean, the you-want-me part, I get, but . . ."

Decker kissed her, and his mouth was so soft. "Sleep," he said. "As in must. Now. Me. Please, may I share your couch and blanket?"

Tracy nodded.

"Thanks, honey," he said, and he wrapped his arms around her and pulled her back so that they were both lying on the couch.

"Mmmm," he said as he realized she'd never found her bra and shirt, as he discovered and covered her bare breasts with the warmth of his hands. "This is a bonus." He nuzzled her neck. "You always smell so good . . . so sweet. . . ."

And with that, he fell soundly asleep.

# CHAPTER
# SEVENTEEN

Jimmy sat in the dark living room, looking out the big sliding glass doors at the desert.

The moon was full and its light cast shadows on the rock- and brush-cluttered surface of the hillside.

Nothing moved—it was as if the world were in a vacuum. Or as if this house had been built on the surface of the moon.

Jimmy heard Tess coming—she wasn't trying to be quiet. She also didn't turn on any lights, which was good, because he didn't want to see her eyes.

He spoke first. "You read fast."

"I skimmed," she admitted as she sat down, way on the other end of the sofa. "I'm going to go over it again, more carefully. I've marked seven ops that made me go *huh*. Some of them are because I worked support on a related op. Some of them, I'm not sure why, but I figured this was a good time to trust my gut. Watch your eyes."

She reached over then, and clicked on the lamp that sat on the table beside her.

Jimmy squinted, but the light was dim enough and his eyes adjusted quickly. She was holding out his entire massive list, and he took it from her because she seemed to want him to.

"The yellow are the seven in question," she told him.

But there were other marks, all the way down the page, slashes of pink, highlighting almost every single black op mission that he'd listed there. It was entirely like Tess to use color coding, but . . . He flipped it over, and the pink marks were on the second page, too. And the third and . . . It was only on the last page—those listing the ops he'd done after "leaving" the Agency—that the pink disappeared, and he couldn't figure out what that meant.

"The pink are the ops I knew about," Tess told him quietly. "Granted, I didn't know *everything* about them, but I knew enough."

Jimmy looked at her, shocked.

She nodded. "Yeah. Despite the covert nature of the Agency's black ops division, they kept information on these assignments in your file."

She'd hacked his file, years ago, back when she was working for the Agency's support staff.

But that didn't make sense. He knew he had a regular Agency file but . . . "Information about *these* jobs were in there?"

"Yup," she said. "And—for the record? About four months ago, I have to confess that I hacked back in. You were acting crazy and I wanted to see if you were still working for the Agency. But there were no additional entries in your file—in fact it was marked *Closed*. At the time, I assumed you had a separate file for black op assignments. I dug for it, but I couldn't find it. But you don't have one, Jimmy." She tapped the paper that held his list. "These assignments that you listed here were in that closed file. Except for the last page. Those are all new."

"Mother of God."

Tess nodded. "We need to stop looking at the Agency, and instead look hard at former Agency operatives and especially former Agency support. People like me, who could still have access to Agency files and information. People who have the information—and the power—to make former operatives believe that they're still being hired to work for the Agency."

And there it was. He'd been doing black ops for someone who wasn't part of the Agency. But when he'd gone into the Agency's D.C. annex and pushed his way into Doug Brendon's private office to talk about his "ongoing" association with the black ops division, Dougie had kicked his ass out into the street. No investigation, no inquiry, no nothing. Which meant Brendon was either involved—or a moron.

"You okay?" Tess asked, and he turned to look at her.

She was sitting there looking back at him exactly the same way she always had. With interest, expectation, intelligence, humor, love, and, yes, not an entirely small amount of exasperation.

"I wish you had trusted me," she whispered. "That's all I've ever wanted from you. Trust and honesty and respect. You say you love me, but without the trust—"

"There's too much to tell," Jimmy said. "Where do I start? With my mother? She sucked and I left her behind. Because that's what you do— you decide if you're going to live or you're going to die, and I chose not to die. I found people who saved me, only they sucked, too, and I went to jail out of loyalty, for something I didn't do. And I don't want to talk about *any* of it because, like Deck always says, it's over and done."

"Fair enough," she said—which was something else Decker always said. "But—"

"What if there's no but," Jimmy said. "What if there's just me, relieved beyond belief that you aren't avoiding eye contact and backing away from me because of everything on that list. What if there's just me, promising to be honest. Promising"—he choked it out, because he knew what was coming—"to respect you."

"Really," she said, but she didn't sound particularly convinced.

"We've started over," Jimmy told her.

"Yeah," she pointed out. "Too many times to count."

"No," he said. "Not like this. I died, Tess. On that chopper. I died, and I knew it, and I was apeshit, because I also knew you needed me. And there was this light, this beautiful light, and it was so warm and peaceful and the pain was gone and it freaked me out." It still freaked him out to think about it. "I tried to scream, but nothing came out, so I tried harder and . . . I don't know what I did, but I did it."

"The paramedic said you scared the crap out of him," Tess whispered. "That he used the defibrillator on you and it wasn't working, and then you just suddenly started . . . roaring, he said." She laughed, but there were tears in her eyes.

"Yeah. I don't know exactly what happened," Jimmy admitted. "But I knew I was back because it hurt like a bitch. But that was a good thing. Because as warm as that light was, I knew I wouldn't find you there." He took her hand. "I didn't choose to come into this world the first time around.

But that day, in that chopper? That *was* my choice. I want to be here and
I'm not going to screw it up this time around."

Tess reached over and turned off the light.

It seemed like a strange response, a little distant and cold, like she was
going to walk away, but then Jimmy realized that there were headlights approaching, way in the distance, down along the road.

And his heart started to pound.

Tess stood up and moved to the intercom on the wall. Pressed the button. "We've got a vehicle approaching."

"Roger that." Alyssa Locke's rich voice came through the speaker,
calm and relaxed. "It's Ric and Annie. Sam and Jules are going down to
meet them at the gate."

Jimmy closed his eyes. Holy Mary, he was jumpy.

"Have you talked to Jimmy?" Alyssa asked.

"I'm doing it," Tess said.

"Let me know what you decide." Alyssa signed off.

Tess turned toward him, but her face was in shadows—backlit the way
she was by the window and that gorgeous moon.

It was respect time. And the pain he'd felt in that chopper was nothing
compared to the way that this was going to hurt.

"You want to go back to San Diego," Jimmy said, managing to keep his
voice even.

"I need to," she said. "I have to look at Tracy's computer—at the actual
hardware. I can't do it remote, and I won't allow it to be sent here."

"Deck's gonna be pissed. He doesn't want you there."

"Decker doesn't want *you* there," Tess told him. "And he thinks you're
incapable of being a team player. He thinks you're a child—that you won't
stay back unless I'm here to hold your hand. *And* he thinks—as do the rest
of the Troubleshooters team—that your injuries would make you a burden
if you insisted on going with me."

"Don't hold back," Jimmy said. "Say what you really mean."

She returned to the couch. "You're amazing, Jimmy. No one thinks
that you're not. It's incredible that you're up and walking so soon. But
you're *not* up to speed. And you're also not fighting this battle alone. You're
part of this team. And right now, the best thing you can do for all of us is to
hang back, and to promise me—and Sam and Alyssa and Jules and
Decker—that you will, absolutely, remain here."

*So, let's see, me and the gay actor and the baby . . . We'll hide in the panic room while, hours away from here, where I couldn't possible reach you in time if something went wrong, these monsters are going to try to kill you?* Jimmy clenched his teeth over the words that he knew he couldn't say.

Tess sighed. "I know how hard this is for you, but you're not going to be sitting in the panic room twirling your thumbs. I need your help with research. I need more explicit details on these seven events I've marked on your list. I'll be calling you to get that information. It's not like I'll be out of touch."

Jimmy managed a nod.

"But eventually, you *are* going to have to deal with that," she told him quietly. "If not now then later. Because I'm good at what I do, and I'm going to be sent on jobs without you, the same way you're sent out on assignments without me. Which is hard for me, too. You know, it works both ways."

"But this one," he tried to explain. "This goatfuck . . . it's my fault. They're after *me*."

Tess shook her head. "It started with you, but now they're after all of us. And if they thought they had problems when they went after you . . . ? They're about to meet the Troubleshooters team, and boy, are they going to regret ever messing with us."

Jimmy nodded again. And he made himself say it: "Go to San Diego. But you better finally goddamn marry me when this is over."

Tess was no fool. "Promise you'll stay here. Say the words."

"I promise I'll stay here goddamn it."

"Then, yes, Jimmy, I'll marry you." She kissed him so sweetly and when she pulled back, he saw that she had tears in her eyes. "Thank you so much for coming back."

"You do the same, okay?" he whispered. "Just promise me you'll always do the same."


"This is a mistake," Dave said. "We should wait for Tom."

"We waited for Tom," Sophia reminded him, as she adjusted his arm around her shoulders and took more of his weight as the hotel elevator door closed. "He's downstairs, with the car."

"That's not good," he said. "That I didn't remember that. What else don't I remember?"

"You promised to buy me a boat," Ken said from the far corner of the elevator. He'd apologized, in advance, to Sophia, for being unable to help her carry Dave downstairs. As their bodyguard, he needed both hands completely free. "A shiny red one that goes *real* fast."

"Yeah, Ken," Dave said, wincing from the pain in his side. "I'm pretty sure I didn't do that. But nice try."

He glanced at Sophia, and she could tell from his eyes that he was hurting far worse than he'd let on. His wound was swollen and inflamed, and she could *not* believe that he hadn't mentioned that it had gotten so much worse. She still wouldn't have known, if he hadn't done that nose-dive onto the hotel room floor.

"That wasn't a dream, was it?" he asked softly. "What you said to me."

"Nope," she said, as she stared up at the changing numbers over the door—fourteen, twelve, eleven—willing this thing to move faster.

"Marry me," he said. "Will you marry me, Soph?"

She didn't answer right away. She wanted him to wonder and maybe even to sweat. It was stupid. She was being stupid and a little petty—giving him a ten-second punishment for hiding his pain from her. As if that would make him think twice next time.

And there *would* be a next time.

As frightened as she was at the idea of losing him, she was *not* going to make him sacrifice his career for her.

But Sophia didn't answer Dave's question about getting married right away, and then she couldn't answer, because the elevator dinged and the door opened on the eighth floor.

And everything went into slow motion.

Two men—one tall, dark-haired, and almost too handsome, one shorter and wearing a hat—were standing on the eighth-floor landing.

Ken stepped in front of the open door. "Sorry, gents, you'll have to catch the next—"

There was a sound, like a pop, and the SEAL took a jerky, halting step back as Sophia was sprayed with . . .

Blood?

Dear God, she was covered with what had to be Ken's blood as she heard the popping sound again, and this time Ken fell to his knees.

He was shouting—something—Sophia couldn't make out the words. And Dave was shouting, too, as he pushed her roughly, almost brutally down onto the floor of the elevator. "She's hit," Dave was screaming, "she's hit, too, she's dead, you killed her," his eyes lit with his fear and apology, and with . . .

Resolve? His mouth moved—*I love you*, he told her silently.

"I'm not," she tried to tell him, "I'm okay—"

But Dave swung and hit her and the world turned gray and vanished with another of those awful pops.


Decker woke up feeling if not quite refreshed, then pretty damn close.

He'd wrapped himself around Tracy, who was still asleep, breathing slowly and steadily.

His hand was still on her breast. And even though he knew it would probably wake her, he couldn't keep himself from touching her, letting all that smooth, sleek skin slip beneath his fingers, brushing the softness of her nipple against the too-sensitive palm of his hand.

She hadn't understood the significance of what he'd told her, when he'd said that he didn't just want—he wanted *her*.

It hadn't been that way with Emily. He'd wanted. Anyone. And she'd walked into the bar, and into his life. He'd loved her because he was with her—not the other way around. And on some level, she'd probably always known that.

And then there was Sophia—another random anybody. Made worse by the fact that he'd known she was desperate when he'd let her unfasten his pants.

And maybe he was lying to himself—he was pretty good at that—but he couldn't imagine having that random kind of sex-for-the-sake-of-sex with anyone, especially not a stranger, no matter how beautiful and alluring, on the desk in his office.

But for Tracy . . . ?

He'd planned it. He'd done it. And now, after the fact? He wasn't beating himself up about it. In fact, as he lay here on his couch, smiling at the memory, with Tracy's breast in his hand and his incredibly happy dick pressed tightly against her heart-rate-revving posterior, he could imagine—in the very near future—breaking his rule all over again.

Her nipple had tightened and peaked beneath his touch, and she stirred and stretched and pressed herself more fully into his hand. "I like that," she murmured.

"Mmm, me, too."

"You know, that's an often neglected erogenous zone," she told him.

"It won't be with me around," he told her.

"No." She laughed and took his hand. "Not me, *you*. This." She brought his hand to her mouth and kissed him, right on his palm. "You like touching things, don't you? You're into the tactile. You know how I know? I've seen you stop yourself from doing it, from reaching out—like you're afraid it might overload your senses."

She moved his hand back to her breast, and keeping his fingers open, she drew circles on the center of his palm with the very tip of her taut nipple.

And he went from semi- to fully, painfully aroused—a fact that she couldn't fail to notice, considering their proximity. "Hmm," she said, laughter in her voice. "That's going to be fun to experiment with."

Decker laughed, too, as he turned her to face him. "I think," he said, "*that* has more to do with you than me. We're not going to get the same reaction if, say, a big fat man touched the palm of my hand with a pencil."

"Hang on," she said, as she smiled into his eyes, "we can check. Because I think I've got a big fat man in one of my 'massively huge' suitcases."

He laughed again as he kissed her, shifting further so that she was on top of him. "This," he said as she sat up, straddling him, pushing her hair from her face, her bare breasts full, her soft skin beautiful in the dim glow of the light he'd left burning on his desk, "*I* like."

She smiled down at him, her lower lip caught between her teeth as she reached between them to unfasten his pants. "Bet I can make you like it even more."

He shook his head. "It'd be pretty stupid to bet against that."

She freed him from his jeans and his shorts, her hands soft and cool against his stomach. "This right here is nice," she said, touching the muscles in his abdomen, "the way it kind of sweeps down and leads the eye right"—she wrapped her fingers around him—"here."

Decker reached for her, too, to unzip her jeans, but she shifted back.

"Uh-uh," she said as she caressed him. "Nope. I'm in charge." Somehow she managed to hide her smile as she gazed coolly down at him. "No talking, no touching. I'll tell you what I want you to do, and you'll do it—is that clear? Nod. Once."

Okay. Moment of truth. There was sex in the office and then there was *sex* in the office. And yet, Deck found himself trapped by her gaze and nodding. Once.

"No smiling," Tracy said as she continued to stroke him, harder now, and suddenly, it wasn't all that difficult to not smile.

It *was* hard, however, not to touch her. He wanted those jeans off, wanted her breasts in his hands, her mouth on his mouth, his dick buried inside of her.

But she had other plans.

"Hands behind your head," she ordered. "Like this . . ." She let go of him to show him, putting her arms up, elbows bent, hands clasped.

He wanted to ask her to stay that way so he could get his camera because Jesus. Instead, he silently did the same, and if his injured arm hurt, he didn't feel it. It was inconsequential, a mere inconvenience. He was hyper-aware, though, that he was already breathing hard, his bare chest rising and falling with each breath he took.

She nodded her approval, taking hold of him again, but loosely, with only one hand this time, as she reached out with her other and—lightly—ran her fingers down the smooth underside of his upraised arm, where the nature of his position made his bicep bulge. "Very nice." She ran her fingers back up the other way. "*I* like this."

It took everything he had in him not to move because what she was doing felt unbelievably, erotically good. Try as he might, he couldn't keep his hips from tightening, couldn't stop himself from pushing himself more fully into her hand.

She held his gaze as she tightened her grip on him, but then, again, she let him go.

She leaned forward, whispering, "Don't move," and then she kissed him, her lips gentle against his mouth.

He had to fight not to respond as she licked him, her tongue warm and sweet—and gone way too soon.

She kissed his chin, his neck, his chest—swiftly licking the nipple above his pounding heart. But then she went back up to his arm and kissed the same expanse that she'd touched so lightly—"Mmm"—humming her approval.

She moved back to his other nipple, then trailed kisses down his stomach. He knew what was coming, he *knew* it with a certainty that redefined his faith in God, and yet it *still* damn near killed him when her mouth landed on him, when she kissed him and licked him and sucked him—but he couldn't touch her, couldn't speak, couldn't move.

All he could do was watch. She knew his vantage point was a particularly good one, because she made sure to give him plenty of eye contact. Or maybe she was just policing him. Either way, it worked for him. Completely.

All of his muscles were tight and tense as he held himself still, as she used her hand to add to the pleasure she was giving him with her mouth. He could feel her laughing, the vibration adding to the sensation of her lips, her tongue, and he had to close his eyes, because it was too much, too good, no, it was too fucking *great*—and he was going to . . .

"Don't move," she said again. "*Don't. Move.*"

Jesus, he had to . . . He needed . . . Colors flashed behind his eyelids as he clenched every muscle in his body even more tightly, as he gritted his teeth and tried to silence the moan, the *growl* that he could feel building in the back of his throat.

"Don't move," she ordered him again. "Just come. *Now.*"

And Decker let go.

He let go, and all that there was, was *yes*.

It roared through him, consumed him, incinerated him. He was everything and nothing, light and darkness. The world ended and kept turning. Time stopped and rushed forward. Life had meaning and he was both here and gone. Exploding, cartwheeling, shattering, obliterating, for the first time in an eternity, Decker truly, completely, totally let himself go.

He didn't know how long it was that he hung, suspended, in that place of sheer pleasure. He didn't know how long it was that he lay there, gasping, still not moving, his hands still up behind his head—he was nothing if not a rule follower. But he slowly became aware of his surroundings, of Tracy's hair fanned out across his chest, the weight of her head on his stomach as she, too, caught her breath.

He wanted to slow it all down, to hold on to it, to make it last, because it was sex to the nth—sex unlike any sex he'd ever had, ever. But it was already over. Already done.

And he recognized, immediately, that part of what had made it so great was that he'd stopped thinking. He hadn't brought anything with him—no baggage, no analysis, no sense of what he should or shouldn't be feeling.

It was just him and Tracy. And pleasure the likes of which he would never have believed possible.

And he already, absolutely, couldn't wait until they did it again.

She lifted her head then, her hair sliding across his stomach as she sat back up, still straddling him, still bare-breasted, still breathtakingly beautiful.

And in love with him.

She'd told him so.

"You have my permission to smile," she said now, still in that stern voice.

He did just that, laughing a little, as he held her gaze. "What I really want," he whispered, "is permission to do that to you."

The look on her face was beautiful, but as she opened her mouth to answer him, someone knocked on his door.

She froze, and Decker quickly sat up, covering her with the blanket, just in case the lock didn't hold.

"Deck?" It was Lindsey out there. She knocked again. "I'm really sorry to wake you, sir, but there's been a clusterfuck of some magnitude, and we need you out here, right away."


Decker was furious. Tracy could tell because he got very, *very* quiet. "Why wasn't I told about this?"

His T-shirt was also on inside out. She hoped for his sake that no one else had noticed that, but . . . No such luck. Jo Heissman was sitting at the conference table, looking from Decker to Tracy and back, with a curiously bland expression on her face.

Lindsey, meanwhile, stood her ground against Deck's wrath, chin out. "Because Tom was handling it. He *is* still the boss here. And he told me I should let you sleep."

Complications had developed from the knife wound Dave had gotten in Boston. Apparently, an infection had set in, and he'd passed out at the hotel while Tom Paoletti was bringing his family here to the office, for safety.

It made Tracy want to look beneath Deck's bandage, to check that bullet wound in his arm.

To be honest, she hadn't even known Kelly and Charlie Paoletti were here—they must've arrived while she and Deck were sleeping, et cetera. Apparently, they'd already left, rushing over to the hospital to be with Tom.

Who had been shot at by a sniper on the street outside the hotel—at about the same time SEAL Chief Ken Karmody had taken two bullets to the chest, and one to the leg in the elevator, which had stopped on the eighth floor.

Tom had leaned over to pick up his sat phone from the floor of his car, and a bullet that otherwise would have killed him instantly merely left a two-inch furrow just behind his left ear. It hadn't knocked him unconscious—not quite. But it had bled heavily and created quite a scene as he'd staggered into the hotel, weapon drawn.

The elevator in the lobby had opened to reveal Karmody, critically wounded. Sophia had been in that elevator, too, unwounded but unconscious.

Dave Malkoff was nowhere to be found.

"Where's Sophia now?" Decker asked tersely.

"Lopez and Cosmo are bringing her back from the hospital," Lindsey reported.

"They're bringing her here," Decker clarified.

"Yes, sir. They should arrive soon. They drove Kelly and Charlie over there to be with Tom. The FBI has already arranged for guards to be placed on both the chief and Tom. Everyone agreed that it would be best if Cosmo and Lopez got Sophia here immediately."

Ken was currently in surgery, as doctors raced to repair the damage done by bullets at close range. No one had said as much, but Tracy knew from the extent of his injuries that it would be a miracle if he survived. His wife, Savannah von Hopf, of *the* van Hopfs, had chartered a jet out of New York and was flying in.

Tracy had always been jealous of Savannah, who worked as a high-powered attorney despite having bushels of inherited money, but she didn't even remotely envy the other woman now.

Tom, meanwhile, was in the hospital, because an X-ray had revealed a hairline skull fracture. Such injuries could result in bleeding in the brain, and he was undergoing the first of what would no doubt be a night of observation and cat scans.

Tracy made a note in the office calendar to send flowers to the nurses who were going to have to live through *that*. Knowing Tom, he was going to be pissed and insisting he get back to work. Kelly was going to have to get out the whips and chains, and okay. Suddenly that seemingly casual expression held a whole new meaning.

"Alyssa's on her way," Lindsey reported to Decker. She looked at her watch. "ETA ten minutes."

Decker nodded. When Alyssa arrived, as company XO, she'd be in charge. Until then, he was in command. "I need Commander Koehl on the line, and I need him now."

Tracy stood up. "I can do that."

Deck shook his head. "No," he said. "This is going to need finessing. Lindsey . . ."

"I'm on it." Lindsey vanished down the hall.

He realized how negative his words had sounded. "I didn't mean—"

"I know," Tracy reassured him. Lindsey's husband Mark was on Koehl's SEAL team. "She'll get through to him before I will. Jo and I'll go to the lobby and wait for Sophia. I'll let you know as soon as she arrives."

He nodded. And beneath his layers of grim, beneath his anger, Tracy could see an echo of all the intimacies they'd shared over the past few days. And beneath that, she could see his fear for Dave.

"We'll find him," she told him quietly. "We'll get him back."

He nodded as he looked into her eyes, but then he glanced at Jo Heissman, who was sitting there, pretending not to listen.

He gestured with his head, and Tracy followed him out into the hall.

"You really have that much faith that that *Secret* thing works?" he asked her.

"No," she said, touching his hand down where no one could see them. "But I have that much faith in you."

He didn't say anything, but he held onto her, linking just one of his fingers with one of hers, so she added, "In case you don't have time to, I don't know, say good-bye or . . . In case you have to leave quickly? I'm just going to say it now. Be as careful as you can, without getting too inside your head about being careful. I'll be here when you get back."

She felt tears start to form in her eyes, and she blinked, hard, because getting all weepy would only undermine her message.

"Lew Koehl on line one," Lindsey shouted from her office. "Jackpot! Am I great, or am I the greatest?"

Deck dropped Tracy's hand and was already moving.

She chased him down the hall. "Sir."

It felt weird calling him that, and indeed, he shot her a look.

"Chief," she corrected herself. She lowered her voice. "You really need to fix your shirt."

He looked down. "Ah, shit."

"No one noticed," she said, following him to his office door. "Well, except me and Jo. And Lindsey."

He laughed as he went inside. "Only everyone in the room." He picked up his phone, nodding a dismissal. "Commander. I'm sorry to bother you, sir, but our situation's escalated. . . ."

Tracy closed his office door and headed back to the conference room, where Jo had already gathered up her things.

And okay. *This* was going to be awkward.

Jo knew it, too. It was there in her Mona Lisa therapist smile.

So Tracy went point-blank as she led the way down the hall. "Peter Olivetti. Michael Peterson. Did he call you *my princess,* too?"

"*Queen,*" Jo said. "*My Queen,* or *My Liege. My Lady.* In retrospect, it's astonishingly unappealing. Like a renaissance fair gone horribly wrong."

"He smelled good," Tracy said. "And he listened."

"He did do that," Jo agreed. "All that charisma, all of his focus . . ." She paused. "And then there was the fact that he looked the way he looked."

Tracy nodded as she turned on one of the standing lamps in the Troubleshooters lobby. At the time, Michael *had* seemed unbelievably well put together. Of course, that *was* before she'd seen Decker naked. "I wonder if anything he said was true. I mean, I know he doesn't really teach first grade. Although what does that say about me, that I found that so attractive?"

Jo sat down on the leather sofa where she'd been camped out earlier. "It says that you like the idea of a man who has a strong calling—a connection to his work. Because, let's face it. People, particularly men, don't become teachers for the money. You're also of an age where you're seeking to fulfill your biological imperative, so a man who likes children *would* be particularly attractive to you. There's nothing wrong with that." She paused. "In the same way, it makes sense that you'd be drawn to someone older, someone you perceive to be steady. Someone you might think is ready to settle down. Or maybe even just settle."

She was talking now about Decker. "No," Tracy said firmly. "No, thank you. I'm definitely not interested in your opinion about—"

"He's an incredibly complicated man."

"And one who would be understandably upset to find *anyone* indulging in office gossip about him," Tracy countered, even though she'd done it herself in the past.

"I'm merely offering advice," Jo said. "Things have changed radically in the past hour. You *do* know it's possible that Dave Malkoff will be recovered, not rescued."

A living person was rescued, a dead body was recovered. As awful as it seemed, it *was* certainly a possibility. At this point, they didn't even know if Dave was still alive.

"If Dave is dead," Jo pointed out, "Lawrence Decker's connection to Sophia Ghaffari—"

"Do you honestly think," Tracy asked emphatically, "that if Dave is dead, I'll be concerned with more than the awful, dreadful, *horrible* fact that *Dave* is *dead?*"

"Oh, God, no . . ."

Tracy looked up to see Sophia, her face totally white, and—dear Lord—her clothes stained with the dark red of drying blood, standing by the main entrance. It was obvious that she'd just come in and had heard only the end of Tracy's sentence, and even though Tracy said, "No!" she crumpled to the floor.

Lopez was there, thank goodness, and he caught Sophia and lowered her to the carpeting. He, too, looked devastated. "Dr. Malkoff is dead?" he asked.

"No," Tracy said again, "Well, we don't know. I was just . . . Shoot! *Decker!*" She forsook the intercom system and went with what was the standard here at Troubleshooters Incorporated—the interoffice bellow. "Lindsey! Deck! We need you in the lobby, *now!*"

Jules arrived to find the Troubleshooters office in an uproar.

Decker was channeling his inner caveman as he moved Sophia in a he-man cradle carry from the floor to the lobby sofa.

It was hard to tell with everyone talking at once, but apparently Tracy had told Sophia that Dave was dead, when in fact Dave's status remained only missing.

Tracy looked stricken—it was clear that, whatever she'd told Sophia, her intent had not been even remotely malicious.

But the emotional energy that got consumed was enormous as Sophia finally roused and, finding out the truth, burst into tears of relief. After more noise and apologies all around, Lindsey helped her up and into the locker room, because—just to make everything even more horrible—Sophia was still dressed in the clothes she'd been wearing when Navy SEAL Chief Ken Karmody had been gunned down in that hotel elevator.

Tracy stood, as if to help Lindsey with Sophia, but Decker stopped her. "Don't. You've done enough."

To Jules's surprise, the receptionist got in his face. "That's *not* fair. She walked in on a *what-if* conversation I was having with Dr. Heissman, and she completely misunderstood. She's my friend, Deck. May I please go and help her find something to change into? She's not going to fit into anything Lindsey has in her locker, and I've got two suitcases full of clothes."

Decker nodded. "Go," he said. It was only then that he turned to Jules.

"Hey, Deck," Jules said. "How's it going?"

"Where the fuck is Alyssa?" Decker was apparently eager to relinquish command.

"She and Sam are outside, doing a perimeter check with Cosmo and Silverman," Jules reported. They were looking, in particular, at the security cameras that surrounded the building, because Lopez believed the system had been compromised. They'd brought in an expert to look at it—Tess—but Jules wasn't going to mention that here, with all the extra ears in the lobby. "Dr. Heissman, nice to see you, ma'am." He nodded at the woman, then turned back to Deck. "Do we have a description yet, of the men in the elevator?"

Lopez spoke up. "Chief Karmody's still in surgery, and Sophia didn't see much. From what I understand from her recall of the attack, she was covered in the chief's blood, so Dr. Malkoff starting shouting about how she was shot, too. I think he believed the gunmen were intending to kill her. He actually hit her—knocked her out so she would appear to be dead. They grabbed him, and ran."

"*Dave* knocked Sophia out?" Decker repeated. "Jesus."

"It saved her life," Lopez said somberly. "Oh, and Chief?" He handed Decker a pair of envelopes that looked like they'd been through a war zone. They were crumpled and stained with blood. "Karmody has these in his pocket. Best guess is he was holding on to them for Dr. Malkoff."

One of them had Decker's name on it. The other had been opened, and it looked as if it were . . . Yes, it was Dave's will. Crap.

As Decker opened the second one, Jules could see even from several feet away, that like the first, Dave had handwritten it in his nearly illegible scrawl.

As he watched, Decker skimmed it, flipping the page over and . . .

"Oh, Jesus," Deck said. He glanced up at both Jules and Lopez as he jammed it back into the envelope, and pocketed it. "It's personal."

Jules cleared his throat. "I'm going to have to ask you to—"

"Yeah," Deck said shortly. "I know. I'll let Alyssa see it. If she feels it's necessary to share it with you . . . That'll be up to her."

Jules nodded. Worked for him. "I've got some information that falls into the bad-news department," he said. "Can we go into your office or. . ."—he glanced again at Dr. Heissman, who was sitting quietly off to the side—"somewhere else we can shut the door?"

"I'll hang here," Lopez volunteered.

"My office," Decker said, leading the way.

He was silent as they went down the hall, silent as he led the way into his office.

Jules closed the door behind him. The small room had a lived-in smell—common among law enforcement and counterterrorist specialists, who didn't exactly keep bankers' hours.

Jules couldn't count how many times in the course of his career he'd slept in his clothes in his office—on the couch or sometimes even on the floor. You'd sleep, you'd eat, you'd sweat, you'd change your shirt, maybe wash up in the sink if you felt you could take a few minutes' break.

But mostly you just sat there and got more and more ripe.

Except the gym locker fragrance in here had a soupçon of something lovely mixed in. Perfume.

And sure enough, as Jules looked around, he could see that the somewhat Neanderthalish Decker had been sharing his cave, so to speak.

A sweater was on the floor along with some notepads filled with loopy handwriting, a blanket was on the sofa, and a pair of high-heeled sandals had been kicked under one of the chairs.

Huh. And Deck's desk was curiously, absolutely clear.

And—oh, ding—something small and white and silky and just the right size to be a style of underwear that absolutely would never fit Decker peeked out from behind a throw pillow that had landed on the floor in the far corner of the room.

Well, you go, D-Dawg.

Jules worked to keep his expression neutral, instead of wide-eyed and openmouthed in amazement. Tracy—and it had to be Tracy. Those shoes did *not* belong to Jo Heissman or Jay Lopez. And, yes, Tracy was pretty dang cute, but probably the dead-last person in San Diego Jules would have ever imagined hooking up with someone as grim and perpetually, quietly angry as Decker.

Except, this fiasco with Dave aside, Decker currently didn't seem to be quite as angry. Way to go, Tracy.

"What have you got?" Deck asked as he sat behind his clutter-free desk. "An address from the plate numbers on Tracy's picture of Michael Peterson would be nice."

Jules sat in one of the chairs instead of on the sofa, where, despite the clear desk, the aura of a recent happy-fun-time lingered. "Yeah, a friend of a friend in San Diego PD. I pulled some favors and she ran the plates, completely on the lowdown. We got a name—Karen Michaelson—and an address. An empty apartment in Spring Valley. I got Yashi and Deb out here—both on their own time—seeing if they can't track her down."

"Michaelson, huh?" Decker shook his head. "Girlfriend? Wife?"

Jules shrugged. "No idea. But in the event that she is? I'm going to want to show her those photos of our man Peter-slash-Michael doing the naked thang with the doc."

Decker nodded. He clearly understood that jealousy was often right up there among the possibilities when it came to making a family member of a suspect spill the proverbial beans. "Dr. Heissman's been cooperative, so let's be careful not to let those pictures get distributed too widely."

"Of course," Jules said.

"What else?" Decker, perceptive as always, asked. "You said *bad* news."

"Yeah." Jules sighed. "When the lab report on the knife Liam Smith used to stab Dave came back, it sat on CIA Special Agent Bill Connell's desk. He was supposed to notify both Dave and the hospital, but he says it allegedly slipped through the cracks. Guy's a total dick, by the way, and if Dave dies, I'm going to make sure he's looked at for negligent homicide. I may do it anyway—throw an *attempted* in there. Motherfucker."

"Bill Connell," Decker repeated.

Jules nodded as he watched Deck store the name in his permanent memory banks. Bill didn't know it yet, but should anything happen to Dave? The man was totally fucked. "Bottom line, the weapon was a biological nightmare. The amount of bacteria was . . . Well, knives are rarely antiseptic, but this one?" He shook his head.

"It was intentional," Decker said. It wasn't quite a question, but Jules answered it anyway.

"Had to be," Jules agreed. "The other knife on the scene contained normal trace amounts of ick and germs. Alyssa has a copy of both lab reports, if you want to see them."

"I do," Deck said.

"It's a hard copy. Don't spill your coffee on it. We're not sending anything via e-mail that's not completely scrambled," Jules said, "and there wasn't time to fix this document. Speaking of there wasn't time, we brought Tess back with us, to check out Tracy's computer."

Decker was not pleased. "What the fuck?"

It was clearly a rhetorical question, but Jules tried to answer it anyway. "There was no way we could risk bringing that computer to the safe house, and it may hold some answers."

"And you think Nash is just gonna sit still while—"

"Yes," Jules said. "He is. He's walking, but not without a cane. He's in no condition to jump onto the roof of a speeding train, or whatever it is you former Agency operatives do to catch your suspects. And he knows it."

As an agent with the FBI, Jules usually did a lot of math in the course of an investigation. And then he drove to the address of the suspect in a really nice car, put on a bulletproof vest, and followed the SWAT team inside. It wasn't every day that he was actually the one to kick in the door. Of course, having done it more than once, he *could* understand the appeal.

He could also understand how excruciating it would be, to be injured and forced onto the sidelines while his life partner took incredible risks.

But the words Tess said to Nash had apparently resonated. They were a team. Not just Tess and Nash, but all of them. They were in this thing together. And wasn't *that* the truth?

"I gotta call him," Deck said.

"I'm sure he's not sleeping," Jules again agreed.

Decker brought himself back to the issue at hand. "Theories on the knife?" he asked.

"I'm thinking our bad guys were shaking the tree, seeing what fell out. They target Dave—known to be a friend of Jim Nash, with the hope that, after being attacked, Dave would either run to Nash, or Nash would reach out to Dave. But if nothing happened within a certain time frame, even if Dave went underground, by using that extra-dirty knife, they could pretty much bank on him resurfacing for a return trip to the hospital. Which is where he needs to be, by the way. Intravenous antibiotics. As soon as possible."

"You think they're going to contact us?" Deck asked. "Attempt a trade? Dave for Nash?"

"Nash thinks it's more likely that they'll try enhanced interrogation first. Gosh, that sounds almost lovely, doesn't it. *Enhanced.*"

Decker swore. "Dave doesn't know where Nash is. Torturing him won't . . . Shit."

"He wouldn't tell 'em even if he did know," Jules said. "He's Dave. So. What do we do, Chief? Do we tell Sophia about the knife or . . . ?"

"We tell her," Decker said, nodding grimly. "*I* tell her."

Jules nodded, too. "That's not going to be much fun. If you want, I'll—"

"No."

Jules sighed. "All right." He stood up. Looked at the door. Looked back. "Chief, do you think of me as a friend?"

"Yes, I do," Decker answered, no hesitation.

"I'm having a hard time with the murdered seven-year-old," Jules confessed. "When we find the guys responsible, I'm going to kill them. I thought you should know that. I don't give a fuck if it's the head of the Agency or the Queen of England. No quarter, no mercy. They are fucking dead."

Decker nodded. "I hear you."

"And when it's all said and done? I'm probably going to need a new job," Jules told him. "If my marriage is recognized in California after November . . . I may be knocking on your door."

"You're welcome here," Decker reassured him. "Always."

"Thank you," Jules said. "So. In the spirit of our excellent friendship? You definitely need a few tips on how to 24/7 it in your office. One, air freshener. Two, put your shit back on your desk, so that you and everyone else in the office can pretend you weren't using the surface for non-work-related activities. Three, there's no such thing as an underwear elf. Even when it goes missing, it's somewhere in the room. So make sure you find it." He pointed to the corner.

"Oh, hell," Jules heard Decker say as he firmly shut the door behind him.

# CHAPTER EIGHTEEN

Jimmy was sitting in the panic room with the actor and the sleeping baby, listening to Robin's theories as to why Sam and Alyssa had named the kid Ash instead of after Sam's Uncle Walt—a member of the illustrious Tuskeegee Airmen and a WWII hero—who'd been the father figure and positive role model in Sam's life.

Apparently there was some spooky little boy named Walt on the TV show *Lost*, and neither Sam nor Alyssa wanted people thinking they'd named their kid after him.

So they'd gone for their second choice, which was a nod not to the punk who'd married Demi Moore, but rather to the Bruce Campbell character in the classic Evil Dead movies.

At least that was Robin's current theory.

"How are you doing?" Robin interrupted himself to ask.

"The helicopter should've gotten them there by now," Jimmy said.

"Yeah, I know, I'm watching the clock, too." Robin nodded. "But they're not going to walk in and say, *Excuse me, Elite Task Force, I must go call my significant other.*"

"Yeah, I know that," Jimmy said tersely. "It's just hard." Especially knowing that the bastards—whoever they were—had Dave.

"I wish I could tell you that you get used to it." Robin sighed. "But you don't."

Their phones both rang, almost simultaneously. And yes, it was Tess calling him. Jimmy opened his phone.

"Look, I've been thinking," he said, going point-blank as Robin, who was more mobile, took his call from Jules out in the hall. "We've gotta get Dave back and—"

"We're going to." Tess's voice was filled with conviction. "You're going to have to do your job there, while we do ours here."

He closed his eyes, because he didn't want to be a helicopter flight away from her. And it was driving him crazy to think about where Dave surely was, right now. "Yeah, *I'm* working hard."

"Well, it's good I came back here." She ignored his sarcasm. "The security cameras' signals have been pirated."

*Pirated* meant the signal was going out to another receiver. And yes, dealing with that kind of problem *was* right up Tess's extremely talented alley.

"One of the SEALs—Lopez—noticed a glitch in the system, and when we checked it out, sure enough," she continued, with that note of thrill in her voice that happened when she was in techno-nerd mode. It was another reason to curse the fact that he wasn't there, because he loved watching her when her eyes lit up and she glowed with the excitement of a challenge. "It's creepy, I have no idea how long they've been watching us, because it wasn't something that would've been noticed on a standard system check. But there's been some kind of short, which makes the digital signal from the camera freeze—which is what brought it to Lopez's attention. After I get off this call, I'm going to pirate the pirate and give ourselves the ability to send our watching friends only those images we want them to see. It's tricky: I can't just create a simple loop, because the sun's going to come up. I have to get creative."

"Damn that pesky dawn," Jimmy said.

"Yeah." She laughed. Paused. "You sound almost okay."

"I'm not," he admitted. "I know what they're doing to Dave, and it's making me—"

"We're one step closer to finding him," Tess said. "Remember Russ Stafford? On the flight over, I figured out why that name sounded so familiar."

Jimmy sat up. "You think Russ is our man?"

"I do," Tess said. "His name sounded familiar because it was. It came up during an assignment in 2003."

Which was back when she'd worked, like him, for the Agency. Only she'd worked a desk down in Support.

"But there's something I need to ask you first," she said. "Have you ever skimmed funds from money that you seized while working an Agency op?"

"Define *skimmed*," Jimmy said. "Because when you're out in the field, and you need to make a quick escape, you take what you need to survive." Which sometimes included the contents of someone else's wallet. "A trip to the ATM isn't always prudent, so—"

"No," she said. "I'm talking about *significant* amounts of money. Like, enough to slow you down while you figure out a way to transfer it into some offshore account."

"Slow me down?" he said. "Not a chance. Most of my assignments were in places where if I was found—by anyone—I'd be killed. Arranging to transfer money takes time and contacts who don't want to kill you. Although if I saw a situation where large sums of money were going to fall into, say, al Qaeda's hands? I'd intervene. Maybe push it in another direction. An anonymous donation to the local orphanage."

"Okay," she said. "Maybe that's what happened, which is too bad because it means I'm probably wrong about Stafford."

"How much money went missing?" he asked, knowing that this was where this conversation was going.

"Fifteen million dollars," Tess told him.

"Shit," he exhaled on a laugh. "No. That would require a truck to move. That's not a slip-an-envelope-through-an-orphanage-mail-slot deal. Can you give me details?"

"Abida Talpur," she said. "September 1999. His deletion was on your list." She managed to say it without the pause that most people added before the word *deletion*, but then she added, "For his terrorist activities—"

"I know what he did," Jimmy interrupted her. Abida Talpur was responsible, in 1998, for taking out an Air Kazbekistan jet carrying the K-stani minister of defense—and two hundred and twenty other men, women, and children, all of whom had died. Talpur had planned it, paid for it, and celebrated it. And so, in 1999, Jimmy was assigned to erase him from the surface of the earth. Which he'd done, gladly and, as it turned out, rather easily.

He'd gone in, done the job, and gotten out.

"I didn't get close to Talpur," he told Tess now. "I took a sniper shot from a mountainside. I didn't even go into the city. I hiked out, across the border."

"Okay," she said. "Good. Then Russ Stafford's back on our list. Because when Talpur died, he had assets of close to forty million dollars. I don't know if you paid attention to the political and financial ramifications of Talpur's death—"

"I did," Jimmy said. "But it's been a while."

"Talpur didn't have a son, didn't have any surviving male relatives," Tess told him, "except for this one brother who'd been exiled. So Hersek Khosa, the friendly warlord next door, moved in and absorbed Talpur's property and holdings. His empire, so to speak. But in the spring of 2003, Talpur's brother manages to get back into the country, and he cries foul— claiming that Abida was killed by a squadron of U.S. soldiers, who were in league with Khosa."

"Not a soldier in sight," Jimmy confirmed.

"By 2003, we'd pulled our embassy and all troops out of the region, and the borders were locked down, pretty tightly. We were looking for a reason to get operatives in, so we sent an 'official' team to investigate. I was on support for that assignment. And here's where it gets really interesting.

"I was digging through intel," Tess continued, "just doing my job, collecting all the information I could find for the agents in the field, and I come upon a discrepancy in Talpur's bank records. We'd been watching his assets pretty closely before his removal, because of his terrorist ties, and we had what seemed to be a very accurate accounting of his funds— which, like I said, totaled about forty million, give or take a few hundred thousand.

"But we're also watching the assets of Hersek Khosa, because we're keeping track of everyone in the region who has money, and I notice, huh. Khosa absorbed Talpur's assets, but the numbers are off by fifteen million dollars. It's just gone. And I check and I recheck and I pull all sorts of files and it's just not there. And I'm getting worried, because a terrorist can do a lot of damage with that much money. So I write up a complete report, including all kinds of information like the name of Khosa's Agency handler—and okay, the fact that Khosa even had an Agency handler alone is something of a surprise—"

"Not to me," Jimmy said.

"Well, it was—and it still is—to little ol' naive me," Tess said. "And yes, Khosa's handler was Matt Hallfield—the former head of Agency support. Although Russell Stafford's name also came up because he'd had plenty of in-person dealings with Khosa, too. You said he was Hallfield's assistant?"

"That's right. Although why *he* would have gone to Kazbekistan is beyond me. Hallfield, yeah, he was a field agent himself in his day, but Stafford? That's flat-out weird."

Tess agreed. "Stafford's wasn't a name I recognized, so I flagged it. And I gave the entire report to—wait for it—Doug Brendon, who was my immediate supervisor, and he goes *Good eye, Bailey, but it's being handled.*"

Yeah, that sounded like Dougie Brendon, the current head of the Agency and prick extraordinaire.

"A week later," Tess continued, "the missing fifteen million shows up on the reports about Talpur's assets, with an asterisk. Someone's added a note, saying that the money is missing and the subject of an ongoing investigation. As far as Khosa's files? They were gone. They didn't just lock me out—"

"Which wouldn't have worked." There was no such thing as hackproof as far as Tess was concerned.

"They were completely erased," she told him. "Good-bye. I tried to figure out where they'd moved them, but I never did find them." She paused. "Except for the copy I had made, to include with my report."

"Please tell me you still have that."

"I do," she said. "It's on a flashdrive, with all of the other reports I wrote when I worked for the Agency. It's . . . somewhere safe. Deck actually recommended I do that—keep a record of everything—back when I first left the Agency." She paused. "And, in fact, I'm pretty sure now that *that's* what they were looking for when our apartment was ransacked in July."

Their apartment had been completely trashed, their sofa slashed, every dish they'd owned broken. The place had been searched, but it was a search with an attitude—and a threatening message.

"But okay," Tess continued, "back in 2003, I see that asterisk on the report, and I go back to talk to Brendon, who tells me, off the record, that the ghost group operative who took out Abida Talpur was being questioned, but that these things happened—that operatives of this sort often took their own bonuses. It was a part of doing business with the men and women who had those kinds of special skills. Wink. Wink."

"No one ever asked me anything about any missing money," Jimmy said.

"Well, all right then," Tess said. "There's where we start. With Russell Stafford and Doug Brendon."

"So this is about money," Jimmy said. "Jesus Christ, fifteen million isn't even that much by today's standards."

"It's not just about money," Tess said. "It's about accountability and, well, treason. On the chopper flight out here, I dug to see if there was any additional information—recent info—on either Talpur or Khosa in the Agency files, and turns out Hersek Khosa not only had al Qaeda ties, but his name came up in connection to perpetrators of the 9/11 attacks. He was an al Qaeda leader, and he went on to help fund the Bali bombing as well as set up terrorist training camps in Indonesia, Afghanistan, Algeria, and Kazbekistan. The real kicker is that there were reports—that had been conveniently buried or best case negligently overlooked—that confirmed this information as far back as 1997."

Fuck. "So you think Russell Stafford brokered the murder of Abida Talpur in exchange for fifteen million dollars from Hersek Khosa," Jimmy said, "*knowing* he was putting money and power into the hands of an al Qaeda leader?"

"I think," Tess said, "that in 1999 al Qaeda didn't mean the same thing it does now. It was just another random terrorist group that posed a threat to people living in already dangerous places. So, yeah. For fifteen million dollars, Stafford brokered that deal, got the Agency—and you—to do the dirty work, buried the reports on Hersek Khosa, and went on his merry way. According to his personnel file, he was in line to take over Matt Hallfield's job. Instead, he vanished. I think 9/11 happened, and everyone started looking hard at anyone with money in the region. And Hallfield—out of the blue—commits suicide on October 4, 2001. Yeah, he's got cancer, but everyone's shocked—"

"Oh, tell me you think that Russ Stafford killed him."

"I *do* think Russ Stafford killed him," Tess said. "I think Hallfield correctly made the connection between Khosa and al Qaeda, and was going to create trouble for both Stafford and the entire Agency. And although I think Doug Brendon may not have been involved, I think he knows enough to go to jail." He could hear her smile. "We got 'em, Jimmy."

"You *do* know that I think it's beyond hot," Jimmy told her, "that you're so freaking smart . . . ?"

Tess laughed. "*We* got 'em."

Yeah, right. "So how do we use this information to make 'em give us back Dave?" Jimmy asked.

"That," Tess said, "is where it gets even more tricky. . . ."

Sophia was sitting in the Troubleshooters women's locker room, wet hair pulled back into a ponytail, wearing Tracy's jeans and a T-shirt, with her own sneakers—left in her locker last week—on her feet.

At her request, Lindsey and Tracy had left her alone.

She'd needed to throw up again, and she didn't want her friends to see or hear her. She didn't want them to know that she was pregnant. She couldn't risk one of the team leaders—Alyssa or Jules or Decker—deciding that she was too fragile to help rescue Dave. And she *was* going to help rescue Dave.

She'd already started working out a plan. Apparently, the men who'd taken Dave had access to all of the information on Tracy's computer. So Sophia would send an e-mail from Tracy's computer—it didn't matter to whom. She could send it to herself, and they'd receive it.

She would tell them that she was willing to trade whatever information they wanted in return for Dave. Except they wouldn't want information, they'd want Nash, and seeing as how that would piss off Tess. . .

Okay. So, Sophia would tell them that she was willing to trade *herself* for Dave. She would be their hostage in return for them dropping Dave at the nearest emergency room. His knife wound needed immediate treatment—it would buy the TS Inc. team at least a little time.

And really, as far as being their hostage went, what could they do to her that hadn't already been done before?

Except, dear God, this time she was pregnant. It wasn't just her own life she'd be risking.

A soft knock on the door made her look over to see Lindsey peeking in at her. "You dressed?"

"Yeah," Sophia said. "I'm just bracing myself to come out there."

"Deck wants to know if it's okay if he comes in," Lindsey asked, and Sophia stood up, her heart instantly lodged in her throat.

"There's been no news about Dave," Deck said, pushing the door open so that she could see him. And she could, indeed, see his words confirmed by the calm certainty on his face, in his eyes.

"Sorry," Lindsey said. "Crap. Of course you'd think . . . God, I'm sorry."

"May I come in?" Deck asked. "I thought this would be a good place to talk privately."

"I was so glad to hear about Jimmy," Sophia told him. "So glad."

He nodded, and even smiled—and she looked at him harder. What was different? Something was. It wasn't his clothes. He had on faded blue jeans with those giant boots that she'd sometimes seen him wear during PT. Dave had told her it was an old SEAL trick. Anyone could run five miles in sneakers, but doing it in boots, in soft sand? *That* was a workout.

His T-shirt was standard, too. A faded shade of grayish green, with a faded blue trim around the crewneck collar and sleeves. He must've bought a dozen of them, on sale, in different colors. He usually wore a shirt over it, to hide his shoulder holster, but his holster was currently nowhere in sight.

Okay, so that was unusual, but . . . The difference was more in the way he was standing, in the energy that radiated from him. He was somehow less tense, less tightly wound.

Which didn't mean he wasn't still exuding buckets of grim. He was. His concern for Dave was clear. And yet there was a peacefulness to him that she'd never seen before.

"It was hard," he told her, "keeping the truth about Jim from everyone like that. I'm sorry, because I know it must've been—"

"You don't need to apologize," Sophia reassured him. "We were part of your cover. Dave and I both understood that. And I *am* incredibly glad that you didn't lose him, Deck. That *we* didn't lose him. I'm glad for Tess, too."

Decker nodded. "May I . . . ?" He was still standing in the door.

"I'm sorry," she said. "Of course, come in." She forced a smile. "As long as no one out there needs to, you know, pee."

"They've been cleared to use the men's." Decker nodded his thanks to Lindsey as he let the door close behind him. He came over to the cluster of easy chairs in the corner, where she was standing. "This is nice. We don't have anything remotely like this in the other locker room."

"My guess is that you're probably not doing a lot of breast-feeding in there," Sophia said. After Ashton was born, Alyssa had started bringing the baby with her into the office. But she found it difficult to switch instantly from company XO to mommy, which was frustrating for both mother and child. And everyone else in the office, too, considering Ash's healthy lungs.

Tracy had been the one to come up with the solution—to create a quiet place here in the women's locker room that would allow Alyssa to leave the chaos of her office and relax during Ash's feedings. Tracy had also repainted the walls a soothing shade of blue—coming in on a Saturday and Sunday to do the work herself. She'd bought lamps and new dressings for the window, and a plush throw rug for the tile floor.

The entire transformation had taken place over the course of one single weekend, and Alyssa had hugged Tracy when she'd seen it. Which was saying something, because the XO wasn't exactly the president of the Tracy Shapiro Fan Club.

Deck now hovered near the second easy chair, unwilling or more likely *unable* to sit before Sophia did. The man was nothing if not terminally polite.

"Please." Sophia sat. "You've really never been in here?" she asked. "Even after hours, when no one's around?"

"Never." It was such a Decker thing to say, a Decker thing to do. And, in another Decker move, he cut to the chase. "Dave needs to get to a hospital. The samples from the knife that Liam Smith used to stab him started growing all kinds of bacteria in the lab. Do you have a sense of when his infection started?"

She shook her head and forced herself to breathe past the fear that filled her throat. "He seemed fine, right up until he face-planted. But he changed the bandages himself after we got to the hotel."

"Okay," he said. He looked out of place sitting there, on the very edge of that chair, elbows on his knees as he leaned slightly forward, eyes narrowed as he. . . . Ah, yes. He'd caught sight of the bruise that was forming on her cheekbone and around her left eye.

She angled her head so that he had better light with which to see it.

"You all right?" he asked, searching her eyes as if to make sure she wasn't going to lie about it.

"It hurts."

"It must've been a surprise—having him hit you like that."

"It was," she said. "But he thought they were going to kill me and he wanted—"

"He ever hit you before?" Decker interrupted.

Sophia laughed. "Please," she said. "Dave?"

Decker nodded, but then said, "You know how when you go to the emergency room, and the triage nurse is required to ask—"

"He's never hit me before," she said. "These are not the questions you need to be asking. I'm fine." She stressed her words. "Dave, however, is not." She leaned forward, too. "Who's got him, *where* have they got him, and how are we going to get him back so we can get him to the hospital?"

Her proximity made Decker sit back in his seat—he never did like to let anyone get too close. No, make that *her*. He didn't like to let *her* get too close.

"We're working on it," he said.

"Great," she said. "What have you got, because I want to work on it, too."

He was silent, then, just looking at her.

Dave would have been talking a mile a minute, using diagrams and other visual aids to make sure she understood every single thing that he knew about the situation.

"Why did Dave rewrite his will before leaving your hotel room?" Deck finally asked—and she sat back in her seat, too.

Dave rewrote his will? This was the first she'd heard about it.

"See, I can't figure out why he would've done that, unless he somehow knew this attack was coming. Is it possible that he was in contact with the kidnappers?" Decker asked her. "Was he being, I don't know, blackmailed—because they tried that with Nash, and I know this Anise Turiano thing was a big problem for Dave a few years back. If they somehow threatened to resurrect it—"

"They did," Sophia said. "They resurrected it. You *know* that they killed a CIA agent to make it look as if Dave . . ." Oh, God. She exhaled hard. "Deck, I've been with Dave pretty much constantly over the past few days—"

"*Pretty much* isn't constantly," he pointed out.

"It's close enough, considering that the times I wasn't with him he was under guard, or with an FBI agent, or with Tom and Chief Karmody."

"You slept though, right?" he said. "So it's possible—"

"It's possible," Sophia said sharply, "that Lindsey's going to come running in here to announce that she's won a Nobel Peace Prize. But it's not at all likely."

"And you have no idea why Dave would, essentially, get his life in order? Cross all his t's, dot all his i's," Decker asked quietly as he dug in his pocket for something—a folded-up envelope. "Because he didn't only write a will. He also wrote this. Karmody had it, but it was addressed to me."

He took what looked like a letter from the envelope and held it out for her. So she took it and yes. This was Dave's familiar handwriting. She unfolded it and . . .

*Lawrence,* Dave had written.

> *I don't know what's going to happen over the next few days. I'm determined to come through this, but I fear determination alone won't win the day. I'm uncertain as to the identity of my enemies. I know only one thing for sure—I will not put Sophia into any additional danger.*
>
> *She wanted me to ask for your help—you are, after all, the one and only Decker—so I am doing that now.*
>
> *Please don't let her come after me. If I don't come back within a few days, it's because I'm dead. But the threat will be gone—provided the instructions in my will are followed and the trail of my assets doesn't lead back to Sophia. Make sure that doesn't happen.*
>
> *I believe firmly in fate, and if I don't return, it's because it was meant to be. I can only hope that my death brings you and Sophia together.*

"Oh, my God," Sophia said, looking up at Decker.

"It gets worse," he said.

*I think you've long been holding the assumption that loving Sophia would be painful or difficult. I assure you, it is anything but. She's worked hard to put the past behind her, although there is one topic she and I have never discussed.*

*The death of her husband.*

*I went to Kazabek recently to get the answers to questions that Sophia seemed unwilling or unable to reveal. And I discovered the awful truth by talking to a number of women who worked in Padsha Bashir's palace while Sophia was held prisoner there.*

*Bashir used his sword to behead Dimitri as Sophia stood by, powerless. The blade was sharp enough, and he was strong enough to do the deed in a single blow. But the horror didn't end there. As we well know, Bashir "married" Sophia, and took possession of her assets—but this apparently happened while her husband's body twitched, while she was covered with the still-warm spray of his blood. Bashir claimed possession of Sophia as his bride shortly after—in any other culture this would have been called* rape— *with Dimitri's head on a table beside the bed.*

*Yes, you read that right.*

*I was told that it remained there, locked with her in her room, until it started drawing too many flies.*

*I'm telling you this because I feel confident that Sophia herself will never speak of it. But I wanted you to know.*

*It was meant to break her, to change her, to weaken her, to control her. To make her passive and hopeless, unwilling to resist or run.*

*And yet, when the opportunity arose, Sophia used Bashir's very same sword to run him through. She tried to kill him, and then she escaped.*

*Sophia is not a victim, she's a survivor. She's not fragile or weak, she's unbelievably strong. She's not filled with despair or depression over all that she lost—and she lost a man whom she loved with all of her heart. She grieved that loss, and has since acknowledged—with gladness—that she's still alive.*

*And hers is not a life that she's willing to live grudgingly, filled with regret and weighed down by remorse. With Sophia, each day is a glorious celebration, a joyous tribute to life. With Sophia, each day is a blessing and a gift from God.*

*Which brings me back to where you found her in Kazabek, all those years ago.*

*She's told me very little about what went on between the two of you after she fled Bashir's palace. I can only imagine how frightened—practically feral—she must have been when you first met. What I know about the event in question, I learned from you, a day or so after it transpired. She's long forgiven you—you need to look her in the eye and let her accept your apology. It's long past time for that.*

*And then—if I'm truly gone—you'll be able to take her hand and see the Sophia that I see, the Sophia that I love. And I know that you will be unable to do anything but love her as completely as I do.*

*Of course, if I'm still here and you do that, I'll challenge you to a duel, but I suspect if you're reading this, you don't need to worry about that.*

*Please, please make her happy. It would take such little effort. Just close your eyes, dear friend, and let go of the past.*

He'd signed it *Dave*, but then added a P.S.

*If, someday, someone asks you if I killed Anise Turiano? You can say with certainty that you heard it directly from me that I did not. I was, if anything, guilty of loving too easily and too foolishly. But not so with Sophia. I loved Sophia with all my heart—even when it wasn't easy to do so. But it was well worth it. You can tell whoever asks that I died having lived my dream.*

Sophia was crying when she put Dave's letter in her lap. It was so un-fair—she'd long prided herself on not being the kind of person who burst into tears every fifteen minutes. And it wasn't just her hormones, crazy as they were, that had done it—it was the way Dave's voice came through in every word he'd written.

"It sounds, from reading that," Decker said quietly, "like he was planning to leave."

"No," Sophia said. "I mean, yes, it *sounds* that way, but . . . No."

He shifted in his seat. "Sophia, I don't like asking this, but I have to. Before we risk more lives, I have to know if there's a chance that Dave went with them intentionally—the men in the elevator."

"No," she said again. "Absolutely not."

"Intentionally doesn't mean willingly," he told her. "If he was working with them, he was surely pressured—"

"No," she said adamantly. "He must've written this before Jimmy called. The reference to Anise Turiano . . . ? When he wrote this, he didn't realize that the attack in the parking lot was really all about Jimmy. But it *was*. After he spoke to Jimmy, he was certain that it was." She could see that Decker wasn't convinced. "Dave asked me to marry him in the elevator, moments before the attack. He wouldn't have done that unless he thought he had his life back."

Decker nodded. "I do believe that he loves you. Very much."

"Yes, he does," Sophia agreed, the lump back in her throat. "Please, let's focus on getting him back instead of—"

"He's never written a will while on assignment before—"

"God, you can be so stubborn—"

"Careful," Deck corrected her. "I'm being careful—"

"*Too* careful," she said hotly. "You *always* were—"

"No, not always," he countered.

And there it was—right there, as if it were sitting between them—everything that they hadn't said to each other for the past four years, since she'd tried to kill him in another ladies' room, very different from this one, on the other side of the world.

They'd come full circle, and Sophia had to wonder—because he was Decker, and he *was* so damned careful—if he hadn't intentionally chosen this place to have this conversation here and now.

But he swore under his breath, as if he'd realized, too, exactly what she'd been thinking. "Jesus, maybe it's true what they say about always returning to the scene of the crime."

"There was no crime," Sophia said emphatically. "I didn't kill you, and you didn't kill me. And I'm sorry, but the sex was completely forget-table."

"Not for me," he said tightly.

"Yeah, well, for me? You were one of scores of men that I . . . I . . . *serviced* in those months right after Dimitri died. And I considered myself lucky if all they wanted was a blow job before they sent me back to my cell."

He was silent.

"I know that still bothers you," Sophia said quietly.

"Bothers?" he asked. "Yeah, it *still bothers* me."

"I did what I did to stay alive," she told him. "I used to beat myself up for that, but I don't anymore."

"Well, I do," he admitted, his voice rough. "I still beat myself up be-cause I didn't help you. Because I took advantage—"

"So *what*?" she said. "Get over it already! You were human and you made a mistake, although you know, if I'd been in your shoes, I would have killed me. Right there. A bullet to the brain. *Good-bye.* But you didn't do that. You also didn't take me to the police, you didn't bring me to Bashir's palace—and either one of those things *would* have been a death sentence for me. My head, Deck, on some other woman's bedside table, as a warning to her. Maybe some fourteen-year-old he'd married, who hadn't yet realized how hopeless her life truly was."

"Jesus," Decker said.

Sophia leaned forward. "So what if you didn't help me right at that moment. And if you don't think that helping me later—searching for me, protecting me, getting me out of there, lending me money, getting me this job that I love with these people I love—all the things you've done for me, Decker . . . If you don't think that makes up for one small, *human* mistake, then help me *now*. Look into my eyes and believe me when I tell you that Dave had his reasons for writing that will, and that it's personal. I know what it is, and he didn't want me to tell *anyone*. Not even you—or he would have told you in here." She waved the letter. "Kind of like you not telling us about Jimmy."

He still didn't say anything. He just looked at her—that quiet, compli-cated, dreadfully damaged man whom she'd once thought she wanted. What a mess *that* would have been. She hadn't known it at the time, but he'd needed to heal as much as she had. A fact she was now well aware of.

"Help me now," she whispered. "I want Dave back. I love him, Deck. I really do."

Decker sat in the Troubleshooters women's locker room, looking at Sophia, and realizing that the words Dave had written were true.

She wasn't a victim—not even that of his own poor judgment. A *human mistake*, she'd called it. He'd made it, he was human—no doubt about that—and, yeah, despite that mistake, she'd survived.

The sex they'd had all those years ago was completely forgettable, she'd said—but it wasn't, not to him. But its unforgettable stature wasn't because it was Sophia's mouth, Sophia's hands, but rather because it had been so dangerous on so many levels. *And* because it seemed to confirm his fear that there was something wrong with him—for loving that mix of danger and sex so very much.

But Tracy was right—the only thing wrong with him was that he was a freaking prude. The sex he'd shared with Tracy just a short time ago had been off the charts. Best sex ever. *Ever.* And Tracy had been completely willing and eager. The danger she'd helped create was of a different kind.

There wasn't just hope for him, there was a real chance at serenity hanging out there on the horizon of his not-so-distant future. Serenity, embellished with moments of joy and true happiness.

A few days ago, he never would have believed that possible.

"Please, let's find Dave," Sophia whispered, and as he gazed into her eyes, as he looked at her tired, anxious, and yet still stunningly beautiful face, he said—at the exact same moment that she did—"I trust you."

He had to smile. "That's good," he said.

But she had more to say. "I'm pregnant," she told him. "That's what Dave didn't want anyone to find out, because he believed it would put me in danger. But I *do* trust you completely, Deck, so there's really no reason why you can't know."

She was . . . "Wow," he said. "Is this . . . good news—you know, something that you . . . wanted . . . ?"

Sophia laughed. "You don't know me very well, do you?"

Deck shook his head. "I guess I, uh, really don't."

"It's unplanned," she said, "but wanted. *Very* much wanted."

"That's great," he said quietly, and yeah, he felt a twinge of something that wasn't quite envy. It was awareness. Acknowledgment of something that might've been possible if they'd met in a different lifetime, or on a different planet.

But they hadn't. And it was clear to him that whatever she had, at one time, felt for him, it was nothing compared to what she now felt for Dave.

"Please don't tell anyone else," she warned him. "And don't even think about wrapping me in gauze and telling me what I can and can't do. I'm healthy and strong. And I'm going to help you get Dave back. So tell me what you know. How are we going to find him?"

# Chapter Nineteen

"Anything?" Deck asked quietly.

Tracy looked up from her reception desk, where she was monitoring incoming e-mail from the company's main, untampered-with computer, coordinating the arrival times of the remaining Troubleshooters, and still trying to unearth operative PJ Prescott, who was nowhere to be found.

Decker had come up less than dry with his latest call to Commander Koehl. Not only were the SWCCs unable to come save the day, but the TS team was going to lose most of their SEALs, too. Everyone but Lopez—who'd recently had a surgical procedure on an old injury to his shoulder, yet hadn't mentioned it to anyone—was being called back in and going wheels-up, which meant they were getting on an airplane and leaving the country.

The commander was heading overseas, too, but not for a few more days. Because of their lack of manpower, Koehl himself was coming to join the search for Dave. Not that the TS Inc. team was actually in a position yet to do any physical searching. But they had a lead—a former Agency support staffer named Russell Stafford.

And Jo Heissman had finally made herself useful. She remembered Stafford quite well from their shared years at the Agency.

Relatively slight of stature, he was somewhat rotund, with thinning hair and glasses. Not exactly the monster Tracy had been imagining.

Jo had told them that Stafford was quiet. The times she'd met him, he'd stayed in the background. Like some support staff members, he seemed disdainful and resentful of the field agents, which made him unpleasant to be around. Jo reported that she herself had felt uncomfortable with him, and avoided him whenever possible.

"Most of the times I encountered him," the doctor told them, "he was with his boss, Matt Hallfield—who had a very large personality and cared a great deal about his staff's allegiance. I always assumed Stafford's unswerving loyalty was the reason they were inseparable."

Stafford was loyal until—if Tess's theory was correct—Hallfield discovered Stafford's embezzlement and treason, at which point Stafford killed his boss, making it appear to be a suicide.

Monsters, Jo had reminded Tracy, came in all shapes and sizes.

Her physical description of Stafford was invaluable information, but best of all, Jo was able to provide a list of other operatives Stafford had worked with, particularly from 1999 until 2001.

Tess was taking that information and digging to find out if any of the men—and they were all men—on Jo's list had also left the Agency around the same time Stafford did.

Sooner or later they were going to find the information that would lead them to Dave, and when they did? Tracy was making damn sure that they'd have enough operatives to help break him free.

"Nothing yet," she told Decker now as she glanced at the clock. "But it's only been a half hour."

They'd used her laptop—the one that Michael had compromised—to send a message to Stafford and the other men who'd kidnapped Dave and wanted Nash dead.

Alyssa, Jules, and Decker had all agreed that the best approach was to write an e-mail as if it were from Sophia: *I don't know who you are, or why you've taken Dave. I do know it has something to do with James Nash—who is not dead as we'd all believed. He is in hiding—I don't know where. I am not any kind of operative—I work client interface at TS Inc. But I am Dave's fiancée. If you can guarantee his safe return, I will find out whatever you want to know.*

The consensus was that Stafford and Michael—it was hard to think of him as Gavin Michaelson, which apparently was his real name—would respond by telling Sophia they were interested in nothing less than a direct trade. Nash for Dave.

Not that anyone on this side of the battle was willing to do that. But "Sophia" would attempt to negotiate. She'd ask for proof of life.

And Tess would analyze each e-mail they received, which would perhaps give the Troubleshooters team additional information to help them track down Dave.

Who was not only desperately ill, but probably being tortured.

That was the only certain thing they knew—that Dave Malkoff needed rescue, fast.

"I hate this," Tracy told Decker now. "I keep thinking about Dave and wondering . . ." If he were locked in some basement somewhere. Having been locked in a basement by a psycho who'd wanted to harm her, she was feeling extra anxious. But she shook her head, forced a smile. "What can I get you?"

He looked a little surprised. "Nothing," he said. "I, um, brought you coffee?"

She looked down, and indeed, he'd set a mug—the one with the smiley face—on her desk.

"You never have it the same way," he added, "so I thought I'd let you . . ." He'd brought her a few packets of both sugar and sweetener, and a couple of those tiny milk containers, too.

It was so unbelievably sweet.

Or maybe it was her consolation prize. He had, after all, just spent a long, *long* time with Sophia in the ladies' room. *Hey, honey, I brought you coffee and wanted to let you know that I'm marrying Sophia. Thanks for the great sex. See you around.*

"What, no scone?" she asked him.

He laughed at that, the worry-grooves at the corners of his eyes turning into laughter lines. She felt her heart lurch as she lost herself in the warmth of his eyes.

"Yeah, no scone," he told her. "Even if we had any, why would I bring you something I know you don't like?"

"Yeah, I was just stalling," she admitted.

"Stalling?" He was either the best actor in the world, or he really didn't understand.

"You're not here with bad news?" she asked.

"No, just coffee," he said. "And . . ."

Here it came.

He leaned closer. Lowered his voice. "I wanted to make sure that you knew it wasn't your fault," he said. "The thing with Gavin Michaelson."

After spending that long, *long* time in the ladies' room with Decker, Sophia had looked at Tracy's photo and had identified Michael-Peter-Gavin as one of the men from the elevator who'd shot Ken Karmody and was probably, right now, torturing Dave. Tess had chimed in with the information that Michaelson had, at one time, worked as an Agency operative, but had left after being marked as too reckless, too unreliable, too unpredictable, and, oh yeah, possibly too psychotic. He was described in his file as vengeful and amoral. Remorseless and erratic. Off-balanced and unstable.

And at that final confirmation of her own naive stupidity in dating the man in the first place, Tracy had escaped into the very same ladies' room to cry.

She'd only been gone for maybe ninety seconds—just long enough to grieve and rage in private and then splash some cool water onto her face. She wasn't wearing any makeup, so there'd been nothing to fix after her tears. She'd come right back out.

She'd thought no one had seen her. Apparently, she was wrong. And now she was going to cry again, for an entirely different reason.

Decker had brought her coffee—and comfort.

"You were conned," he now reminded her.

"Deck, I slept with this guy," Tracy said.

"No you didn't," he said quietly. "You slept with Michael. Who turned out to not be real. That's what you should be upset about. That your perfect man was an act."

She had to smile at that. "Perfect, except for the part where he moved to Maine. That sucked."

He smiled, too. "Perfection's overrated, anyway. If he was real, you'd've been bored in a month. No one to argue with."

"I don't argue. I just sometimes disagree."

"Vehemently," he said.

"Passionately," she corrected him again, and ooh, there it was. That look in his eyes that promised passion, indeed. But they couldn't go there, not here at her reception desk, out in the front lobby, although that was a lovely fantasy. Besides, he was listening—really listening—to her, so she told him the main reason she'd gone into the bathroom to cry.

"I feel as if I let Jimmy and the entire company down," she admitted. "I was such an easy target. I didn't ask enough questions, I didn't—"

"It didn't matter," Deck said with that absoluteness that she loved so much. "He would have figured out a way to play you, regardless of that. Don't beat yourself up for something that you didn't have the training to guard against. You're not going to make that same mistake again. And that picture you took? It's been vital."

She sighed. "I guess. I just keep thinking about Dave."

"I know," he said quietly. "I do, too. Bad memories, huh?"

Tracy nodded. "I know what it's like to face this near-certainty that no one's going to find you and . . ." She knew precisely what it felt like to feel death's inevitable shadow and yet still hope and pray that help was on its way.

"We found you," Decker told her. "And we're going to find Dave. Weren't you the one who said you had faith?"

She smiled at that. "In *you*."

"Yeah," he said softly. "It's kind of crazy how much I love hearing you say that."

Love.

He leaned closer, and speaking of crazy, for several totally insane seconds, Tracy was convinced that Deck was going to kiss her, right there in the front lobby. True, they were alone, but . . .

"Deck." It was Jules. "Whoops, sorry, but it's important."

"No." Decker straightened up. "I was, um . . ." He cleared his throat. "What's up?"

"Yashi called," the FBI agent said. "We've got an address for Gavin Michaelson. And we have good reason to believe that Dave is there."

Alyssa and Jules didn't have to include him in the decision-making process. But Decker was grateful that they had. He stood with them at the front of the conference room as they laid out their plan—as vague as it was with their limited intel.

Limited intel, and seriously limited manpower.

"Sam will lead the take-down with Decker as his XO," Alyssa had decided as Decker looked around the table. They had only a single SEAL for this op—Lopez. Cosmo was already gone, and Silverman and Gillman, who were outside standing guard, were going to leave for the Navy base as soon as this meeting was over. "They'll pick their team after we get there and we have a chance to assess the situation."

They had only five Troubleshooters—Alyssa, Sam, Decker, Lindsey, and Tess. FBI agent Jules Cassidy—and Lopez—brought their total up to seven.

Two other FBI agents had been working—off record—for Jules, but they were guarding Karen Michaelson, who'd provided the key information as to Dave's whereabouts. They couldn't let her go, or even bring her to the local FBI office—not without the risk that the Agency would get wind of their discovery.

They still didn't know if Agency head Doug Brendon was directly involved, or if Stafford's access to Agency information was something he'd set up, illegally, via their computer system before he'd left.

Whatever the case, it left the TS team completely unable to tap any law enforcement—the FBI or even local police—for additional assistance.

They had to rely on their own limited ranks. And hope that other TS team members, such as Jones, whose plane had yet to land due to morning fog, would eventually arrive, like the cavalry to the rescue.

"Who's staying behind with the civilians?" Lindsey asked. The civilians being the non-operatives, as in Tracy, Jo, and Sophia.

"Oh, no." Sophia was quiet but certain. "I'm going."

Alyssa opened her mouth to argue, which was when Deck stepped in.

"Let's take a surveillance van," he suggested. Their vans had heavy-duty armor. Anyone inside would be safe. "That way no one has to stay behind to stand guard. We've got limited manpower as it is, and we have no idea what kind of army Stafford employs."

Tess chimed in. "I don't think he's got an army. I think he's working with a small, tight group. Five, six . . . I've got seven possibles—former Agency operatives who have dropped off the map. Michaelson, by the way, previously worked out of the Agency office in Malaysia. My best guess is that he met Stafford through his connection to Hersek Khosa—the fifteen-million-dollar man." She reeled in her tendency to distribute unnecessary information. "My point about this is that you can't be invisible, the way Stafford's been for so many years, if you've got a huge army." Then she immediately countered herself. "But if we get there, and find out I'm wrong . . . ?"

"We're also not talking about leaving just one operative behind,"

Decker reminded Alyssa and Jules both. "And frankly? Even if we leave two guards back here, *I'm* not going to be comfortable with that. Yeah, we did it earlier with Lopez and Lindsey. But we've been here for hours now and—"

"Excuse me." Tracy spoke up, ready as usual to argue and even interrupt. "But I don't think you should be worrying about unlikely scenarios. Take Sophia. I'll stay here with Jo. We'll lock the doors—"

"No." Decker wasn't going to let that happen. "Stafford knows that we're here. It would piss me off royally if we got Dave back—only to lose Tracy or Dr. Heissman. And I do mean *lose*. And I don't believe it's an unlikely scenario. This is the man who blew up the Seaside Heights motel."

With that, Tracy turned to tell Alyssa, "I agree with Deck—we definitely should come with, in one of the vans."

Alyssa looked at Tess. "How do we move one of the surveillance vans without broadcasting that fact to Stafford?"

The vans were parked down at the back entrance to the building, where one of the pirated cameras was located.

Tess didn't look happy. "It'll take me, wow, at least forty minutes to find the footage I need to override that camera's signal."

The plan, as it currently stood, was to leave all of their cars in the front lot, in case one of Stafford's gang did drive-by surveillance.

And as far as electronic surveillance via the pirated signal from the Troubleshooters security cameras, Tess had already used the magic of digital video editing to superimpose footage she'd found in their security archives of the sun rising—and the morning sunlight growing stronger as the fog dissipated—on the completely empty Troubleshooters parking lot, which included a clear shot of the building's main entrance. She'd glued that footage over a Photoshopped-to-include-daylight digital image of all of their vehicles, just sitting there. Stafford and his cohorts would see that and—hopefully—assume they were all still here, scrambling to figure out who'd taken Dave.

Meanwhile, as the camera sent that false information, the Troubleshooters team would gear up and exit the building—as covertly as possible. They'd also be able to get back inside—undetected—if they needed to.

The plan was to move to the street, where they'd be met by Commander Koehl, who'd engineered the delivery of a passenger van from the base. He'd have his SUV, too.

"So we put the civilians in Koehl's SUV," Sam suggested. "With luck, it has tinted glass. It's not optimal—"

"I don't like it." Alyssa turned to Tess. "*Forty* minutes?"

Tess stood up. "It's the sunrise that's killing us. If it were midnight, I'd be set. But the sun's going to come up, and I've got to find footage that fits. A quiet, foggy morning, where all of the vans are in position right where they're currently parked, with no movement in or out of that back door. It's going to take me—"

"Send Lopez out for coffee," Tracy spoke up again. She turned to the SEAL. "You can walk out the back door—let them see you go, let them watch you get into the van and drive away. The convenience store on the corner is open twenty-four hours; it's where I go when the Starbucks is closed. It'll take you three minutes to get there and back. You don't even need to get coffee—just grab the paper trays and cups and lids. Tell Ronnie, the guy who works the late shift, that you're a friend of mine and that I'll be by later to explain. Then, when you come back here, you can park on the street, out of range of the cameras. Stafford might wonder what you did with the van, but I'd bet his gang's more concerned with knowing where you are. And they'll see you come back in, carrying coffee. One man leaves, one man comes back."

And they'd have access to that van. Decker nodded. "It's worth the gamble that Stafford doesn't have the manpower to come out to investigate."

"I agree," Jules said. He'd been quiet up to this point. "Way to rock it, Tracy."

Decker nodded to her, too. "Good idea."

Her smile was beautiful, and as she met Decker's eyes, there it was again. That spark, that warmth, that sense of faith that they *were* going to get Dave back, and then all would be right with the world.

Alyssa nodded at Lopez. "Three minutes. Go."

Lindsey went, too, to secure the door behind him.

"I want body armor on everyone," Alyssa announced. "And I mean *everyone*. Let's do it. Someone grab gear for Lopez."

"Make sure your radio headset works," Tess chimed in as they headed for the equipment locker, adding, "Double-check it, people."

Alyssa shouted out assignments. "Lindsey and Tess with Tracy and Jo;

Deck, you've got Sophia. Get 'em into the van as quickly as possible. Lindsey, I want you driving, Tess shotgun. Deck, catch up to Sam—I want you riding with him."

Decker could see, over in the corner, that Lindsey was helping Tracy put on a bulletproof vest. As if feeling his eyes on her, Tracy looked up.

*Stay in the van*, he told her, speaking clearly so that she could read his lips across the noisy room.

She pretended not to understand, giving him a big questioning face and mouthing, *What?*

He shook his head at her. She knew exactly what he'd said.

Tracy smiled at him. And her certainty, her total conviction that they were going to get Dave and bring him home, lit her from within and made her shine. But that wasn't all she brought to the table. She had a resilience, a strength that he more than admired.

She wasn't afraid of him. And if things went south, if they didn't get Dave back, if the day didn't end as it should, Decker knew that Tracy would, without a doubt, wrestle him to the ground and make him process it, and deal with it, and yeah, even cry about it, if he had to. Just as she'd promised she would.

And what he did next was really just a test, to see if she really couldn't understand him. It was done on pure impulse. The words weren't even voiced. He just moved his lips very slightly.

*I love you.*

Decker wanted to turn away after he said it, because she froze, her eyes huge and almost frightened in her face. And in that moment, he was afraid, too—that maybe *she* would run from *him*, screaming. God knows he would run from himself if he could. But he wasn't a coward, so he made himself stand there and wait for her to respond.

His gift was the sweetest smile he'd ever seen in his entire life. But it was uncertain, as if she didn't quite believe what she'd seen. And she said, again, *What?*

So he said it again—the thing that was most important for her to understand: *Stay in the van.*

This time she nodded. *I will.*

Jules tapped Deck's arm as he went past, startling him. "We're going to need you here, fully focused, Chief," the FBI agent said. "Is Lopez back?

Because we're going to need medical supplies. I want to bring whatever we need to start IV antibiotics on Dave right away—even before an ambulance arrives."

Deck knew that they couldn't have an ambulance waiting. Calling one in advance could well tip Stafford off.

"Oh, and someone grab Tracy's laptop," Jules added, "in case Stafford decides that now's the time he wants to contact us."


Dave inched his way across the cold concrete of the basement floor, exploring the limited area that he could reach, picking out names for the baby.

*Be quiet. . . . Be quiet. . . .*

He liked Marianne. Marianne Malkoff. It sounded like the name of a woman who could become President someday. Of course, he had no idea if the baby truly was a girl. She could be a boy. In which case Marianne wouldn't work as well.

*Be quiet. . . .*

He didn't want to do that Dave Junior thing. He knew kids, growing up, who were saddled with their fathers' names, and it had never seemed quite fair. More than half the time they went running to their mother, only to find out that she was calling their dad instead.

Of course, if their dad were dead? Then it could work.

Dave heard footsteps overhead, and he rolled back to the center of the floor where they'd left him. He closed his eyes, willing himself unconscious.

But it was not to be.

A bucket of water in his face—a refreshing change from having it jammed down his throat—made him gasp and cough.

When he let the water drip from his hair and face, and he opened his eyes, there were still only four of them. And he wished that they hadn't taken his cell phone out of his pocket, so that he could call Decker and say, *You know how I'm always bitching about all you SEALs and former SEALs? Well, I apologize. Because you and Sam and Tom and Cosmo could absolutely make yourselves useful. You could kick down the door of this crappily built house in a heartbeat, and get me the hell out of here.*

He'd seen and heard only four men, holding him here. The same four men. Which didn't mean there weren't more outside.

Although, he'd spent quite some time listening to the sound of footfalls overhead, to the water running through the pipes, to the toilet flushes—and he would've bet the bank that these four were it.

And the one in charge—the older, paunchy man—was losing the confidence of the others. Dave had made note, right away, of the fact that the guy with the glasses was positively spooked.

It was just a matter of time before he made some excuse—gotta pick up a pizza or run to the drugstore—and vanished into the night.

Or day. It was hard to tell down here exactly what time it was.

But regardless of the movement of the earth and the position of the sun and the stars in the sky, whenever the whole gang joined Dave here in the basement, it was time for only one thing.

A little game called *No Way, No How*. His opponents, sadly, still believed it was called *Everyone Has a Limit—Let's Find Dave's*. They'd yet to comprehend that his was death.

It always started the same way. With a little friendly conversation. With an invitation to sit like a person in a chair.

Well, not quite like a person, since his hands were cuffed behind his back, and it was getting harder and harder—as he became more and more ill—to do much of anything besides lie on the floor.

So as Paunchy watched, Glasses, ugly guy, and the sadistic dreamboat manhandled him up, wrenching his elbows so that his cuffed hands went behind the back of the chair, so that his arms held him there, in place. Humiliating and painful, but effective.

"How are you doing, Dave? Are you ready to talk to us?"

"I'm doing just great, thanks, but my throat's a little sore so I should probably save my voice. How are you?"

"We're doing much better now that we have Sophia."

Words to make his blood pressure rise. But he knew if they had her, they would show, not tell. "Sophia. Sophia. I don't think I know a Sophia. But I do know a *lot* of Navy SEALs, and they are going to track you down and kill you. In the middle of the night. You know, you can go high-tech, you can go guards—" He aimed his words at the guy with glasses, because he knew the threat was freaking him out.

"Shall we bring Sophia down here?"

"—but it doesn't matter, because they're like phantoms. They'll get into your bedroom and you won't even wake up. Well, not until your throat's slit and you're—"

This was where he usually got slapped, hard enough to rattle his fever-riddled brain, and sure enough, he wasn't disappointed.

But he kept going, "—bleeding out."

"Just fucking kill him!" Glasses was losing it.

"You're going to give us what we want to know, sooner or later, Dave. So just tell me, where's James Nash?"

Silence also worked, since Dave's goal was to run Glasses off, not get another knife in the gut. Because the stab wound he already had was plenty bad enough, thanks.

"This all ends, Dave, right here, right now. All you have to do is tell me where he is."

"Is that supposed to be a philosophical question? Because everyone knows that James Nash is dead. I don't believe in hell, and even if I'm wrong, he was a good man, so I'm sure he wouldn't go there, so . . . I'm going to go with . . . he's in an urn on his girlfriend's fireplace mantel."

That got him a punch from Sadistic McDreamy, right where his bandage was—assuming his bandage had stayed on through the last round of waterboarding. It was impossible to check with his hands cuffed they way they were, even when he was left alone down here.

This time the pain from the blow didn't just make his eyes water, it made the world dance and spark and sputter and fade and . . .

Sophia was there—right at the edge of his vision.

"Shh. Be quiet," she said, smiling in that way that she had that always telegraphed her secret plan to get him naked, ASAP. He didn't have the heart to tell her that her plan was never much of a secret due to that smile. She held out her hand. "Come on."

"I can't," he said. "I'm a little tied up at the moment. Bah-dump bump."

"No," she said. "Come on. Come on, Dave. But, shh! Be quiet."

He reached for her hand, but she shimmered and vanished, and he realized he was back on the floor, alone in the basement. He was soaking wet and shivering from the cold—they must've waterboarded him again, but he remembered none of it.

Which kind of defeated the purpose. He was supposed to fear it, and talk to keep them from doing it again.

Dawn was leaking in a strip of window that was too small for him to squeeze through, even without his hands and feet bound, without him being tethered to a workbench that was built into the wall and extremely solid. And he knew it was the sunlight that had caught his eye and made him imagine Sophia.

And yet her voice whispered in his ear. *Come on. Come on, Dave. . . .*

And he realized they'd cuffed his hands in front of him to lay him back on that bench, and they'd failed to switch the cuffs around after they were done—no doubt assuming he was too weak, too ill, too broken to be much of a threat.

They'd still tethered him, tying a rope from his feet to that workbench they used, along with copious amounts of water, to persuade him to talk.

With his hands in front he could untie that rope, but his feet were locked together with plastic bands that he'd need a knife to cut through.

He couldn't get his eyes to focus quite right, and his hands were numb, his fingers thick and useless. Still, he was alive. He was breathing. And he wanted, more than anything on earth, to see Sophia again.

He wanted to meet little Marianne.

So he grit his teeth and he set to work.


Sophia's phone rang in the parking lot.

She'd set it on silent, but it was in her pocket so she felt it vibrate. She pulled it out and—

Decker nearly tripped over her. "Don't stop moving—"

"I'm getting a call from Dave's cell phone," she told him.

He pulled her back over to the building, where Sam was locking the place up. He held a finger to his lips and gave Sam the hand signal for *go*. Sam understood exactly what was happening and gave the international signal for *call me* as he nodded and hurried to the vehicles, even as Sophia pushed *talk*.

"Dave?" she asked, knowing it wasn't him, it couldn't be, as she pushed the speaker button so that Decker could hear, too.

But they'd tried, with the e-mail they'd sent, to make Sophia sound like she was in completely over her head, and out of her league.

"No," said a male voice. "And I'm not with Dave, so your friends shouldn't bother tracing this call. And even if they do? I'm on the move and I'm keeping this short. They won't find me, and Dave will die. One phone call from me, and he's dead, do you understand?"

And okay, she *was* in completely over her head. Her hands were shaking as she looked at Decker, who was the embodiment of steadiness and calm. He nodded encouragement and mouthed the words *proof of life*.

"Yes," she said, and she didn't have to force the wobble in her voice. "I understand. But I need to talk to him. To make sure he's all right."

"He's not all right," the man said. "And he'll be less all right if you continue with this bullshit attempt to negotiate. We have him, you want him. You'll do what we say and you'll do it now or he's dead. You stall or argue, he's dead. You tell *anyone* about this phone call, he's dead. You say anything to me but *Yes, I understand*, he's dead. Do you understand?"

Sophia couldn't help it, she started to cry. "Yes, I understand."

"You make an excuse, and you leave—by yourself," the man said. "We know where you are, we're watching. Anyone other than you gets into your car, Dave is dead. Anyone leaves the building after you, Dave is dead. We're monitoring calls, both from your cell phone and from the Troubleshooters office. Anyone makes a call about this, Dave is dead. Your friends are going to tell you that I'm bluffing, that we don't have the technology to do that, but we do. The choice of whom to believe is yours, but if you believe *them*? Dave is dead."

Decker nodded his encouragement, and through a tight throat and frozen lips, Sophia managed to say the words, "Yes, I understand."

"Winston Park," the man said. "Drive completely around the park— make a full circuit before you pull over and park on Barrett Boulevard. There's a webcam near the fountain. When we see you, we'll call with further instructions. You have ten minutes to get there."

"Ten minutes!" Sophia said. "I mean, *yes, I understand*, but—"

The connection had been cut.

"We can do this," Decker said, despite the fact that Winston Park was in the dead opposite direction from the place they believed Dave was being held. But he was already unlocking the front door, his sat phone to his ear as he called Tess.

"Get moving," he said into his phone. "We've been contacted by the kidnappers. I've got Sophia—we'll catch up. We're shutting down the bogus signal to the security cameras. No one should come back until this is over, or until they contact me—spread the word—but first tell me how the hell to do this."

After Tess climbed in, Lindsey pulled the surveillance van away from the curb.

"Wait," Tracy said. "Where's Sophia?"

And Deck? Where was Deck? She was counting on getting at least another glimpse of him as he delivered Sophia to the van. She wanted to look into his eyes and see if she'd been hallucinating when she'd seen him say what she thought he'd said.

She didn't even dare to think it—that he might actually love her, too. True, he'd made clear his intention. She knew without a doubt that after this was over, after Dave was safe, she and Decker were going to spend a significant amount of time locked, alone, in her apartment.

She was guessing it would be several days, at first. Then, he'd come home with her every night after work, when he wasn't OCONUS. And after a few weeks had passed, after the sense of urgency wasn't quite so fierce, they'd fall into a comfortable pattern where he'd visit a few times a week and maybe stay over on the weekend.

Tracy had been ready for that. She'd been willing and even content with the idea that her relationship with this incredible man would last only as long as it lasted. She'd resigned herself to the fact that, having completely fallen for him, she *was* going to end up hurt.

But that was far into the future—far enough to push away, out of sight and out of mind.

But then he'd gone and said what he'd said—maybe. He might've been saying *I love zoos.* Or *I love shoes.* Or *I lurk, too.* But her twisted sense of perception had seen it as the big proclamation with *love* as the verb, and now she was filled with the kind of wanting that could, way too quickly, turn desperate and unattractive and painfully needy.

And, if she weren't careful, everything she said or did would telegraph her single-minded goal, which was *please, please, please love me forever.*

So she swallowed her question—*Where's Decker?*—aware that Jo Heissman was sitting quietly behind her, and instead asked Lindsey, "What's going on?"

Lindsey and Tess were both talking on their sat phones.

"Uh-huh," Lindsey said as she drove. Tracy couldn't keep herself from turning in her seat to watch out the rear window as they left TS HQ behind.

"The program is running on a laptop that I've hooked into the main system," Tess was saying. "It's on my desk, in my office."

"Uh-huh," Lindsey said again. "Roger that, ma'am. We're on the move." She looked at both Tracy and Jo in the rearview. "Alyssa said that Deck said to get moving. Sophia's been contacted by the kidnappers. They're dealing with that."

"*Dealing?*" Tracy asked. "How exactly are they *dealing?*"


Decker couldn't get the fucking computer to work.

He had Tess on the phone, on speaker so Sophia could hear her, too, and she was saying something about the system parameters and how her laptop was connected to the main computer and, Jesus, time was running out.

He interrupted her. "If I simply pull the plug—if I disconnect your laptop from the main system—will that do the trick?"

"Well, yes, but you're not going to get it up and running again by—"

"If I don't go out there, right now," Sophia spoke over Tess, "if they don't see me on that camera, in the parking lot? They're going to kill Dave." She grabbed and pulled before Decker could stop her.

"Wait," he said, but it was too late.

"Oh, no." She immediately realized her mistake. She should have let Deck go out first, so he could hide in her car. "Oh, *shit.*"

"Tess, I gotta go." Deck hung up his phone. "Okay," he told Sophia as he hustled her to the door. "It's okay. The north side of this building has a blind spot between two cameras." She knew this—they'd all helped design the security system here at the Troubleshooters office. They'd put in a blind spot for this very reason—as an alternative escape route. "I'll go out the conference room window."

"Those windows don't open," she told him.

"Every window," Decker said, "opens. Go—take a left out of the drive, pull over in front of the hydrant. I'll meet you out there."

She nodded and pushed open the door.

"Soph," he said, and she turned back. "Wait there for me. I'm right be-hind you. Do *not* leave without me, do you understand?"

"Yes, I understand," she said—it was the phrase of the hour—and went out the door.

Jimmy got a call from Tom Paoletti on the secure phone line, with an up-date on Ken Karmody's condition. The SEAL had survived his surgery and was in ICU. He wasn't out of danger, but at least they'd finished sewing him back together.

"I'm still here in the hospital, too," the CO said. "It's driving me frig-ging nuts. I'd walk out but . . . like you, I'm under the protective eye of guards."

"I don't know what's worse," Jimmy admitted. "Getting updates or not getting updates." He laughed. "Tess keeps calling me with little jobs to do. Research. I'm working support for her."

"She's a good operative," Tom said.

"Yes," Jimmy agreed. "She is. And I'm sorry, sir, I've got to go—she's calling me right now." He clicked over. "Yeah."

"www.WinstonPark.org," Tess said. "Click on their webcam. What do you see?"

Decker grabbed a length of mountain-climbing rope from the equipment locker, digging for the key to the section that was kept double-locked—the section where the C-4 was stored.

They didn't keep much of it on hand—the building's insurance policy didn't allow it. But they kept enough.

And right now he didn't need much. He tore off a chunk—it was like putty or modeling clay—and grabbed a fuse and blasting cap, then locked the cabinet back up. As he headed for the conference room—and the win-dow in question—he rolled the explosive in his hands like he was making a Play-Doh snake for Charlie Paoletti or Haley Starrett.

It was strange to think that Sophia was going to have a child, that she was pregnant. And that, in turn, made him think about something Tracy had said, just a few days back—Jesus, it seemed like a lifetime ago. But she'd accused Decker of imagining Dave and Sophia's relationship as being G-rated, and yeah, he definitely had. Because he couldn't think about Sophia having sex with *anyone* without thinking about all of the pain and abuse she'd lived through in the months after Dimitri had died. And now he had that added image of Dimitri's head on the table beside her bed—thanks so much, Dave.

And Jesus, Dave was a better man than he was, to be able to look past all that horror, to just wipe it away and be able and willing to start fresh. But Dave truly loved her. Dave had always loved Sophia, enough to get past anything.

Deck put the strips of the C-4 on the window—it wouldn't take much, and it didn't have to be artful—and he attached the fuse, which didn't have to be very long.

"Fire in the hole." It was stupid to say it aloud when he was alone, but say it he did, after lighting the fuse and ducking into the hall. He used the time to secure the end of the rope around the entire conference room door and . . .

*Poof. Csssssssh.*

The explosion was junior-sized—most of the noise came from the window shattering, and even that seemed subdued. It had broken as he wanted it to—inward—and he crunched over the glass on the floor as he tested the rope.

It held against his weight, so he went out the window and down the side of the building, and ran out into the street toward Sophia's waiting car.

"Where's Winston Park?" Jules asked. "What's the terrain?"

Dawn had broken, giving the fog an unnatural, almost alien glow as Alyssa looked into the backseat where Jules and Sam were sitting as they rode with Commander Koehl in his SUV.

Which was kind of weird. Koehl's leadership style was vastly different from Jules's. He was one of those *I am God, obey me*–type commanders.

But Koehl shook his head now, as did Alyssa. "I don't know it," he said.

Sam did. "I took Haley and Charlie over there—it's near the 5, south of the Nature Center. It's not big like Mission Trails or Balboa. It's a city park. Fountain in the middle, playground, chess tables, sidewalks, and lawn. A coupla blocks long at the most, little parking area at one end. Really little—pretty useless—but there's street parking. You can pretty much drive around the park until a spot opens. I think there's one of those old-time bandstand stage things near the fountain, although they might set it up and take it down as needed. We went to see some kind of dog show—an agility contest—and they were using the stage to give out the awards."

"We should call Decker with that information," Jules said.

"Deck knows the park—we ran into him there," Sam said. Both Alyssa and Jules looked at him, so he shrugged and explained. "He told me he volunteers at a local animal shelter. He'd brought one of their dogs out to compete, maybe find her a home."

And okay, that wasn't *the* most surprising thing about Decker that Jules had discovered today, but it was pretty close.

Alyssa wasn't quite as amazed. And she was, understandably, a little freaked out by her decision not to divert any additional support to back up Decker and Sophia. But how could she? They didn't have the personnel to split into two groups—one of them about to attempt the take-down of a not-yet-surveilled location.

As it was, Sam was going to need to replace Decker as his second-in-command. It shouldn't be Jules, because if something went wrong, he was needed to call in the local FBI.

Which he couldn't do in advance, because that information would be received by the Agency—God, he hated this. But one thing he was going to love? After this was over, he was going to love walking into the Agency and arresting Doug Brendon's ass. Tess had been pretty certain that the Agency head was at least loosely involved. The man had—at least—participated in a cover-up.

Alyssa was back on the phone with both Lindsey and Tess. "Any word from Jones?"

"Why did Stafford call Sophia now?" Sam mused aloud. "Unless they know we're coming and they're trying to delay or divert us."

"Maybe they were waiting for dawn," Jules said. "Decker said they mentioned the park's webcam. You ever look at a webcam shot at night? Not much to see." He aimed his words at the CO. "Excuse me, sir, can this thing move any faster?"

Koehl stepped on the gas even as he said, "There's no way we're going to get there, do the surveillance we need, and execute the take-down within that ten-minute time frame." But he was telling them what they already knew.

Sam, meanwhile, was playing devil's advocate. "Okay, so Sophia shows up at the park. What's to keep 'em from taking a sniper shot?"

"They don't want to kill her." Jules was virtually certain. "Dave's not talking. They want her as leverage."

"So they're going to try to grab her."

"Yup."

"She better fucking not get out of her car."

"Whatever happens," Decker told Sophia as they sped toward Winston Park, "whatever they say, whatever they tell you, do *not* get out of this car."

She nodded, her knuckles nearly white on the steering wheel as she drove.

"I want to hear you say it," he said. "*I will not get out of the car.*"

"I will not get out of the car."

"What you need to do is stall," he told her, but she didn't respond. "Sophia, I'm not convinced you're listening to me. They're not going to kill Dave, okay? They're going to keep him alive, because they know if he's dead you're not going to help them. You have the power here. So you circle the park. You keep moving. And you tell them that you want proof of life, and that they're going to have to be on *your* timetable now. Tell them to call you back in ten minutes, and this time you want to hear Dave's voice on the phone. Tell them that you want to talk to him. He's going to have to answer your questions so that you know it's not just a recording. You tell them all that, okay?"

She nodded.

"Take it slowly when you're talking," he said. "Repeat yourself. We're buying time. And right now, we're doing great on our travel time," he tried to reassure her.

His phone rang. It was Nash. "Yeah."

"I am here, in Safety Central, looking right now at the view from the webcam over at beautiful, downtown Winston Park."

Decker put his phone on speaker so that Sophia could hear Nash, too. "Tell me more."

"The camera's positioned on top of what looks like some kind of statue in the middle of some kind of fountain," Nash continued. "It's pretty fucking stupid—every few minutes the fountain shoots its wad and the water completely obscures the view. I don't know, maybe it's supposed to be artistic, but I'm finding it annoying."

"Can you see the cars on the street? And you're on speaker, by the way, so try your best to keep it clean."

"Yes, I can see the cars—but only on Fremont Street. Barrett, where they want Sophia to park, is out of the webcam's range," Nash reported. "And hello, Sophia. By the way, I'm not dead."

She actually smiled at that. "Yes, I heard a rumor about that."

Nash continued. "I can not only see the cars on the street, I can see into them. The quality of this camera is pretty intense. High-def. If you hide in Sophia's car, anywhere but in the trunk? They're going to see you. Or the suspicious-looking blanket that you use to cover yourself."

"You're not hiding in the car," Sophia told Decker. "I won't risk that."

He nodded and told them both, "I'm going to get out three blocks from the park." He dug in her glove compartment and came up with a map. "I want you to pull over, a block after that, and look at this map as if you're lost. Let me go past you. Give me enough time to get in place."

She nodded, but Decker wasn't convinced she was going to remember anything he said. So he signed off with Nash, and tried to bring her back into a world where there was more than just her anxiety and fear.

"When's the baby due?"

She glanced at him as if he'd spoken in Japanese.

"The baby," he said again. "Your baby. Dave's baby. How long until—"

"I don't know exactly," she said. "I haven't been to the doctor yet, but . . . Early April?"

"Dave must be over the moon."

"He is." Sophia smiled at that, but her smile faded rapidly. "Deck, if Alyssa calls to say that Dave's not there—"

"If he's not there," Deck said quietly, "then we'll find out where he is, and we'll go *there* to get him, okay? We're going to find him."

She nodded. Then she said, "I'm not afraid."

"That's good," he told her.

"But if he doesn't get to a hospital, he's going to die."

"Yeah, well, Dave's pretty tough," Decker said. "And he's got an awful lot to live for."

"I know how serious this is," she said just as quietly. "I read the lab report. I know this could end badly. And I know if we don't find him this morning, his chances—" She cut herself off as she pulled up to a red light. She turned and looked at him. "Sometimes, for such a smart man, Dave can be pretty idiotic. That last bit that he wrote in his letter to you . . . As if he could die and you could just step into my life, as if you and he were inter-changeable—"

"He wants you to be happy," Decker said. "That's all he's *ever* wanted. I think he must've loved you, Sophia, from the moment he met you."

Sophia nodded. "That doesn't make him any less of an idiot, to think . . ." The light turned green and she stepped on the gas. "Lindsey told me about you and Tracy."

"Lindsey did," he said, because he didn't know what else to say. Lindsey, who had been there in the office when Decker and Tracy had . . . They'd tried to be quiet, still. . . .

But when Sophia turned and smiled at him, her smile seemed more genuine, and there was real life and sparkle in her eyes. "Are you actually blushing?"

He looked out the window. Just a few more blocks. "I might be."

"She's smart and she's funny and she's beautiful and very sexy—"

"She sees me for who I am," Decker interrupted. "And she treats me like a man. Like an equal. Not some hero or . . . I don't know what. She's not afraid of me. She says what she thinks, she never pulls her punches and . . . I like the way she needs me. I really do. It's clean and . . . honest."

"And guilt-free," Sophia added.

He nodded. "Yeah, that's part of it. It's complicated—like every rela-tionship is. But I can relax around her." He searched for the right words. "I feel . . . safe when I'm with her."

"It's weird," she said. "I'm both jealous . . . and not. Because I'm safe, too, when I'm with Dave." Her lips trembled and tears filled her eyes. "Deck, I can't lose him. I can't."

"We'll find him," he promised her. "Just remember to stall, okay? We're getting close—you better pull over and let me out."

Sophia signaled and pulled to the curb. "Whatever happens," she said, wiping her eyes with the heels of her hands, "I'm glad that you're happy. I really, truly am."

"Whatever happens," Decker told her, "don't get out of this car."

# CHAPTER
# TWENTY

What little strength Dave had left was in his legs. He was shaking so much from the fever that his arms were nearly useless, his hands unable to grasp much of anything—and certainly not one of the loose two-by-fours that he'd found in the corner of the basement.

It was exactly what he'd been looking for—a baseball-bat-long remnant of solid wood. Wielded correctly, it could smash an opponent's skull.

But he could no longer wield it.

His captors had made a mistake, but it had come too late—except there was Sophia again, dancing in his peripheral vision, a golden flash of warmth and light. *Come on, Dave. . . .*

"I love you," he told her.

*Come on. . . .*


Sophia was circling the park for the second time when her phone rang.

"I told you to park on Barrett Boulevard."

Stall. She had to stall. "I wasn't sure which side of the park you meant."

"Just pull over," ordered the man on the other end of the phone—Stafford, or more likely one of his minions. "Right there."

Sophia gunned it past an open parking spot. "Right where?"

*Don't get out of the car* went hand in hand with *don't park the car.*

Decker had said to keep it moving, but she'd just learned something valuable from that interchange. According to Jimmy Nash, she currently wasn't on the part of the street visible via the webcam on top of the fountain.

Which meant that the man on the phone was able to see her without that camera. Translation: He was nearby.

"Park and get out of the car," came the order. "And walk north on Barrett Boulevard."

Where was he? Or more likely *they*. If she were going to grab someone from a public park, she'd need muscle and she'd need a driver. And she'd need some kind of cargo van. Or a vehicle with heavily tinted windows. This being sunny San Diego, there were plenty of those. Too many.

But what she'd also need was an opportunity to *not* commit a crime on camera. If Sophia walked north on Barrett, Jimmy had confirmed, she'd be well out of the webcam's range.

"I came alone," Sophia said. "I'm here. You can obviously see me and I'm not going anywhere else. Because I know that your threat to kill Dave is just a threat. If he's dead, you have nothing—you'll get nothing from me." She spoke quickly, not allowing him time to interrupt as she zipped into a parking space almost directly beneath the webcam. "I also know that he's desperately ill, so here's what I'm going to do: I'm going to sit here, in this park, right under this camera. And I'm going to wait for a phone call— from Dave, telling me that he's been dropped off at a hospital emergency room. At which point I *will* walk north on Barrett."

She didn't wait for a reply and, flashing both hot and cold, praying that they wouldn't realize she was lying, knowing that Decker was going to be furious, she got out of her car and hurried toward the fountain plaza.


The street address for Gavin Michaelson was at the very end of a new development that had obviously fallen victim to the financial disasters sweeping the country. Construction had been halted, with very few out of nearly a dozen McMansions completed. Two of the four that had roofs had foreclosure signs in front of them, the other two had for-sale signs. But most pathetic of all were the foreclosure signs on framed shells or stark foundations that were already starting to be overgrown by weeds.

Tracy watched over the van's video monitor as Lopez used a minicam to do a quick surveillance of the area. The house in question was garish and ugly, with a driveway of brick pavers that didn't quite match the Southern plantation–style architecture. A single car sat in front of the house, and Lopez gave them a close-up of the plates.

Radio communication was open between the van and the SUV.

"Are we in the right place?" Sam sounded incredulous. "There's no security. No cameras—"

"There looks like an alarm system," Alyssa pointed out.

"A bush-league civilian one," Sam scoffed. "What the hell? Are we going to kick down this door and find some family eating breakfast?"

Jo Heissman spoke up. "We don't know much about Michaelson, but the lack of security fits Stafford's profile. He sees himself as so much smarter than the rest of the world. He would have absolutely no expectations that he'd ever be found."

Tess was on the phone with Jimmy. "There's an MLS real estate listing for this address. Jimmy found a floor plan. He's sending the images now."

"He can do that?" Tracy asked. Could he do that with the webcam images from the park, too? She was chewing her fingernails off, waiting for word from Sophia or Deck.

"Got it," Sam said. "Everyone take a good look. We'll go in both back and front doors. Front team sweeps upstairs, back sweeps down."

Jules's voice came over the speakers. "Car is registered to Russell Stafford," he reported. "I am getting a warrant as we speak. Sam's team, get ready to go inside."

"Koehl—front door with Lopez and Jenkins; Bailey, you're at the back with me," Sam said. "Lock and load. I want everyone else watching windows and doors for squirters. Let's do this—let's go!"


As Decker watched, Sophia parked and got out of her car.

"What the hell?" he said aloud, but of course, she didn't answer him, because she was too busy getting out of her fucking car.

Decker took out his phone. He knew it wasn't worth it to dial Sophia's number. She wasn't going to pick up—she was clearly still on her phone with the people who wanted to grab her and torture her in front of Dave, to convince him to talk.

Instead he dialed Nash.

Who answered mid-ring. "What the hell is she doing?" Nash was incredulous. "She's fucking with them—I can see her clearly—she didn't park on Barrett, the way they said."

And with a flash of clarity and understanding, Decker knew. "They're here," he told Nash. "She knows they're in the area—they're not just watching her on the camera. She's trying to draw them out so we can catch them and find Dave."

"She's going to get grabbed," Nash warned. "Someone Sophia's size—it'll happen in a heartbeat."

Decker was well aware of that. And although the idea of apprehending one of the kidnappers was a good one, she was seriously underestimating their adversaries.

"I need your eyes," Decker told his friend as he looked around at all the people—the joggers, the dog walkers, the nannies with children—as he tried to move quickly toward Sophia, without drawing attention to himself. "My vantage point is limited. Help me find them, Jim. They're going to try for her."

"Okay," Nash said, as he watched through the webcam. "Okay. I got something. Two men came into the camera's frame. One's wearing a sweatshirt—a dark color: maroon—with the hood up, the other's got a baseball cap pulled low. Dark pants, dark shoes. Both are being careful not to let me see their faces and—fuck me! The fountain just went off! Deck, I got nothing but water!"

Dave was hallucinating, big-time. He recognized that. He was lying in a puddle on the basement floor—although he was pretty certain *that* was real—as Anise Turiano—definitely a hallucination—came down the stairs.

"Look what you've done," she said, because he'd failed to hide the fact that he'd untied himself from the tether. "And look what you've found. What on earth were you planning to do with *that*? Did you really think you were going to be able to hurt somebody?"

She used her foot to push the two-by-four away from him, and when her back was turned, Dave used his leg—his beautiful, strong, reinforced-by-the-other-two-by-four leg—to kick *her* legs out from underneath her.

She shouted as she fell onto the concrete—shouted and morphed into the ugly man who'd laughed as he'd pulled Dave's fingernails out with a pair of pliers.

The *son* of a *bitch*.

Dave brought his leg down hard on the man's head and pain ripped through him as he felt something give in his knee as the two-by-four he'd hidden up the pants leg of his jeans did damage to himself, too.

But not as much damage as it did to the man—who stopped shouting.

The pain was a good thing, sending shock waves through Dave with each blow he struck. He was alive, he was alive, he was alive. . . .

But enough—it was enough. Ugly man had stopped moving, and Dave rolled him over to search through the man's jacket as he heard more footsteps on the stairs.

*Come on, Dave. Come on . . .*

Tess was with Sam, positioned at the back door, when she heard first one gunshot, and then another—definitely from inside the house, from what sounded like the basement.

"Go," Sam said into his radio, even though the official word on the warrant hadn't yet come down from Jules. There were exceptions to the rule within the letter of the law—and shots being fired were up at the top of that list.

Sam had already jimmied the lock on the door, and Tess followed him in, weapon up and ready to fire. And the world went, as it often did in this type of situation, into crystal-clear slow motion.

*Clear,* Tess signaled as she swept both a laundry area and a bathroom that was off the kitchen.

*Clear,* Sam confirmed that the kitchen and a dining room were also empty.

The house was quiet. She could hear Koehl and Lindsey already moving stealthily up the stairs. Lopez, however, joined them in the kitchen, pointing downward. He, too, believed the gunshots had come from the basement, and Sam nodded his agreement.

A door that hung open was right where it should have been—according to the floor plan—and a quick look confirmed that, yes, it led down to the house's lower level. Tess reached to open it, but Sam caught her arm. Typical SEAL—always wanting to go first.

Although the look on his face was not one of eagerness. And he didn't say it aloud, but she knew what he was thinking.

This could be bad.

*Ready?* he signaled.

Tess nodded.


Sophia saw them coming. Two men—both careful to keep their faces covered. Heading straight for her.

She ran for her car, but glancing back at them she saw a glint of sunlight as the one with the sweatshirt pulled out a gun.

It was meant to stop her, but she didn't slow down. She'd had sufficient weapons training to know that it was hard enough to aim and hit someone with a handgun, let alone to do it while running. You had to stand and plant and shoot—unless, of course, you were the Sundance Kid.

The crowd scattered at the sight of that gun, which was a good thing, because it gave Sophia plenty of room to maneuver.

She scrambled into her car, fumbled with the key in the lock—please God, come *on*—and started the engine with a roar.


"Hey!" Decker shouted, as everyone around him ran for cover at the sight of his weapon, and the man in the sweatshirt turned.

And hesitated.

It was all that Deck needed as he squeezed the trigger, and the man dropped. But then, shit, Deck's weapon jammed and the other man, the one in the baseball cap, spun and fired.

As Deck felt the bullet hit him and knock him down, he could see Sophia clearly through the windshield of her car. "Go," he shouted at her. "Go!"


Jimmy couldn't believe what he was seeing.

The fountain had subsided, and Decker—like some kind of federal marshal from a western like *High Noon*—calmly blew the man in the sweatshirt away.

Jimmy couldn't find where Sophia had gone. The other guy, the one with the Lakers baseball cap—which seemed wrong—took aim at Decker, who, for some stupid-ass reason, didn't blow him away, too.

Decker fell, and Jimmy watched as he slammed his weapon with his other hand, and he knew with a sick certainty that, as he sat here in Safety Central, as he called it, he was going to watch his friend die.

But then Sophia's car moved, lurching forward, up over the curb and onto the park's lawn. And the Lakers man stopped shooting and dove out of the way as Sophia drove her car right where the man had been standing, providing the shield Deck needed.

There was a dead man slumped near the bottom of the stairs.

Tess couldn't see him clearly enough to know whether or not it was Dave, but she could smell the blood and the death.

She could feel her heart pounding as she quietly followed Sam down into the basement. They moved soundlessly until one of them—it might've been her, it might've been Lopez—stepped on a stair that squeaked.

"Freeze! Hands in the air where I can see them!" The voice giving the order was little more than a whisper, but they all froze.

Sam was giving her a signal to move back, but she didn't. Instead, she said, "Dave?"

There was silence from the shadowy darkness of the basement, and then, "Tess?"

"Yeah," Tess said. "It's me. And Sam and Lopez. Are you alone down here?"

"I'm not sure," Dave replied. There was a clatter as if he'd dropped a piece of wood on the concrete floor, and Sam's weapon was back to up-and-ready as the SEAL squinted into the dimness. "I think I . . . I think . . ."

"Dr. Malkoff, is it okay if I turn on the light?" Lopez asked. Tess looked up and saw a switch at the top of the stairs.

"Please," Dave said, and the light went on.

As usual, Sam said it best: "Holy fuck."

Dave was sitting in the middle of the otherwise empty room, holding a sidearm despite the handcuffs that bound his wrists. He was bloody and beaten, his clothes wet and torn, his pallor a deathly shade of green-gray.

And in addition to the body at the bottom of the stairs, another man was beside Dave—and what was left of his head was in a growing pool of blood.

Sam spoke into his radio headset as Lopez pushed past them both, ever the hospital corpsman. "Lys, we got him. Repeat, we have got Dave. Cassidy, we're going to need that ambulance, stat!"

Dave looked from Lopez, who gently took the gun from his hands, to Sam, to Tess. "Sophia," he said. "Is Sophia all right?"

"Get in!" Sophia shouted as she leaned across the car to open the door for Deck. "Can you get in?"

She had no idea how badly injured he was, but he was able to scramble into her car as she jammed it into gear.

The man with the ballcap had rolled back to his feet and, taking a potshot that spiderwebbed her windshield with cracks, had started running north through the park, away from them.

The man in the sweatshirt was dead, his exposed face staring sightlessly up toward the webcam. And although identifying him was going to help, he wasn't going to tell them where Dave was being held.

Decker was healthy enough to kick out the windshield and shout, "Go!" as he dug for a backup weapon.

So Sophia hit the gas, and followed the man in the ballcap, because she wanted Dave back.

But then Deck grabbed his leg, so she shouted, "How badly are you hurt?" as the man in the cap launched himself into a waiting SUV, which peeled off, north on Barrett Boulevard.

She followed, laying down a rival strip of rubber as she went after him, the wind in their faces. The man in the cap knew where Dave was, and she was going to catch him and make him tell her. Because she wanted. Dave. Back.

"I'm fine," Decker said, which was such a Decker thing to say, only maybe it was true, because like her, he was wearing body armor and he didn't seem to be bleeding, and the grabbing-the-leg thing was because his phone was ringing and . . .

His phone was ringing and he answered it and then said the words she'd been praying she'd hear, words that made her pull to the side of the road and let the SUV roar away.

"They got him. They found him," Deck told her. "Dave. He's alive, Sophia. He's safe."

It was over.

The ambulance had arrived, accompanied by what looked like the entire volunteer fire department and half of the local police.

They were getting ready to move Dave up and out of the house as Tracy paced, waiting for her phone to ring.

Rumors were flying.

Sophia and Decker were going to meet them at the hospital.

Lindsey had spoken to Tess, who had spoken to Nash, who thought that it was possible that Decker had been shot. Again. No one knew how badly, but when Tracy finally caved to temptation and called Decker's phone, she got bumped right to voice mail.

"Hey, just making sure you're okay," she said, which was totally lame, but less so than not leaving any message at all and registering on his phone as a missed call. She hung up, and as long as she was being pathetic, she dialed Jimmy Nash's number.

He answered on the first ring. "Tracy?"

"Yeah," she said, moving farther away from the van because the reception was so crappy. "Hi. I just wanted to squelch a rumor that's going around that Deck was shot. You know how worried people get. I wanted to get the facts straight."

Nash laughed. "*People?*" he said. "You seriously expect me to buy that? You're calling because *people* are worried? And speaking of rumors, I've heard a doozy about—"

"Please," she said. "*I'm* worried, okay? Is he all right?"

"I saw him go down," Nash told her. "Tess told me he was wearing a vest, but . . . You're going to see him before I do. This'll give you a good excuse to undress him."

"Don't," Tracy said. "Please. You know that kind of teasing would make him really uncomfortable."

"Wow," Nash said. "You're serious."

"Very much," she admitted.

He sighed. "I'm just going to say this, okay? I like you, Tracy, you know I do. And I love Deck like a brother, but . . . He's been hung up on Sophia a long time and seeing her with Dave has got to be hard for him. I just want you to be careful that you don't get too attached."

"Are you telling me that I'm a rebound?" she asked, turning to watch as Dave emerged from the house on a hospital stretcher. He was already hooked up to an IV, courtesy of Lopez—and Jules, who'd made arrangements for them to carry the supplies and antibiotics with them.

"Rebound," Nash said. "Yes. I know you don't want to hear this, but—"

"Do you even *know* him?" Tracy interrupted as the wheels of Dave's stretcher magically vanished as Lopez and the paramedic loaded him into the back of the ambulance.

"Do I even—Yeah, I know the man pretty damn well."

"He loves me," she told Nash.

That silenced him.

"If you talk to Deck, tell him to call me," she said, and then she froze, because Michael Peterson was standing directly in front of her. He was carrying a gun, but it was concealed under his jacket—and aimed right at her.

"Hey, Tracy," he said with a smile on his handsome face—that smile she used to find so appealing. "It's been a while."

She slipped her phone into her pocket. "Michael," she said as she remembered Tess's description. Unstable, erratic. Psychotic. "Or is it Gavin?" She couldn't keep her voice from shaking, but she raised it so that Jimmy could hear her. "Is that a gun you're holding or are you just happy to see me?"


Dave knew he was in bad shape, because even Alyssa teared up when she saw him.

"Hey," she said. "You kicked some ass in there, huh?"

"I don't remember much," he said as he felt the painkiller slipping through his veins and making him even woozier than he was from the fever. "Was Sophia there?"

"No," she said, "but you're going to see her soon."

"Ken Karmody?" he asked, fearing the worst.

But Alyssa smiled. "He's hanging in. Still in ICU, but Savannah's with him. He's pretty tough."

"Did I get 'em all?" Dave asked. It was so foggy, what had happened. "I don't remember getting 'em all. There was Anise Turiano and I took her gun and shot the older man—"

"*Her?*" Alyssa asked, straightening up, morphing into the former naval lieutenant and team leader. "There was a woman holding you?"

"A woman?" Dave repeated. "Did I say . . . ? No. No woman. Men. Four men."

"Four?" she asked. "Are you sure? Because Sam said you told him there were only three. The two you killed and the man with the glasses that you chased away."

"Did I?" he asked. The world was so fuzzy. He counted them on his fingers. "The old guy, the handsome guy, the ugly guy, and the guy with glasses." That definitely made four.

"Excuse me," Alyssa said, "I have to get this information to Jules."

"No worries," Dave said as he felt his eyes go even further out of focus. "I'm not going anywhere."

Gavin Michaelson was holding a gun on Tracy. "Don't scream. I *will* shoot you."

She hadn't hung up the phone—she'd left the line open—and Jimmy heard everything. "Robin," he shouted. "I need you to call Jules—right now!"

"This is your fault, isn't it?" Gavin asked Tracy. "I saw the picture that was circulating. You took that with your phone, didn't you? Always taking pictures of me, driving me fucking nuts."

Jimmy couldn't hang up. If this crazy motherfucker took Tracy somewhere, this could be their only link.

"What'd you do, get a shot with the plate number of my car?" Gavin continued. "Dumb luck. *Dumb* luck. And wasn't *that* the last thing I expected—a bimbo like you hooking up with Lawrence Decker? How the mighty have fallen."

"*I'm* a bimbo?" Tracy was not only pissed, but her unsteady voice sounded as if Gavin was pushing her forward.

"Scream," Nash told her, even though she couldn't hear him. "Scream and let him shoot you, but do *not* get into a car with him. *Robin!*"

"I'm not the one who was stupid enough to use my own car when I was conning someone—"

"So it was my plates, and it *was* your fault—"

"My fault?" Tracy said. "It's my fault that you're a liar and a traitor and a thief?"

"*Killer*," he said. "Don't forget *killer*."

"I got bounced to Jules's voice mail," Robin called. "What's going on?"

"Call Tess," Jimmy said. "Now!"

Tracy stumbled as Michael pushed her into the ambulance, where Dave was lying on a stretcher. Lopez was with him, and he reached out to catch Tracy, which was when Michael hit the SEAL, hard, with the butt of his gun.

And then it was Tracy who was holding Lopez, who'd gone suddenly, frighteningly slack. Her ankle twisted and she went down into a pile with him, as Michael closed the ambulance door behind him.

"We're in, you can go," he called to the paramedic—a woman—in the front seat, who turned around to look at him.

"Where's Lenny?" she asked, but then she saw the gun, and she put the truck in gear.

Tracy scrambled to regain her footing, wincing at the pain in her ankle, searching for something, anything to use to defend herself.

Which was when Dave rose up behind Michael, like some kind of apparition—battered and bruised and bloody, but unstoppable. He looped his plastic IV tube around the man's throat and pulled it tight.

Michael dropped the gun as he clawed for air, and it bounced on the floor before Tracy grabbed it. "Stop the truck, stop the truck!" she shouted, and the driver hit the brakes.

The sudden lurch knocked Dave off balance—or maybe Michael had managed to pull the IV tube free from his arm.

"I'm going to kill you," he snarled, and as Tracy looked into Michael's eyes, she knew that he meant it. His words were more than a threat—they were a promise.

So she squeezed the trigger, and the gun went off, throwing her back and down, on top of Lopez again. But Michael didn't fall. And before she could aim the gun again, he opened the back door and jumped from the ambulance.

Dave managed to get the doors shut and locked. "Drive," he shouted. "Back up the hill!"

The driver did a hard U-turn, tires squealing, which sent both Dave and Tracy onto the floor again with Lopez, who, thank God, was starting to stir.

"Are you all right?" Dave asked Tracy as he took the gun from her and set the safety.

She nodded through tears that she couldn't hold back. "I tried to shoot him. Did I shoot him?" she asked.

"God, I hope so," Dave said.

The driver braked to a less dramatic stop as they were met, halfway up the hill, by half a dozen police cars and the entire Troubleshooters team.

"I can't believe you did that," Tracy said, laughing through her tears. "With your IV . . . ? You were like, totally, James Bond."

Dave nodded. "Do me a favor," he said. "Don't tell Sophia . . ."

# CHAPTER
# TWENTY-ONE

T he paramedics moved Dave quickly from the ambulance and into the ER.

Decker grabbed Tracy as she, too, emerged, ready to hustle her away from the hospital entrance. But she had a splint on her ankle, and he must've had a terrible look on his face when he saw it because she said, "I think I just sprained it when he pushed me."

He *pushed* her.

Gavin Michaelson had grabbed her, held her at gunpoint, and pushed her—and if he'd had the chance, Decker had absolutely no doubt, he would have killed her.

And even though a nurse's aide was bringing out a wheelchair, Decker swept Tracy into his arms and carried her into the hospital.

"Are you all right?" she asked him. "Jimmy said he saw you get shot."

"I'm fine," he said curtly. "Body armor. I'm just a little bruised."

Another nurse tried to stop him. "The triage station is up front—"

"You'll have to do it in the back," he told her. "I'm getting her away from these windows."

Jules Cassidy was right behind him. "FBI," he told the nurses, giving them his trademark adorable smile. "Sorry for the disruption. And just to make things even more exciting, there's going to be some guards coming in. We'll try our best to comply with as many rules as we can."

Tracy was not happy as Decker carried her into an empty room. "We didn't catch him—Gavin?"

Jules shook his head. "Not yet."

"But we will," Decker promised her.

And as she gazed at him, into his eyes, she nodded. "Good," she said. She glanced at Jules, who was standing in the open door, and said to Decker, "You can put me down now. People are already starting to talk. I know how much that bothers you."

Decker put her down. And then he kissed her, because she looked as if she had another fourteen paragraphs to say about the fact that people were talking about them, and how he should be worried about that, when in fact, he didn't give a flying shit.

"I'll, uh, just . . ." Jules cleared his throat. "Let me know when you have a minute—I need to, um . . . Good." Decker heard the click as the FBI agent closed the door.

But then he tasted salt, and he realized that Tracy was crying.

"Hey," he said.

"I wanted this to be over," she told him. "I'm sorry to be such a baby, but I wanted—"

"I know."

"I should have shot him," Tracy said. "He was three feet away—how could I have missed?"

"Because you're a receptionist?" he said.

She smiled, but it was far too fleeting.

"The truck was moving," Deck reminded her. "You've never fired a handgun before, so you pulled your shot way left. You also probably closed your eyes, which doesn't help with aiming. The good news is that you scared Michaelson away—and you didn't hit Dave."

"Yay, me," she said, but again, she got serious really fast. "Deck, he said he was going to kill me. And Tess says he's crazy enough to—"

"I'm not going to let him get near you," Decker promised her. He took a box of tissues from the counter and handed it to her. "Look, I'm going to go talk to Jules. See what he has in mind, okay?"

She nodded as she wiped her eyes and blew her nose.

"If this is too much for you," he started, but he wasn't exactly sure what he'd do if it was.

"It's not," Tracy said, but he knew she was lying, which twisted his stomach into a knot.

He cleared his throat, trying to push aside all of his doubt. "I'll be right outside."

Tracy nodded and forced a smile.


Tess couldn't believe what she and Lindsey and Dr. Heissman were hearing.

Tracy and Decker were having a fight, right in the middle of the ER.

Tracy's ankle had only been sprained, but she was adorned with an Ace bandage and crutches—this after hours of being X-rayed and schlepped from one end of the hospital to the other.

Always with a small contingent of guards.

The plan—as Tess understood it—was for Tracy and Decker to return with Tess, Jules, Sam, and Alyssa to the safe house. The plan was for Dave and Sophia to be moved there, too, as soon as Dave was able to travel.

The plan was for them all to take a deep breath, during which time Gavin Michaelson would—hopefully—be apprehended and would cease to be a threat.

Tracy, apparently, didn't want to wait.

And then, it seemed, there was the not-so-little matter of a phone conversation she'd had with Jimmy. In which Jimmy—amazingly—had told Tracy that Decker was using her as a rebound.

And of course, since this was Decker who was fighting with Tracy, it was all being done very quietly, but still loudly enough for them all to overhear.

"It's not a rebound," Decker said. "But Nash was right about . . . He doesn't want you to get hurt."

"So don't hurt me," Tracy said, her voice shaking. "I've been honest, haven't I, about what I expect—or *don't* expect? And believe me, I don't expect much."

"But you should," Decker said. "You should be with someone who can give you what you deserve—"

"And you can't," she said. "Or you *won't?*"

Deck was grim. "I'm so fucking bad at this, I've got so much to deal with and you deserve better."

"That's such crap." Tracy got in his face. "It's testosterone-speak for *thanks for the sex, but anything more than that requires too much emotional effort.* If you don't love me, Deck, just say so. Don't make up this . . . bullshit!"

Decker was silent.

"Yeah," Tracy said. "That's what I thought. Tell Tom I quit. I'm going home. To pack. I'm done with California."

And with that, she hobbled away, surrounded by Deb and Yashi and two other FBI agents Tess didn't recognize.

And Deck didn't do a thing. He just stood there, and watched her go.

Tess couldn't stop herself. Jo and Lindsey tried to hold her back, but she shook them off. "Deck, was this really the right time to have a conversation about—"

"Stay out of it," he said. "Please." And with one last look in Tracy's direction, he turned and went back into Dave's room to sit and wait with Sophia.

# CHAPTER
# TWENTY-TWO

Six Days Later

Dave awoke to find Sophia sitting by his bed, holding his hand.

"Hey," she said.

"Hey." His voice was rusty, his throat dry, and she leaned forward to let him take a sip from a straw sticking out of a cup of water. It felt cool going down his throat. "I heard you tried to run over some guy with your car."

She laughed her surprise. "Yeah," she said. "I was looking for you. I thought he knew where you were being held."

"And that a tire mark across his chest would jog his memory. I assume I'm in a hospital and you're real, not some hallucination? A lovely one, to be sure—"

"I'm real," she said.

He experimented, taking a deep breath. Ow. "What day is it?"

"A good one," she said.

"Hmm," he said. "It's been that long, huh?"

"You've been coming and going," Sophia said. "But you're finally out of ICU." She smiled at him through tear-filled eyes. "I celebrated by throwing up. It's kind of my new hobby."

He laughed and winced. "Ow. I'm both sorry about that and . . . not."

"I'm not," she said. "But the secret's out. I had to tell, because they didn't want me and my 'flu' anywhere near you. And then the nurse kind of told Tom and Kelly, and Lindsey was here when I had to. . . . you know."

"It's okay." He reached up to touch her face—that bruise where he'd hit her in the elevator. It had already faded, and he was glad he'd been unconscious and unable to see it when it was fresh. "I'm so sorry about this."

"You saved my life." She put his hand on her still-flat stomach. "And Mary Anne's life, too."

He laughed his surprise. "What? How did you . . . ?"

Sophia smiled. "You were pretty out of it when they brought you in. You kept asking me if Mary Anne was all right and I . . . did the math."

"Yeah," he said. "I don't know why, but it helped me to, you know, give her a name."

"I like it," she said. "Is it a Malkoff family name?"

"No," Dave said. "It's your favorite character from that Jane Austen book."

She looked surprised, but then laughed. "*Marianne*—one word," she said. "From *Sense and Sensibility*."

Dave nodded.

"But you said you hadn't read it." Sophia was bemused.

"I said that weeks ago," he told her. "I read it on the plane to, um, you know . . . On the plane."

She was looking at him so oddly.

"You told me it was one of your favorite books," he said. "You really thought I *wouldn't* read it?"

"No," she said. "I don't know. I just thought . . . Yeah, I guess I thought you wouldn't want to read it."

"I want to read all your favorite books," Dave told her. "I want to listen to your favorite songs. I want to know what you're thinking. I want to live in your world, Soph. I'm happy—I am—to leave mine behind. Completely, if that's what you want."

"No," she said, bringing his uninjured hand to her lips to kiss. "Dave, no, I was wrong about that. I was scared. But I shouldn't have been, because, dear God, you certainly proved that you can take care of yourself."

"I did?"

She looked at him. "You really don't remember what you did?"

He tried to focus, closing his eyes because her beautiful face was just too distracting. "I remember really wanting to live," he told her. "I remember . . . They must've thought I was beaten, because they didn't bother to cuff my hands behind my back. They cuffed them in the front when they were. . ."—he opened his eyes and cleared his throat—"talking to me."

Sophia pushed his hair back from his face with fingers that were gentle. Her expression, however, was classic *cut the crap*. "Jules told me you were waterboarded repeatedly, which pretty much explains the pneumonia that you're also being treated for." She pointed to his bandaged hand. "So don't bother trying to pass *this* off as a lousy manicure, okay?"

"I was trying so hard to be normal," he confessed. "But I really don't remember much."

She laughed despite the tears that were suddenly brimming in her eyes. "According to the FBI forensics team, you were tied by a rope to the bench where they tortured you. You untied the rope, and—with a 104-degree fever, in excruciating pain, you found a pile of wood—remnants of two-by-fours—and you dragged two of them back with you to the middle of the room.

"One was a decoy," she continued. "The other you managed to put up the leg of your pants. Your right leg, which explains your broken knee."

"I remember that," he said. "I remember thanking God and St. Levi for my wide-leg jeans."

"You somehow engineered it, or you got lucky," Sophia continued, "because one of the four men who were holding you fled. We picked him up, by the way—Matthew Rexton. He was trying to board a flight to Thailand."

"Glasses?" Dave asked.

"Yup."

"He was weak," Dave said. "I knew he would run."

"He did," Sophia said. "Which left Russell Stafford, Gavin Michaelson, and Kevin Taylor. Taylor, by the way, killed the three John Wilsons. Jules confirmed that yesterday morning."

Dave nodded. "We got him, I hope."

"He's dead," Sophia said. "You really *don't* remember, do you? Apparently, he came down to check on you and . . . I don't know how you did it, but you used the two-by-four and your leg to hit him in the head. Several times. And then you took Taylor's gun and shot Stafford. You killed him, too.

"And when Sam and Tess came into the house, to rescue you," Sophia told him, "you were sitting in the basement, holding that gun. But apparently, before you heard them coming down the stairs, you were using Taylor's knife to cut through the plastic straps that bound your feet. You had a broken knee, an infected wound in your side, no fingernails on your right hand, and pneumonia, and you were on the verge of walking out of there."

Dave nodded, unable to keep his own eyes from tearing up. "*Crawling* out of there," he said. "I think I was probably going to crawl."

"Walk or crawl, you were on your way home to me," Sophia said.

"Maybe I can take classes," he said, "to learn to be more boring."

"You were never boring," she said, "And, Dave, if you were *normal*, you'd be dead. I want you alive, and I want you exactly as you are. I want all of you: Lunch Dave and hot, sexy James Bond–super-spy Dave."

He laughed. Ow. "I think you might've pinned the bullshit meter with that one."

"Do you know that you saved Tracy's life?" Sophia said. "In the ambulance? Lopez, too. Gavin Michaelson grabbed her. Apparently, he wasn't in the house with you. The team was watching—they would have seen him if he'd escaped. Best we can figure is he came onto the crime scene with the police and paramedics and volunteer deputies. We found his car. It got parked in by a bunch of cruisers—which was lucky for Tracy. Jules is pretty certain he came back to target her specifically. But because he didn't have access to his car, to take her out of there, he hijacked the ambulance. Which was where you were. You used your IV tube as an improvised garrote and—"

"He got away," Dave remembered that. "Did we get him?"

"Not yet," Sophia said. "Out of the seven who were working with Russell Stafford, he's the only one still at large. Until we get him, we've got guards, 24/7, on all of us, but especially on Tracy. And Jo Heissman, too. I can't say too much about that, except that Tracy's ankle is much better. She's already off her crutches and . . . Oh, you'll like this. The Agency has taken responsibility for the security breach. They're revamping their entire computer system to make it hacker-proof. They're hiring Troubleshooters—Tess—to lead a cyber–red-cell, to attack whatever they put into place, to make sure it's secure. And Doug Brendon's resigned as Agency head. He may face conspiracy charges."

"I should sleep for a week more often," Dave said.

"Please don't," Sophia told him.

"Is Ken Karmody . . . ?"

"Up and walking around," Sophia told him. "Tom's fine, too." She paused. "My father died, though."

"Oh, Soph."

"No," she said. "It's okay. I'm really glad you made me go and see him. And Aunt Maureen even understood why I couldn't come to the funeral." She laughed. "You know how I was afraid he was going to hit me up for cash? He left me some money. I'm going to put in a trust for . . . Marianne."

"What if he's a boy?"

"We got a lot of time," Sophia said. "We'll come up with something."

And there they sat, just holding hands, as the sunlight from the window backlit Sophia and made her seem to shimmer and shine.

She smiled at him. "Yes."

"Did I ask a—" *Question*, he was going to say, when he remembered. In the hotel elevator. He'd asked her to marry him.

Sophia kissed him. "I love you," she told him.

And Dave smiled. He knew.

Ten Days Later

Jimmy Nash prayed.

He was not a religious man, but Tess had what he considered to be more traditional spiritual beliefs, so he prayed to her god.

He figured it couldn't hurt.

"You okay?" Decker was beside him, hunkered down in a first-floor room, mere steps from the front entrance to Tracy's apartment building. Jimmy and Tess's apartment building, too—although this was his first time back here since he'd died.

"Tell me again that there's no way Michaelson could get close enough to take a head shot," Jimmy said as they watched the street through a monitor and a series of minicams.

"There's no way," Decker said patiently. "He's not a sniper, Jim. He's never had that skill. He's going to want to grab her and take her, so he's going to get close."

Which meant Gavin Michaelson was going to come out of wherever he was hiding. And then they were going to end this thing for good.

Tess's voice came over Jimmy's headset. "I'm ready."

Decker looked at him and Jimmy nodded. The entire team was in place. Alyssa, who *was* a sniper—of legendary ability—was up on the roof of the building across the street. He knew she was ready—and able—to take Michaelson out, should the need arise.

Decker said it for him. "We're ready, too."

Jimmy made himself breathe, as Tess's voice came over his headset. "I'm already down the stairs and approaching the door."

He could hear her heels on the tile and the *whoosh* of the door as she pulled it open.

And then there she was, on their video monitor, except it wasn't Tess, it was Tracy—except, no, it *was* Tess. But Decker clearly thought it was Tracy. Jimmy heard him draw in a breath of surprise.

But there was no time to say anything, because there was Gavin Michaelson, right on cue.

"Go, go, go!" Sam's voice came over their headsets, his Texas drawl gone, and Jimmy followed Decker out the window and into the street, their weapons drawn.

A shot was fired and a car window shattered, and Jimmy and Decker both ran for Tess—to put themselves between her and Michaelson, who was there on the sidewalk, a .45 in his hand.

There was another shot, almost immediately after the first, and Jimmy saw Michaelson fall, saw Jules Cassidy leading the charge, throwing himself on top of the man, knocking the weapon from him.

But it was over—it was *over*. Alyssa had taken aim and drilled the motherfucker, right in the head.

Gavin Michaelson was dead.

And Tess was safe in Jimmy's arms. "Are you all right?" he asked, making sure she was still in once piece.

She was, and she stood on her toes to kiss him. "I'm fine."

"What the . . . ?" Decker said, then took a step back when she pulled off the wig she'd been wearing. "Jesus, I was ready to give Tracy hell for coming out here—you walked *just* like her."

"What do you think I've been doing for the past two weeks?" Tess told him. "You needed me to be Tracy, I'm going to *be* Tracy."

Jimmy put himself between her and Deck. "Don't give him any ideas."

She looked at him. "Was that a joke?" She looked at Decker in mock wonder. "Jimmy just made a joke."

Jimmy's heart was still pounding—it was going to be quite some time before his pulse rate dropped to normal. He pulled Tess aside, which was okay with Deck, who was already taking the stairs for the building's front door, beelining it for the real Tracy.

"That was hard for me," Jimmy confessed. "Really hard to watch, but . . . You were terrific."

Tess's eyes were soft as she gazed up at him. "Thank you," she said. She kissed him again. "I love you," she whispered.

Jimmy kissed her back. He knew.

Tracy got the word mere moments after hearing the gunshots—Gavin Michaelson was no longer a threat.

"Was anyone else injured?" she asked.

It took way longer than it should have for her to get an answer—and during that entire time she cursed the fact that there weren't enough headsets for her to have one, too.

On the positive side, there weren't enough headsets because the team they had in place to apprehend Gavin Michaelson was nearly two dozen strong—both Troubleshooters and FBI agents. That was good.

Of course, Decker had made sure he'd be front and center of the action.

But then there he was, pushing his way past the crowd of agents and into her living room, looking for her.

Tracy couldn't help herself. She hurried toward him. "Deck!"

He turned. And grinned. And held out his arms.

She launched herself into them, and he swung her around. "We did it."

"It was really him?" she asked.

"Already got a fingerprint match," he said. "You'll get a chance to do an ID, but it's definitely him."

And then, God, Decker was kissing her. Right there. In front of *everyone*.

The past two weeks had been crazy. They'd determined, early on, that Gavin Michaelson had not only bugged Jo Heissman's computer, but that he'd also tapped her phone and planted a surveillance device in her home.

So Tracy and Deck had staged a public split, right in front of the doctor, hoping that she would discuss it with the guards who were assigned to watch *her*, 24/7, after Michaelson's escape. Decker had been afraid that Michaelson wouldn't feel secure enough to try to attack Tracy if he thought she and Deck had a romantic connection.

But Jo hadn't talked about their faked fight with anyone, so Lindsey had made a point to take a shift at Jo's house, and while there, *she'd* discussed it extensively. She'd also made sure to announce that Tracy was resisting the need for round-the-clock guards, and was, against all advice, preparing to move back to New York.

Fighting with Deck hadn't been that hard to do, although it had made Tracy feel oddly unsettled—until later that night, when he'd climbed in her bedroom window.

Yeah.

For over two weeks, Decker's presence in her life had been covert. During the day, she'd pretended she wanted nothing to do with him— even during the rare few times he'd dropped by to "check in on her." That had been oddly fun.

Still, she'd found herself waiting impatiently for the night, never knowing exactly when he'd show up—he was usually late—or even how he'd get into her apartment. Sometimes she'd just walk into her bedroom to find him reading as he sat, legs outstretched, on her bed. He'd look up at her and smile and . . .

Needless to say, it had been a strange two weeks, her days filled with anxiety and tension over the threat from Michaelson, her nights filled with laughter and intimacy and *the* best sex—despite their having to be quiet and discreet—of her entire life.

And then, today, they'd set up the final part of their con, leading Michaelson to believe that they thought he was on the verge of attacking Jo Heissman. Three of Tracy's guards had gone to provide backup at Jo's house—which had left Tracy underprotected and vulnerable. She made a phone call on a non-secure line, pretending to be exasperated at her "captivity" and expressing her certainty that Michaelson was no longer a threat to her. She proclaimed she was going out, guards be damned.

Tracy had helped Tess with her makeup and wig, and lent her her favorite jeans and jacket, her second favorite pair of shoes, and . . .

It had worked.

And now Decker was kissing her in front of everyone.

Someone—Sam Starrett—started to applaud.

Tracy felt Decker laugh, and she pulled back to look up at him.

"We can finally go out," he told her. "You want to go out to dinner tonight?"

She nodded, but then shook her head. No. "I'd rather stay in," she told him. "It would be nice to be here, just the two of us." And wasn't *that* an understatement. "I could cook you dinner, and, um . . ." *You could lick it off of me.* She didn't say the words aloud, but then again, she didn't need to. Over the course of the past few weeks, Lawrence Decker had learned to read her mind.

He smiled, heat simmering in his eyes. And when he spoke it was not to answer her, but rather to address the FBI agents and other operatives who were lingering in her apartment. "Let's clear out of here, let's go. Move it out."

Tracy laughed. "I'm thinking you want your dinner early."

"Damn straight," he said, laughing too.

"Any chance we could go out tomorrow?" she asked. "During the day?"

He nodded, tucking a stray lock of hair behind her ear. "I can make that happen," he said. "I don't blame you, needing to get some fresh air."

"Actually," Tracy said, "I want to go shopping."

Decker didn't flinch, he didn't wince, he didn't even blink. "I'm up for anything," he said bravely, and she knew at that moment that it was true — those words he'd whispered to her in the darkness, over the past weeks of nights. This man loved her.

"Not for clothes or shoes," she said. "I was thinking we could maybe go to the shelter and . . . pick out a dog?"

Decker nodded, and there was more than heat in his eyes then. "I would love to get a dog with you," he whispered, and he kissed her again.

"I'm the last one out," Sam announced, "and I'm locking the door behind me." It closed with a *clunk*, and yes, they were finally alone.

"Just for the record," Tracy said. "As an FYI? The you-climbing-into-my-bedroom-window thing *really* worked for me."

Decker laughed. "Honey, just say the word and —"

"Game on?" Tracy asked.

"Game," Decker said as he kissed her again, as he pulled her into the kitchen and began to lower all the blinds, "totally on."

## ABOUT THE AUTHOR

Since her explosion onto the publishing scene more than ten years ago, SUZANNE BROCKMANN has written more than forty books, and is now widely recognized as one of the leading voices in romantic suspense. Her work has earned her repeated appearances on the *USA Today* and *New York Times* bestseller lists, as well as numerous awards, including Romance Writers of America's #1 Favorite Book of the Year (three years running), two RITA Awards, and many *Romantic Times* Reviewers' Choice Awards. Suzanne Brockmann lives west of Boston with her husband, author Ed Gaffney.

## ABOUT THE TYPE

This book was set in Electra, a typeface designed for Linetype by W. A. Dwiggins, the renowned type designer (1880–1956). Electra is a fluid typeface, avoiding the contrasts of thick and thin strokes that are prevalent in most modern typefaces.